"Center gives readers a sharp and witty exploration of love and forgiveness that is at once insightful, entertaining, and thoroughly addictive."
—*Kirkus Reviews* (starred review)

"A compelling love story, a tear-jerking twist, and a thoroughly absorbing story. Another winner from Center." —*Booklist* (starred review)

"An emotionally resonant and deeply satisfying love story . . . a moving testament to the power of forgiveness."
—*BookPage*

"Center crafts a heartfelt story of growth and the redemptive power of love perfect for fans of women's fiction, especially works by Jodi Picoult and Elin Hilderbrand."
—*Library Journal*

"Katherine Center's funny, unabashedly sentimental romance unfolds between Cassie, the only woman firefighter in her town, and a new rookie on the squad."
—*Refinery29*

"A novel as vibrant as its cover."
—*Bustle*

THE SENSATIONAL NEW YORK *TIMES* BESTSELLER

Praise for *Things You Save in a Fire*

"Oh, how I love Katherine Center's writing . . . and her newest novel is a gem . . . a story that reminds us that the word emergency has, at its heart, a new beginning. Just read it, and thank me later."

—Jodi Picoult, #1 *New York Times* bestselling author of *A Spark of Light* and *Small Great Things*

"An absolute gem of a novel about a tough, heroic female firefighter who, when faced with family illness, must learn to embrace vulnerability and slowly relearn what it means to live a truly openhearted life (in the Brené Brown sense)! Elegant writing and a wonderful story."

—Emily Giffin, #1 *New York Times* bestselling author of *The Lies That Bind*

"Center gives readers a sharp and witty exploration of love and forgiveness that is at once insightful, entertaining, and thoroughly addictive."

—*Kirkus Reviews* (starred review)

"A compelling love story, a tear-jerking twist, and a thoroughly absorbing story. Another winner from Center." —*Booklist* (starred review)

"An emotionally resonant and deeply satisfying love story . . . a moving testament to the power of forgiveness." —*BookPage*

"A spirited, independent heroine meets a smoking-hot fireman in Center's smart romance . . . If you enjoyed *The Kiss Quotient* by Helen Hoang, read *Things You Save in a Fire*." —*The Washington Post*

"Center crafts a heartfelt story of growth and the redemptive power of love perfect for fans of women's fiction, especially works by Jodi Picoult and Elin Hilderbrand." —*Library Journal*

"The novel is at its best in the fire station . . . its window into firefighter culture is fascinating. But *Things You Save in a Fire* has a greater ambition, too: shedding a light on trauma victims and the devastating effects of ignoring emotional fallout from a harrowing experience."

—*Newsday*

"Katherine Center's funny, unabashedly sentimental romance unfolds between Cassie, the only woman firefighter in her town, and a new rookie on the squad." —*Refinery29*

"A novel as vibrant as its cover." —*Bustle*

"[*Things You Save in a Fire*] is not only delightfully romantic, but also courageous and inspiring." —*The Christian Science Monitor*

"An emotional story of self-discovery and forgiveness."

—*Fresh Fiction*

"*Things You Save in a Fire* is a profound tale of how a woman makes it in a man's world." —*New York Journal of Books*

"A wonderful exploration of personal vulnerability and strength that takes the reader along on Cassie's journey . . . *Things You Save in a Fire* is sure to be a hit." —*Shelf Awareness*

"I don't even know how to explain how much I adored this book . . . This is a story of love, of family, and of learning how to be vulnerable—and trust me, Cassie's life journey is one you don't want to miss."

—Siobhan Jones, Book of the Month Club

"A love story full of courage, forgiveness, and steamy chemistry."

—*Woman's World*

"This book is so good! Loved the juxtaposition of the hero's and heroine's roles. She's the expert and he is the rookie. Fabulous forgiveness theme. Humorous and touching!" —Leigh Davis, *USA Today*

Praise for *How to Walk Away*

"In *How to Walk Away*, Katherine Center masterfully weaves together the wonderful, horrible, funny, painful, messy parts about being human to create a heartbreak of a novel that celebrates resilience and strength. Through her characters, she shows readers that no matter what happens, hope and love are more powerful than tragedy and loss."

—Jill Santopolo, bestselling author of *The Light We Lost*

"If you just read one book this year, read *How to Walk Away*. Katherine Center has written a beautiful and strong survival novel for the soul. If you have friend who is lost in life, do them a favor and hand them this novel."

—Nina George, *New York Times* bestselling author of *The Little Paris Bookshop*

"Warm, witty, and wonderfully observed . . . Katherine Center's *How to Walk Away* reads like an intimate conversation with your best friend. I wish I could go have coffee with Margaret now!"

—Emily Giffin, #1 *New York Times* bestselling author

"Sympathetic and refreshing!"

—Elinor Lipman, bestselling author of *The Family Man*

"Laugh-out-loud funny while simultaneously deeply moving, *How to Walk Away* is a book about survival, resilience, strength, and forgiveness. A book that will resonate with readers long after the last page is turned."

—Karen White, bestselling author of *The Night the Lights Went Out*

"I can't think of a blurb good enough for this novel. . . . Poignant, funny, heartbreaking."

—Jenny Lawson, bestselling author of *Furiously Happy*

"Don't start *How to Walk Away* if you've got somewhere to be. It's a cancel-all-plans kind of book, a call-in-sick-to-work kind of book, a just-one-more-chapter kind of book. . . . I laughed a lot and cried

a little. But mostly? I wished Katherine Center would move in next door."
—Catherine Newman, author of *Catastrophic Happiness*

"Center has a sharp eye for social dynamics and the comedy they produce and knows how to keep the reader engaged."
—Graeme Simsion, bestselling author of *The Rosie Project*

"I picked up *How to Walk Away* with the intention of reading the opening paragraph, just to see what it was all about. One hundred pages later, I realized I had missed six emails, two phone calls, and lunch. I never miss a meal. But Katherine Center's voice did what great fiction is meant to do: It pulled me in so immediately and completely that I forgot about real life. . . . This generous story about family secrets, love in sickness and in health, and the resilience of the human spirit has serious Nora Ephron vibes. I loved it and I think you will, too."
—Taylor Jenkins Reid, author of *The Seven Husbands of Evelyn Hugo* and *Daisy Jones & The Six*

ALSO BY KATHERINE CENTER

How to Walk Away

Happiness for Beginners

The Lost Husband

Get Lucky

Everyone Is Beautiful

The Bright Side of Disaster

Things You

Save in a Fire

KATHERINE CENTER

This is a work of fiction. All of the characters, organizations, and events portrayed in this novel are either products of the author's imagination or are used fictitiously.

Published in the United States by St. Martin's Griffin, an imprint of St. Martin's Publishing Group

www.stmartins.com

Designed by Devan Norman

The Library of Congress has cataloged the hardcover edition as follows:

Names: Center, Katherine, author.
Title: Things you save in a fire / Katherine Center.
Description: First edition. | New York : St. Martin's Press, 2019.
Identifiers: LCCN 2018057650 | ISBN 9781250047328 (hardcover) | ISBN 9781466847712 (ebook)
Classification: LCC PS3603.E67 T48 2019 | DDC 813/.6—dc23
LC record available at https://lccn.loc.gov/2018057650

ISBN 978-1-250-62212-9 (trade paperback)

First St. Martin's Griffin Edition: May 2020

10 9 8 7 6 5 4 3 2 1

For every woman who has ever had to be brave.

And for the folks in the world who make a choice to be helpers.

And for my hilarious and good-hearted volunteer firefighter husband, Gordon. This book would be about ten pages long without his help. He told me a hundred hilarious and heartbreaking firefighting stories, walked me through all his EMS skills, read draft after draft for accuracy, and fielded countless questions like, "What is firefighter slang for 'vomit'?"

Things You Save in a Fire

One

THE NIGHT I became the youngest person—and the only female ever—to win the Austin Fire Department's valor award, I got propositioned by my partner.

Propositioned.

At the ceremony. In the ballroom. During dinner.

By my partner.

There we all were, the entire B-shift from Station Eleven, in our dress uniforms, using salad forks—and there I was, in my crisscross tie, getting more and more nervous at the prospect of having to walk up on that stage in front of all those people under all those lights. The winter before, a busload of schoolchildren had slid off an icy road into a ravine, and I had climbed inside to push the kids out through a window, one by one, as the water rose. That's why we were here. The newspapers were calling me the School Bus Angel.

And Hernandez, of all people, chose this moment to hit on me.

Hernandez, my partner of three years. Hernandez, who I'd never once thought of that way. Hernandez, who was so perfectly, mechanically handsome that he didn't even register as handsome anymore.

He was like a Latino firefighting Ken doll—so bizarrely perfect, he wasn't even real. He lifted weights, and flossed, and preened, and he used his washboard stomach and perfectly aligned white teeth to snare more unsuspecting ladies than I could count. He wasn't just in our department's calendar—he was on the cover. Picture-perfect Hernandez, the last guy on earth I would ever think of as anything other than a health-food-eating, CrossFit-training ladies' man, leaned over close to my ear, right there at the banquet table, and asked me to spend the night with him.

"Maybe tonight's the night," he said.

I kept chewing. I honestly didn't see it coming. "Tonight's the night for what?"

He looked at me like, *Duh*. "To finally do something about all that sexual tension."

I looked around to see if the other guys had heard him.

He had to be joking.

Somebody had to be making a video, or taking a photo, or poised to jump out and start laughing. There was no way this was anything but an epic firehouse *Candid Camera* prank. I surveyed the rest of the crew. Pranksters all.

But everybody was just sawing away at their chicken.

I decided to call Hernandez's bluff. "Okay," I said. "Great idea."

He lifted his eyebrows and looked delighted. "Really?"

I gave him a look like, *Come on*. "No. Not really."

"I'm serious," he said, leaning closer.

"You're not."

He gave me a look like, *And who are you to judge?*

I gave one back like, *You know exactly who I am.* Then I said, "You're never serious about anything. Especially women."

"But you're not a woman. You're a firefighter."

"Yet another reason I'd never go home with you."

"I think you want to."

I shook my head. "Nope."

"Deep down."

"Nope."

"I could dare you," Hernandez said.

I never backed down from a dare. But I shook my head, like, *Not even that, buddy.* "I don't date firefighters. And neither do you."

"This would hardly be a date."

I tilted my head. "You're like my brother, dude."

"I can work with that."

I flared my nostrils. "Gross."

"Seriously. Why not?"

I squinted at him. Was he serious? Could he possibly be serious? I glanced up at the stage. In a few minutes they were going to start the awards ceremony. This was a big night for me. Huge. The biggest night of my career. Did we really have to do this now?

"We work together, man," I said. I shouldn't have even had to say it. Firefighters don't date other firefighters. It's not just against the rules, it's against the culture.

He didn't care. "I'd never tell."

"That doesn't change anything."

He gave me a serious, evaluating look. "You need to let yourself have some fun."

I shook my head. "You're not my kind of fun."

He leaned in a little closer. "You never date anybody. How is that possible? It's such a waste of a good woman. Stop holding back."

"I'm not holding back," I said, like we were discussing the weather. "I'm just not interested."

He glanced down at himself, approvingly, and then met my eyes. "You're interested."

I shook my head.

"You've thought about it," he said.

"Pretty sure I haven't."

He lowered his voice. "You're thinking about it now, though, aren't you?"

"Not in a good way."

"You need to stop living like a nun," he said. "What if I'm the cure for all your loneliness?"

That got my attention. I stabbed a carrot in my salad. "I'm not lonely."

He frowned like I was certifiably insane. "Guess what? You're the loneliest person I know."

To be honest, that smarted a little. I pointed at him with my fork. "I am *self-sufficient*," I corrected. "I am independent. I am in charge of my own life."

"You are also in need of some . . ." He gave a meaningful pause. "Company."

I refused to take his meaning. "I don't have time for company," I said. I had my shift at the station, my second job as a self-defense instructor, ten hours a week of volunteering with Big Sisters, a marathon to train for, and weekends helping my dad build an addition to his house. I barely had time for sleep, much less "company."

"Whose fault is that?" Hernandez asked.

Was that a real question? "'Company' is not a priority for me. I'm not romantic."

"This is not about romance. It's about warmth. Connection. Human closeness."

"Sounds like romance to me," I said.

"Call it what you want. You need some."

What was happening? This was *Hernandez*. There was no way he could be serious. And yet his face looked so earnest. I kept scanning for some tell—maybe a little side smile, or a spark of mischief in his eyes—but all I could find was that intense, unwavering, weirdly earnest gaze.

I hesitated. "You *are* kidding, right?"

He had to be kidding.

It was beyond off-putting for this person I'd been in mutual disinterest with for so long to suddenly, out of nowhere, claim to be interested. It was as if we'd agreed to play checkers and he suddenly announced it had been chess all along.

He lifted his hand to the edge of the table and absentmindedly touched his finger to my unused knife handle. "What if you're wrong about your entire life?" he asked then, lowering his voice almost to a whisper. "What if I'm exactly what you've needed all this time? Don't you want to find out? Won't you always wonder if you don't?"

I repeat: This was *Hernandez.*

This was the guy whose favorite joke was to try to throw me on the couch and fart on me. There was not one moment that had ever passed between us that could be classified as flirty or suggestive—or even *personal.* But now he had me locked in this crazy conversation. His intensity with women was a famous hypnotic force. I'd seen him use it on countless targets with near-perfect success. He'd just never tried it on me.

I should have been immune. But I was a little off-balance, in this fancy hotel, anticipating walking up on that stage. It's a hell of a thing to be recognized, to be *honored,* and it was clearly stirring my emotions in unexpected ways. And truthfully, Hernandez wasn't a hundred percent wrong about me. Despite everything I knew about him, and life, and firefighters, and myself, I confess: Something about his whole shtick right now wasn't entirely *not* working.

I guess you can't keep your guard up all the time.

Maybe I was lonelier than I'd realized. Maybe I did need something more. Maybe nothing in my life was quite what I thought.

The problem was, he'd just said things that were surprisingly true. Which seemed unfair—to know me so well and then use it against me. Trapped in this strange moment, I was suddenly blinking at my entire life through a different lens. Was he right?

Maybe I didn't even want to play checkers.

It was the strangest moment of all the time I'd spent with him. Stranger than the disco party, and stranger than the pie-eating contest, and stranger even than the karaoke night that went off the rails.

Hernandez. Of all people.

We both watched his finger on the knife handle. He pushed it closer to me. "You're tempted."

I wasn't. Or maybe I was. Just a microscopic fraction. I thought about my sad, spartan apartment and its neat little row of herbs on the kitchen windowsill. I thought about my bed, always made with military precision, hospital corners and all, and how I'd never once had anyone in it besides me in all the time I'd lived there. I thought about how quiet it would be when I got back, just the tick-tick of the kitchen clock.

I knew exactly what going home to that apartment tonight would look like, and feel like—the slight tightness I always felt on my face after I'd washed it with soap, the whiff of my laundry detergent as I slid my pajama top over my head, the sound of the sheets as I pulled them back and slid between them and tucked them carefully under my arms. The same bedtime routine, over and over, endlessly—as safe and repetitive and dull as always. I could play it out to the minute in my head.

I could even tell you what I'd think about as I fell asleep. The same thing I always did: I'd imagine making chocolate chip cookies, each step in soothing detail, from mixing in the butter to adding the vanilla, from cracking in the eggs to stirring in the chips. I'd watch the mixer blades spin, and scrape the sides of the bowl with a rubber spatula, and scoop the dough with little half-sphere tablespoons, dropping them one by soothing one onto the cookie tray in neat, perfectly spaced rows.

I hadn't baked cookies in years. But I thought about doing it every single night.

What would it feel like to shake up that routine?

You're the loneliest person I know, Hernandez had said.

Suddenly, I knew that was true.

But that wasn't a reason for me to sleep with him. Sex was hardly a cure for loneliness. More likely the opposite.

Hernandez. It was like if your high school chemistry partner suddenly propositioned you. Or your dry cleaner. Or your doctor.

I was not, absolutely not, going to sleep with Hernandez. That would definitely never happen.

Probably.

Without even realizing it, I held my breath.

And then, off to the side, three seats over, across the table, I heard a familiar, distinctive, telltale sound: the muffled, closed-mouth snort that our engine operator, Big Tom, always made whenever anybody got pranked.

My eyes snapped toward it.

There was Big Tom, hand clamped over his mouth and nose, hunching down into a guffaw that he couldn't contain any longer.

I'd seen him do that a hundred times. He was the one who always broke.

"Oh my God," I said, turning away.

I scanned the rest of the table. The guys from our shift were all there to cheer for me on my big night. They'd been perfect gentlemen all night long, chewing with their mouths closed and everything. But once Big Tom broke, they all broke. In one scan, I saw it on every single face: glee. Triumphant, practical-joke-infused glee.

They'd gotten me.

I turned back to Hernandez and punched him on the shoulder. Hard. "Seriously?"

They'd never gotten me before. And not for lack of trying.

What can I say? Nobody's perfect.

Once the guys' restraint collapsed, it collapsed hard. They all started pointing. And raising their arms in victory. And cackling so hard they made the table shake. Reichman, Nolan, Trey, Big Tom, and especially Hernandez—now hooting with delight, leaning back for air, turning red.

I let them have a minute. They'd earned it.

Then I started laughing, too—at the relief of it—as the world shifted back into a recognizable pattern and became familiar again. I took a deep breath of comprehension: Hernandez had not propositioned me. He had *pranked* me.

Only a prank. Thank God.

When Hernandez finally settled enough to talk, he pointed at me. "You totally bought it."

I punched him in the shoulder. "You freaked me out, dude! Tonight, of all nights."

"We thought you could use a distraction," Hernandez said. Then he pointed at Big Tom. "You torpedoed me, man! She was about to say yes."

"I was not," I said.

"You were," Hernandez said. "If there's one thing I'm good at, it's getting girls to say yes—"

"I'm not a girl. I'm a firefighter."

"—and you were *one second* away."

I threw a dinner roll at him. "You wish."

But he'd made some good points, I'd give him that. Maybe a few too many.

Hernandez dug into his pocket for his wallet. "Man! I just lost twenty bucks."

The other guys pulled theirs out, too. "Never bet against Hanwell," Big Tom said, giving me a wink.

The money came out and got shuffled around the table as the guys paid up, counting bills and collecting them.

I watched Hernandez pay out and punched his shoulder again—harder this time. "You bet against me?"

He shrugged with a sly smile. "I know what I know. I'm irresistible."

Up onstage, the program was starting.

An emcee fired up the mic as the waitstaff cleared away the plates and people rerouted their attention to the stage. "It's my great pleasure," the emcee said, "to help honor our city's fire and rescue heroes here tonight."

A huge cheer roared up from the room. Then the guys at my table started chanting, "Cassie! Cassie! Cassie!"

I shushed them and made a "cut" gesture at my neck.

But I smiled anyway. Knuckleheads.

I gave Hernandez one last glance. Just a prank. And it had been a good distraction.

Then we all got quiet, I sat straight in my chair, and all my nervousness roared back. I clasped my hands together on my lap, noted how cold they were, and then took a second to appreciate the ridiculous fact that nothing scared me—except, apparently, stages at banquets.

I stared straight at the podium as they started calling up the honorees—fully dreading the moment when I'd hear my name.

I was wearing pumps, of all things, with my dress uniform, and I was having a few issues with balance. I was not exactly a person who loved the spotlight. Plus, I'd have to speak. We'd been given two minutes each to say our thanks at the microphone, and two minutes seemed impossibly short and impossibly long at the same time.

I had conscientiously typed out a paragraph I figured I could read out loud. How hard was reading, after all? Though as I watched the other honorees come up and read their prepared remarks, I started to think it must be harder than I remembered. They stumbled, mumbled, lost their place, and tripped on simple words over and over. I found myself wishing I'd practiced in advance.

Because I was the youngest-ever honoree for my award, and a female, of all things, and because this was the most prestigious award the department gave, and because the School Bus Angel was all over the news, they'd saved my award for last. I was the grand finale of the night. The mayor himself was going to come out, hand me the award, and bask with me in the glory.

I counted down as all the others walked up and then back to their places, my chest feeling tighter and tighter with nervousness.

Finally, it was my turn. Almost done. I just had to get through the next five minutes, and I could go home to my plants and my smooth sheets and my quiet, locked apartment.

"Folks, we've saved the best for last," the emcee said, as the guys from my shift all started whooping and drumming on the table. "Our final honoree is the top of the top, and to present this last award, we've got a very special treat. A VIP is joining us tonight. We had hoped to have the mayor with us, but even though he got called away at the last minute on city business, never fear! We've got the next best thing! It's now my pleasure to cede the podium to Austin's very own homegrown city councilman—"

The emcee turned to gesture toward the side of the stage, and in that second's pause, I heard myself say, "Oh, shit."

Not the mayor.

This was bad.

Because I just knew—somehow—the name he was about to say next. I felt it coming.

And I was right.

"Heath Thompson!" the emcee called then, in a loud *Price Is Right* announcer's voice as if some lucky audience member had just won a new washer-dryer.

And then it was like everything downshifted into slo-mo. The sounds of the words got deep and syrupy, and the clapping started to sound like five hundred people beating on snare drums, and I watched in disbelief as the guy himself, Heath fucking Thompson, walked out from stage left to join the emcee there.

Actually, strutted was more like it.

I'd know that strut anywhere: The utterly infuriating gait of a man who fully believed the world would always let him have anything and everything he ever wanted—and had never once been told any different.

Should I have seen it coming? Should I have known better than to dare to want something for myself? Should I have assumed from the start that life would find a way to ruin this moment?

Because I didn't. I hadn't. I was so gobsmacked to see Heath Thompson step onto that stage that I forgot to breathe. Entirely. Until Hernandez saw me frozen there and slapped me on the back.

Then, everything I knew blurred into one tiny pinprick of comprehension: At the proudest moment of my entire life, one that was supposed to honor everything I had worked so hard to achieve and become, I was going to have to receive my award from Heath Thompson.

Heath. Thompson.

The only person in the world who could ruin it.

Two

AS HE TOOK the stage—commanded it, really—the roar of the crowd mutated in my head into a howly, wind-on-the-moors sound that drowned everything else out.

The change in sound was so real, I wondered at first if something had gone wonky with the sound system. I looked around, but nobody else looked disturbed. Nobody else looked like something crazy—something impossibly insane—was happening before their eyes.

Everybody else was fine.

That's when I decided it had to be a nightmare. There was no way this moment was actually happening. As I embraced that idea, the weird howl in the room became comforting proof that I must be fast asleep, tucked in bed, making it all up in my head. As usual.

I wasn't really here in a hotel ballroom at the proudest moment of my life, about to receive Austin FD's highest service award—from *Heath Thompson*.

Life couldn't possibly be that unfair.

But there he was. Still. Talking into the microphone, up onstage, in the lights, like reality was his birthright. I blinked again, as if I could clear my eyes. He was a thousand miles away. My eardrums started to throb, and then, just as I heard his distant, almost unintelligible voice call my name, or thought I did, I felt nausea welling up through my torso—from my stomach to my rib cage to my collarbones to my throat—

Hernandez poked me on the shoulder.

I turned to him and, in slo-mo, he pointed at the stage and waved me toward it.

I looked around. Every face in the room was trained on me. Smiling. Clapping. Cheering. The guys on my shift stood up for a standing O, and the rest of the room followed. My next move was clear. I'd won an award, and now all I had to do was one simple thing: Walk up to the stage and take it.

I swallowed, and stood. Mind over matter. Just stand, walk, take plaque. Simple. *Simple.* I swallowed again, then stood, cursing those ridiculous pumps, and moved through the crowd, winding past the tables like a blinking fish through a coral reef.

Somewhere between my seat and the stage, I dropped my prepared remarks. I felt them flutter from my fingers, but it was like it had happened to somebody else. *Oh well,* I thought. *No speech, then.* Least of my worries.

There was a step at the stage. Then another, then another. My ankles wobbled on those dumb heels. Then I was approaching the podium, my stomach feeling heavy inside my torso, like a water balloon tied to my rib cage.

I wouldn't look at him, that's all. Or touch him. And I wouldn't stop moving. I'd keep in motion like a shark, and I'd keep my eyes averted at all costs. Get in, get out. Don't stop. Don't look back. Pretend it's not happening.

Just take it and go. Take it and get to the back of the stage. I coached myself through this the way I'd coached myself through every other hard thing in my life. The way I'd add just one more mile to a ten-mile run, or one more set of reps in the gym. I'd navigated a collapsing staircase. I'd held a dying man's skull together. I'd jumped from a collapsing roof. I could do this.

I stopped in front of the podium, eyes fixed on the plaque itself, trying to mentally Photoshop the person holding it out of the frame.

Was I actually going to have to shake Heath Thompson's hand?

No. No way.

I could make myself do a lot of things, but I wouldn't make myself do that.

I saw the plaque come my direction in slo-mo and clasped my fingers around it, trying to ground myself by focusing on how solid and heavy it was. *What wood was that? Oak? Walnut?* It weighed a ton.

Take plaque, move away. But before I could, Heath Thompson—*Heath Thompson*—grabbed my free hand. To shake. The way every other presenter had done for every other recipient.

Except he wasn't every other presenter, and I sure as hell wasn't every other recipient.

Heath Thompson had made sure of that.

The shock of his touch was like a burn from an electrical wire—sharp and mean and fast. It registered as pain somehow, and then, in response, on instinct, I looked up into his face.

There he was. Older and beefier and more hair-sprayed than he had been ten years ago, and wearing a smug city-councilman expression, as if the entire world existed for him to grandstand in.

I knew in that instant: He recognized me.

He'd just read my name out to three hundred people, so it stood to reason.

But I'd changed a lot—my hair was darker, and shoulder length now, and I'd worn it down when I was younger but now wore it tight back in a braid or a bun every day. I'd gotten contacts. And I had about twice the muscle mass I'd had in high school. Not to mention my dress uniform, its blazer buttoned all the way up with its padded shoulders and little crossover tie.

Something about that combination—his beefy, self-satisfied face, his pompous grin, his self-serving posture, and then, finally, the recognition in his eyes . . . Let's just say it altered my emotional landscape. In a flash, my insides shifted from cold shock to burning rage.

There must have been a photographer there, because Heath Thompson was squeezing my hand, holding me in place, smiling offstage, and holding a pose.

Somewhere far off, I heard Big Tom from the crew shout, "Give 'em hell, Cassie!"

And then, just as I was congratulating myself for holding it together—for coping with such grace under the most astonishingly horrific circumstances—I felt something pressing against my butt.

Not just pressing against it, like I'd backed up to the podium or something. *Cupping* it.

The only thing it could possibly be was Heath Thompson's other hand.

The fact of it hit, the flashbulb popped, and then that hand gave my butt-cheek a bold, entitled, proprietary squeeze.

And I lost it.

Given everything, it's a miracle I didn't literally kill him.

There was nothing else I could possibly have done. I turned and whomped Heath Thompson on the head with my oak-and-metal plaque so hard, I knocked him unconscious and gave him a concussion.

I NEVER WANTED to be a firefighter.

There are people who dream their whole lives of becoming firefighters. There are little kids who ogle fire trucks, and wear toy fire hats, and dress up in bunker gear for Halloween.

Boys, mostly.

I was not one of those kids.

In fact, on career day in kindergarten, I famously announced my goal of growing up to be the Tooth Fairy. Which I still think would be a great job.

I never even thought about being a firefighter before it happened.

And it happened essentially by accident.

I was on my way to med school, in fact, planning to be an ER doc. I was a freshman in college looking for a campus job, and I got recruited by a cute guy in my dorm to work as an EMT for the university. It was an easy sell. I needed practice working in medicine, and I also needed a job. Done.

Once I started working as an EMT, I didn't want to stop—like I didn't even want to go off shift. I loved everything about it, from the medical training to the sirens to the life-or-death moments.

It wasn't just the adrenaline. There was something profoundly satisfying about helping people—about stepping into these terrible moments over and over and making things better. The feeling of doing something that actually mattered was addictive. I'd had lots of jobs over the years—dishwasher in a pizza joint, lifeguard, dog sitter—but I'd never had a job like that.

My roommate, in contrast, had a campus job serving fro-yo.

No comparison.

Being an EMT was a whole new world. It was glorious. I stuck people with needles, and pumped chests for CPR, and reset bones. My first week on the job, I helped save a physics professor in cardiac arrest with a defibrillator.

Not bad for ten dollars an hour.

All to say, it just turned out I had a knack for it.

When I wasn't on shift, I was waiting until I could go back on shift. I worked holidays. I covered for coworkers. I dreamed about lights and sirens.

I did that for two years before my supervisor recommended I get certified as a paramedic and go to work for the city. All firefighters are EMTs—firehouses handle far more medical calls than fires, in fact—but not all are paramedics. It takes a year of extra training to get your paramedic certification, and you have to really love medicine to do it, or be "forced" because the department needs you.

I really loved medicine.

I worked as a paramedic for a year, and then, after graduation, another supervisor talked me into applying to the Fire Academy.

Things just kind of snowballed from there.

Somewhere along the way, I realized this was what I was born to do.

There are lots of qualities that make a good firefighter. It doesn't hurt to be big and strong, because that makes it easier to handle all the equipment. It's nice if you're good-natured and low-key, because it's the textbook definition of a high-stress job. Wanting to help people is a plus. And if you happen to deal with anxiety by running around in your underwear, or dumping water on people's heads, or wrapping toilet bowls with Saran Wrap? Even better.

You'll fit right in.

Oh, and if you can be a guy, be a guy. That's definitely an advantage.

I was not a guy.

But I was a really good firefighter.

Maybe that sounds cocky, but you just know when you're good at something, you know?

For one thing, I was the top student in my graduating class at the academy. The number one top student. I knew the Merck Manual backwards and forwards. I could start an IV in my sleep. Plus, I was strong—for a girl, and even for a lot of guys—and I didn't get offended easily. I was totally comfortable in the firehouse with the guys. I wasn't shy. I didn't get scared. I never panicked. I had a single dad who was a high school basketball coach—so I grew up playing hoops constantly, and talking trash, and beating the boys at everything.

All that helped, but what really made me a good firefighter was a funny little personality quirk that I never even knew I had until I started using it. It takes guts to walk into a burning building or staunch an arterial bleed—no question. But it also takes a special kind of brain. Firefighters think differently from other people, and this is especially true of me. Because when everybody else is panicking, when the entire whole world is freaking the heck out—that's when I get calm.

It's like some circuit in my brain is reversed.

Everybody in the fire service has this reverse wiring to some extent. When herds of panicked people are running out of a burning building, that's when we're calmly strolling in.

But I've never met anybody who has it like I have it.

Normal humans see the explosion, or the flames, or the twenty-four-car pileup and think: *Run!* My brain just thinks: *Huh. Cool.* Everybody else is sprinting away, wild-eyed and shrieking, because that's what evolution wants us to do—get the hell out of there. I just slow to a stop and look around.

I must get a tiny squirt of adrenaline—but only just the right amount. Enough to make me beautifully, brilliantly alert. Everything comes into sharp focus and gets quiet, and I can see what's happening with exquisite clarity. For everyone else, it's a blur, but for me, it's details, textures, colors, connections. Insights.

Sometimes I feel like that's the only time I ever see anything clearly.

Anyway, that's why I didn't wind up an ER doc. You don't want me *just after* the emergency. You want me *during* the emergency.

It's a strange thing to know about yourself, but there it is: I'm at my very best when things are at their very worst.

And so, even though my dad was sure the "fireman thing" was "a phase," four years later, here I was, still at Station Eleven in Austin, still the only girl on B-shift—except for our badass female captain—and still loving every impossible minute.

THAT'S WHY THE night I got the valor award should have been just another easy, inevitable step in my unblemished, pure-hearted firefighting career.

But I have to confess something. I didn't just hit Heath Thompson, city councilman, with that wooden plaque when he squeezed my butt.

I beat the crap out of him.

I pummeled him. I *mauled* him. Even after I'd cracked his head with the plaque itself, I landed a punch to the face, a knuckle strike to the windpipe, and at least one jab to the solar plexus before adding a few good kicks to the ribs with my pumps after he hit the floor. Nobody saw it coming, not even me, so his reaction time was a little slow—which worked to my advantage.

I cut my hand on his teeth, but it was worth it.

I don't remember this part, but according to Hernandez, the whole time, I was shouting, "Touch me again, douchebag! Touch me again and see how long you live!"

He did not touch me again.

Lucky they didn't book me for assault. I could have—should have—spent the night in jail. It's no small thing to pummel a city official into a bloody, quivering pulp on a stage in front of three hundred of the city's bravest public servants. That kind of thing just doesn't happen every day. Or ever.

Of course, it's no small thing to grab a firefighter's ass, either.

They whisked us both off the stage and bandaged his face and my hand while the emcee tried to get everybody to sit back down and finish their desserts. The police came, but Heath Thompson refused to press charges. "It's fine, it's fine," he kept saying through his swollen lips. "Just let her go."

I bet he wanted them to let me go. There were news cameras out in the lobby. And a thousand bucks says I wasn't the only thing he had to hide.

In the end, they snuck us both out the back door. I don't know what kind of strings he pulled, but nothing about it showed up in the papers. I'm not sure, ultimately, if that was a good thing or a bad thing.

Later that night, after I was home, and had showered and bandaged up my hand in my quiet apartment, Hernandez showed up at my door.

I saw him through the peephole—holding my cell phone in one hand and my plaque in the other. In all the commotion, I'd left them behind.

It took me a minute to undo all the dead bolts. When I swung the door open, he held out the plaque—tied in a plastic bag.

"It's pretty bloody," he said.

I nodded as I took it. Then I reached for my phone, but he held it back, out of my reach.

"What just happened?" he asked, not crossing the threshold.

I looked at my phone held hostage in his hand. I shrugged.

"Are you okay?" he asked.

I nodded.

"Do you want me to stay for a bit?"

I shook my head.

"You knew that guy in high school?"

I nodded again.

Hernandez assessed me for what felt like a long time. Then he said, "Am I guessing right that he has something to do with why you never date anybody?"

I held his gaze until he had his answer.

Then he nodded, like, *Okay*. He let out a definitive sigh. "Nice work, by the way. They took him to the hospital."

I gave a tiny little smile. "I try."

"My offer still stands, you know," Hernandez said.

"Offer for what?"

He gave a little shrug. "For company. *Actual* company."

I knew he meant well. But I shook my head. "I'm better always on my own."

Next, still holding my phone, he opened his arms to offer a hug. "Come on. Bring it in. If anybody ever needed a hug, it's you."

I would have said no to that, too. But just then, my phone rang.

That was it. The moment was over. He held out the phone to me, I took it—and then I used it to salute a farewell before I re-dead-bolted the door and answered it.

Three

IT WAS MY mother. On the phone.

"Thank you for answering," she said.

I closed my eyes. "It was an accident."

"I need to talk to you," she said.

"I figured," I said.

She'd been after me for weeks, and I'd been avoiding her—insisting to myself that I was legitimately too busy to talk.

Her first call came in while I was at work, during one of the busiest shifts I'd had in weeks. We'd run nonstop calls for a suicide attempt in a high school bathroom (failed), a structure fire in an abandoned warehouse (arson), a sushi chef with a severed fingertip (reattached in the ER), and a cow wandering loose in a residential neighborhood (adorable).

By the time I went off shift at seven the next morning, I had not even looked at my phone, much less listened to the messages from my semi-estranged mother.

I had too much else to do.

Plus, I didn't want to talk to her.

If she really needs to talk to me, I decided, *she'll call back.*

Which she did.

She called back the next day while I was folding laundry, but I let it go to voicemail.

She called again while I was out on a run. Then again while I was at the grocery store.

Honestly, at some point, it got a little stalkerish.

"What do you need?" I asked, when she finally had me.

She took a breath. "I need to ask a really, really big favor of you."

I braced myself for the question. Whatever it was, the answer was no.

"It's going to sound very abrupt," she went on, "but that's partly because it's hard to get ahold of you and I'm afraid you're going to hang up any second."

She was right. I might hang up any second.

She took a breath. Then, in a burst: "I need you to come to Massachusetts and live with me."

I blinked.

"Just for a while," she added. "Not forever! A year at the most."

"A year?"

"At the most."

I was stunned by the question. Stunned that she had even asked it—or thought to ask it. We were not estranged, exactly, but we sure as hell weren't close. It was such a ridiculous, never-gonna-happen thing to propose, I couldn't believe she'd even said the words. "I'm not moving to Massachusetts, Diana. That's bananas."

I hadn't called her "Mom" in years. Ten years, to be exact. Not since the day she'd walked out on me and my dad. The same day I'd started calling my father "Ted."

At first, it was just to annoy them, to say that if they wanted to be treated like parents, they'd have to act like parents and stay miserably together. But the longer they stayed apart, the more it became a way of turning them into adults of no special significance that I just happened to know.

By this point, they were just Diana and Ted to me. I could barely imagine that they'd ever been anyone else.

"I'm serious," Diana said.

"You can't be."

"Don't give me your answer right away," she said. "Take some—"

"No," I said.

She hesitated.

"No," I said again, with more emphasis, as if she'd tried to argue.

"You haven't even heard the rest of the idea."

"The rest of the idea doesn't matter."

"One year"—now she was bargaining, like she had any kind of a chance—"and then you go back to Texas like it never happened."

"That's not how it works. I'd have to stay there several years and earn a promotion before I could find a new position."

"I don't know what that means."

"It means if I did what you're asking, I'd give up my whole life. Everything."

"When you put it that way, it doesn't sound very appealing," Diana said.

"That's why it's so simple. *No.*"

"I get it," she went on. "I've been over and over it in my head. You didn't want to move here with me when you were fifteen—"

"Sixteen," I corrected.

"When you actually still needed me," she continued, "and so why you'd be willing to come now, when you're all grown up, and also pretty much hate me—"

"I don't hate you," I said, on principle. But I didn't like her very much, either.

"You have less reason than ever to come, and I knew before I called that you'd say no. But I just had to try."

I closed my eyes. "Why?"

"Because I need you."

Something in her voice was off.

I'd talked to her maybe four times a year in the decade since she'd moved across the country—the obligatory calls on Christmas, Thanksgiving, and birthdays. But I still could read her voice—too well. I'd grown up with that voice. I knew its pitch, and its cadence, and its rhythms. That voice was the model for my own. I couldn't unknow it if I tried.

"What's going on?" I asked.

"I'm having a little eye problem, and I can't see as well as I used to."

"What kind of eye problem?" I asked. I knew a lot about eyes. And problems. "Are you going blind or something?" I asked.

A sigh. Like I was really demanding too much info. "Sort of."

"What does that mean?"

"Only in the one eye. And not *going,* exactly. More like already gone."

I mentally flipped through my medical knowledge of eyes. Cataracts? Macular degeneration? Diabetic retinopathy? "You've gone blind in one eye? Just one?"

"It's glaucoma, or something. Some kind of 'oma. They did a surgery, and there was a good chance I'd lose my sight, and I knew that going in. It just turns out it's harder to see with one eye than you might think. Especially when you've been spoiled for so long with two."

I wasn't sure I'd call having two eyes being "spoiled," but okay.

"Why didn't you tell me about this before?"

A sarcastic pause that read, *Please.*

"You let them do surgery on your eye, but you can't even tell me what's wrong with it?"

She gave a sharp sigh. "I'm not really a details person, Cassie."

That flash of irritation in her voice gave me permission, suddenly, to be irritated, too. Was it really too much to expect her to retain the most basic details of her health situation? The woman was in her midfifties, and she was acting like a ninety-year-old biddy.

But I couldn't keep the irritation going. Even though it's so much easier to *judge* than to *relate,* I couldn't help but feel empathy. It must be a hell of a thing to lose half your sight. For anybody—but especially an artist, of all people. Her entire professional life was about looking, and seeing, and perceiving. Of course she was irritated. Probably panicked as well.

"How is the other eye?" I asked then, more softly.

"Okay for now."

It's never a good idea to feel too much empathy for patients. But she wasn't my patient, I reminded myself. She was my mother.

"Anyway," she went on, "it's not so bad. I just can't seem to get a handle on spatial relationships. I keep pouring coffee and missing the cup. Tripping, too. Palms, knees—all scraped to hell. Fell down the stairs the other day. And there's no driving anymore. I doubt that's ever coming back."

"You fell down the stairs?"

"I'm fine. Point is, I could use some help. Not forever."

"A year at the most," I repeated.

"Exactly!" she said, like we were getting somewhere. "While I adjust. There's a therapy you can do to help speed things along. Learn to use the one eye like a pro. But it takes a while."

"A year?"

"Nine months to a year. Then we're done."

You had to admire the optimism.

I pushed the empathy back. I was not going to feel sorry for her. People suffered worse things all the time. We'd just picked up a guy last week who'd severed his hand cutting boards to make a playhouse for his kids.

But my mind was on alert now. This was happening. She was really asking. A *year*. That was a lifetime. I didn't have a year to give away. "Can't you hire a caregiver?"

She burst out with a laugh, like I had to be joking. "Sweetheart, I'm an artist!" Then, like it went without saying, "I am dead broke."

"Can't Ted help you?"

"Why on earth would he even consider doing that?"

She had a point there.

I tried again. "But you have health insurance, right?"

"It's terrible. It's worse than not having insurance at all."

"Don't you have friends?" I asked.

"Of course I have friends!" She sounded insulted. "But they have their own families to look after."

"But I live in Texas!" I said, feeling my argument weaken.

"It's just a two-day drive," she said, like, *Easy*. "You can stay with me. For free! I have a spare room in the attic with white curtains with pom-pom trim and a window that overlooks the harbor."

She waited, like pom-pom curtains might do the trick.

Then she added, "Think of all the money you could save on rent! Just for a year. Maybe less."

I shook my head. "I have a life here. Friends."

"A boyfriend?" she asked.

"No boyfriend."

"Someone you're sleeping with, then?" Then, like she was making air quotes, she added, "A sex buddy?"

"Mom!" I shrieked, forgetting I didn't call her that anymore. "That is not the term."

"Sorry."

"I'm too busy for that, anyway," I added.

"Too busy for what?"

"Too busy for dating. I don't have time."

There was a pause, and then she said, "I don't understand."

"Look, I just don't do love," I said. How had we landed on this subject?

I could hear the frown in her voice. "You don't *do* love?"

No way out but through. "It's not my thing."

"You don't do any kind of love? At all?"

"I don't do romantic love," I specified. "The dumb kind."

She paused a second, and I could tell she was deciding whether to take that topic on. "Great, then, I guess," she said at last, letting it go. "One less thing to hold you back."

This was the most substance we'd worked into a conversation in years.

"I do love *my job,* though," I said, to get us back on track. This might have been a good moment to tell her that I had just received an award for valor. But I didn't.

"We've got firemen up here, you know," she said, as if that made any sense.

"Fire*fighters,*" I corrected.

"And we've got plenty of fires," she said, sounding almost proud. "Tons of them. This whole part of the country's a smoldering tinderbox just waiting to go up in flames."

What was her point?

"There are fire stations on just about every corner," she went on. "Maybe you could do some kind of exchange."

"That's not how it works, Diana. I'd have to give up my job."

"Just for a year."

"I'm not a foreign exchange student," I said. "They don't hold your place."

She let that one pass. Then, with new determination, she said, "When have I ever asked you for anything?"

I sighed.

"Never," she answered for me. "I have never asked you for anything."

True enough. She had once asked me to forgive her, in a letter—one I hadn't even replied to. But that wasn't something we talked about.

"Just this once," she said. "I promise I will never, ever ask you for help again."

It was too much. My head was spinning. I just needed to shut this day down. I thought about tonight, and the guys, and the way they chanted my name at the banquet. Then I thought about what it would feel like to leave them, and I said something so true it was mean.

"I'd really like to help you, Diana," I said. "But I just can't leave my family."

NOT TEN MINUTES after I hung up, as I finished rinsing off my plaque in the sink, my phone rang again. I thought it would be my mom, trying again, and I planned to ignore her . . . but it was my dad.

I never ignored my dad.

"Your mother just called me and told me you said no," he said when I answered.

What were they—in cahoots? "You knew?"

"When she couldn't get you last week, she called me."

"Why would she do that? You two are divorced."

"This matter concerns the whole family."

"Not really."

"How could you say no to her?" he demanded. "She needs you."

"Can we talk about this later?" I asked.

"It doesn't matter when we talk about it," my dad said, rolling out his most authoritative voice. "You're going."

"I already said no."

"Change your mind."

"I'm not going to change my mind," I said, like he was completely nuts.

"She's your mother, and she needs you, and you're going."

"You're telling me to leave my job, my apartment, my life—everything?"

"You're young. You'll make it work."

"Ted," I said. "I don't want to make it work."

"That's not relevant."

"I barely know her. She's practically a stranger."

"Bullshit. That woman *made* you. She gave you life."

"She *left* me. And she left you, too, buddy, by the way!"

"Are you still mad about that?"

"Yes. No. Both."

"You can't stay mad forever."

"Wanna bet?"

"You've got to move on."

"You moved on with a new wife. I can't get a new mother."

"True. But your old one is knocking on your door."

In a way, I'd felt abandoned again when my dad started dating Carol. And I won't say that Carol was awful, because she wasn't technically a bad person, though she was a little prissy for my taste.

The point was, my dad and I had been lonely together for years, like it was our thing. Like we were in a special club of two: *People Abandoned by Diana Hanwell.* But then he found Carol, an administrator at his school—a divorcée, in her pastel culottes and espadrilles—and then, of all things, he decided to marry her. That was that. He couldn't be in our loneliness club if he wasn't lonely anymore.

He left.

Or maybe I kicked him out.

But some part of me flat-out refused to leave that club. It was the principle of the thing. In some funny way, I was still standing up for my teenage self.

Because if I didn't, who would?

Now, here was my dad going over to my mom's side. "Why are you advocating for her?" I demanded. "She left you! You loved her, and you were good to her, and she cheated on you."

He knew all this, of course.

"These things happen, Cassie," he said. "Life is messy. When you're older you'll understand."

The fact that he wasn't mad made me madder. "I hope not."

"Nobody's perfect," he said.

What was he doing? Was he trying to model behavior for me? Was this some kind of teachable moment about growth and change? It seemed so patronizing. I might not know everything about forgiveness, but I sure as hell knew you didn't get there by pretending earth-shattering betrayals had been no big deal.

Your wife cheating on you is a big deal. Your mom abandoning you is a big deal.

I wasn't going to insult my teenage self and all she'd been through by just shrugging and saying, *Nobody's perfect.*

"I think you've forgotten how bad it was," I said. We'd eaten SpaghettiOs for a solid year.

"I probably have," my dad said.

"Well, I haven't."

"Don't you know that expression, 'The best revenge is forgetting'?"

"Seems to me like the best revenge would be *revenge.*"

"Tell me you're not plotting revenge on your mother."

What would that even look like? It was far too late for revenge. "Of course not," I said, though, in a practical sense, by keeping my distance for so long, that's what I'd been doing for years. "I'm just refusing to give her a pass."

"Sweetheart," my dad said tenderly. "Let it go."

"She's the one who called me!"

"It's been a *decade.*"

"A decade I've spent building a nice little life for myself—*in Texas.*"

"She needs you."

"I won't dismantle my entire life and move across the country for a woman I'm not even close to."

"I think she'd like to be closer."

"Too bad. She can't just demand closeness. She gave up the right to be close to me when she left."

"She's not demanding. She's asking."

"I can't believe you're defending her!"

My dad was quiet for a second. Then he said, "You know, there are people who have no choice but to spend their lives avoiding their mothers. People whose mothers are mean, or toxic, or drunk. People whose mothers hurt them every time they let their guard down. But you are not one of those people. Your mother is actually a nice lady."

That was a lot of verbiage for my normally strong-but-silent dad. Practically a soliloquy. "How can you say that after what she did to you?"

"People make mistakes."

"You can't make me forgive her," I said, barely able to believe how petulant I sounded.

"You're right," my dad said. "I can't make you."

For a split second, I thought I'd won.

Then he went on. "But you're going to go anyway."

"You're wrong," I said.

"I'm right," he said. "Because you were raised to do the right thing. And she's the one who raised you."

Four

THE NEXT MORNING, I was on shift by 6:30 A.M., the cut on my hand bandaged, ready to keep plowing forward with my life.

But the captain must have been watching for me, because as soon as I walked through the doors, she said, over the loudspeaker, "Hanwell. In my office. Now."

I was passing Hernandez right then, and he crossed himself at the tone of her voice.

I walked to her office all chastened, with my head tilted slightly down, but just as I stepped through her door, my phone went off.

My mother. Again. And it turned out, the guys on shift had changed my ringtone to "Big Bottom" from *Spinal Tap*. Because that's what firemen do.

Captain Harris watched me like, *Really?* as I scrambled to silence it.

"Close the door," she said.

I closed the door.

"Take a seat."

I took a seat.

She shuffled through some files on her desk and let me wait. Captain Harris had been one of the first women to join the Austin Fire Department, back in the eighties. She was also the first-ever African American female captain. I idolized her, and admired her, and feared her, too. She'd seen everything and then some, and then some more.

She was about as close as a regular human could get to a superhero. And guess what? She really didn't put up with nonsense.

I waited for her to light into me. I waited for her to tell me in unflinching detail how much I'd humiliated the department last night with my behavior. I waited for her to punish me somehow—a suspension or a demotion. Something.

She just kept her eyes on her paperwork and let me wait.

Finally, she looked up. "How long have you worked here, Hanwell?"

"Four years last month."

She studied me a little. "You're a good fit here, aren't you?"

"I think so," I said.

"The guys like you. Even after you raised Big Tom's underwear up the flagpole."

"I suspect they like me *because* I raised Big Tom's underwear up the flagpole."

"You seem to be very admired. For a woman."

I blinked. "Thank you."

"I called you in here for several reasons—not just your temporary insanity last night. But don't worry, we'll get to that."

I waited.

"First, we need to discuss your performance on the Lieutenant's Exam. The scores are in. This was your first time taking it, correct?"

I held very still. "That's correct, Captain."

"You realize most people don't pass that exam the first time?"

"Yes, Captain." Everybody knew that.

"Some of our best guys have tried three or four times before passing."

My heart wilted a little, anticipating bad news. I'd studied for months for that test. "Yes, Captain."

"It might surprise you to hear, then, that not only did you pass, you got the number one score in the entire city. You scored two points below me."

I sat up.

She lifted her eyebrows, just a sliver, in admiration. "Strong work."

I didn't know what to say. "Thank you, Captain."

"Ordinarily, of course, that would mean a promotion to lieutenant."

I nodded.

"But your circumstances at the moment are not exactly ordinary."

I glanced down at my hand, which was throbbing a little. I might need to splint a finger.

Worth it.

I lifted my eyes back to the captain.

"I need you to know that the chief and the mayor have had their eye on you for a while now."

"They have?"

She nodded. "You've been on the city's radar ever since that feature the *Statesman* did on you last summer, but that top test score clinched it." Now she was looking me over. "Until last night, you were a perfect representative of the best of our department. You're young, and fit, and wholesome. No visible tattoos." She studied my face another second, then added, "Pretty, but not too pretty."

I frowned. "Thank you."

"Tell me this, Hanwell," she said. "Why did we put the hoses on that warehouse fire last month when it was burning too hot for the water to do any good?"

We both knew that answer. A hundred-person crowd had been watching us, and then the news helicopters showed up. And even though the only way that fire was going to go out was to burn itself to the ground, we put water on it anyway. Because that's what people wanted us to do.

"Hydraulic public relations, Captain," I answered.

She nodded, like, *Exactly*. "Image matters. When they see us coming, they need to know we're the good guys. They need to let us get in and get to work."

I nodded.

"Do you know what the trouble with women is, Hanwell?"

I shook my head.

"Women don't look like firefighters."

No argument there.

"You know Austin is a very progressive department," she said next.

I did know that, of course. Anyone who'd seen our rainbow flag flying, or shopped at one of our vegan/kosher bake sales, or seen our fire marshal tooling around in a Prius knew we were a progressive department.

"The city wants to update our image," she said. "And—again, up until last night—I would have said you were a perfect candidate to lead the way. You're smart as hell, and you're strong as an ox, and you don't seem to be scared of anything."

"Thank you."

"I'm not saying you're reckless. I mean you have a steadiness about you that's particularly well suited to the job."

I nodded.

"You're not just a token female, is what I'm saying. You're actually good."

I'd assumed that went without saying, but okay.

"After we announced you were getting the valor award, the mayor and the fire chief met and made it official," the captain went on. "They wanted to enlist you as part of a PR campaign to redefine the look of the fire service. Billboards, TV interviews, bus ads. You and a few others. They put together a whole multicultural A Team."

Whoa.

"But that"—she pulled her reading glasses down her nose—"was before yesterday."

I nodded but didn't say anything.

She studied me. "What the hell happened, Hanwell?"

What the hell did happen? How to even begin? I stared at my hands.

"I want to help you," the captain said. "But I can't help you if you won't talk to me."

It wasn't that I wouldn't talk to her. I wasn't sure if I could.

I took a breath. "The councilman?" I began. "From last night? I knew him in high school. He was a senior when I was a sophomore."

She waited, all impatient patience. "And?"

But I couldn't seem to arrange my thoughts into words. Subject-verb-object. It shouldn't be that hard. I opened my mouth, but no sounds came out.

She shook her head. "You've got to give me *something*."

I nodded. Something. Okay. I leaned forward and looked right into her eyes. "He's a bad person," I said at last.

She waited for more, and when it didn't come, she lifted her hands. *That's it?*

I nodded. That pretty much summed it up. I leaned a little closer. "He's a very, *very* bad person."

Then her face shifted. She seemed to get it somehow. Not that she suddenly, telepathically knew the specifics of *how* he was a bad person, but she got that on some level the specifics didn't matter. She knew me. She trusted me. I had proved myself over and over to be a moral person, and a brave one, and a selfless one. In that moment, based on my expression, she knew.

She knew in that way that other women just know.

I wasn't joking around, and I wasn't being flip, and I hadn't lost my mind, and—most important—I had my reasons. She didn't need more details, and she wasn't going to push for them. If I said he was bad, then he was bad. Case closed.

She sighed and dropped her shoulders.

"They're willing to overlook it."

I blinked.

"They can't put you on the PR team, of course, because it would be a media fiasco. But they're still willing to promote you to lieutenant and chalk it up to an 'interpersonal conflict.' You're certainly not the first firefighter to ever get in a fistfight." I saw the corner of her mouth trying to avoid a smile. "Though you might be the first lady firefighter to ever pummel a smug politician to the ground."

I looked down at my hand.

She said, "I hear he got a concussion."

I gave a tiny shrug. "He deserved it."

I wasn't sure what to make of what she was saying. I had felt certain last night, back alone in my apartment, that I was facing a suspension, at the very least.

Not a promotion.

"We could," she went on, "just let this all blow over, give it a year or so, and then quietly promote you. How does that sound?"

I met her eyes. Safe to say, this was not the conversation I'd expected. "It sounds too good to be true," I said.

"The point is not to let one bad night define the rest of your career," she said, then added, "or your life."

I nodded, noting the irony.

"They just need you to do one quick thing," she said then, closing up her folder like we were almost done here.

"What's that?"

"Apologize."

I blinked at her. "To who? To the chief?"

She frowned, like, *Hello?* "To the city councilman."

My head started shaking before my mind had formed the words. "I can't do that."

She gave a little sigh, like now I was being difficult. Which I suppose I was. "A formal apology. You don't have to mean it. Just get it on the record."

"I'm not going to apologize," I said, just to be clear. Again.

"He and his friends on the council, they control our budget." She gave a head shake. Then she added, "He could press charges for assault."

But I didn't think he would. We had too much history, and he had just as much to lose as I did. "He won't press charges," I said.

"You don't know that," she said. "And more importantly, the chief doesn't know that. He wants full assurance that this is all over. That's his deal: Apologize, and we all move on."

"I can't apologize," I said. "And I won't."

She assessed me then. Was I really going to go there? Was I really going to dig in and not budge?

Apparently, yes.

"If you don't apologize, I have to terminate your contract," she said. "Chief's orders."

Terminate my contract. That was my choice. Apologize, and I got promoted; refuse to apologize, and I got fired.

"I won't apologize."

She leaned in a little closer and shook her head. "Just do it. Get it over with. Let's move on. You're a phenomenal firefighter. You deserve to do what you love. You need us and we need you. Don't let this derail you."

"I can't," I said. Anything else, but not that.

I held still.

She leaned back. Then she let out the long sigh of a woman who'd seen, and survived, far too much to mess around. She peered at me over her reading glasses, like, *Fine.* "You're sure that's what you want to do?"

I nodded.

She looked back down at her file and retreated into formalities. "Then as of this moment, you are terminated for gross insubordination and conduct unbecoming."

Terminated.

Oh my God. *Terminated.*

A fog of panic rose up through my body. Who was I if I wasn't a firefighter? What did I do if I didn't do this? This was the life I'd worked for, trained for, dreamed about. This was the only thing I wanted. This was my reason for going to the gym, for eating broccoli, for *living.* This was my whole identity.

Terminated.

But even facing that, I still wasn't apologizing.

There was no other choice I could make, and here was my consequence.

Then I suddenly remembered one other possibility—and no matter how out-of-the-question awful it had seemed yesterday, today it was suddenly looking better.

"What if there's another option?" I asked.

"Like what?"

"What if I transferred? To another department?"

She frowned.

"My mother is ill," I said. "She's been asking me to move to Massachusetts and help her out as a caregiver. Maybe I could move away and work at a different fire station. Make myself disappear."

Maybe this could work. Anything was better than *terminated.* Plus, something else struck me: This wouldn't be the last time I ran into Heath Thompson. The man was everywhere in this town these days.

Maybe it was time, after all, to get the hell out of here.

The captain frowned. "If this comes out, if it leaks to the press or he presses charges, you'll be terminated anyway."

"He won't press charges."

She stared at me while she ran through my remaining options in her head. I could see her weighing everything. She liked me, that much I knew. I wasn't just a good firefighter, I was great. She didn't want to see me terminated either. She started nodding, like this could work. Finally, she said, "I didn't even know you had a mother."

"Sometimes I forget, myself."

"Okay. We'll try your plan B. The promotion's out, though. You'll have to start all over. Stay there a few years at least. Work your way back up."

Starting over, I could handle. Terminated? Not so much. I closed my eyes. "Thank you."

The captain opened my file back up to make some notes. "Where does she live? I know of some openings in Boston."

"She lives in Rockport—about an hour north, on Cape Ann."

"Maybe there's something closer, then. I'll ask around."

She was going to ask around.

I wasn't terminated.

For a second, I felt relief—then, right on its heels, a thickness in my throat that I realized, with horror, was the feeling you get before your eyes fill up with tears. I coughed to clear it, and then coughed again. I had not cried in years, and I sure as hell wasn't about to start now. But these guys—this shift at this station—they were my family. The idea that I had to leave them all behind created a kind of weather system inside my rib cage.

A wet one.

Not good. I wasn't really a fan of being overcome by emotion. In fact, I'd structured my life around lack of emotion. I'd built it around routine, and safety, and order. Feelings were a lot of trouble. I avoided them as much as possible.

I swallowed. I held very still. I ordered myself to be tough. I wanted to bolt for the door, but I was afraid that if I moved, I might lose it.

Was I seriously about to cry—in front of the captain—on top of everything else?

It wasn't looking good.

Suddenly, all deus ex machina, the tones went off for a jackknifed eighteen-wheeler on Highway 71.

Work always saved me. I stood up, felt all those unruly emotions drain away, and shifted into all-business work mode.

"Hanwell?" the captain said, as I reached the door.

I turned back to her, my hand on the knob.

She looked at me over the top of her reading glasses. "You would've made a goddamned great lieutenant."

Five

WITHIN A WEEK, the captain was able to find me a position in a small city called Lillian, about twenty minutes from my mom's place in Rockport. A shift at Station Two had two positions open because a pair of brothers who'd worked together thirty years were retiring together—moving south to Florida to fish and drink beer for the rest of their lives. They'd found a rookie for one of the spots, but they wanted somebody with experience for the other.

Captain Harris called me in after a conference call with the battalion chief and the station captain, a guy named Murphy.

"I let them know that you're a big deal," Captain Harris said. "I talked you up for a long time. I told them about your test scores, and how much we don't want to lose you. I gave them some of your best saves: the double cardiac arrest at that rib joint; the infant you pulled from that car fire when no one else heard the cries; what you did to those frat boys who set that swimming pool on fire. I told them about your being the youngest person ever to receive our valor award—though I conveniently left out how you clobbered the hell out of the presenter on the stage."

"Thank you."

"All to say, I made sure he was totally sold on you before I broke the bad news."

"The bad news?"

I guessed that she was referring to my alarming capability for random violence, but instead she shrugged, like, *Duh*. "That you're a female."

"Oh." I nodded. That. "What did he say?"

"Honestly," she said, "that guy Murphy's accent is so thick, I didn't catch everything. But I'm pretty sure he told me that women are the worst, and they have no place in the fire service, and that in the hundred and twenty years of the Lillian FD, they'd never hired 'a lady' before. Then he added, 'Not to fight fires, anyway.'"

"Did he really say, 'Women are the worst'?"

She squinted. "He doesn't seem to have much of a filter."

"Did he realize that he was talking to a woman?"

"If he did, he didn't care."

"Did he realize he can't discriminate?"

"If he did, he didn't care."

I took all that in. Then I let out a long sigh. My brain flipped through my options. I could sue the Lillian FD for discrimination, I supposed, but that wasn't going to help me get to Rockport any faster. Plus, I'd never sued anybody in my life—and I was really rooting for fewer lawsuits these days, not more.

I didn't want to fight for justice. I just wanted to fight fires.

I let out a breath. "Maybe I can look in Boston," I said next, trying to stay productive. "An hour commute isn't impossible."

The captain looked up. "Oh, no. They want you in Lillian."

I frowned. "They do?"

"Yes. Captain Murphy ended his lecture on how women in the fire service will be the downfall of human civilization by admitting that they actually do really need somebody, and beggars couldn't be choosers, and at this point, they'd take, quote: 'Anybody with experience and a pulse—even a lady.'"

I kind of hated that word, "lady." Made me sound like I had ringlets and a petticoat.

"And the chief agreed," she added. "So you're in."

"So," I said, summing up, "they don't want me, but they're so desperate, they'll take me anyway."

"That's about the size of it."

I thought for a second. "Well, I'm desperate, too. So I guess we're a good match."

"You're a terrible match," the captain said. "But your only other option is Boston. And I can't imagine they want a lady either."

I nodded.

"So you'll take the position?"

I nodded again. What choice did I have?

"And what will you do?" she asked.

I wasn't sure what she meant. I frowned. "I'll get a map of the city and learn the territory before I get there. I'll show up on time ready to work, and I'll work hard—"

The captain cut me off. "That's not what I mean." She leaned across her desk to hand me a blank piece of paper.

I took it.

Then she found a pen in a drawer and flung it at me.

I caught it.

"How did you wind up here?" she asked then.

"I was recruited straight out of the academy."

"Having graduated at the top of your class," she added, "easily passing both the written and physical tests—and then I handpicked you to come here. And you've been a valued asset, a tireless worker, and a rising superstar ever since."

She waited for me to see her point.

I didn't, though.

She leaned closer to spell it out. "You have no idea what it's like to work in a place where you're not wanted. You've been recruited—welcomed—into every job you've ever had."

She wasn't wrong.

"But all that's over now," she said. "The day you walk out of here, all that's gone."

"Is it going to be that bad?" I asked.

"It's going to be worse."

I looked down at the sheet of paper. "What's the paper for?"

She leaned back in her chair. "I'm going to give you some hard-won advice. And you're going to take notes."

"Okay." I popped the cap off the pen and waited.

She paused for a second, like it was hard to know where to start. Then she began. "First: Don't expect them to like you," she said. "They dislike you already, and they've never even met you. These guys will never be your friends."

She looked at the blank paper under my hand. "Write it down."

I wrote it down.

She went on. "Don't wear makeup, perfume, or lady-scented deodorant. ChapStick is okay, but no lip gloss—nothing shiny, no color. Don't paint your nails. Don't wear any jewelry, not even earring studs. And cut your hair off—or keep it back. Don't take it down or shake it out or play with it—ever. Don't even touch it."

I wasn't going to cut my hair off. That was where I drew the line.

"So the idea is to make them think I'm a guy?"

"They will know you're not a guy. The boobs are a dead giveaway."

I corrected: "To make them *less aware* I'm a girl?"

She nodded. "Whenever possible." She went on. "Don't giggle. And don't laugh too loud. Don't touch anybody for any reason. Don't carry a purse. Don't use the upper registers of your voice, but don't allow too much vocal fry, either. Don't sing, ever. And if you make eye contact, make it straight on, like a predator."

"Are you joking?"

She raised one eyebrow, like, *Do I ever joke?*

No. She was not joking. I was going to have to look up the term "vocal fry."

"Follow your orders," she went on. "Don't ask questions. Know the rules. Go above and beyond at every chance. If your captain says to run a mile, run two. If he wants you to dead-lift one fifty, do one seventy-five. How much can you dead-lift?"

"Two hundred."

"Impressive. How many pull-ups can you do?"

"Twenty." A lot, even for a guy.

"You need to do thirty, at least—and with ease. Get on that. Forty would be better. And make sure you can do at least a few one-handed."

I wrote down *40 pull-ups*.

"Don't ever act afraid. Don't ever hesitate. Don't ever admit it when you don't understand."

"What if I don't understand, though?"

"Figure it out. Like a man."

I had no idea what that meant, but I wrote it down, too.

"Don't back down from a challenge," she went on, "and if you go up against somebody, make damn sure to win. No fear! If your hands start shaking, sit on them. If you get an injury, ignore it."

"You always tell us *not* to ignore injuries."

"New rules: Never admit to being hurt. Pain is for the weak."

I wrote down *PAIN = for the weak*.

"They will ignore you. They will exclude you. They will resent you. Being nice won't help. Working hard won't matter. Just by your very presence there, you are attacking them, trying to steal something that's rightfully theirs, trying to infiltrate and dismantle their brotherhood. You'll be a hen in a wolf-house, and they will eat you like a snack the first chance they get."

She paused, and I thought about where all this advice was coming from.

She was trying to help me face my future, but she was clearly talking about her own past, about the path she herself had walked to get where she was. My admiration for her went up another thousand percent—even as my own confidence started to flag.

I tried to regroup. Maybe things had changed. She'd joined up thirty years ago. They'd barely invented the sports bra back then. I thought about the friendly camaraderie I'd always known at our station—what a solid brother- *and* sisterhood we had.

The captain sounded like she was describing some distant dark ages.

I wondered if it could still really be this bad.

"You can't let anything bother you," she went on. "You can't get offended. You can't be girly. They will test you and test you before you earn a place among them—and you might still never get one. They'll tease you relentlessly, and it might be good-natured, or it might be cruel, but it doesn't matter either way. They will burst in on you while you're in the bathroom. They will goose you on the butt. They will dump ice water on you while you're fast asleep in your bunk. And don't get me started on the duct tape. It is what it is. It's the life. Don't get mad. Don't file reports. Your only choice is to laugh about it."

I circled the word "laugh."

"And don't talk too much, either. Remember: What women think of as sharing, men see as complaining."

I could feel my shoulders starting to sink.

"Here's another one: Don't have feelings."

"Don't have *feelings*?"

"Don't talk about them, don't explore them, and for God's sake, whatever you do, don't cry."

"I never cry."

"Good. Keep it that way."

I wrote the word "feelings," circled it, and drew a line through the circle. *Feelings: bad.*

"Last, but not least," she said, tapping the paper with her finger like she really wanted me to pay attention. "No sex."

She waited for me to protest, but I didn't.

"No sex with firefighters," she went on. "Or friends of firefighters. Or relatives of firefighters. Even acquaintances of firefighters." She pointed at me. "If they even get a whiff that you're attracted to somebody anywhere near the station, you're a goner. That's the biggest rule, and I saved it for last: Do not sleep with firefighters."

"So I need to live like a nun." Not a problem. Tragic celibacy for the win.

"Until you've proved yourself, yes. Because there's no faster way for you to go down in flames than to screw one of the guys."

"Just hypothetically," I said then, already knowing the answer, "would the guy go down in flames, too?"

The captain took off her reading glasses and gave me a look like, *Please.*

"I like you," she said then. "I've always liked you. You've had it easy, and now you're about to get the opposite. Maybe it'll break you, or maybe it'll make you. If you play it right, your struggles might even lead you to your strengths."

I had no idea how to play it right.

Then she said, "My best advice to you? Find one person you can count on. Just one."

I looked the sheet over. "So, to succeed in my new job, I basically need to be an asexual, androgynous, human robot that's dead to all physical and emotional sensation."

She sat back in her chair and nodded, like, *Yep. Simple.*

I nodded.

"Just be a machine," she said. "A machine that eats fire."

Six

THE DRIVE ACROSS the country gave me a lot of time to think things through.

I didn't even turn on the radio.

I just drove with the window down, the air roaring in and swirling around me.

Had all that really just happened? Had I really just torpedoed my career—the best thing in my entire life? Had I beaten up Heath Thompson on a stage in front of three hundred of my most esteemed colleagues? Had I given up a promotion to lieutenant by refusing to apologize? What the hell?

One thing I couldn't decide: Had refusing to apologize been standing up for myself—or sabotaging myself? I could see arguments both ways. As I left behind everything and everyone I cared about back in Texas, and as I pictured my emptied-out apartment and my dad's garage filled with storage tubs of my stuff, and as I watched the road ahead of me stretch out farther and farther into uncertainty, the question lingered.

It could have been worse, I kept telling myself.

I kept thinking about a woman I'd rescued from a plane crash not that long ago. The pilot, her boyfriend, got caught in a crosswind during landing and cartwheeled. The guy walked away without a scratch, but the woman was so burned, crushed, and wedged, we had to strip the plane apart with the hydraulic cutters.

During the extrication, she told me they had just gotten engaged. On that very flight.

Then she insisted it was the happiest day of her life.

After a while, in the fire service, calls start to blur together in your mind. But a rare few stand out. Something about that woman stayed with me—something about the way I'd glimpsed her future before she did. Her life as she knew it was gone, and I was the first one to know.

That's how life is. Things happen. Lives get broken. Some people never can put themselves back together.

I wondered if she would.

I wondered if I would.

All I'd had to do was shake the man's hand and walk off the stage. Instead, I put him in the hospital. Which was still a lot less than he'd done to me. But what was that old saying my dad loved so much? *The best revenge is forgetting.*

I clearly hadn't forgotten a thing.

Despite all my efforts.

In my defense, I hadn't expected to see Heath Thompson there. I'd had no warning. It was supposed to be the mayor—a friendly, portly fellow I'd met several times before. It was the shock of seeing the monster himself. I hadn't had time to prepare. If I'd known it would be him in advance, maybe I could have acted differently.

Or not.

Maybe, if I'd known, I would have skipped the banquet entirely.

Maybe I wasn't as completely fine as I wanted to think.

And now—insult to injury—I was moving in with my mother.

The last person I would have picked.

She didn't even know the real reason I'd agreed to come. She thought I was just being nice—just doing my daughterly duty.

Or maybe she thought I'd softened toward her. Or even decided to forgive her. Was she expecting bonding? Was that on her agenda?

There would be no bonding.

I was going there to do a job. I would help her until she'd adjusted to her new eye situation, and then I'd find somewhere else to live. If I could prove myself at the Lillian FD, I'd move to Lillian. If not, I'd move somewhere else. Somewhere closer to home—preferably some place with tacos. A year at the most, she'd said. But it would take much longer.

Oh my God. I was moving back in with my mother.

How long had it been since I'd lived with her? Not since before she'd left us—on the night I turned sixteen.

A lifetime.

Would she notice how different I was now?

Would it bother me when she noticed?

Would she try to change me back?

And if she did that—if she insisted on comparing and contrasting who I'd been before with who I'd become now—what would that do to me? Would it drown me in sorrow for everything I'd lost?

I sucked in a deep breath and sat up straight.

I needed a strategy. The one thing I couldn't do right now was to become emotionally destabilized. I had worked too hard and come too far.

The only safe approach I could see was to keep my distance. Yes, I had to live in her attic, but we'd be housemates and nothing more. I'd go to work, and take long runs, and work out, and do whatever chores she asked of me, and that would be it. My mother—and life, and circumstances, and Captain Harris—could force me into this situation. But nobody could make me like it.

ARRIVING IN ROCKPORT, I spotted my mother's house right away. I didn't even have to check the address.

It was a tiny, classic New England saltbox shape, with gray shingles, just as I'd seen everywhere on my drive up, but it was covered, doorstep to roof, in painted flowers.

The front door, and all around it, and the windows and shutters and window boxes—all brightly, lovingly hand-painted with folk-art reds and pinks and oranges. The tiny front yard overflowed with real flowers as well, in a colorful, tangled jumble, draping over the picket fence.

Yep. This was Diana's place.

She'd lived in Rockport for a full decade, but I'd never visited. She kept on inviting me, and I kept on declining.

Some part of me had never wanted to see the life she'd left us for.

Now, here I was, moving in.

I stood at the garden gate, but I couldn't seem to make myself walk through it.

The sheer cuteness of her painted house felt disingenuous. The world might pass this sweet-looking house and decide that an equally sweet person lived in it. But I knew the truth. No amount of painted flowers could cover the truth. She was still the person who'd left us. She was still the person who had disappeared when I really, really needed her.

She was still one of the greatest disappointments of my life.

I tried to get oriented by looking around at the town's sheer, unadulterated, almost aggressive New England charm.

It wasn't like I hadn't been warned. According to Diana, if you'd ever seen a movie that featured a "charming seaside village" for any amount of time, it was Rockport. She could rattle off ten of them in as many seconds. And her house, she swore, was at the epicenter of the cuteness—in a historic fishing village nestled on a narrow jetty called Bearskin Neck that curved out into the harbor.

She'd described it before, of course. I just hadn't been paying attention.

Quaint little dollhouse-like stores decorated with weathered wooden buoys sold everything from T-shirts to jewelry to ice cream. Shutters were painted cheery pastels, and planter flowers bloomed everywhere. It was too idyllic to be true, and next to my big, hot, multicultural, gritty, authentic, beloved home city of Austin, this place felt absolutely fake.

Yet it felt like my mom, too. She herself was charming, and well groomed, and lovely. I could see why she would feel drawn here. It felt like her in a way Texas never had. I felt a surge of jealously toward this adorable town and all it had to offer. It had gone up against Austin, and won. But the real loser was me.

Just then, the front door opened. And there she was. My long-lost mother. Not literally lost, since, technically, we made an effort to see each other from time to time.

But lost all the same.

It had been a year since I'd seen her—for coffee, the last time she'd been passing through Austin—and I felt the familiar sensation that seeing her always gave me in the years since their divorce. A particular kind of numbness that happened when my heart wanted to flood with all the things people feel about their mothers—but I flat-out refused to let it.

There she was. The lady who had always been my mother. Exactly the same.

Except, wearing an eye patch.

It was so strange to see anyone in an eye patch, let alone my own mother. Then there was the patch itself, homemade out of blue calico fabric with flowers—which was even more off-putting than the fact of it in the first place. Who had a homemade eye patch?

That had to be the eye with the mysterious 'oma, of course. The sight of the patch made her situation—and by extension mine—seem real for the first time.

It also made her seem a little larger than life.

Or maybe that was just her.

I reminded myself again that she was only Diana. Of course, our parents get an extra dose of importance in our minds. When we're little, they're everything—the gods and goddesses that rule our worlds. It takes a lot of growing up, and a lot of disappointment, to accept that they're just normal, bumbling, mistaken humans, like everybody else.

Her hair was grayer now, and she wore it in a short bob that curled forward under her ears. She'd never been a big one for makeup. She wore the same canvas apron she'd always worn, with a lifetime's worth of smears and drips of glaze on it in every color known to nature, over wide-leg linen pants and a linen shirt that were both somehow the exact right ratio of wrinkled to pressed.

I'd forgotten how beautiful she was. I could say that without softening toward her, couldn't I? That was just a cold fact. She was beautiful.

But also, for the first time in my life, I thought she looked old.

She tried to step toward me, but she stumbled over a corner of the welcome mat and had to bend down to study the two steps down to the sidewalk.

By the time we reached each other, the resentment I'd been feeling had mixed with so many other feelings and impulses—sorrow, regret, loneliness, protectiveness, admiration, affection—that it became something else completely.

Complicated.

She moved in for a hug in slo-mo. I saw her lean in, and I thought, *Don't hug me. Don't hug me.*

Then she hugged me.

I stepped back when she released me.

"You made it," she said then, raising her one good eye to take me in.

"Nice eye patch," I said.

She touched it, like she'd forgotten it was there, then smiled as if I'd embarrassed her. "A friend made it for me," she said. Her fingernails had clay under them, as always, and she had a paintbrush tucked behind her ear.

"You found your way okay?" she asked.

"I always do."

"Thank you for coming, Cassie."

I shrugged. "There wasn't really a choice."

"There's always a choice," she said. She half-turned to lead me inside. "Can I help you with your bag?"

The idea was almost funny, as I watched her work her way back up the two little steps. "I don't think you can," I said.

Inside, the house was tiny—and not just because everything's bigger in Texas.

Just past the door was a living room barely big enough for a love seat and two chairs in front of a stone hearth. Beyond that was a kitchen area with a farmhouse table. That was it. Past the kitchen door, out back, I could see a garden, and beyond that, the water. From the living room, a crooked little eighteenth-century staircase crossed in front of a window, up to the second floor. There didn't seem to be a right angle in the whole place, and the wind outside made the house creak like a ship.

"This place is like a dollhouse," I said.

She smiled like I'd offered a compliment. "Isn't it?"

Nothing about any of this felt real. I felt like a live person who'd just showed up in a Disney cartoon.

Yet here I was.

"Can I fix you a snack?" she asked, almost like I was a kid just home from school. She assessed my state. "Or get you a drink? Or would you rather just unload your things and get settled?"

No, she could not fix me a snack. What was I, twelve? "I'll take my stuff up," I said.

"My bedroom and studio are the next floor up," she said, "and the whole attic is yours. It has its own bath, so you'll have everything you need."

"Is it always this windy?" I asked.

"Always," Diana said, like it was a selling point. "Because we're out here on the jetty. We're not just near the water, we're on it."

I looked around. "This place must be two hundred years old."

She nodded. "Two hundred and fifty. A fisherman named Samuel McKee built it. He and his wife, Chastity, raised eight children here."

"There's some irony there."

"There are stains on the kitchen floor where they used to pickle the fish."

Off to the side was a porch the length of the building that Diana used for a pottery studio and shop. She had made up a profession for herself: She was a dishmaker. It wasn't a real category, and I'd spent my life explaining it when people said, "Huh?" But here in the house, it seemed plenty real. She made dishes and cups and saucers—threw them on the ceramics wheel, then hand-painted them with glaze and fired them. She specialized in gardens and animals, bright colors and polka dots. She made whole sets. And the shop was bright and cheery like the dishes. She sold other fun kitchen items to round out the selection—tea towels and aprons and napkins—all in charming patterns and fabrics.

"It's a terrible living," she told me once, "but it's fun."

I could tell it was fun. Just from looking.

"How did you find this place?"

"Oh," she said, glancing out the window, "it belonged to Wallace."

Wallace was the man she'd left my father for. The cheater. We didn't talk about him. "He gave it to you?"

"Left it to me," she said, nodding. "After he died."

A pause. I'd never met Wallace. I knew about him, but I'd refused to meet him in the same way I'd refused to visit Rockport. I'd blamed him. I'd been angry. I'd been far too absorbed in the pain he caused me—and my dad—to see Wallace as anything other than the source of all my problems. Now, of course, it was too late. He'd died when I was in college.

"It'll be yours one day," my mom added then.

"I don't want it," I said, too quickly. She couldn't just make me move here and then give me a house.

She blinked. "Oh, well, that's okay. But I'll leave it to you anyway. In my will. You can sell it, of course, if you want."

"You don't have to leave it to me."

"Who else would I possibly leave it to?"

"Let's not talk about it."

"No. I agree. Hardly our first order of business."

I looked around the room.

"I'm so grateful to you for coming," she said after a minute. "I know you gave up a lot to be here."

There it was again. That magic she had for draining my anger: her gratitude, her sympathy. She didn't make things easy. With my dad, things were always simple. He was dedicated, true-blue, kindhearted, and tough. You knew exactly where you stood with him, always. No layers of conflicting feelings to sort through. He was just a good guy, plain and easy.

But there was no feeling I had about my mom that wasn't mixed with other feelings—often opposite ones. Everything was always tinged with something else.

Plus, I couldn't get over the eye patch. It gave her a strange, incongruous vibe—as if Laura Ingalls Wilder had turned pirate.

Assessing her gave me a flutter of fear through my chest, and in response to fear, I always got all-business. "Let me take a look at that eye," I said, stepping toward her and reaching toward the patch, relieved for something to do.

She lifted a hand to block me. "Not sure that's a great idea."

"You do know what I do for a living, right? I see this stuff all the time. You can't shock me."

"I know," she said. "This is different."

"I might be able to help you," I said.

"I don't think so," she said.

"Just let me take a look."

She wasn't going for it. "I've got a whole team of doctors. Don't concern yourself with it."

"Isn't that the reason I'm here?" I asked. "To concern myself with it?"

She shook her head. "You're just here to help me up and down the stairs. And do the driving. And buy the groceries."

"That's really all you want?" I asked. Seemed like just about anybody could do that.

"That's what I *need,*" she said. Then she took my hand and squeezed it. "What I actually *want,* after all these years, is to spend a little time with my long-lost daughter."

Seven

DINNER WAS HOMEMADE lobster bisque and a salad with greens from her garden—and I felt both grateful for and annoyed by how delicious it was. I'd been thinking I'd just take a sandwich up to my room, but she'd cooked everything already and set the table. With her own charming dishes.

Plan B: Eat quickly and say good night.

Having dinner together was worse than I would have expected. Apparently, we'd forgotten how to talk to each other. Attempts at chatting just flared and died. "This town is too cute to be real," I'd say. And she'd say, "I agree." And then we'd listen to the wind creak the house until somebody came up with another idea.

All of it made worse, in my opinion, by the fact that it never used to be like this back when she was my mother.

We'd been close, before. We'd watched every movie Jimmy Stewart ever made, side by side on the sofa. She hadn't been like the other moms, all rules and criticism. She'd been more like a friend than a parent. No minivan, for example: She drove an emerald-green, highly impractical vintage Volvo that she'd named Barbara. It was in the shop half the time, so we had to take the bus, and when I begged her to get a better car, she responded that she'd had Barbara longer than she'd had me. Case closed.

"Do you still have Barbara?" I asked her then.

"Yes," she said, "but she's in the shop."

"As usual," I said, and it was nice to share the memory.

My mom had married my dad, she'd once told me, because he'd told her she was fascinating.

"Who doesn't want to be fascinating?" she'd said.

But they weren't much alike. She was a dreamer who had trouble keeping straight what day of the week it was, and he was a high school math teacher with a buzz cut—all practicality—who coached basketball. Still, he was kind, and fair, and loyal.

I had not seen it coming when she left. Neither had he. We had thought we were happy.

It was on my list of things I would definitely never ask her about.

Across the table, Diana made another attempt. "I know it's a big change, coming here. I'm glad to introduce you around town."

I waved her off. "No thanks. I'm good."

She frowned. "Just a little jump-start on making friends."

I shook my head. "I'm not here to make friends."

I sounded like a contestant on a reality show. She held on to that frown. "What *are* you here for?"

"I'm here to"—I paused a second. "I'm here to do my duty."

"Your *duty*?"

"Yeah," I said, not appreciating her mocking tone. "You're old, you're half blind, you're broke, and it's my duty to come here and help you." Okay, I'd also come to avoid getting fired. But the truth—the real truth—is that I would have come anyway. I would not have held to that no. Eventually, guilt would have prodded me into doing the right thing, even if the threat of being terminated had sped things up a bit. "I'm here to help you, as requested," I said. "For one year."

She looked disappointed.

What more did she want? I'd shown up, hadn't I? Did she really have to guilt-trip me for not being happy enough about it? "What?" I demanded.

"It just doesn't sound very fun."

"I'm not here to have fun."

Her shoulders went up in a little shrug. "Is fun out of the question?"

"Yes," I said, with a decisive nod. "Fun is out of the question. I have too much to do. I have to take care of you. I have to get in better shape. I have to prove myself at a firehouse that already hates me. I have to rebuild my life."

"Without fun."

She was like a terrier with this "fun" thing.

I stood up, pushing my chair back with a scrape. "Time for bed," I said.

She looked at the clock on the wall, then raised her eyebrows. "It's seven thirty."

I wasn't letting her win. "I'm an early riser."

She nodded, then, after a second, said, "I just wanted to invite you to come to crochet club."

Crochet club? I gave it a beat.

"It's right next door," she said, gesturing. "At my friend Josie's house."

"I don't crochet."

"You don't have to crochet. You could knit. Or wind yarn balls."

"You want me to wind yarn balls?"

"It's very soothing. Or sew something. Maybe a little potholder?"

"I don't sew potholders either."

"The point is, it's more about hanging out and visiting."

"I'm just not really a joiner. Of clubs." That was true. Human connection had its upsides, but it sure was a lot of work. The risk-reward ratio was low, at best.

"You joined the fire service," she pointed out, as if she might win this conversation.

"That's not a club. That's a job."

"Pretty clubby for a job, though."

She wasn't wrong. "I avoid the clubby parts."

"Just come for ten minutes. You'll love it."

Did she really think she could tempt me with the phrase *sew a pot-holder*?

"And it's not just crochet," she went on. "We usually put on a rom-com, too."

She was not helping her case. I shook my head. "I have one day left to finish memorizing all the streets and fire hydrant locations in Lillian."

"Good grief," she said.

"It's called knowing the territory."

"You have to memorize them *all*?"

"I've been working on it ever since I got the job. I've got flash cards. Maps."

She nodded, sighing with resignation.

I took my plate to the sink, rinsed it, and put it in the dishwasher. She watched me the whole time. Did she really think I'd come here to *crochet*? Or watch rom-coms? This was exactly what I'd feared. She wanted to bond. But I didn't bond. With anyone.

I walked toward the staircase.

She followed me.

"It's not going very well, is it?" she said, as I started up.

"What?" I asked.

"This. Now. Tonight."

"It's an odd situation. We're suddenly living together after ten years of . . ." What to call it? "*Not* living together."

"Feels kind of like a first date or something. An awkward one."

"I wouldn't know," I said then, hoping to shut the conversation down. "I don't go on dates."

She peered at me. "What does that mean?"

Oh God. Now I'd started a conversation. "My generation doesn't really date," I said.

"Why not?"

I shrugged. "I guess it just seems kind of artificial."

"What do you do instead?"

I kept thinking each answer I gave would be the last one, and then

I'd be released to go on up. But she kept stopping me—snagging me there on the staircase. "We hang out. Usually in groups."

"But then how do you ever get close to anybody?"

"I guess it depends on how you define close."

"How do you have conversations? Get to know each other? Fall in love?"

"I told you," I said. "I don't fall in love."

"Surely you do, a little bit."

"Nope," I said. "Love is for girls."

"You are a girl," Diana pointed out.

I didn't even try to hide the scorn in my voice. "That doesn't mean I have to be girly."

Did we really have to have this conversation? I lifted my foot to the next step. I just wanted to go memorize fire hydrants. I sure as hell didn't know how to explain it to her if she didn't get it already. "Love makes people stupid," I said at last, hoping to cut to the chase, "and I'm not interested in being stupid."

"Not always," she said.

"Women especially," I added, not bothering to hide my impatience. "It makes them needy and sad and pathetic. And robs them of their independence."

"Independence is overrated," my mom said.

"Love is overrated," I countered. Then my notes from Captain Harris popped into my head, and I added, slapping the banister for emphasis, "Love is for the weak."

I needed that on a bumper sticker.

She wasn't letting that stand. "Love is not *weak*," she said, like I couldn't have shocked her more. "It's the opposite."

I took another step up. "We're just going to have to agree to disagree."

But she wasn't releasing me. The wind creaked the house. "Choosing to love—despite all the ways that people let you down, and disappear, and break your heart. Knowing everything we know about how hard life is and choosing to love anyway . . . That's not weakness. That's courage."

I have to give myself credit here for not snorting and saying, *We can talk about courage after you've walked through actual fire.* She wanted to talk about courage? I could talk about courage all day. And you weren't going to find it in a rom-com.

But I really just wanted to go to my room. "Okay," I said in a pleasant voice. "Whatever you say."

Now she pinned me with her stare. "It's my fault," she said, after a second. "For leaving."

"It's not your fault," I said, but there was that anger again, swirling itself into the mix. It kind of was her fault. She had been the first person to show me how terrible love could be.

The first, but certainly not the last.

She nodded now, like she'd figured something out. "You were fifteen when I moved out—"

"Sixteen," I corrected again. "It was my sixteenth birthday, the night you left."

Who does that, by the way? Who leaves her husband—her family—on her daughter's birthday? One of the great unanswered questions of my life, but I wasn't asking it now. We'd be here all night.

"You were so infatuated with that boy you liked. What was his name? Hank? Harold?"

"No one in my generation is named Harold," I said. "It's like asking if his name was Egbert."

She was squinting at me now, like she had me cornered. She snapped her fingers at me. "What was his name, though?"

I sighed. We had to do this? Right now? "His name," I said, ready to get it over with, "was Heath Thompson."

Saying it released a funny, acidic sting in my chest. The second person who had ruined love for me. Also on my sixteenth birthday, as luck would have it, on the very same night in a spectacular one-two punch of abandonment. My sixteenth birthday. The night I'd spent pretty much the rest of my life trying to recover from.

She barely even remembered it.

But I was not—*not*—going to get into that. I glanced up the stairs like I was late for an appointment or something.

"You were in love with him. I could tell. You doodled his name constantly."

I held very still.

She pointed at me like she was winning, like we were reminiscing about something pleasant. "I thought you were going to give yourself carpal tunnel."

"That wasn't love," I said, totally poker-faced. "That was delusion."

But she looked pleased with herself, like we were really getting somewhere. "Whatever happened with him?"

I took a second to marvel at the question.

I knew, of course, that there was no way she could be aware of "whatever happened" with Heath Thompson. I never told her. I never told anyone. In fairness, I couldn't resent her for that. But something about the chitchatty tone of her voice as she asked about it, like she was just getting the update on some friend's vacation plans or something—maybe even the idea that she could just *not know*, could have spent the past ten years obliviously making tea and watering hydrangea beds in this stupidly cute town—that, suddenly, really pissed me off.

I looked at her, so polite and friendly in that goofy calico eye patch.

"Nothing," I said. "Nothing ever happened with him."

She responded slowly, like she somehow knew I was lying. "Oh," she said. "That's too bad."

"Not really," I said. "He turned out to be a dick."

The language made her blink. "Did he?" she said.

I thought I was doing a pretty good job of mimicking a normal conversation—until I realized I was shaking. Not trembling, the way your fingers do when it's cold, but rumbling deep inside my core, as if my emotions were colliding with each other in plate tectonics.

Could she tell?

I wasn't waiting to find out. "I really do have a lot of work to do," I said then, taking another step up. The stair squeaked.

She read my expression, and my voice, and my urgency, and I could see her mentally back off. She'd gone too far, she suddenly realized. Tried too hard. Violated the essential rule of human relations that if you chase too hard, everyone eventually runs away. "Of course," she said, taking a step backwards. "Not tonight. To be continued."

"Or not," I said.

She saw her mistake. In trying to pull me closer, she'd pushed me away. She met my eyes one last time and gave a sad smile. "Now I've got my work cut out for me."

I'd already turned away. I paused and looked over. "What work?"

"Getting you to change your mind about love."

I shrugged, like I was sorry to break it to her. "I'll never change my mind," I said. "I know too much."

"Maybe you don't know enough."

Why wouldn't she just let me go upstairs? I let the irritation in my voice leak out. "Just look around at the world—at the lonely and the cheated on. The violent. The abandoned. I know exactly what people do to each other. I've seen enough ruined lives to last forever."

"None of that is what I'm talking about," she said. "None of that is love."

"There's conquest, and there's status, and there's porn. Love is something girls invented so they could feel better about it."

I'd shocked her. Good. "If that's what you truly believe," she said, "then I feel so sad for you."

"I feel sad for all the women out there dragging their boyfriends to Bed Bath & Beyond and making them shop for throw pillows. They want the fantasy more than they want the truth."

"What's the truth?" she challenged.

"The truth is that love doesn't exist."

I meant for that moment to be my win—I meant it to convey to her that whatever it was she remembered of me, or expected of me, or wanted from me, it wasn't happening. We weren't going to watch *It's a Wonderful Life* and be besties. We weren't going to talk about boys or braid each other's hair or treat this whole long year like a slumber party. That one fierce statement was meant to settle how things were going to be.

The girl she remembered was gone.

My mother should have nodded, looked down, and given up. But she didn't. If anything, the words seemed to spark more resistance in her.

She stood up a little straighter and looked me over like she was really seeing me for the first time all day. Then she said, "Sounds like you just threw down a challenge to the universe, lady."

I narrowed my eyes. "What does that mean?"

"It means," she said, looking a little triumphant, "that you clearly, obviously, any second now, are just about to fall in love."

Eight

WAY TOO MUCH conversation. I spent the next two days fiercely avoiding my mother.

No easy feat in a house the size of a shoe box.

I skipped dinner. I went for runs. I made "visual inspections" of the town of Lillian. I did the grocery shopping and picked up a lavender neck pillow for Diana at the pharmacist.

When I did interact with her, helping her on the stairs, say, I kept my interactions short, polite, and action oriented. I would not have another conversation like that with her. I hadn't come here for therapy, or to have my mind changed—about anything. I'd only come here because I had no choice.

Basically, I was just holding it together until I could start my first shift at work.

I had already timed the drive from Rockport to Lillian, twice, and scouted the station so I'd know how to get there. I'd been to HR downtown to fill out reams of paperwork, get fingerprinted, and pick up my mask, gear, and uniform—both dress and everyday—and make everything official. I picked up my brass nameplate and my ID badge with my firefighter/paramedic designation.

Then, the morning of my first day, I set three alarms for four thirty so I'd have no chance of being late.

I followed Captain Harris's instructions to the letter: no makeup, no jewelry, no cleavage. I even made an attempt at "no boobs" by clamping mine down with a bra that was part spandex, part corset. I put my hair in a low, decidedly unbouncy bun at the back of my neck. Actually, it wasn't even a bun; it was more like a wad. I just wrapped the ponytail holder as many times around it as it would stretch. Message: I care about my appearance exactly as little as a guy.

I even hesitated on the ChapStick because when I took off the cap, the wax looked slightly pink.

When I left the house at sunrise, Diana was also up, sitting meditation-style out on a bench in the garden, eyes closed, face turned to the breeze riding in from the ocean. She wore a silk kimono, and she had a different eye patch on. This one was red with cherry blossoms. In two days, I'd never once seen her without one.

I opened the back door, but she didn't hear me.

"I'm heading out," I called.

She turned and opened that one eye. "At this ungodly hour?"

"*You're* up," I said.

"Not by choice."

"Insomnia?"

"Something like that."

"What are you doing?"

"Breathing."

I squinted at her, like, *Um. We're all breathing.*

"Meditating," she corrected.

"Oh," I said. "That doesn't sound as good as sleeping."

"It has its upsides."

"Do you need anything before I go?"

She gave a little head shake. "I'm good. If I get in a fix, I'll call Josie next door. Her husband travels for work all the time, so we look out for each other."

I couldn't help but note that there'd been no mention of Josie back when Diana had been pressuring me to move here. But it was fine. Great. Backup. Less to worry about.

Time to get moving.

"It's crochet club again tomorrow night, in case you'd like to come."

I gave her a look. "That's a nope."

"See you tomorrow, then," she said. Then she winked her good eye at me and said, "Have fun."

I ARRIVED A half hour early and waited in my truck until it was time to go in, not wanting to look overeager.

At quarter to six, I grabbed my gear and reported to Captain Murphy's office.

I'd never walked into a firehouse cold like this before. Every job I'd had, I'd eased into. I'd known some guys who worked there, or I'd been encouraged to join by someone on the crew. It's one thing to be invited somewhere, but it's quite another to just show up.

My stomach felt tight. This was the moment of truth. This was the moment when I'd find out exactly how much I'd given up by moving here—and if I could ever get it back. As strange as it sounds, friends, apartments, and even cities were all replaceable. But the job—this particular job—held something for me that I couldn't find anywhere else. It gave me access to my favorite part of myself. That calm, centered person who knew exactly what to do.

I'd endure anything to get back to her.

Failure was not an option.

Maybe they didn't want me here. Maybe they'd resent everything about me. It didn't matter. I needed to secure my place here, however I could.

If I lost this, I lost the one part of myself I couldn't do without.

I'd Googled Captain Murphy already, of course, because I'd Googled them all, and I knew him by sight. Midfifties, stocky, ruddy from a life spent outside—and sporting a spectacular walrus mustache that made him look more like a cartoon of a fireman than a real one.

Captain Murphy did not seem to be expecting me. "Yes?"

"I'm Cassie Hanwell," I said, and when I didn't see any recognition, I added, "Here for C-shift."

Then came the nod. "Got it," he said. "The rookie beat you. And he brought doughnuts."

Had it been a race? "I'm fifteen minutes early," I said.

"Our battalion chief always says if you're fifteen minutes early, you're half an hour late."

I frowned. But I said, "Yes, sir."

"Don't be late again."

I couldn't tell if he was joking.

He tilted his head back and angled his coffee mug above his mouth so that the dregs ran out in a trickle. Then he clapped the mug back on the desk, scooted his chair back with a honk, and said, "Follow me."

I followed him—out the door and down the hallway into another office. He grabbed the PA system mic and flipped it on. "Attention, please. There's a stripper at the kitchen table. Repeat: Stripper at the kitchen table."

He gave me a little wink and headed back into the hallway.

"You do know I'm not a stripper, right?" I asked, following him.

He kept walking. "Of course I do." Then he pushed through the swinging doors to the kitchen. "That's just how we call all our meetings."

The guys from C-shift were gathering at the table. Some were already reading the sports page or checking their phones, and some were arriving from other parts of the station. I hung back near the kitchen work area.

Captain Murphy stood at the head of the table and started talking before everybody was settled. "It's just another C-shift today, boys, but it's not just another C-shift. Today, while the Patterson brothers are sunning their flabby Irish asses on a Florida beach, we welcome not one but two new members to the finest crew on the finest shift in all the departments of the great state of Massachusetts."

The guys cheered.

I'd studied them all, the same way I'd studied the territory. I'd learned all their names beforehand: Jerry Murphy, Joe Sullivan, Drew Beniretto, Tom McElroy, Anthony DeStasio. Add me and the rookie, and that was the whole crew, though we were too new to be up on the website. I scanned the group and matched the photos I'd seen with their real-life faces. Quite the contrast from my shift back home, which had been almost universally young, fit, clean-cut, calendar guys. There were seven of us on this shift, and, with maybe two exceptions, nobody fit that description. Even the guys who weren't middle-aged kind of looked middle-aged. All scrawny and grizzled, with a gray, northeastern paleness to them. Down in Texas, everybody had been robust and tan. Here, they looked like ashtrays. And one, McElroy, was fat. Much fatter than in his photo. Genuinely fat. Heart-attack fat.

Nobody in the room looked anything like a rookie.

Captain Murphy went on. "Some of you might be wishing we didn't have to break in two newbies at once, but I'm here to tell you it'll be worth it. These are impressive new recruits, and that's no lie. The first one rose through the ranks of the Austin FD down in Texas like some kind of a comet before moving to our neck of the woods for family reasons. But we'll save the best for last. First, I want you to meet our new rookie, a fourth-generation Massachusetts firefighter. Some of you may know his father, Big Robby Callaghan out of Ladder 12 in Boston. This kid's fresh out of the academy, and now it's our job to make him a man."

Captain Murphy paused a second to look around the room. He frowned a little.

"Guys, where's the rookie?"

The guy I recognized as Beniretto cleared his throat. "He might be duct-taped to the basketball pole, Captain."

"Already?" The captain shook his head. "Sullivan! DeStasio! Go cut him loose. He's missing his own introduction."

Two guys stood and headed for the bay doors. I recognized Sullivan from his picture, but he was much bigger—at least six-four—than you could tell from the website. The other, DeStasio, was much smaller.

The captain watched them a second. "Look at that," he said to the group, like it was a profound life lesson. "The Irish and the Italians working together. Who says we can't overcome our differences in this country?"

Again: I couldn't tell if he was joking.

But I didn't have long to wonder, because a second later, the bay doors burst back open and the two came jogging back in—this time, carrying a sideways body.

The rookie.

He was sopping wet—clearly, they'd turned the hose on him—and his ankles and wrists were duct-taped together, hands behind his back. Sullivan and DeStasio smiled as they laid him facedown on the dining table.

"Not sanitary," one of the guys called out, as the rest broke into applause.

DeStasio pulled out a utility knife and approached the rookie.

I should mention that when firefighters work, they work hard—and when they play, they play just as hard. Firehouses are full of guys with too much energy who are stressed-out adrenaline junkies haunted by plenty of tragedy. Goofing around is nothing short of a survival skill.

Everyone in the room knew that the soaking-wet rookie was just the fun new firehouse toy—but I had a very strange half a second when I caught sight of DeStasio's face as he moved toward the rookie with that knife, and I realized he wasn't laughing. He was the only person in the room who wasn't. Even I—not yet technically in on the prank—was smiling a little.

But not this guy DeStasio.

I felt a flash of alarm as he leaned in toward the rookie with that knife, like he might have some kind of psychotic break and just gut him like a fish in front of all of us.

But that's not what happened.

Instead, DeStasio cut the duct tape at the rookie's boots to free his legs, then cut the tape at his wrists. The rookie flipped himself around to sit up on the table.

And then something truly, unspeakably horrible happened—far worse than anything DeStasio could have done with that knife.

The rookie lifted his head.

He shook out his wet hair like a dog after a bath, and then he gave the rest of the guys a big, goofy grin, just as I froze in place at the sight of his face.

His stunning, heartbreakingly appealing face.

Oh, no, I thought. *No, no, no.*

Because the second I saw him—laughing, breathing hard, muscles still tense under his wet shirt—and saw his affable, all-American, Norman Rockwell–esque smile, I had all the symptoms of a heart attack.

I stood there, in a room full of EMTs, silently diagnosing myself with a possible myocardial infarction. It was comforting, in a way, to know that I was standing in a whole room of guys who could save my life if need be.

But then the rookie met my eyes and smiled at me, and I had to admit to myself that it wasn't a coronary.

It was worse.

It was the rookie himself.

I was having a reaction to the rookie. A romantic reaction. The dumb kind.

A full-body reaction, too. Like someone had lit a Fourth of July sparkler inside my chest. It was so terrible. So humiliating. So . . . girly.

That kind of thing never happened to me. Not ever.

It's worth mentioning that he wasn't a *calendar* firefighter. He wouldn't have stopped traffic or anything. He was just a normal guy. There was no reason at all that the sight of him should have hit me like that.

But it did.

I couldn't turn my eyes away—which was okay, because everybody else was watching him, too. He climbed off the table and stood next to the captain, dripping. Then he took a few bows.

Get a grip, I thought. *Pull it together.*

I'd seen a thousand firefighters in my life. Tough ones, handsome ones, ripped ones. Hot firefighters were a dime a dozen. Heck, I'd spent three years working shoulder to shoulder with calendar-*cover*-guy Hernandez. I'd built up a solid immunity, and the rookie should have been no different.

What was it? The straight nose? The square jaw? The friendly curve of those eyebrows? What was I seeing in that face that was reverberating through my eyeballs, into my brain, and off to every corner of my body?

Maybe it was his teeth. They were so—I don't know: so *straight.*

Good God. What was happening to me?

"Guys, meet the rookie," Captain Murphy said, and the guys all shouted hellos and welcomes. "He's a homegrown real deal from a long line of brave heroes."

Not helping.

Time slowed down as I watched the rookie meeting all the guys one by one, stepping forward and reaching out with his wet, muscled forearm to shake hands over and over. Smiling at everyone with those heartbreaking teeth, including whoever had just duct-taped him to the basketball pole and turned the hose on him, with the most agonizingly good-natured crinkles at the edges of his eyes.

It goes without saying, but this was not good. *Not good* doesn't even scratch the surface, in fact. Firefighters don't feel sparklers for other firefighters—not if they want to keep their jobs.

Don't panic, I told myself. *It's physical. He'll turn out to be dumb, or rude, or narcissistic, or overly fond of fart jokes—and all this weirdness will dissipate. You'll be fine.*

I'd better be. Because there's no *attraction* in a firehouse.

There's no longing. There are no goo-goo eyes, or savoring glances, or secret trysts. Firehouses are temples to heroic masculinity, and ladyish things like heart sparklers are the absolute antithesis of everything they stand for—because there is absolutely nothing girlier than falling in love. As I'd just explained, with many eye-rolls, to my mother.

In fact, one of the reasons I'd always considered myself uniquely qualified to be a female working in a firehouse was that—whether by luck or design—I had always been totally immune to all that nonsense.

Until right now.

Because on the very first morning of the very first day of the rest of my firefighting life—the very moment I needed that immunity more than I had ever needed it before—I lost it.

Nine

THAT'S WHEN THE captain started introducing "our other newbie." Me.

That's also when I started to wonder if anybody had mentioned to the crew yet that the other new guy was a girl.

Later, I would reflect back on the captain's pronouns as he introduced me. Did he ever actually use the word "she"? Maybe not, after all.

Because when he finished describing the new member of the crew to the team, everybody looked around the room.

And kept looking.

Like I wasn't even there.

I mean, there I was, a total stranger in their kitchen, wearing department-issue Dickies and an unmistakable FD uniform shirt. I walked over and stood next to the captain, for Pete's sake. I was the only unaccounted-for person in the room. There was no one else it could possibly have been. But their eyes swept past me—more than once—as the room murmured in confusion.

Was this really possible? Could *what you expected to see* alter so much what you actually saw?

Finally, somebody said, "Check the basketball pole."

That's when the captain, who seemed to be enjoying how flummoxed they all were, finally decided to clear things up. "Friends," he said, sweeping his arm in my direction, "meet the new guy."

The room fell silent.

"We thought she was a student," one guy said.

"We thought she was *the stripper,*" another guy corrected.

"Sorry to disappoint you," Captain Murphy said, meeting my eyes. "New guy—meet the crew."

Next, the introductions. The captain pointed at the most calendar-like guy in the room. "The ladies' man right here with the six-pack is Drew Beniretto."

"You're too pretty to be a fireman," Beniretto said to me.

I gave him a look. "Right back atcha, pal."

The crew chuckled at that, and the captain added, "We call him Six-Pack."

Six-Pack lifted his shirt to show us his abs, and a couple of guys threw things at him—a paper cup, a Nerf football, a set of keys.

The captain went on. "The plump dumpling next to him is Tom McElroy. We call him Case."

"'Cause Drew's got a six-pack . . . ," one guy called out.

The rest joined in: "And Tom's got a case!"

McElroy smiled and slapped his round belly. "Tight as a drum," he said to me.

"Not sure that's a good thing," I said.

Case took a step closer to me. "Punch it."

I shook my head. "You really don't want me to do that."

The captain kept moving, now pointing at Sullivan. "This is Sullivan, our engine operator. Stand up, Sullivan."

Sullivan stood up. I revised my earlier guess. He was six-five, at least. Maybe six-six.

"What do you think we call this guy?" the captain asked me.

It was a challenge—to see if I could think like a firefighter.

"It's either Shorty or Tiny," I guessed.

All the guys burst out with laughs and shouts. "She got it!"

Tiny took a bow.

The captain gave me a nod of respect and went on with the introductions. "The cranky one with back trouble is DeStasio. I'll give you a thousand dollars if you can ever make him smile. Whatever you do, don't park in his space. He's taking over cooking duties in the wake of the Patterson brothers' departure. He can make a total of three different meals, and they're all burned."

DeStasio didn't say hello. In a voice of pure dismay, he asked the captain, "Why is the new guy a girl?"

The captain nodded, like, *Good question*. "I thought you guys could use a little surprise. Plus, she's a hotshot medic. And we were desperate."

Then Six-Pack said, "I for one am all for it. I'm tired of looking at you ugly bastards."

Another cheer of rowdy laughter and protest.

The captain put his hands out to settle them down. "Now, I know what you guys are all thinking about women." Here he paused, seeming to think about women himself for a minute. "But this is who the chief hired, and you can be men about it or you can whine like little—"

He caught himself, glanced over at me.

"Puppies," he continued.

Case piped up again. "But where is she going to sleep?"

"Where's she going to *crap*?" Tiny said. "We don't even have a ladies' room."

"Where is she going to put her lady products?" DeStasio demanded, and the whole room moaned in disgust like there was nothing on earth that could be grosser than that. As if these guys hadn't seen every unspeakably nasty thing in the world. As if they hadn't literally walked over slimy dead bodies and charred human remains. As if any of them could be shocked by a tampon.

But I was actually wondering those same questions myself. In Austin, our firehouse had been pretty close to brand-new—out in a newer suburb, with plenty of natural light and gender-neutral accommodations, and even flexible sleeping areas for different groupings of men and women on different shifts. This firehouse, in contrast, was at least a hundred years old and had not, shall we say, been built with a progressive eye toward gender politics.

"There's only one shitter," Tiny called out, "and it's mine-all-mine."

"No ladies in the poop zone!" Case chimed in.

"Where *is* she going to sleep?" DeStasio asked.

The captain had a ready answer. "I asked the chief the same question. The guys up top said to put her in the supply closet."

I squinted at him. Was he kidding?

"I'm not kidding," he said. "When you take the shelving out, there's room there for a bed." He gave me a wink. "We'll paint it pink for you, sweetheart, so you'll feel right at home."

I gave him a look.

"Unless," he went on, "you want to sleep with all the guys."

"You can sleep with me, baby," Six-Pack called out, and they all laughed.

In truth, I wasn't sure. I didn't love the idea of the supply closet, away from the group, but whether sleeping in a big room with these guys would help or hinder our sense of camaraderie was going to depend very much on the guys.

"What's it going to be?" the captain asked.

I shrugged. "Whichever room has the least number of farts," I said.

A burst of laughter.

"Don't sleep near Tiny, then!" somebody shouted.

"If she takes the supply closet," Case asked, "where will we keep the supplies?"

"Are you talking about a certain stack of supplies that we keep on the bottom shelf?" the captain asked.

"A certain stack of supplies that's been handed down from crew to crew for decades?" Six-Pack added.

"I'm talking about the supplies that"—Case glanced at me now, wanting to make his meaning clear to the others but not to me—"some of the guys in the house spend time with when they are feeling—" He looked at me again. Words seemed to fail him.

"Restless?" Tiny offered.

Captain Murphy tried to take the high road. "We will find new storage spots for all supplies. Don't worry, Case. Your porn is safe."

Six-Pack burst out with a laugh. "'Cause that's the only exercise Case gets."

A couple of guys reached out to pat Case on the shoulder.

"Okay, rookies," the captain said, turning to the rookie and me.

I raised my hand. "I'm not a rookie."

"Noted," the captain said, and then began again. "Okay, rookie and newbie, let me tell you a little bit about Station Two. We play hard, but we work harder. I'll joke around like anybody else, but when I give an order, you don't think about it, you don't question it—you follow it. Lives depend on our chain of command, and the one thing I will not tolerate is insubordination."

The rookie and I nodded in unison.

"I expect everybody on our crew to pull their weight and do their share. There's no complaining here. You do your job, and you're grateful for the opportunity. And you stay in shape. How you do that is up to you, but twice a year, we run the obstacle course out back in a crew competition. Even Case," he said, with a glance at the fat guy.

"We're going to tease you and prank you and bust your balls," the captain went on. "Don't worry about it. Worry if we *don't* prank you. Otherwise, no matter how mean we are, just know we're glad you're here." He looked at me. "Even the lady."

Captain Harris had been right. Not much of a filter.

Next, the captain turned to the crew.

"I know what you're all probably thinking," he said. "You're thinking having a girl here is going to kill all the fun. We won't be able to play the way we like to, or relax the way we like to, or joke the way we like to. You're thinking she's going to have no sense of humor and get offended at everything. She won't let us curse. She'll be weak and terrible. It'll feel like having your mom around all the time, nagging you to pick up your underwear. I get it. In a hundred and twenty years, our station's never needed a woman for anything. Not to do with the job, anyway. But things change, boys." He jabbed his thumb in my direction. "This one's supposed to be very good, for a girl. Her chief said she was a rising star down there in Texas, and not just because promoting a female looked good on paper."

"Her captain said she was actually good?" DeStasio asked, like it was impossible.

Murphy shrugged like he was just as baffled as the next guy. "That's what she said."

"She?" Tiny called out.

"Her captain was also a woman?" Case demanded, like, *What next?*

The whole room broke out in speculation and questioning. Was a woman captain even qualified to judge a woman firefighter? Was it possible she'd lied about me to help me get this job? Could we ever take her assessment as anything other than affirmative action for females?

Unanswerable questions, all.

But I had an answer for them.

Looking back, maybe it wasn't the best idea. My plan had been to lay low at the beginning and get my bearings—to be strategic about how I presented myself. Maybe if the outrage over my non-maleness had dissipated in some reasonable amount of time, I would have let it go.

But it didn't. If anything, it fed on itself, like a runaway structure fire.

And I didn't have the patience to let it burn itself out.

I guess you can only watch people willfully underestimate you for so long.

Finally, I shouted, loud enough to halt all conversation, "How many pull-ups do you think I can do?"

They all turned to stare at me.

"Three," Tiny guessed, after a minute.

"Two," Captain Murphy said.

"Women can't do pull-ups," Case announced, like I'd tried to pull a fast one.

"Fifty bucks," I said then, "says I can do at least seven."

Wallets started hitting the table.

I should note: The only one who didn't bet against me was the rookie.

They walked me out back to "the course," which turned out to be a military-sized obstacle course, complete with poles, hurdles, monkey bars, ropes, and a ten-foot climbing wall.

We stopped under a pull-up bar, and the guys gathered around.

Here's a problem I didn't anticipate: This pull-up bar was high. Built for six-foot guys. Standing under it at five foot five, it was pretty clear that I couldn't reach.

As I waited for the snickers and offers to spot me to die down, I felt a creeping sensation that this idea was going to backfire. Had I just invited them all out there to watch me jump like a munchkin for a bar I'd never catch? Had I just gotten everyone's attention only to humiliate myself?

I stared up at the bar.

I waited so long that a few of the guys started to walk back toward the station.

"Wait!" I said.

I wrapped my arms around one of the poles that held the crossbar, and I climbed. At the top, I grabbed the bar and swung out. A few splinters—but worth it.

There was a murmur of appreciation that I'd solved it.

I grasped the bar with my fists, hung there for a second, and then, very deliberately, when I had everyone's attention, took one hand off the bar, lowered it, and planted it on my hip.

The whole group went silent.

I began. As I lifted myself up, one armed, I crossed my ankles and held myself in tight form. With each pull, I exhaled with a sharp *shh* and then inhaled as I let myself down. I could usually do seven, but I knew that today adrenaline would give me a little boost.

Eight one-hand pull-ups in quick succession.

And then an extra one for luck.

At the end, I dropped down and landed in a crouch. Then I stood and took a minute to walk off the burn in my shoulder. When I turned around, no one had moved.

The guys were just staring at me, mouths open.

Then they broke into applause.

And started handing me money.

Which felt like a pretty good start to the day.

Ten

THAT NIGHT, ON my cot in the storage room, it took me a long time to fall asleep. New place. New sounds. Lumpy cot. Sleeping wasn't my greatest skill in the first place. Plus, there was a weird bug on the ceiling I had to keep an eye on.

I finally dozed off, only to be woken seconds later by a loud stampede of firefighters whooping and hollering and bursting through the storage closet door.

I should have expected them. I *did* expect them. But they scared the hell out of me anyway.

In response, I shouted and launched up into a jujitsu crouch on top of my mattress. The first face I saw was Case, who had been trundling toward me gleefully—but as soon as he saw me flip up into self-defense mode, he froze and put his hands up.

They all froze, actually.

I must have forgotten to mention I'd had a second job as a self-defense instructor.

In the still of that moment, as we all stared at each other, I got why they were there: Of course. They were hazing me.

I looked at their shocked faces. They'd clearly assumed it would be easier than this.

"Are you guys here to haze me?" I asked, lowering my arms.

Tiny gave a little shrug. "We're supposed to duct-tape you to the basketball pole."

I nodded and relaxed out of my crouch. Fair enough. "Okay, then."

Tiny didn't step forward, so I waved him toward me.

"Let's get it over with," I said.

He gave a little shrug and stepped closer, and I bent over his shoulder so he could carry me out the door, down through the engine bay, and out back to the parking lot.

Along the ride, I realized that they'd grabbed the rookie, too.

Next thing I knew, they had pressed us together, standing back to back against the basketball pole, running a roll of duct tape around us to keep us there. It was late summer and starting to get chilly. I'd been sleeping in a T-shirt and boy-shorts-style underwear. I felt glad in that moment that I always slept in my sports bra when I was on shift. I'd caught a glimpse of the rookie on the way down—and I felt pretty sure he wasn't wearing much of anything at all.

Please, God, I thought. *Don't let him be naked.*

We stood obediently as the crew duct-taped us from shoulders to hips, accepting our fate with as much dignity as possible, waiting for the guys to go back inside.

The guys knew their way around a roll of duct tape, I'll give them that.

After they left, we were quiet for a good while. I could hear the rookie breathing. At one point, he coughed, and his elbow grazed mine.

"I'm spending a lot of time with this pole," he said then.

"At least they didn't turn the hose on us," I said.

"That is lucky."

"You knew they'd have to haze us."

"Sure," the rookie said. "Of course."

"It's part of the fun," I said, starting to shiver.

"You bet," he agreed.

"Rookie—" I started, but that was as far as I got.

"You can call me by my name, if you like."

He hadn't been on the crew list I'd studied. I didn't remember his name. "I think I'll stick with 'rookie.'"

"Okay."

I asked, "What temperature would you guess it is?"

"Sixty?" he guessed. "Sixty-five?"

"Kind of on the chilly side."

"For sure."

"What's your clothing situation?"

"Just—" He hesitated. "Just, um, boxer briefs."

So. Not naked. Relief.

But still pretty close.

I tried not to picture him in his boxer briefs, but my mind seemed bent on conjuring the image. He wasn't a real firefighter yet, but he sure did look like one. An image of him with his sandy blond hair falling over his forehead—longer in the front, shorter in the back—just drew itself in my mind, despite every protest. In some ways, even as a total beginner, he fit in better than I did. Everything about his tall, broad, earnest demeanor shouted "helper." He looked the part. He'd grown up in this culture. He was so . . . *male.* Even his Boston accent—*mah-ket, gah-den, disappeah*—was right out of Central Casting.

Not cool. And now my mind was drawing him shirtless. "Not even a T-shirt?" I asked, hoping to be wrong.

"Nope," he said, awfully cheerful for a person who must have been covered in goosebumps. "But at home I sleep naked, so the underpants feel like a lot."

Perfect. Now an image of him asleep in his bed at home, naked, curled up in his sheets, popped into my head. I squeezed my eyes closed to blot it out.

What color would those sheets be, anyway? I found myself wondering. White? Heather gray? Maybe like a faded blue chambray?

Just then, an upstairs window slammed open and the guys hurled a blanket down toward us—though it landed a good two feet away.

We both stood staring at the blanket.

"What do you think the chances are," the rookie asked, "that the guys'll come down and move it a little closer?"

"Nonexistent," I said.

So near, and yet so far.

"I think we should work our way down to a sitting position," I said, after a while.

I could feel his shoulders shrug. "Okay," he said, and I felt him bend his knees.

I bent mine, too. Our shoulders pressed and rubbed against each other as we worked our way down the pole, finally getting seated on the concrete down at the base. The cold concrete.

"Are you cold?" I asked when we were settled. Somebody was shivering. I just wasn't sure which one of us it was.

"Just my butt," he said.

"I think I can reach the blanket," I said, stretching my leg out sideways.

I managed to pinch it with my toes.

"You are amazing!" the rookie said, as I pulled it closer.

What we were going to do with the blanket, I didn't know, since our arms were duct-taped at our sides. I pushed it toward the rookie until he was able to grab a corner of it with his fingers.

"Don't you want it?" he asked.

"You take it," I said.

"But you're the girl."

"But you're the person in nothing but underwear."

"I'm serious," he said.

"*I'm* serious," I said. "You're way more naked than I am."

In the silence that followed, I wondered if I could have phrased it better.

Then the rookie had a bizarre question. "Are you wearing a shirt?" he asked.

"What?"

"Like, a T-shirt?"

"What kind of a question is that?"

"Because I'm not. So they duct-taped me right to my skin."

"That's going to be a bitch to take off."

"But I'm thinking you're probably wearing a shirt of some kind. And maybe the tape is just on your shirt. Which means you might have a better chance at wriggling."

At *wriggling*? "There's no way we're escaping. If there's one thing these guys know, it's duct tape."

"But you might be able to work your way around to the pole to get closer to me."

A beat. "Why would I want to do that?"

"For warmth," the rookie said.

"Are you seriously proposing that we *snuggle*?"

I could almost see his frown. "I wasn't going to call it that."

"On our first night here? Do you realize we would never live that down? Do you have any idea how much crap those guys would give us if they came down in the morning and found us *snuggled together*?"

It hadn't occurred to him. "I was just trying to think of ways to keep warm."

"I'd rather freeze to death," I said. "And trust me: so would you."

When I was quiet for a minute, he said, "So, you're saying no?"

"Let me put it to you this way, rookie," I said. "Is there anybody else on this shift that you would offer to do that with?"

"Um . . ."

"Would you snuggle with Tiny? Or the captain? Or up against Case's big belly?"

Now he was smiling—I could hear it in his voice. "You might be the only one I'd *enjoy* doing it with . . ."

"Exactly. That's your answer, right there."

"What is?"

"If you wouldn't do it with DeStasio, you can't do it with me."

"Fair enough. Good tip."

"Just pretend I'm a gross old dude."

"I will do my best."

I closed my eyes and leaned my head back against the metal pole. A dog barked. A car honked. We sat in silence for a while, biding our time and doing exactly what I hated doing most—sitting still. Alone with my thoughts was my least favorite place to be. If I had to be alone, I always had the radio going, or a book to read, or something else to distract me. Here, there were no distractions. I couldn't even fall asleep. I had to just let my own consciousness gather around me like a thickening fog.

"Can I share something else with you?" the rookie asked after a while.

"Only if you have to."

"I kind of need to pee," he said.

I shook my head. "Going to be a long night, rookie."

"It definitely is."

The crew came out to free us at six thirty with blankets and hot coffee, just as the next crew was arriving for shift. I opened my eyes to a delighted crowd of firefighters standing around us, the captain announcing we'd gotten off easy. "In my day," he told the crowd, "they stripped you down naked, greased you up with Crisco, and taped you to a backboard out in front of the house for all the neighbors to gawk at."

"They did that to you, Captain?" Case asked.

"Buck naked," the captain confirmed with pride. "Except they made a little splint for my johnson with tongue depressors and sterile gauze."

"Well, that's a visual you can't unsee," Six-Pack said.

"You're welcome," the captain said, and—again—I couldn't tell if he was joking.

The moment they cut us loose, the rookie sprinted to the bushes to pee. I caught an accidental glimpse of his naked back before I looked away.

Too late. Those broad shoulders—and that little butt in those red boxer briefs—were burned permanently into my corneas. I blinked my eyes over and over on the drive home, trying to blot the image from my memory.

I left that first shift completely flummoxed. And it wasn't the hazing, or the sleeping in the supply closet, or even the mental visual of the captain's johnson in a splint made of tongue depressors.

It was the rookie.

I'd just spent an entire night with the guy, and he hadn't done even one annoying thing. He hadn't farted, or hocked a loogie, or even snored. The worst thing he'd done was try to come up with ways to keep me warm in the cold night air. I already suspected he was easygoing, and then last night he couldn't seem to stop being considerate, and now, as of first thing in the morning, I knew for certain that he had an adorable butt.

Disaster.

I needed some flaws on this guy, stat.

Otherwise—seriously—I was in trouble.

Eleven

WHEN I GOT back to Diana's after shift, it was eight in the morning, and I was exhausted. In many different ways.

Diana was having coffee at her kitchen table with a friend—a cute African American lady with poofy hair, maybe ten years older than me. Their cups were full, with steam rising, and they both cradled the mugs in their palms, savoring the warmth. They looked up and smiled when I walked in.

Diana had changed her patch to a blue-and-white gingham.

"Meet my friend Josie," Diana said. "She owns the yarn shop next door, and she reviews movies on her blog."

I had the weirdest feeling they'd just been talking about me.

It's strange to say, but it surprised me for Diana to have a friend. I'd created an idea of her in my head as a lonely old lady, isolated in her house, making pottery all day with her eye patch on. Like, if I'd been mad at her for ten years, the rest of the world must have been, too.

I lifted my hand. "Hello."

But Josie was already plunking her coffee down on the table and scooting back her chair and launching into an excited jog—almost a prance—to come over to me. She held her arms out and up, and her whole face was a smile. "OMG!" she said. "It's you!"

Getting a good look at her, I suddenly wondered if she might be a little bit pregnant. Just a hunch. I had a knack for spotting pregnant people. Though, if she was, it was only barely.

I didn't ask.

Then she was hugging me—tight, and with no hesitation, the way you'd hug a dear friend, even though we'd never met before.

I wasn't a fan of hugging, but I held still and endured it, anyway.

She let go but kept smiling at me. "Sorry," she said. "I'm a hugger."

"You're good at it," I said. "I can see why."

Then she hugged me again.

I didn't protest—even mentally. Who could resist all that enthusiasm and warmth? Plus I loved her style. She had a polka-dot bandana and blouse with a Peter Pan collar. Big, bangly bracelets, too.

She was, in a word, adorable.

"I love your shirt," I said.

Her smile got bigger. "I made it," she said.

"You made it?" I said. I wasn't sure I'd ever seen a piece of homemade clothing.

"She's very crafty," Diana said from the table.

Josie was still standing very close to me. On impulse she grabbed my hands and squeezed them. "I'm just so happy to meet you," she said.

It was off-putting in a way. Growing up with my dad, who was not exactly a talker, life was pretty quiet. We each spoke mostly when spoken to, in a kind of negative feedback loop. He was not a person you'd describe as effusive, unless he was watching sports. In everyday conversation? A minimalist, for sure.

Maybe I'd absorbed too much of his reserve, without ever intending to.

But I already liked Josie.

"Josie's heard a lot about you," Diana said, taking a sip of her coffee.

I looked at Josie. "That's worrying."

"We're in crochet club together," Diana said, "so, as you can imagine, we chat a lot."

Nope. I could not imagine a crochet club.

"We're actually the only two people in the crochet club," Josie added.

"Co-founders and co-presidents," Diana chimed in.

"Unless you'd like to join," Josie offered.

"No, thanks," I said.

Diana went on. "I've told her about the time you yanked out your tooth on the playground at school and tried to sell it to another kid in your class."

Oh God. I'd forgotten that.

"So resourceful," Josie said.

"And the time you got lost at the zoo and we found you, an hour later, all the way on the other side, at the lion cages. Perfectly happy. No sense at all that we'd shut down the entire zoo to look for you."

I'd forgotten that, too.

"Adventurous," Josie added.

"And the time you found that plant with the green berries in the backyard and ate a whole stalk's worth and then very proudly came inside and announced, 'Mama! I ate your peas!'"

They looked at each other like they could barely stand the cuteness.

"Had to call poison control for that one," Diana said.

"Your mom's very excited you're here," Josie said in a pretend whisper.

"It is exciting," I said, not sure if I sounded sarcastic.

"Come join us. Tell us all about your first shift," Diana said then, pulling out the chair next to her.

"Can't," I said, too fast. "I'm beyond tired. They kept us up all night."

All of which was true. But that wasn't why I wouldn't stay.

I wouldn't stay because I needed to keep my life in order.

Ever since that night at the banquet, I'd been off-kilter. It was as if seeing Heath Thompson again had cracked some load-bearing wall in my sanity, and now everything I did had to be about shoring it back up. Moving here hadn't helped, either. Starting over with a new crew, having that weird reaction to the rookie—none of it was helping.

I needed the things I always needed. Running. Working out. Organizing a schedule for my time. Arranging my life so that it was sensible and ordered. I needed quiet, restorative time alone.

I did not need to lounge around in this kitchen with two women I barely knew, cooing over stories about how cute I'd been as a child. I did not need to create emotional bonds that could tug at me. I needed fewer variables—not more. I needed to be alone.

UP IN THE attic, I forced myself to shower, even though the only thing I wanted to do was flop down on the bed. Then I put on pajamas and climbed between the velvety white sheets. Diana had good taste in linens. I'd give her that.

But then I couldn't sleep.

Too much to process, I guess.

As far as I could tell, I had three major problems to solve before I could make a life for myself here.

One: The station was in terrible shape. Really terrible. Life-threateningly terrible.

I had suspected that the Lillian station would be different from what I'd known in Austin, but I'd had no idea.

Instead of a spacious, ultramodern concrete-and-chrome building, the Lillian station was a hundred-plus years old and brick. Instead of a plate of fresh-baked vegan brownies, the kitchen table had a box of Twinkies. Instead of stainless gear racks, this place had wooden pegs. No central air, just window units wedged in with foam. No ergonomic Ikea furniture—just sweat-stained La-Z-Boys lined up in front of the TV. No solar panels on the roof, no organic garden out back, no compost heap.

No vent, even, for the diesel fumes from the engine below.

The radios looked at least ten years old, and the light fixtures looked even older. Even the updated ones were fluorescent instead of LED. The kitchen was 1970s orange Formica and stained walnut cabinets.

It gave me the girliest urge to redecorate.

Even the supplies were different. I'd been shocked to see that there were no infrared cameras. Also, no cyanide-antidote kit, which was shocking given how much modern stuff—from furniture to carpet—released hydrogen cyanide when it burned.

So: not just different, but dangerous.

When I'd asked if we had a cyanide antidote, Captain Murphy had burst out laughing.

"Is that a no?" I asked.

The captain was still laughing as he shook his head. "Those are two thousand bucks a pop."

Two thousand bucks or not, we needed them. It was a real concern. There were all kinds of ways to get cyanide poisoning, from running out of air in your tank to having a bad seal on your mask. Breathing that stuff would kill you. Having an antidote was a no-brainer.

In Austin, we'd had three.

"We should have at least one," I said.

"Find me two thousand dollars, and we'll get one," the captain said, like he'd asked me to find him a pot of leprechaun gold.

It wasn't an unreasonable request. "It's crazy we don't have one," I said.

"It's crazy we don't have a lot of things," the captain said. "Like radios that work."

If I'd been taking a sip of something, I would have done a spit take. "Our radios don't work?"

"Some days are better than others." Then he shrugged. "Built by the lowest bidder."

Here was the upside: The captain was joking when he told me to find him two thousand dollars, but I could actually do that. I'd written a bunch of grant proposals for our firehouse in Austin. I'd gotten us a snazzy new gear-drying rack, a top-of-the-line exhaust removal system for the engine bays, and a "community relations" grant to landscape our side yard and install picnic tables made of recycled plastic.

And this station—all due respect—could use a few picnic tables.

To say the least.

I'm not saying I wanted to go crazy. I knew better than to march in as a newbie with flower vases and throw pillows. But working radios? Cyanide kits? Those things weren't frivolous—they were essential.

I found myself Googling "firefighter grants" on my phone instead of sleeping, for my own safety, if nothing else. But I also started wondering if raising money for the station might be my way of creating a place for myself there. If I could help them get things they needed, maybe that would raise my value.

Off the top of my head, I could list a hundred things this station could use: a fresh coat of paint, new self-contained breathing apparatuses, air masks with radios embedded instead of handheld radios, new mattresses, central air, a motorized hose wheel or two, new lockers, a new washer-extractor for bunker gear, and a new hydraulic cutter—or several.

It was a good start.

The second problem keeping me awake was the course out back.

It really was too tall for me. Half the structures there were going to be hard for me to reach—and the other half were going to be impossible. It was set up with two identical runs side by side, and guys had told me they didn't just "do" the course twice a year, they held massive high-stakes competitions, with full bragging rights going to the winner—and the opposite, I supposed, going to the loser.

I knew one thing for sure. I needed to figure out how to ace that course. Not losing, at the very least—but I wouldn't say no to winning.

But I couldn't just grow taller.

I was going to have to get creative.

I started thinking about something the guys used to do back in Austin called parkour. It was a way of running, leaping, climbing, and vaulting through the city as if it were a giant playground. They used to watch videos on techniques around the table in the kitchen.

I Googled it on my phone, and sure enough there were hundreds of videos breaking down techniques.

Like, you really can run up the side of a wall, if you know the right angle to approach and then how to tilt your body. And if you've got three surfaces at right angles and you do it right, you can use momentum and positioning to just leapfrog up to a second story.

Watching the videos was mesmerizing, and I stayed awake far too long, watching one clip after another of people doing impossible things with ease—and then showing everybody else how to do them, too.

I could stand to learn a few impossible things.

A new hobby. Not exactly crochet, but it would have to do.

For a morning spent lying in bed, it was remarkably productive.

A way to make myself useful to the crew? Check.

A way to conquer the course? Check.

Then there was my third problem. Which was, of course, the rookie.

And as for the rookie?

I closed my tired eyes. Maybe that answer couldn't be found on Google. Maybe I'd just have to figure that answer out for myself.

Twelve

SETTLING IN AT the station was both easier and harder than I'd expected.

Over the next few shifts, I noticed a few important things about the crew.

One: They insisted on treating me like a lady. Sort of. To the extent that they could remember to.

In a way, this was a good thing. It wasn't the blistering hatred that Captain Harris had led me to expect. It was still a problem, though. They wouldn't curse in front of me, for example. I'd walk into a room just as Tiny was saying, "What the fuck?" and he'd duck his head, guilty, and change it to "frick."

"You can say 'fuck,' Tiny," I'd say.

But then he'd scold me. "Watch your mouth."

"Stop treating me like a girl!"

"You *are* a girl."

I couldn't shift anyone's thinking. Curse words were not for females. Same for bawdy conversations, bodily functions, and jokes in general.

Case wouldn't even say the word "fart" in front of me. He'd just glance my way and say "toot." If I was in the room, they held everything back that wasn't PG. Over and over, I'd walk into the kitchen and watch them all fall silent.

"What?" I'd demand.

"Not for your ears," Case would say. "Scram."

I don't think they were actually trying to exclude me—not consciously, anyway. It was a type of chivalry, I think. They were trying to be polite, and possibly respectful. But their idea of what it meant to be female was off, and I couldn't seem to recalibrate it.

I was, for example, a huge fan of cursing. The power of it, the rule-breaking shock of it. The year my mother left, I cursed incessantly—in front of my dad, in fact. *With* my dad. And he was too heartbroken and angry and disoriented to stop me. I'd fix him a drink or two, and fix myself one that was "virgin" (though it wasn't), and we'd sit at the kitchen table eating Pop-Tarts and complaining about everything we could think of. Especially women.

"Women," my dad would say scornfully.

"Preaching to the choir, buddy," I'd say, only half joking. "Women are the worst."

Later, when my dad married Carol, we both had to stop cursing. She didn't like it. If we wanted to curse, she sent us to the garage.

So now, being the reason the guys at the house had to use limp substitutes like "frig" and "heck" and "dang" kind of made me feel like my stepmother.

"Guys," I kept trying to tell them, "I *like* cursing. It's one of my favorite hobbies."

But the captain shook his head. "Not appropriate."

They also kept making the assumption I was weak, which really struck me as odd. Hadn't they all watched me do nine one-arm pull-ups on the first day? I'd bet a thousand dollars that Case couldn't even do one pull-up using both arms and a leg. And yet they opened doors for me. They reached things on high shelves. They'd take heavy equipment from me and say, "I've got it."

In itself, this wasn't bad. I took it in the spirit it was meant. They were being kind. They were helping. It was more than I'd dared to hope for on my drive up from Texas, when I'd feared they were just going to glare at me all the time.

But there was a downside to it: the assumption that I couldn't do those things myself. The guys weren't holding doors for each other, or helping each other carry equipment. If they had to carry the hundred-pound roof saw for me, I was the last person they were going to hand it to when it was time to use it.

It's easy to fixate on the size difference between men and women, but there are actually plenty of ways that being smaller can benefit you in a fire. You're lighter. You're lower to the ground and more nimble. You can squeeze through spots no big guy can navigate.

Remember that valor award I got in Austin for rescuing a school bus full of kids? That bus had slid off an icy road into a ravine and crumpled like an accordion. I'd been the only one small enough to wedge myself in. I was the one who pried all those kids out because I was the only one who could fit.

We all have our different upsides.

But that's not how the guys saw it.

I didn't want to reject the kindness when one of the guys tried to carry the hose for me—but I *did* want to reject the notion that I couldn't do it myself. I finally settled on a phrase for every time one of the guys started to do something for me: "I've got it," I started saying. "Keeps me strong."

Half the time, they'd do it anyway.

It was kindly meant. And limiting. Both.

The other thing the guys kept insisting was that women had no sense of humor. Where did this idea come from? Over and over in those early weeks, I'd crack jokes that nobody laughed at. Jokes I knew would've been funny in Austin.

I guess it makes sense, in a way. Part of thinking something is funny is expecting it to be funny. So if you've already decided that women aren't funny, then it's a bit of a self-fulfilling prophecy.

Firefighters are, on average, very funny people. All the sorrow you absorb in that job makes you funnier. You have to balance out the pain somehow, and joking around is one of the best things about the job. There's so much death in that world, but laughter is life.

You need it.

It left me thinking a lot about how much *what you think you're going to think* matters. If you expect something to be funny, it will seem funnier. And if it seems funnier, it *is* funnier—by definition.

The only person who laughed at my jokes was the rookie. Of course, he laughed at everything. He was just that kind of guy. Another likable quality that I resented like hell.

So that was my life at the new station. No cursing. No comedy.

And then there was basketball.

In the afternoons, after the dishes were done, and the trucks had been washed, and all the chores were complete, the guys liked to play basketball out back. Shirts versus skins. And they wouldn't let me play.

"You'll get hurt," the captain said.

"You'll get *destroyed,*" Tiny said.

I suspected they all assumed I'd be bad at it. Even though I'd told them that my dad was a high school basketball coach and I'd spent my weekends shooting hoops with him since infancy. Even though I stood on the sidelines and explained—loudly—that I'd played varsity basketball in high school for four years and been the captain of the team.

"I am actually really good," I kept saying.

But I was only five foot five. And a "lady."

I finally decided to throw some money at the problem.

One afternoon, just as a game was starting up, I planted myself in front of the hoop, held up a fan of cash, and challenged them to a shooting competition.

The guys all laughed. That was funny, I guess.

I lifted the money higher and waved it at them. "I can crush all of you, if you like, or we can save time: You pick your best guy and I'll just crush him."

More laughter.

At six foot five—a full foot taller than me—Tiny was a shoo-in. They didn't even have to nominate him.

He just stepped toward me, bowed a little as he gestured toward the hoop, and said, "Ladies first."

I shook my head. "Balls before beauty."

Tiny gave me a little smile and walked to the free-throw line, which was really just a crack in the pavement.

He didn't even have to try. He made the first ten shots without moving anything but his hand at the wrist, and they swished through the net in perfect arches. The guys counted out loud for him as he went. "Eleven. Twelve. Thirteen."

Finally, at his fifteenth shot, he pushed just the tiniest bit too hard with his pinkie finger and the ball's trajectory shifted off to the left. I knew the minute it left his hand that he was going to miss. And he did. The ball hit the rim and bounced off to the side.

The guys all high-fived him, like he was impressive.

Tiny lifted his eyebrows at me, like, *Beat that, little girl.*

Now it was my turn. I took my place at the free-throw crack, but before I lifted the ball, I said, "When I beat Tiny, you guys have to let me play."

"Safe bet," Six-Pack said.

"No one beats Tiny," Case said.

"What if you don't beat him?" Six-Pack asked.

I shrugged. "I'll take bathroom duty for a month."

The guys all high-fived like this was their lucky day. All except the rookie, who had his arms crossed and was studying me like he suspected they were all getting played.

"Deal?" I confirmed.

"Deal."

Of course, I knew I was going to beat Tiny. I'd been raised by a lonely, divorced basketball-coach father who had no idea how to talk about his feelings. Shooting hoops in the driveway was our only means of communication. For a while there, my ability to shoot hoops in our driveway was my dad's only reason to live. Possibly mine, too.

I was fucking *fluent* in basketball.

I dribbled for a second, which made the guys laugh.

Then I lifted the ball on my middle finger and made it spin, Globetrotter style, and watched them stop laughing.

Then I started shooting, and I just didn't stop. Perfect arc after perfect arc. *Five. Ten. Fifteen.*

After a while, I shifted to using the backboard, aiming it smack in the middle of the faded square every time, and hitting the spot in a satisfying ka-swish, ka-swish, ka-swish. *Twenty. Twenty-five.* Then I busted out some tricks. I stood on one leg and shot. I shot with my left hand. I kneed the ball in. I head-butted it. I was at thirty-seven with no misses—not even near-misses—when the tones went off in the station for a call.

I turned around and threw my last shot backwards, and without even waiting to see if it made it, I walked back toward the station.

The rookie saw me coming and held the door open. As I closed the gap, he shook his head in admiration. "You're my hero."

"Did it go in?" I whispered as I passed.

"Nothing but net," he said.

I high-fived him without even breaking stride, and I never looked back.

DESTASIO SHOULD HAVE ridden with us to the call, but his back was giving him trouble, so the rookie came instead.

Firefighters don't talk about "pain." They don't admit that things "hurt." The most you'll ever hear them admit to is "discomfort." DeStasio had fallen during a roof collapse and been injured so badly that for a few days it was unclear if he would walk again. But he did walk again—part of his legend. Everybody knew he was in constant pain, but all anybody ever said was that his back was "giving him trouble."

Basically, DeStasio suffered in silence every day, and the crew admired the hell out of him for it.

And on bad days, he got a pass and snoozed in the Barcalounger by the big-screen TV.

The fire call turned out to be for an "eight-year-old female, not breathing"—which sent us all into extra-high gear.

We were loaded up in forty seconds.

The rookie and I rode in the back as we ran full lights-and-sirens—pushing through intersections, veering around parked cars—to make it to the scene in under eight minutes.

Fast, but probably not fast enough.

Brain damage sets in after one minute without oxygen, and it's irreversible at five. But "not breathing" could mean more things than you'd think, and with kids especially, you never give up hope until you have to.

Kids always break your heart.

There's nothing anyone in the service wouldn't do for a kid.

One of the first runs I'd ever made in Austin had been for a drowned girl about this same age, and I'd never forgotten her. We'd done CPR on her for thirty minutes—all the way from the scene to the hospital—without even thinking of giving up.

We never got her back, though.

With kids, it doesn't matter. You try beyond hope, no matter what.

We entered the neighborhood and found the street. School was out for the day by now, and kids just home from school stopped on their front walks to watch us go by.

At the location, a tiny grandmother stood in her driveway. She waved her arms like semaphores. I knew even from the street that her eyes would have that look eyes always get when the souls behind them are recoiling into shock.

"This way," she said, leading us into the house.

We followed, steeped in that sensation of focused attention that accompanies every call. You never habituate to it. You never tire of it. No matter how many calls you go out on. No matter how many unspeakable, hilarious, tragic, ridiculous, heartbreaking, disgusting things you see. That moment of anticipation, as everything in the world disappears except for the one life-or-death task in front of you, is always exquisitely the same.

There's not a name for that feeling. But it's really something.

"Over here," the old lady said, turning the corner into a living room. The TV was on too loud. In a recliner up ahead, an old man was fast asleep with a cup of coffee beside him.

I frowned. "Him?" He was *geriatric,* not pediatric.

She didn't break stride, urging us past the chair. "No."

Behind him, on the floor near the kitchen, lay a pile of bath mats, and on top of the pile, unconscious and unresponsive, was a Chihuahua.

"Here," the old lady said, the expression on her face urgent.

But it didn't compute for me. I was looking for an eight-year-old child. "Where?"

"Here," she repeated, gesturing at the dog.

The four of us looked down: brown-and-white Chihuahua. Dead as a doornail.

We looked back at the old lady.

She gestured at the dog. "My baby," she said, and her voice broke into a genuine sob.

Eight-year-old female.

Six-Pack and Case looked at each other, then turned right around to walk back out the front door without a word. Only the rookie and I stayed.

My heart, which had clenched in preparation for a child, relaxed. I felt a wash of relief. Compared to the drowned girl, whose wet eyelashes I still saw sometimes when I closed my eyes, a dead Chihuahua seemed almost delightful.

I took a step back, then let out a long breath that I expected to be a sigh—but it came out instead as a laugh.

The old lady's eyes questioned mine, like, *You think my dead dog is funny?*

And I tried to make mine say back, *Sorry! Not funny. Just—funnier than a dead child.*

That's when the rookie made attempts at comfort, saying things like, "It was just her time. She's in a better place now."

But the old lady's voice flooded with grief. "No," she said. "Please."

The job hardens you, there's no question about it. That's the only way to survive. You take in too much. One horror after another soaks through your skin, swirls in your lungs, echoes in your ears. You can't think too hard about what it means, or how anybody feels, least of all you. You can't help them if you become them—and the only reason you're there is to help.

Of course, my laughing hadn't exactly *helped*.

The job hardens you, but it shouldn't make you cruel. *Her baby.*

So I decided, for my own sake as much as hers, to pretend to try to save her dog.

Even though that's not what 911 is for.

It was hopeless, of course.

I took another look at the dog. Still dead.

I knelt down anyway. I opened the medical kit and pulled out the oxygen tank and a flexible pediatric mask, curling it into a cone shape around the pup's snout. The rookie followed my lead, dropping to his knees and starting chest compressions with his fingertips.

And that's how we—paid, professional firefighters for the esteemed city of Lillian, Massachusetts—wound up doing CPR on a Chihuahua.

I gave the rookie a look, like, *You are never telling anybody about this.*

And he gave me a look back, like, *Oh, I am telling* everybody *about this.*

The rookie pumped the chest, and I administered the oxygen, and the old lady wiped shaky tears from her cheeks with knobby fingers, watching us like nothing else would ever matter in the world.

I'll give it three minutes, I thought.

Then I gave it seven.

Finally, I sat back and flipped off the oxygen.

"I'm sorry," I said, meeting the old lady's eyes. And I was.

The rookie and I bowed our heads for a moment of pseudo-respectful silence, and that's when—I swear to God—that crazy Chihuahua gave a snort as loud as a backfiring car, flipped up onto its pointy little paws, and blinked at us.

I gasped and dropped the mask.

The rookie jumped back. *"Holy shit!"*

"I don't like that language," the old lady said, like a reflex.

Then we all stared as the dog bent low and clenched every single abdominal muscle as tight as stone until a pile of dog-food-smelling vomit flopped out of her mouth with a splat. Next, she shifted position, and a metal thimble came flying out of her face like it had been launched by a slingshot.

It hit the window with a clank and rolled to a stop next to the still-sleeping old man.

We looked back and forth between the dog and the thimble, which seemed to have a circumference wider than the dog's own throat.

Then the dog looked at us for a second, like she couldn't imagine what we were doing there, before peeing on the floor and then trotting off through the doggie door to get on with her day.

Next thing I knew, the old lady—surprisingly strong—had clamped us into a group hug, and my face was in the crook of the rookie's neck, my cheek registering some sandpapery stubble and my brain registering panic over being so close to him. The old lady held us there a minute, snuffling tears of relief and saying, "Thank you, thank you," before grabbing both our hands and leading us to a broom closet in the kitchen.

Inside, down on the floor, was a box full of fat, squirmy puppies.

"Take some," she said, urging us down toward them.

She wanted to give us puppies? "No thank you, ma'am," I said. "We can't accept—"

I was going to say "gifts," but as I watched the rookie bend right down and pick up and cradle one of those little squirmers in his arms, I finished with "puppies."

The rookie stood back up to show me, his face bright with good fortune. "Look at these little guys!"

"Half Chihuahua," the old lady said, "and half poodle." Then she tilted her head to gesture next door. "The neighbors."

"A Poo-huahua," the rookie said, nuzzling his face down into the puppy's fat belly.

"Rookie," I said, shaking my head. "No."

"Don't you think the station needs a mascot?"

"Shut it down, rookie," I said, as menacingly as I could.

But he held the puppy up to me. "Look at that face."

That was it. I drew the line at puppies. "I'm out," I said, walking away.

When the rookie caught up with me a minute later on the front walk, I did not turn back to look. "Tell me you don't have a puppy in your arms."

"I don't have a puppy in my arms," he said from behind me, pleased with his own restraint.

"Good, because—"

"I've got him in a basket."

Thirteen

I DEVELOPED A strategy for dealing with Diana: one-word answers only.

It turned out, I was right all along. She didn't just want me to help her with groceries and stairs. She wanted to hang out. She wanted to be friends.

She wanted forgiveness.

She claimed she was just glad to have me around, but her actions made it clear that she wanted more. Wherever I was, she'd show up there. If I tried to read a book in the living room, she'd read a magazine in the living room. If I was making a snack in the kitchen, she'd make a pot of tea. If I took a stroll down to the rock jetty, she would coincidentally be in the mood for a stroll of her own.

She was companionable. She was low-key. But she failed to comprehend something important: I didn't want to be her friend.

Quite the opposite, in fact.

In the years after she left, I built my entire life on a foundation of routine and order and low drama. That meant setting schedules and keeping to them. It meant going to the same place and eating the same things and following the same routines over and over. It also meant doing everything in a careful, controlled, regimented way.

And that was before I'd even moved here. Now I'd turned everything inside out. I had ten times more chaos than I could handle. The last thing I needed was to hash out old disappointments with a woman I'd already given up on.

I was here to be helpful, and pleasant, and do my duty. I was not here to play Bananagrams, or to learn the art of crochet, or to bare my soul. To anybody.

But Diana didn't get it.

"Answer a question for me," she said one night as I tried to escape after dinner to practice a little parkour.

"Busy," I said, at the door.

"You're always busy."

"Sorry."

"There's something I need to talk to you about."

I just shrugged and gestured toward the road. "Working out."

The house was so tiny that those nighttime escapes had become a kind of salvation. I'd jog the narrow streets of the jetty and then on into town and around the coast, vaulting, leaping, climbing, and swinging. It did make it feel like the whole town was a playground.

Usually, by the time I got home, Diana was fast asleep with her white noise machine running. But on this night, she waited up. When I walked back in, she was perched in the living room like a spider.

"Come talk to me for a minute," she said.

"I'm not really a big talker," I said.

"You used to be."

"I used to be a lot of things."

I sat down, as requested, but I chose the chair closest to the stairs, and I perched at the edge, ready for my quick getaway. As I sat, she studied me. "I want something from you," she said.

I met her eyes. "What?"

"I want you to forgive me."

Well, that was blunt. "We don't always get what we want."

"I don't want you to do it for me. I want you to do it for you."

I drew in a long breath. "We're not going to be friends, Diana."

"This isn't about being friends."

"Kinda seems like it is."

She frowned at me. "I'd like to be your friend, I would. I can't deny it. In addition to loving you—I've always just really, really liked you. So I'm not going to pretend like I feel the same way about you that I would about some stranger off the street. But that's not what I mean when I say I want you to forgive me."

I waited.

"This is about something far more fundamental than that."

I waited again, as long as I could, before finally giving in and asking, "What?"

"This is about you finally setting down all that anger you carry around with you everywhere you go."

She wasn't wrong. I did carry anger around. Maybe not everywhere—but almost.

And it was a lot heavier than you'd think.

I could have lied then, I guess. Or gone up to bed. Or even fled back out the front door into the night. But I just didn't. Did I want to set down all that anger?

Of course I did.

I let out a long sigh before saying, "I just don't know how to do that."

She leaned a little closer, waiting for more.

I'd already started. Might as well finish.

"I always kind of thought that forgiveness would come with time," I said. "That the bitterness would slowly fade like a scar until I couldn't even really find it anymore if I looked. But that's not what happened. It didn't fade. It hardened. Other things around it faded, but the memory of the day you left is still as sharp as if it just happened. I can still see your car pulling out of the driveway. I can hear the pop of the tires as they rolled over those seeds from that Chinese tallow tree. I can see the side of your face, absolutely still like a wax figure as I banged on the window. I can feel every emotion I experienced that day in slow motion. If anything, the memories have gotten stronger."

Those memories were tied to other memories, of course, and there was no way I was going to share anything more with her. But what I was saying was true enough. "I know that forgiveness is healthy. I know the only person you hurt when you hold on to bitterness is yourself. But I literally wouldn't even know how to start. How do you forgive people? How does it even work?"

These were meant to be rhetorical questions.

"You're in luck," Diana said then. "I happen to be kind of an expert on forgiveness."

"Who have you had to forgive?" I asked. As far as I could tell, she was far more likely to be the victimizer than the victim.

"Myself, for starters," she said. "And then lots of other people. You don't get to be my age without disappointments. My parents, in some ways. Various friends. Your dad."

"Dad?" I said, like, *Please.* "Dad is perfect."

"He's hardly perfect."

"He was good to you."

"Yes, he was."

"He was good to you, and you cheated on him."

She snapped to attention. "I never cheated on your dad."

I gave her a look, like, *I know all about it*.

"Is that what he told you?"

"That's what he told Aunt Caroline. I just overheard him."

"I did not cheat on your father," she declared again.

"You left him for another man," I said, like, *Case closed.*

"Yes. But I didn't cheat."

I couldn't help it. I crossed my arms.

"The semester I came up here as a visiting professor, I was desperately lonely," she said then. "I didn't mean to fall in love with Wallace. But I sat by myself every day at lunch—the art teachers were a strangely snobby crew—and he started sitting with me every day. He was terribly funny. And charming. He wore these gray cable-knit sweaters, and he had the most wonderful gravelly voice. He always smelled like gingerbread. I don't know how to describe it. We just had a spark. The more I saw him, the more I wanted to see him. His wife had left him not too long before we met, and we were both just so . . . alone. He very quickly became the best thing in my life up here. And I'm sorry to say it, because your dad is a really good person, but as much as I did love him, I was never really *in love* with him. I married him because he was practical and helpful and good—but not because he ever swept me off my feet. I'd never felt that feeling in my life before I met Wallace. I didn't even know it existed. It was like being caught up in a windstorm. But I never slept with him or even kissed him in all that time. We held hands a few times—passionately—but that was it."

Diana rearranged herself on the sofa and kept going.

"I don't know if you've ever been in love—"

I shook my head.

"But it's a hell of a thing. It's all-consuming. You can't think about anything else. There I was, middle-aged but consumed with fire like a teenager. I didn't just want to be with Wallace, I needed to. I came up with a plan that I would wait until after you left for college. It was only two more years. I figured I could hold out that long. But then, on the night I confessed my feelings to Wallace—and the plan—he told me that he was sick."

Diana closed her eyes for a second. Then she went on. "He had a disease I'd never heard of called pulmonary fibrosis, and there was no cure. His lungs were basically shutting down. They thought he had maybe two years left. Suddenly, it turned out, we were running out of time."

This was new information to me. I knew she'd left us to be with a man named Wallace. And two years later, I heard that he had died. But I never knew until this moment that she'd known he was dying when she left.

"I had an impossible choice to make then," she said, rubbing at some dried glaze on her finger.

He'd been dying when she left.

It tinted the story a slightly different hue, I'll give it that.

"But *you had to leave on my birthday*?" I said, my throat feeling thick. "My sixteenth birthday."

She nodded. "He had a surgery scheduled that Monday morning. He was healthy enough to try a lung transplant at the time, though it didn't ever take the way they'd hoped. I waited until the very last minute, but then, by the afternoon of your birthday, I had to go to make it in time. He was scared and alone."

"*I* was scared and alone." It came out like a whisper.

But she heard it.

She nodded. "I thought if I stayed until your birthday, it would be like splitting the difference. I could be with you in the morning, and see you, but then get to him in time to take him to the hospital."

My chest felt heavy, like it was sagging.

"That's become a defining fact about our lives," she said then, "that I left on your sixteenth birthday—and it was horrible timing, I admit. But I was trying to stay as long as I possibly could. I wanted to take you with me, if you remember."

I did remember. She'd asked me to come, too. But I couldn't leave my dad—and I was so indescribably angry at her for tearing our family apart that I didn't even want to talk to her, much less move across the country.

But that didn't mean I wanted her to go.

I wanted her to come to her senses and stay with us.

"Why didn't you just tell me about Wallace being sick?" I asked.

"I hadn't even told your father yet. I didn't know how much he could handle. He cried so hard when I told him, I was afraid he might hurt himself. I thought maybe I could explain better after things settled down. I was making the best decisions I could. I honestly didn't realize when I drove away that day that you'd never speak to me again."

I gave her a look like, *Come on*. "I'm living in your house. Not sure it's accurate to say I never spoke to you again."

She gave a nod, like, *Fair enough*. "But I lost you."

She wasn't wrong. She had lost me.

Now was probably the time to confess to her about the other big event of my sixteenth birthday. I recognized, as I watched her lift a shaky hand to readjust her eye patch—blue-and-yellow check today—that it wasn't entirely fair of me to let her go on thinking that she alone was responsible for all the misery in her wake. Now was probably the time to give her a real answer to that breezy question about whatever happened to Heath Thompson.

But I couldn't. I had never talked about it in my life, to anyone. And up until this moment, I'd believed I never would.

Instead, I changed the subject. "So," I said, more to fill the silence than anything else. "How does forgiveness work?"

She nodded, like we'd come back to the point. She gave a businesslike sigh and sat up straighter. "There are a lot of different methods for chipping away at forgiveness. Just saying the words 'I forgive you,' even to yourself, can be a powerful start." She did not pause to see if I'd say them but kept right on. "Forgiveness is about a mind-set of letting go." She thought for a second, then said, "It's about acknowledging to yourself that someone hurt you, and accepting that."

Done, I thought.

"Then it's about accepting that the person who hurt you is flawed, like all people are, and letting that guide you to a better, more nuanced understanding of what happened.

Flawed, I thought. *Okay. Check.*

"And then there's a third part," she went on, "probably the hardest, that involves trying to look at the aftermath of what happened and find ways that you benefited, not just ways you were harmed."

I gave her a look. "That last one's a doozie."

"Agreed." She nodded. "The biggest—and the best."

"Are you telling me I need to try to find upsides that came from your leaving?"

"It sounds greedy of me, doesn't it?"

"A little."

"But that's just the way it works. I'd tell you the same thing if we were talking about anyone else."

"You know a lot about this."

"I've had a lot of time to study." Next, she tilted her head. "Can you think of any upsides? Can you think of any good things in your life that wouldn't be there if I hadn't left?"

I let out a long breath. I frowned. I thought about it for a long time as I stared at the floor.

Then, at last, I said, "I got very, very good at basketball."

Fourteen

MY STRATEGY FOR avoiding the rookie was much like my strategy for avoiding Diana. And about as effective. As determined as I was to get away from the rookie, the captain was just as determined to throw us together. We had to sit side by side at meals in the wobbliest two chairs. We had to clean the bathroom together, and do the chores nobody else wanted. We had the worst two parking spots, the farthest away.

For a while, we always got lumped together as newbies.

I worked hard to change that. Practically speaking, this meant pulling pranks on the rookie—establishing that I was a prank-*er,* not a prank-*ee*.

So: Hiding his clothes while he was in the shower? Me. Pouring ice water on him while he was fast asleep? Me. Filling his shoes with water and putting them in the freezer? Me. Whatever the guys needed done, I did it. I *volunteered.* I thought it would separate us. I thought it would distinguish me with the crew. I thought, at the very least, it would annoy the rookie and discourage him from being so nice all the damn time.

But it didn't. He was Big Robby's kid. He'd practically grown up at a firehouse. He knew the honor of being pranked. He laughed every single thing off, and I never saw him look even mildly irritated. Pretend OJ made out of mac-and-cheese powder? Awesome. Mayonnaise on the toilet seat? Epic. Fake poop in his bed? Hilarious.

One morning, I convinced him to pee in a plastic cup and leave it on the captain's desk.

"You don't want to mess around with drug testing, man," Six-Pack chimed in. "We all turned ours in at the start of shift."

"You don't want him to think you're hiding something," Case added, all casual, from his perch in front of the TV.

The rookie looked around at all of us, deeply suspicious. But he took the cup off the table and started to walk out. "Don't forget to label it with your name," Six-Pack called after him, and flung a Sharpie at his head.

Ten minutes later, the captain came busting into the kitchen. "Callaghan!" he bellowed.

The rookie looked up from making a sandwich. "Yes, sir?"

"Why is there a goddamned cup of lukewarm piss on my desk with your name on it?"

The rookie squeezed his eyes closed as we all fell out laughing. He suppressed a smile and then shook his head. "I'm sorry, sir. I was told you were collecting urine samples today."

"And who the hell told you that?" the captain demanded.

But the rookie didn't rat us out. "I can't remember, sir."

With the crew, my strategy worked. But with the captain, it backfired. As soon as he stopped thinking of me *as* a rookie, he started wanting me to *deal with* the rookie.

Which meant he threw us together even more.

Especially since, in the wake of my opening a can of whoop-ass on Tiny in B-ball, I now had a new problem. Nobody wanted me to play hoops because I was *too good.*

Ironic.

Somehow, in the afternoons, just as any pickup game was starting, the captain would send me off to practice essential skills with the rookie.

Which meant the one guy in the world I was desperate to get away from was forced to spend hours every shift putting his hands all over me. Repeatedly. Slowly. For long periods of time.

While the guys shot hoops out back, I had to let the rookie check my spine alignment with the pads of his fingers—all the way up and all the way down, again and again. I had to let him splint my hands, my ankles, and my knees, and strap me to a backboard and put me in a C-collar, leaning across and brushing against me as he worked the straps. I had to take off my shirt and sit in my sports bra while he practiced placing EKG pads in the right order on my chest. And all the while, the closeness of him would wake up all my senses like static electricity. The mouthwatering scent of his laundry detergent and his general manliness would waft past me in relentless waves.

In my real life, I never let anybody touch me.

But the station was different. I could—and would—withstand anything for the job. Even a beautiful man touching my body.

It was torture, but not the kind I would have expected. In general, I didn't let people touch me because it stressed me out to be touched. But, for some reason, the rookie had the opposite effect. The more he touched me—moving my hair back to check my C-spine, sliding the stethoscope over my chest and back, wrapping my arm with the BP cuff—the more I *wanted* him to touch me.

Weird.

Maybe it was the frequency of it. The captain really did make us practice a lot. Maybe we crossed some basic barrier of familiarity I'd never gotten to with anyone else, where I could relax into it.

Because, relax I did. At a certain point, all he had to do was pull out the EKG kit and my body started tingling like I was sinking into a hot bath. Full-immersion anticipation.

It was funny, because I'd done these things with other people in other trainings and it had never, not once, been so, um . . . evocative.

I guess context really matters. My crazy crush tinged even the most pedestrian interaction—passing in the hallway, eating dinner, practicing a blood draw—with electricity. Plus, that was just an effect the rookie had on people: He put everyone at ease.

It was so good, it was bad. It was so wonderful, it was terrifying. It was so delicious, it was awful.

And it just kept getting better—and worse.

It stirred up something ancient and powerful inside me—some unfamiliar longing I had no idea how to handle. And I hated things I didn't know how to handle.

But how I felt about any of it wasn't relevant. The captain said to teach the rookie everything I knew? I taught him everything I knew. The captain said to spend hours letting the rookie put his hands all over me for the benefit of the fire service? I did it. Chain of command. No questions asked.

Whether or not the rookie was turning my body into a symphony of emotion was not relevant.

No matter what, I gave it my all. I showed him how to make an eyewash out of a nasal cannula and an IV bag. I helped him practice his bowline knot and his clove hitch. I taught him to operate the handheld radio with his left hand so he could take notes at the same time. I taught him that if a patient's wearing too much nail polish for the pulse oximeter, you can turn it sideways to get the read.

I also taught him not to look into his critical patients' eyes. Pro tip.

"Why not?" he asked.

"It haunts you," I said, shaking my head a little. "It just haunts you."

"You mean, if they don't survive."

"Once I've left the hospital," I said then, dead serious, "I always tell myself they survive."

Other advice: Carry extra pens, because once a homeless guy covered in lice has used your pen to sign a waiver, you don't exactly want it back. Never cut open a down coat with your trauma shears unless you want to be covered in feathers for the rest of the shift. And always cut pants off on the *outside* of the leg. A guy in Austin famously cut a patient's pants off from the inside with a little too much enthusiasm—and he got called "the rabbi" for the rest of his career.

The rookie paid attention.

But not every part of the job came naturally to him.

I'll give him this: He was one of the fittest guys on the crew, and he could lift anything. He was endlessly good-natured and very well-intentioned. He was decisive, and physically strong, and mentally committed. He was up for anything. And okay, fine. He was handsome, at least to me—though maybe that's not a job requirement.

He also—with some frequency—fainted at the sight of blood.

The first time it happened—though certainly not the last—was the first time he started an IV on me.

The thing about blood is, you can't overthink it. If you really focus on how odd it is to stick a metal tube into another human being's vein, it will freak you out. The trick to doing anything well in medicine is to get so familiar with it that it doesn't seem strange anymore.

But we could all tell from the rookie's face on pretty much every medical call that he was not there yet. He needed a lot more practice.

His hands felt cold as he tied the tourniquet and felt for a vein in my arm.

"Great veins," he said, giving me that smile of his and a quick glance up at my eyes.

"Sweet talker," I said. Then, trying to get back to business: "They're easy to find, but they roll."

He frowned a little. "Okay." Then he felt my other arm.

I could tell from his breathing he was nervous.

"Don't be nervous," I said. "I'm tough."

"Maybe not as tough as you seem," he said.

If it had been any other guy in the crew, I'd have argued. The rookie was the one guy I didn't feel like I had to prove myself to. Partly that was because he was so inexperienced—I clearly had authority over him—but it was also just something about him, the way he was. The expression on his face when he looked at me always seemed to be some version of admiration. The things I was good at—he saw them.

He wasn't competing with me, either. He didn't mind when I was better than him, and he seemed to love it when I was better than the other guys.

I just always had this feeling that he was rooting for me.

But I still needed him to hurry up and jam that needle in my vein.

"Just get it over with," I said.

"Sticks are not my strong suit," he said.

"Don't overthink it," I said.

He looked up then, trying to read me. Then he unwrapped a needle, pressed it to the vein he'd chosen, pushed it in—and spurted blood all over both of us and the room.

"Oh, shit," he said, taking in the sight of all the blood—then he wavered in his chair for a second before he collapsed and hit the floor.

"Rookie?" I said, peering down at him with the needle still in my arm.

People often come to just after fainting, because with a simple vasovagal attack, all that's wrong is not enough oxygen's getting to the brain. This happens all the time at weddings, for some reason. There's a whole subcategory of videos on YouTube with people melting to the floor at weddings. But as soon as you're down flat, the blood equalizes, and you're back up pretty fast.

Sometimes, it takes a few minutes longer.

I pulled out the needle and cleaned up the mess, and then, when he still wasn't up yet, I knelt down beside him. I meant to rouse him right away, but the opportunity to just gaze at him for a second was too appealing to skip. What was it about that face of his? Why did it have such an effect on me? I'd spent so much time trying to figure that out, but I still didn't know for sure.

It had to be subjective. He wasn't *perfect.* I tried to catalog his flaws. He had slight bags under his eyes—but of course it just gave him a sweet, puppy-dog look. He had an incisor that was darker than his other teeth. And he had funny earlobes, now that I thought about it. A little too plump for the rest of him. There. He *wasn't* perfect. Just as flawed as the rest of us.

He should be nothing special at all.

But he just was.

My best guess was something about his eyes—how smiley and kind looking they were. I remember reading an article years ago about a study done on the shape of people's eyes that found people with smiley eyes wound up happier overall. Statistically.

Maybe that was it.

I could have stared at him all day. But of course I didn't. He had a lot more needles to stick me with before we were done.

I reached out to wake him. I meant to push on his shoulder, but my hand decided to cup his jaw instead. At the touch, his eyes blinked open and I yanked my hand away.

"What happened?" he asked, frowning and starting to sit up.

"You fainted. Take it slow." I helped back him up to the chair.

"That's embarrassing."

I sat back in my chair. "I won't tell anybody."

"Thank you."

"You should practice on an orange," I said. "It's about the same surface tension as skin."

"It's not the skin I have trouble with," he said.

"Not a big fan of blood, huh?" I asked.

"Not really."

"You'll get used to it. After a year, blood will seem as harmless as fruit punch."

"That's a disturbing thought."

"You're just going to need to do a lot of blood draws. You need to do so many, it becomes like brushing your teeth."

"Hard to imagine, but okay."

"You can get your sea legs with me, and then we'll sic you on the rest of the crew."

"Thanks, Cassie."

I think it was the first time I'd ever heard him—or anyone at the station—say my first name. I didn't even realize he knew it. Everybody just called me Hanwell.

I held my breath for a second, then forced myself to let it out. Then I held my arm out to him. "Okay," I said, "let's go again."

"Now?" he asked.

"Right now," I said, giving a *don't try to fight it* nod. "Make it happen, buddy. That blood's not going to draw itself."

Fifteen

THE ROOKIE SAW some dark stuff with us that first month. We got a call for a grandpa who'd choked on a piece of steak (fatality), a tree fallen on a house (no one home), and a kid with his head stuck between the steps of a playground slide (close call). We got called to the scene of an abused woman who'd finally had enough and went after her husband with a shotgun (mutilation—not pretty).

It wasn't long before the rookie had acquired what we called "the stare of life," that shell-shocked look new firefighters get before they've figured out how to manage, compartmentalize, and deal with all the horrific tragedy.

Not that you ever entirely figure it out. It's a learning curve.

You eventually get to the point where it doesn't bother you. As much. You put it on a different screen in your mind that's separate from your real life somehow. But it takes a while, and in the meantime, all you can do is cope.

The more stressed the rookie got, the more we joked around with him. For his own good.

Case sent him looking for a left-handed screwdriver. Six-Pack filled his locker with packing peanuts. We hung his boxer briefs from the flagpole. One day, we set his bed on four empty soda cans and remade it so it would collapse when he got in that night. And nobody ever missed an opportunity to dump water on him.

After he delivered his first baby on the box, the guys said, "How was it?"

And the rookie, shaking his head in disbelief, said, "It was like watching an avocado getting squeezed through an apricot."

That night, the guys hung a bag in his locker with a snorkel, dive mask, and flippers, labeled OB/GYN DELIVERY KIT.

To be fair, there were also some funny calls. The lady who called us for menstrual cramps and kept talking about her "groin-icologist." The fierce little poodle that attacked the rookie's bunker-pants leg and wouldn't let go, even as he hopped around trying to fling it off.

Just about the only thing the rookie didn't see in those first weeks was a fire.

Until the day of his—our—six-week-iversary at the station, when we got a call for a garage fire at an abandoned house at the edge of town.

It was a perfect first fire. We ran lights-and-sirens, and we were the first on scene. We got to use the hoses and even worked in a lesson for the rookie about how to read the colors of the smoke.

Afterward, doing demo in the smoldering remains, I heard the captain giving the rookie advice. "A fire's like a living thing," he explained. "You have to treat it like a worthy adversary. It eats and it moves, and it's going to go on eating and moving until we stop it."

I looked at the rookie's face. He looked flushed, and exhausted, and awash with adrenaline.

I knew that feeling.

"Pretty great, huh?" I said, as we walked back to the engine when it was all over.

"What?"

I elbowed him. "Fighting a fire."

We were passing a drain in the parking lot, and I hopped right over it before turning back and realizing that the rookie had stopped to bend over the drain and throw up.

After a minute, he stood back up, wiped his mouth, and kept walking toward me. "Yeah," he said then. "Really great."

THAT NIGHT, I had a nightmare.

Not uncommon. I had lots of nightmares. But I didn't usually have them on shift.

In this one, I dreamed I was suffocating. I must have stopped breathing during the worst of it, because when I woke up, there in my storage-closet bed at the station, I was gasping for air and nauseated—as if I really had been suffocating.

As soon as I woke, I stood up. Then I staggered to the light switch, flipped it, and stood panting for a long while, right there by the door, blinking, repeating to myself, "Just a dream. Just a dream."

I didn't want to go back to bed after that.

I went to the kitchen to get a glass of water.

And guess who was there? The rookie.

I stopped in my tracks at the sight of him. He was *cooking.*

I checked the wall clock. It was 2:00 A.M.

I started to back out of the room, but he sensed me there and turned.

He looked me over. Then he held a pan out in my direction. "Want an omelet?"

"No thanks," I said.

I'd been spotted, so might as well get my water. I shuffled to the sink.

He was chopping at a cutting board while butter melted in a pan, and I found myself watching him.

That knife was like a blur. Tap-tap-tap! A shallot was diced. Tap-tap-tap! A tomato was in pieces. He swept them off the cutting board into a bowl and—Tap-tap-tap!—there went a mushroom. It was the speed, and the confidence of his movements. Mesmerizing. And a whole different side of the rookie. A side that was calm, and confident, and frankly, just from this quick glimpse, totally badass.

"I can't cook," I said, watching. "I'm terrible."

"At least you're not as bad as DeStasio," he said.

"I am worse. I can't even toast a bagel."

That got his attention. He turned to squint at me. "How do you survive?"

I gave him a little smile. "On the kindness of strangers."

He went back to work.

After a bit, I asked, "Why are you cooking an omelet at two in the morning?"

"Oh," he said, waving the question off. "The usual. Just wakeful. What about you?"

"Oh," I said. "The usual." Then I added, "Nightmares."

That got his attention. "Nightmares?"

I shrugged. "Yeah. Just a thing with me. My dad says it's stress relief."

"What are they about?" the rookie asked. He was sautéing now, flipping the contents with the whole pan, in a rhythm. It was kind of like watching a juggler.

Maybe it was the late hour, or the smell of those sautéing vegetables, or just that it felt harder to not answer than to go ahead and answer—but to my own surprise, I heard myself say, "I'm always either being chased, being strangled, or suffocating. Sometimes all three."

"Holy shit," he said, turning to face me.

But I pointed at the veggies. "Don't burn those."

He turned back. "How often?"

"I don't know," I confessed. Had I ever told anyone about this? "It's better not to keep count."

I was kind of enjoying the rookie's sympathy. It made me feel tough and impressive.

"For your whole life?" he asked then.

I shook my head. "Just since I was sixteen."

"Why sixteen?"

I could have shrugged, like I didn't know. Instead, I said, "That was the year my mother left."

It wasn't the whole story, but it was more than I'd ever confessed to anybody else.

We were quiet then while he tended to his cooking. In a few minutes, he slid a perfectly cooked, restaurant-worthy omelet onto a plate and handed it to me.

"In case you change your mind," he said.

I wasn't hungry, but I took a bite anyway—not expecting anything in particular, other than just a basic egg-dish kind of experience. That's not what happened. I don't know what kind of magic he used on those eggs, but the minute that bite of omelet arrived on my tongue, it absolutely overtook my mouth. It infused every taste bud I had with salty, buttery, garlicky, all-consuming pleasure.

"Oh my God," I said, mouth full, blinking at him in disbelief.

The rookie's whole face shifted into a smile. He watched me for a second, seeming to enjoy how much I was enjoying it.

"You can *cook,*" I said, taking another bite.

"Yeah," he said.

"Like, you can *really* cook."

"That's what I did before I came here," he said. "I've been a chef at a little place in the North End for six years."

"But, I mean . . ." I didn't even know what I meant. I couldn't think. I took another bite. "Oh my God. You should go on a cooking competition show and win a billion dollars."

"I'll get right on that," he said.

Later, remembering this moment with the rookie, I would wonder what on earth he was doing fainting at the sight of blood in a firehouse when he could have been off absolutely *writing poetry* with food.

That's not the question that came out in the moment, though. The question that came out was "Why the hell is DeStasio cooking our meals?"

The rookie smiled and looked down. "He likes to cook. I think he needs something to do."

"He's going to kill us all."

"Did you hear that his wife left him?"

I shook my head. "No."

The rookie nodded. "DeStasio was talking about it before bed the other night. She moved to Framingham last Friday to live with her sister. She couldn't take the drinking anymore."

"DeStasio drinks?"

"I guess he must," the rookie said. "You know their son Tony died, right?"

I shook my head. There was a lot I didn't know about DeStasio.

"Yeah," the rookie said, "about two years ago. Drunk driver."

I winced.

"Except that Tony was the drunk driver."

"Poor DeStasio," I said. No wonder he never laughed.

The rookie nodded. "He's had a tough few years. Add the back injury, and he's a superhero for just getting out of bed every morning."

I found myself wanting to come up with ways to fix his loneliness. "Maybe we could set him up on a date," I suggested.

"Would *you* want to go on a date with DeStasio?"

"Maybe we could start a Friday night barbecue club and just start showing up at his place for dinner," I said.

"Have you seen DeStasio's place?" he asked. "It's like a war zone."

"We could clean it up."

"He'd hate that. He'd chase you out with a broom."

I gave the rookie a look. "I'm only trying to help."

"Some guys don't want to be helped."

"We can't just let him suffer."

"I said the same thing to the captain. But he said DeStasio's got too much pride."

"So we ignore him?"

"The captain's going to take him fishing next week."

"That doesn't sound like a long-term solution."

"Neither does tossing him into the dating pool."

This might sound strange, but as sad as the topic was, I found myself enjoying talking to the rookie.

Some—maybe even most—conversations are hard work. With the rookie, it was the opposite. I didn't have to think about what to say next; all I had to do was decide between the options that popped into my mind as I listened. The conversation didn't happen so much as *blossom*.

My mom and I used to have conversations like that, I remembered suddenly. In general, though, in life, they were pretty hard to come by. It made me almost sad to enjoy the conversation so much. I found myself missing it already, even as it was happening.

Bittersweet, for sure.

When it was time to clean up, I wanted to do all the dishes. The rookie had cooked; I should clean. But it was hard for him not to help. He hovered, and kept turning the water on and off for me and handing me the soap.

"You're not supposed to help me," I said.

"I like washing dishes," he said, stepping right up next to me, so close I could feel him there even without touching.

Then the rookie added, "But I always listen to music." He leaned forward to flip on the little radio by the sink. DeStasio kept it tuned to an oldies station. Marvin Gaye came on.

And so I gave in and let him help. We listened to Smokey Robinson and Diana Ross and the Temptations, and scrubbed to the rhythm, and swayed, and occasionally bumped into each other. Which I enjoyed.

When we were done, and there was no good reason left to stay there, and it really was time to go back to bed, the rookie dried his hands with a dish towel and said, "I want to say something to you, but I'm not sure if it's a good idea."

I wasn't sure it was a good idea, either. I glanced over. "Okay."

"I think I know why you avoid me."

"I don't avoid you." Lying.

"You know you do."

"Fine," I said. "When the captain is not ordering you to stick me with needles, I sometimes avoid you. A little."

"Sorry about the needles," he said, wrinkling his nose.

"It's fine."

"The thing is," he said then, "and I don't want you to take this the wrong way—"

"I'll try not to."

"You're tough and strong and capable and totally fearless . . ."

I waited.

"But I wonder if you need a hug."

What? "A *hug*?" I said, stepping back.

He hunched into a shrug. "Of everybody on the crew, I always feel like you're the one who most needs a hug."

"You think I need a *hug*?"

He winced a little, like he knew how dumb it sounded. "I do."

"A hug is like the last thing I need, dude."

"Just—because you're so self-sufficient and you never need any help and you just keep to yourself all the time."

How dare he tell me I needed a hug. What the hell? "Are the guys all going around at work *hugging*, and I just haven't noticed? Did I miss a bunch of hug-fests?"

"No, but—"

"Because I'm not sure what you're saying, but it sounds like there's an insult in there somewhere."

He shook his head. "I'm not trying to insult you." He knew he was fumbling this conversation. "I think I'm just saying . . ." He didn't know where to go. "I think I just want you to know . . ." He shook his head again while I waited. "There's just something about you. Something I feel about you. I don't know how to describe it, but it's a powerful thing . . ."

"What are you saying?"

"I'm just saying that . . . pretty much every time I see you, all I want to do is to put my arms around you."

I held still. That was a hell of a statement. "Well," I said at last, "you can't."

He lifted his hands in innocence. "I know."

"That's on you, man. That's all about you."

"More than likely."

"Maybe you're the one who needs a hug, and you're projecting that onto me."

"It's distinctly possible."

Here is the deep-down truth that I would never admit: I did need a hug. I'd needed one all those weeks ago when Hernandez said it, and I'd needed one every day since. Not just one—a thousand. I would have given anything for the rookie to put his arms around me right then and wrap me up and let me stay like that till morning. I wanted him to. I wanted it so bad, my whole body ached for it to happen.

So, of course, the only response I could muster was to take a step away.

My whole life—everything I'd worked for—hung in the balance. This was not the moment to lose focus. Yes, he was warm, and kindhearted, and surprisingly empathetic, and shockingly good at cooking—but none of that was relevant. As I stood across from him, my brain started issuing alerts about all the disasters that would befall me—and my career, my stability, my carefully constructed sense of order, my sanity—if I didn't get out of there, pronto.

I should have thanked him for the food. I should have said good night, at the very least. But I didn't. I just pointed at him. "Do not hug me."

He took a step back, too, and lifted his hands in surrender. "I'm not going to."

We stood like that, facing off, for a minute. Then I took another step backwards. "Don't ever talk to me about hugging again."

He could tell he'd freaked me out—or insulted me, or something. He lifted his hands a little higher. "Okay."

Another step back. "This"—I gestured down at my body—"is a no-hug zone."

Now deeply regretting he ever brought it up: "Got it."

"Stick me with all the needles you want, pal," I said then. "But if you try to hug me? I will kick your rookie ass."

* * *

A WEEK LATER, the guys pranked me by saying we were going to do ladder drills, convincing me to suit up in my bunker gear and climb onto the roof of the station to "show the rookie how it's done." This prank took a lot of planning, because our station didn't even have a ladder truck.

They had to borrow one from Station Three.

I had a bad feeling, even as I climbed. Still, there it was: chain of command.

I got to the top and dismounted the ladder, and the guys drove away.

It was fine, I told myself. I hadn't been pranked in a while. *Worry if we don't prank you.*

I waved. I bowed. I let them have their moment.

I watched Case and Six-Pack steer the ladder truck off down the street to return it to its proper station, and I watched the rest of them strut back inside, arm in arm.

Finally, I turned and scouted out my new surroundings. I'd be here all night, for sure.

I checked out the views. I took some deep breaths. I told myself this was an opportunity to take some personal time, reflect on my life, and think all those deep thoughts I never had time for. They were doing me a favor, really.

When the sun was gone, I sat against a brick wall, leaned my head back, and closed my eyes, like I might fall asleep.

I wasn't sleeping, exactly—but was definitely starting to drift—when I felt my hackles rise like there was somebody nearby, just as I heard a footstep right beside me.

I popped up like a jack-in-the-box, launched a serious, full-body kick, and didn't realize until I was making impact with my foot that I was kicking the rookie.

He doubled over and hit the ground.

I dropped beside him. "Rookie! What the hell?"

I'd knocked the wind out of him. He was down on all fours.

It's scary to get the wind knocked out of you. It means the impact was hard enough to scramble the nerve signals to your diaphragm. Needing to breathe but not being able to is never an easy feeling.

"Okay," I said, switching from attacker to coach. "Straighten up." I pushed his shoulders back to guide him. He let me. "Put your hands behind your head."

He did it, and with that, his breathing came back.

"That's right," I said, breathing with him, watching his chest rise and fall. "In, then out."

I knelt there next to him while his breathing normalized, keeping a hand on his back.

When he was ready to speak at last, he looked a little mad. "What the hell, Hanwell!"

I gave him a look like, *What the hell, yourself!* "You startled me."

"I wasn't trying to," he said, like that mattered.

"I was fast asleep, pal," I said. Okay, hardly *fast asleep*—but close enough. "What was I supposed to do?"

"I don't know," he said, somehow annoyed and sarcastic and appealing all at once. "Maybe open your eyes and say, 'Hey, rookie! Thanks for being awesome.'"

"What are you even doing here?" I asked.

He blinked for a second, like he thought we should already be clear on that. "I'm rescuing you," he said. Then he gestured across the roof.

Sure enough, I could see the tip of the ladder pointing up over the edge of the roof, in the same spot as before.

He was watching me closely, like he hoped I'd be impressed.

But I refused to be.

"How did you get the ladder truck?"

"I talked the guys into it."

I narrowed my eyes.

"I just, you know, advocated for you during dinner. About how they'd had their fun and it was time to let you down. And then I plied them with some cookies I baked. I guess they got tired of hearing about it, because Case and Six-Pack gave in."

I shook my head at him. "That's not what happened."

He frowned. "Pretty sure it is."

"You only think that's what happened," I said.

"I'm here, aren't I?"

"Yes. But you're not actually rescuing me."

"Why not?"

"Because they just drove away."

To his credit, he didn't turn right away, or run to the place where the ladder had just been. He kept his eyes on me and let all the pieces click into place.

Then he got up, walked to the edge where the ladder had been, and looked down.

"They drove away," he confirmed.

I walked up behind him. "Hey, rookie," I said. "Thank you for being awesome."

That made him smile. I watched the sides of his eyes crinkle up. Then he smacked himself on the forehead.

I said, "That's what you get for being a hero."

He gave me a half-smile. "I can think of worse punishments."

I just shook my head.

"I guess I really must have bugged them at dinner," he said, still putting the pieces together.

"I suspect this was the plan all along."

"You're saying this was a long con to get me up on the roof, too?"

"Bingo."

"How did they know what I'd do?"

"That's just the kind of guy you are, rookie. You're a gentleman."

"You say that like it's a bad thing."

"Not bad," I said. "Just exploitable."

I walked to the edge and waved down at the guys, who were cackling with glee.

"Keep him out of trouble, Hanwell!" the captain called up.

"I'll do my best, sir."

* * *

THE ROOKIE SPENT the next hour confirming that there was truly no way down. No buildings nearby, no trees, no useful ledges. There was a hatch door down into the building, but it was padlocked.

Yeah. We were stuck.

Within the hour, he'd tried shimmying down the drainpipe (fail), lowering himself down to the second-floor fire escape (scary fail), and calling out to passersby for rescue. Triple fail.

You had to admire the optimism.

Once all hope was lost, we sat on the edge of the roof, dangling our feet over and watching the street below, in the quiet camaraderie of people who have literally nowhere else to be. A couple of Harley-Davidsons with no mufflers went by on the street. We watched the riders, noting silently that neither wore a helmet. In EMS, we call motorcycles "donor-cycles."

Then the rookie turned to me. "I'm sorry, by the way."

I looked over. "Sorry for what?"

"Sorry you're stuck up here with me." Then he added, "I feel bad that we started on the same day, and now they're making you babysit me."

"They're not making me babysit you."

He gave me a look, like, *Come on.*

I shrugged. Okay. "All rookies need a little babysitting, at first."

He studied me for a second. Then, like he'd made a big decision, he said, "Speaking of babysitting, I'm wondering if I can ask you to do me a favor."

Oh God. I studied his face. "This can't be good."

"It's not terrible," the rookie said. "But before I ask, I want to remind you of what you just did to me." He lifted up his shirt, revealing a red welt across his stomach.

Also, just—revealing his whole naked, sculpted torso. A shocking sight of its own.

I glanced away, then said, "Are you trying to make me feel guilty?"

His smile was barely mischievous. He bent down to peer at the mark. "I think if you look closely, you can see the boot treads."

"Guilt doesn't work on me," I said. "If anything, it makes me less likely to give in."

"I'll just ask you, then."

"Fine."

"You don't mind, right?"

Was he stalling a little? "I'm not going to physically stop you, if that's what you mean."

"You can say no, I should mention," the rookie said. "It's fine to say no."

I motioned with my hand, like, *Get it over with*.

"Okay." He took a breath. "It's my parents' wedding anniversary this weekend. And we're having a big party."

Oh God. Was he asking me to go? He couldn't do that! It was totally against every single rule. He shouldn't even be *thinking* about asking, much less doing it. My head started shaking on its own.

He went on. "It's their thirty-fifth, in fact. But it's an even bigger deal than that because my dad had a heart attack last year. He wound up retiring from Boston FD, and they moved up here to Gloucester, and when you talk to him, he tells you he's living the dream, but the truth is, he's pretty depressed. My mom says he just watches TV most of the day, wearing dirty socks. And she came up with this idea that if they threw a big party, he'd have to pull it together. She's convinced it's going to work."

It didn't sound like the most promising idea.

"Anyway," he went on, "all my sisters arrive tomorrow."

"All your sisters? How many do you have?"

"Four. It's going to be mass chaos—grandkids and dogs everywhere—and the whole family's counting on this party to be the thing that turns everything around—and I'm going to be the guy to ruin it and break my mother's heart because she's expecting me to bring my girlfriend, Amy—but I haven't told her yet that we broke up."

"Wait—what? You have a girlfriend?" I'd never heard anything about a girlfriend. In all this time, the concept of a girlfriend had not even occurred to me. But my voice had sounded way too shocked at the idea. Calmer, more like we were just making conversation, I added, "Named Amy?"

"Had," he said. "We dated for two years. My family loved her. Polite. Well groomed."

"You make her sound like a poodle. Hey—whatever happened to that puppy you got?"

The rookie grinned. "The Poo-huahua?"

I shook my head at him.

"I gave him to my mom," he said. "She named him Valentino and bought him a little sweater. He pines for her when she walks out—even just to get the mail."

I shook my head again. "Everything works out for you."

"Not everything," the rookie said. "Not Amy."

"What was wrong with her?"

"Nothing. She was fine. Perfectly acceptable. Just a totally vanilla, garden-variety girl."

"She sounds awful."

"My mom really, really wanted us to get married. So did my sisters. So did my dad."

"But you broke up."

"There's not much I wouldn't do for my family," the rookie said, "except possibly marry the wrong girl."

"Fair enough," I said.

"But it was complicated."

"Complicated how?"

The rookie frowned down at the city below, like he wasn't entirely sure what to say next. "I used to have five sisters. My sister Jeannie—the second youngest—died about four years ago from a viral infection in her heart."

"I'm sorry."

He looked down. "She was twenty-three. I was twenty-two. Irish twins."

I let out a slow breath.

"Amy was my sister's best friend when we were growing up, and when I ran into her one night a year or so after Jeannie died, we felt this instant connection and started going out right away. We were both living in Boston, and it was all easy. But it turned out to be kind of like when an old song comes on the radio, and you think, 'I love this song!' but then as you keep listening, you remember you never really loved it—you were just excited for a second because you *recognized* it. That's how it was for me with Amy. But by the time I figured it out, my mother was already planning the wedding."

"You stayed with Amy because you didn't want to disappoint your mother?"

He gave a little shrug. "In a way. But, yeah—I think everybody in my family thought that if I married Amy, it would be the next best thing to getting Jeannie back."

"You do a lot of overly nice things for your family," I said.

He nodded, like he'd never noticed that. "I guess I do."

"That's some pressure."

"You know that feeling you get about people sometimes when it's like they're on some important edge—and even the tiniest breeze could tip them over?"

I nodded.

"That's my mom, ever since my sister died. She acts all bossy and practical with us, but then she goes back into the kitchen and her hands are shaking."

I got that.

"We all want to go easy on her. But no way was I marrying Amy. I didn't feel . . ." He paused. "I wasn't in love with her. I liked her. It just wasn't—the kind of feeling you marry someone for."

"So you broke it off?"

"Just as I was gearing up to end it, my dad had the heart attack."

"Holy shit."

"Yeah. Exactly. So I got busy with my dad, and Amy and I hung on a little longer, and it was fine. But then one night Amy sat me down and gave me the shit-or-get-off-the-pot ultimatum. She wanted to get married."

"And what did you say?"

"I said, 'I just don't think I can marry you, Amy.' And she said, 'Ever? Or right now?' And I said, 'Ever.'"

"That was it?"

He nodded. "She left. That was six months ago. I haven't seen her since. She was pretty pissed."

"I bet."

He shook his head. "And then I just never told my parents. They thought we were dating long distance, with her still in Boston. It turned out to be so easy to just never bring it up."

The rookie took a deep breath and then sped through the rest. "Anyway, my sister Shannon called last night and told me our mom is expecting me to bring Amy to the party, and she's even hoping that all the romance of the lights and the flowers might inspire me to propose. Which of course I won't do because not only did we break up, she moved to California. And Shannon thinks it's too late to come clean to my parents, but that I also can't show up at their party alone, and that my only option for not ruining their thirty-fifth anniversary at this point is to find another female I can bring to distract my mom and cushion the blow, but the problem is, I don't really know very many females right now. I'm in a phase of my life that's kind of female-free."

I waited.

And so did he.

Finally, I asked, "What's the favor?"

"So I don't want to piss off my sister Shannon—'cause, trust me, you never want to piss off Shannon," he said. "And I'm scrolling through my phone trying to think of somebody to ask to this thing when something shocking occurs to me."

"What?"

"You're a female."

"Oh, no."

"Yes. Yes, you are."

I put my hands out like I was trying to soothe an unpredictable animal. "I am a female, that's true. But I'm not that kind of female."

"What kind?"

The kind who gets dressed up. The kind who goes on dates. "The kind who'd say yes to that."

"We wouldn't have to stay very long. Just long enough to distract my mom."

"There's no way I can go with you. That party will be lousy with firefighters."

"But all from Boston. Not from Lillian. My dad doesn't know these guys."

"He knows Captain Murphy."

"True," the rookie conceded. "But Captain Murphy already RSVP'd no."

I shook my head. "It would be all kinds of suicide—career, personal, emotional . . ."

"We wouldn't tell anybody who you are. You'd just be a mystery girl I brought with me."

"We'd get caught."

"I'd make sure that didn't happen."

"Rookie," I said, shaking my head, "don't ask me."

"You can say no if you want to," he said. "But I have to ask."

"Don't do it, man," I said.

He did it anyway.

He turned to me with that heartbreaking face of his and settled his eyes right on mine and leaned in just a little, with his voice something close to a whisper, like he was letting me in on some terrific secret opportunity, and he said, "Cassie, I'm begging you. Please. Will you come with me to my parents' anniversary party?"

The only possible answer was no.

But it was already too late.

Against every single ounce of all my better judgment, I met his eyes and said, "Yes."

Sixteen

SAYING YES CHANGED everything.

When you are all about saying no, one yes is a big deal. It paves the way for other yesses to follow. Yes to dessert. Yes to a late-afternoon nap. The next time Diana and Josie invited me to crochet club, in fact, I said yes.

"Do I have to crochet?" I asked, wrinkling my nose, all judgy.

"Yes," Josie said, just as Diana said, "No."

I'd been avoiding them the whole time. Declining all their invitations for coffee, and tea, and fish tacos. Scurrying up the stairs as soon as they got themselves settled with their yarn and started cajoling me to join them—but then listening from my room at the pleasant murmur of their voices down in the living room, and the rhythm of conversation punctuated with bursts of laughter.

I didn't mean to eavesdrop, but it was a very small house. Honestly, the conversations they had were probably more unguarded and forthcoming without me there than they would have been with me in the room. Without meaning to, I'd learned a lot about both of them.

Josie, for example, was married to a guy who traveled so much, Diana had decided he was a spy. I think his name was Marcus, but Diana only ever called him Double Oh Seven. Diana, for her part, had a little crush on a twenty-seven-year-old guy who worked in the meat department of the grocery store. They called him the Butcher. Josie was indeed pregnant, as I'd suspected, and as happy as that was, it was stressful, too, because it turned out she'd been trying to have a baby for over six years—and she'd had three miscarriages, all of them late, at least midway through. So now, even though she was past her first trimester—well into her second, and starting to show for real—each passing week made her more nervous.

They talked about that a lot: how not to be nervous about being nervous.

Through it all, they cracked a lot of jokes. The sounds of them laughing rose up the staircase like bubbles. They had a great time. Which made me resent them in a way, because it made my retreat to my room seem not just practical, but sad.

I'd been trying to keep myself safe. I'd been trying to take long runs, and eat healthy, and learn parkour, and apply for grants for my firehouse. I had a whole strategy for restabilizing my life.

Then I went and said yes to the rookie.

Which blew my whole strategy apart.

Now, not only had I said yes to going with the rookie to that party—so all rules were off—even worse, I was going to have to actually go.

I really, really needed someone to talk to.

The anniversary party was happening. Soon. And it was more than I could handle alone.

So one night I broke my boycott of crochet club, and I shuffled downstairs in my socks—which felt like both a great defeat and a delightful victory all at once. I felt shy approaching them, like I'd rejected them for so long that they might hold a grudge. But of course they didn't. They made me warm tea, and huddled around me to get the whole scoop, and I wound up telling them everything—and even, in the end, taking them to the Lillian FD website to show them the rookie's picture.

Which didn't really capture him.

So I joined crochet club. Sheer panic can really move things along. I went from full avoidance to full disclosure in a day. If Diana and Josie found the shift surprising, you'd never know. They jumped in whole hog, like we always sat around gabbing about boys.

"You didn't!" my mom and Josie said at the same time when I told them I'd said yes.

I sighed. "I did. And then we slept together."

"You *what*?" Diana shrieked.

"Actually slept," I clarified. "For warmth. Because it was cold up there."

"Like, he held you in his arms?" Josie asked.

I shook my head. "Like, we leaned against a super-uncomfortable brick wall, side by side, and dozed off sitting up."

"So romantic," Diana said.

I frowned. "Kind of the opposite. But I did wind up using his shoulder for a pillow." Technically, you could probably argue that we'd snuggled.

"And now you're going on a date," Josie said.

I put my hands over my eyes. "Let's not call it 'a date.' Let's call it 'a coworker assisting another coworker with a family issue.'"

"Sounds like a date to me," Josie said, and then they slapped a high five.

I pressed my head into a sofa pillow. "I think I just ruined my life," I said, all muffled.

"It can't be as terrible as all that," Diana said.

I sat up. "If the guys in the house find out about this, it will be the end of everything."

"I think it's very kind of you to help out your friend," Diana said. "He can't help it that he's so dreamy. That's not his fault."

I shook my head. "What was I thinking?"

"I just don't see what the big deal is," Josie said. "Who cares who you like?"

"It's breaking the rules. As a girl, you've got two choices. You're either a virgin or a whore. And guess what sleeping with guys you work with makes you?"

They refused to answer that on principle.

"Not a virgin," I finally said.

"Why does it have to be one or the other? Why can't you just be a normal, complex human being?"

"Irrelevant. Those are the rules."

"But you're *not* sleeping with him," Josie protested.

"But I want to!" I said. And then I slapped my hand over my mouth.

They stared at me. I stared at them.

Then I whispered, "Did I just say that out loud?"

"Who *wouldn't* want to sleep with him?" Diana demanded. "He's like human candy."

Josie nodded and we all took another gander at his photo on my phone. "Irresistible."

The way we were joking around about this was comforting in a way. We kept things light. We didn't talk about the real risk that I was taking to do this—or why, knowing everything I knew, I would have even considered saying yes in the first place.

Something to ponder.

Going to this party could very well cost me my job. And yet I'd agreed to go.

That "yes" had just burbled up out of me.

Why? I'd stayed up half the night on that roof, wrestling with that question. The rookie thanked me at least twenty times before he fell asleep, and promised that no one would ever find out. Ever.

But I knew better. The fire department wasn't a job, it was a small town. Everybody found out everything eventually.

It's possible, deep down, there was some self-sabotage involved—some unexamined belief that I didn't deserve to be happy. Or maybe I was looking for a reason to fail.

Or maybe I just really, really liked the rookie. Legitimately.

The more I overthought it, the more the answer seemed frustratingly simple. Why had I agreed to go? Because I wanted to.

I just wanted to.

I knew the risks. But part of me truly didn't care. Part of me really, really longed to be near him. At any cost. Apparently.

"I think it's wonderful," Diana said, refusing to let me beat myself up. "Sometimes we meet people we just click with. That's a good thing. That's a gift from the universe."

"Unless it gets you fired."

"It's not going to get you fired."

"I'm serious," I said. "I already have one strike against me in Austin. I can't be playing around."

As soon as Diana tilted her head and said, "You do?" I remembered I hadn't told her.

I took a breath. "I had an interpersonal conflict," I said.

She decided not to pursue it. This was the first time I'd come to crochet club, and I suspected she didn't want to scare me off. "Well," she said, staunchly taking my side, "this is the opposite of an interpersonal conflict."

"Not sure the fire department will see it that way," I said.

"We'll just have to make sure you don't get caught," Josie said.

"Easy," Diana said then. "Just wear your hair down and clothes that are not your usual style."

What was my usual style? Work pants. Work shirt. Work boots.

"What's the dress for the party?" Josie asked.

I shrugged. "Fancy? Ish?"

Diana looked me over. "Do you have anything fancy?"

I shook my head.

"Do you even own a dress?"

I shook my head again.

"I've got dresses," Josie said then, raising her eyebrows at me. "I've got a whole closet full—going to waste." She patted her belly.

Next thing I knew, the crochet was abandoned, and we were making our way next door and then upstairs to Josie's closet—both of us helping Diana with pavement cracks and stairs to move things along. Then I was standing in front of Josie's full-length mirror while the two ladies pulled out dress after dress, holding them up in front of me, then tossing them in rejection piles on the bed.

Too purple, they'd decide. Or: Too bright. Too dark. Too flashy. Too plain. Too stiff. Too floppy. Too many pleats. Too teenagery. Too old-lady. Too much cleavage. Not enough cleavage. And on and on.

"This is overwhelming," I said.

"Close your eyes," Josie said. "We'll do all the work."

"I'm just not really a clothes person, you know?"

"We know," they both said in unison, not pausing.

Then my mother added, "You can't go to this thing in your bunker gear."

At last, after what felt like hours, they narrowed the whole closet down to one singular, perfect, life-changing dress. Baby blue, midthigh, with spaghetti straps and a fluttery ruffle across the boobs.

"Really?" I said. It looked a little flimsy.

"Hush," Diana said, touching her lips, like, *Shhh*. "Go put it on."

I hesitated. I didn't trust their judgment. It didn't seem to have enough material. And what material there was seemed highly flammable. "It's not even a dress!" I protested, as they steered me toward the spare room. "It's a handkerchief!"

"Go!" Diana said.

"She's such a tomboy," Josie said, after I shut the door.

Was I? I just thought of myself as me. I certainly wasn't girly. My dad had hardly sat around on weekends braiding my hair. This stuff was all pretty foreign to me. Not bad, exactly, just unfamiliar.

I slipped the dress on over my head, but the spaghetti straps did not even begin to cover my racerback sports bra. "Do I take off my sports bra?" I called through the door.

"Yes!" they both called back.

I started over. This time when the dress settled over me, it looked more right.

But also like someone else was wearing it.

"So what kind of a bra do I wear with this thing?" I called through the door.

"No bra!" Josie called back.

"None at all?" That seemed a little extreme.

"You could do a strapless," Josie said, "but you don't need it, and the ruffle over your boobs gives them enough, you know, coverage."

The ruffle did provide coverage. On sight, no one would know there wasn't a strapless bra under there.

Except me.

It was the strangest, most untethered feeling.

It's important to note that this was not a makeover moment like some teen movie where the homely girl becomes a swan. I wasn't homely before this moment, and I wouldn't be homely later, when I clamped myself back into my oxen-harness sports bra and Dickies utility pants. This wasn't a better version of me I was seeing in the mirror—just a different one.

It was like I was meeting an unknown part of myself for the first time.

The flouncy part.

The soft, fluffy, vulnerable, exposed, half-naked, *braless* part.

If you go look up the definition of "vulnerable," in fact, it's a picture of me in that blue hanky dress.

I felt like a mollusk without its shell.

I'm not going to say that "vulnerable" is a bad thing. Still, for a person who's spent her whole adult life trying to be the opposite, it's certainly a change.

It made me keenly aware of every sensation around me—the nubby rug under my bare feet, the silky fabric grazing my thighs, the air moving in and out of my lungs. Not to mention my boobs—unharnessed, with barely a millimeter's worth of fabric between them and the wider world.

"I don't hear any movement in there," Josie called after a minute.

"I'm just getting my bearings," the stranger in the mirror said.

"Come show us!" Diana called, and so I did.

They both gasped at the reveal when I opened the door.

"I feel like I'm headed to the prom," I said.

"What did you wear to your prom?" Josie asked.

"Nothing. I didn't go. Ted had baseball tickets."

They made me twirl around.

"I feel very naked," I said.

"Naked can be fun," my mother said.

Could it? I wasn't sure. Being so bare was both exciting and deeply uncomfortable. I couldn't tell if I liked it. "It's just," I said, "I usually go for, like, the opposite of naked."

Josie nodded. "Good to try new things, though."

Josie pawed through her dresser and found a little cropped cardigan I could put over my shoulders if I got cold, and a matching clutch, and then they started going through the shoe stash. Josie was an eight-and-a-half and I was a nine, but she had a few sandals I could squeeze into. Platform wedges, mostly.

"I feel like a stilt-walker," I said, once we'd strapped on a pair that worked.

"You'll get the hang of it," my mother said.

"*Be* the shoes," Josie encouraged.

I stared at myself in the mirror. I looked like a whole different person. A person brave enough to go braless. A person open to possibilities. A person in all kinds of trouble.

I looked at all our faces reflected in Josie's mirror—theirs with delight, and mine with concern.

"I guess it'll work," I said, chewing my lip.

If nothing else, it was a hell of a disguise.

SATURDAY CAME QUICKLY. Too quickly. And not quickly enough.

Diana made me sit at her dressing table while she gave me a makeover. "Just a little," she kept saying, but I think she used every vial, spray bottle, brush, and tube in every drawer. She plucked my eyebrows. She curled my eyelashes. She dusted me with powders and teased my hair. She frowned and fussed while I sat with my eyes closed, under strict orders not to peek.

When she gave me permission at last to open my eyes, I saw the same me, but different. The eye shadow and lipstick were the biggest shockers.

My eyes looked twice their normal size, and my lips were dark red and extra plump.

"It's like the cartoon version of me," I said.

She gave me a look. "Thanks," she said.

The biggest change was my hair, which they'd insisted I leave down and loose—instead of my usual low bun. A bottle of hair spray and thirty minutes of blow-drying and teasing later, it wasn't just hair. It was a mane. I didn't even look like myself to myself.

The three of us stared at me in the mirror.

"It is a very different version of you," Diana concluded.

"Which is better?" I asked.

Diana gave me a quick squeeze. "I'm very fond of the everyday you," she said, somehow knowing the exact words I was hoping for, "but this is fun, too."

I waited to put on the dress until the last minute so I wouldn't wrinkle it. Same with the shoes—to lessen my chances of breaking an ankle.

When the rookie was a few minutes late arriving, I felt like I couldn't take it.

I pulled out my phone.

"I'm going to cancel," I said, shaking my head at my mom and Josie, who were keeping watch at the front window. "I can't do this."

My hands were cold. Everything felt cold. And hot. Both. At the same time. What was I thinking? We were going to get caught, and I was going to get ridiculed, scoffed at, and then fired, in that order, and my life as I'd known it was going to be over.

"You can run into a burning building, but you can't spend one evening with a nice guy?"

"That's different," I said.

"I agree," Diana said.

Josie added, "This is more fun."

"That all depends on how you define 'fun,'" I said.

It wasn't a date, but it felt like a date. It was too many opposites. I wanted to go just as badly as I wished I'd never offered. I wanted the rookie to hurry up and get here just as badly as I wanted him to never show up at all. I wanted to wear a little flouncy dress for once in my life, but at the exact same time, I wanted to put on my sports bra and a sweat suit—with hood.

My fingers felt like they'd been refrigerated.

At last, a knock at the door—and I felt a visceral jolt of fear in my body. This felt like the scariest thing I'd ever done. How crazy was that? I'd extricated bodies from car accidents, and had guns pointed at me, and literally watched people take their final breaths—but *this* was the scariest thing I'd ever done.

I grabbed Diana's arm. "Maybe I should wear my dress uniform."

"Your *uniform*?"

I nodded. A blazer and some shoulder pads suddenly seemed very appealing.

My heart was glugging like a motor. Without deciding to, I half-hid behind one of the French doors.

But Josie was opening the door, and then Diana was joining in, all normal, as if people opened doors for visitors all the time.

Diana smiled and said, "Hello, rookie. You're late."

"I was early," he said, his voice all apology, "but then I saw a kid wipe out on his bicycle, and I stopped to help."

Of course he did.

Josie and Diana looked at each other, like, *Adorable*.

He'd gotten a haircut since that morning—shorter in back, but still longer in front. He wore a perfectly tailored dark gray suit and a baby blue tie.

He looked unfairly handsome.

And so it was happening. Whatever choices I'd made were playing themselves out. There was nothing left to do but step out and meet him.

Just as I did, he looked up and saw me.

Here was something I noticed: He dropped his smile for a second right then. It was like he forgot everything—what he was saying, what he was doing. He held very still.

Did I look that different? I wondered. Was I that shocking?

In my whole life, nobody had ever looked at me that way.

I guess I could have come up with some self-deprecating explanation for the shock of his expression: food in my teeth, a booger, a sudden nosebleed . . . But I didn't.

I knew that stare. I knew it because I recognized it.

It was exactly the way I was staring at him.

Here's something else I noticed: All my naked agony of anticipation? At the sight of him, it melted away. All my nervousness—gone. His presence in the room made everything okay.

Maybe I was doomed to regret everything later. But I couldn't regret anything right now.

I took a step closer.

So did he—forgetting my mom and Josie altogether. "You clean up good."

"Back atcha," I said.

"Thanks for saving me tonight," he said.

"Just don't tell anybody."

His smile faded again then, and he made a dead-serious *X* over his heart as he said, "Hope to die."

He took a few steps closer, like we were the only people in the room. Then he took my hand to lead me to the door.

"I have to tell you something, rookie," I said.

"What?"

"I cannot walk in these shoes."

"That's fine," he said, holding out his arm. "I'll help you."

"And I feel totally naked in this dress."

He stepped back like he was checking. "You're definitely not naked. That, I would notice."

"And I know this is not a date, but it kind of feels like a date, and I need you to know I've never been on a date before."

He tilted his head. "Never?"

"Never."

"This is your first date?"

"It's not a date."

"But if it were—it would be?"

I nodded. "If it were, it would be."

I think we said good-bye to my mom and Josie, but I don't really remember.

All I remember is the feel of his arm around my waist, and how thin that silky fabric was, and how I was aware of everything: the wind blowing my hair, the late-afternoon sun on my collarbones, the feel of each unsteady step. Every inch of my skin felt awake, every breath I took seemed to swirl in my chest, and every time I dared to glance over at the rookie, my whole body tingled.

Not good—and too good, all at the same time.

He led me to his truck and opened the door for me.

Was I perfectly capable of opening my own door? Yes.

But I liked it.

As I tried to settle into my seat, I didn't know what to do with my legs. Finally, I crossed them, watching one hook over the other with a strange, out-of-body feeling like they didn't even belong to me.

The rookie, settling in on his side, watched them, too. Instead of starting the car.

"I didn't know you had legs," he said then, nodding at them.

"Yep," I said. "Always."

"You kind of keep them hidden."

"Not hidden," I said. "Just, you know—in my pants. Exactly where you keep yours, by the way."

"But you have women's legs," he explained.

"Yes."

"And I don't."

"True."

"I'm just saying, nobody wants to see my legs."

"I'm sure *somebody* wants to see them. Case, maybe."

The rookie grinned and made crinkles at the sides of his eyes. He started the ignition. Then he shook his head. "Hanwell has legs," he said, marveling at the idea.

I smacked him on the shoulder.

Then we were off. We followed the coastline south, and I just let the view and the wind flow past me for a while.

"I won't be drinking tonight, by the way," I said, "so I can be your designated driver."

"Want to keep your wits about you, huh?"

"Something like that."

"Well, it's fine if you change your mind. I never get drunk. I can drink all day and never feel it."

I gave him a look, like, *Please.* "I could drink you under the table, pal."

"I'd like to see you try."

I leaned back against the headrest and let the wind flutter my hair. "Have you decided what you're going to tell your parents about me?"

He nodded. "I thought of a perfect sentence, actually."

"Hit me."

"When they say, 'Where's Amy?' I'll say: 'She couldn't make it, but I brought a friend.'"

"That's actually genius. It's not even lying. Distract and redirect."

"And then your job is to whisk me out onto the dance floor to avoid all further questions."

"I'm not sure I can whisk anybody anywhere in these shoes," I said, "but I'll try."

Seventeen

THE THING ABOUT the rookie at the firehouse was: He was quiet. He smiled a lot, and he was helpful, and he'd do everything anybody asked of him and more—but he wasn't what you'd call a big talker.

But take him to a family reunion with twinkle lights and a disco ball in a room full of Irish cousins and a DJ playing Top 40 hits from every decade?

He never shut up.

From the minute we walked in, folks were grabbing him, hugging him, smacking him, ruffling his hair—and he was doing it all back to everybody else. Pointing at his cousin Mikey, high-fiving his cousin Patrick, telling his aunt Aileen she looked like a million bucks.

He was the life of the party.

I was the quiet one. Standing there all braless in my flammable hankie dress and double-decker shoes and just trying not to fall over.

His sisters were all over him, giving him hugs and cheek squeezes and smacks. He confessed to one of them what we were up to, and in seconds they all knew—like ants in a colony. The oldest showed up with a baby on her hip to get a gander at me.

"This is the decoy girlfriend, huh?" she asked, smiling.

"We're not pretending she's my girlfriend," the rookie corrected. "We're just using her as a distraction."

The sister—Shannon—looked me up and down. "She *is* distracting."

Where was my bunker gear?

Then she pointed at me. "Don't break his heart."

"Shut up," he said to her.

I marveled. Was I passing for a heartbreaker?

"I'm kidding," the sister said. Then back to me, "But seriously. Don't."

It took us half an hour to make it across the room to greet his parents, and by then he'd downed two beers and about twenty mini-quiches, and I'd finished off two virgin daiquiris like a champ.

His parents were adorable. His dad wore his Boston FD dress uniform, complete with cap and epaulets, and his mother wore a pink pantsuit with a corsage on the lapel. The rookie leaned in and kissed them both.

"Happy anniversary," he said. "Colleen and Big Robby, meet—"

His mom interrupted and said, "Where's Amy?"

We'd been expecting it, but maybe not quite so fast.

"Amy couldn't make it—" the rookie started.

Big Robby leaned in and wiggled his eyebrows. "Because our boy's got a new girlfriend."

The rookie and I froze. This was not the plan.

Colleen froze, too. This was not the girlfriend she'd been rooting for.

Big Robby shrugged. "I overheard your sisters talking."

Colleen looked me over. "What happened to Amy?"

The rookie stood up a little straighter. "We're taking a break."

His mother waited for more.

"In truth," the rookie went on, in a spark of impromptu brilliance, "Amy's job took her out to California, and it just didn't make sense for me to move out there with her."

Whatever dismay Colleen felt at the loss of Amy was suddenly tempered by the fact that her son had not foolishly followed her to California. She smiled at me. I might not be Amy, but at least I was local. "And you are?"

"I'm C—" I started, but the rookie suddenly yanked me to his side.

"Christabel!" he shouted. Then, in a normal voice. "This is my friend Christabel."

Colleen looked pleased. "That's one of my favorite names," she said. "If we'd had one more girl, I would have named her Christabel."

"Oh," I said, still a little flummoxed.

"How did the two of you meet?" the rookie's dad wanted to know.

Before I could invent an answer, the rookie yanked me off toward the dance floor. I stumbled off behind him, and when he finally stopped and turned around, I went flying right into his chest with an *ooof*. The DJ was playing Kool & the Gang.

"What are you doing?" I demanded, smacking him on the shoulder.

"You were supposed to whisk me off to the dance floor."

"Well, we had a change of plans."

"No shit. And now they think you're my girlfriend."

"It was super-rude to just walk away from your mother when she was complimenting my name."

"It's not your name," he said. "It's my name. My almost-name. If I'd been a girl."

We stared at each other. The song ended. A new one started. Suddenly, the lights dimmed, and we heard the DJ—yet another cousin—on the speakers. "Welcome to the greatest slow dance of all time. The Bee Gees' timeless classic 'How Deep Is Your Love?'"

"They're watching us," the rookie said then, looking over my shoulder. "Put your arms around my neck."

"I guess we're slow-dancing," I said.

"I guess we are," the rookie said, like it was a dare.

I never backed down from a dare.

I reached up around his shoulders and settled against him. Once again, I was aware of how naked I was under my dress. I couldn't meet his eyes. I stared at the knot of his tie.

I felt dazed. All I could focus on, really, was how strange I felt. I'd slow-danced before, but this was entirely different at the cellular level. I was achingly aware of every part of my body that was touching his—the weight of my arms on his shoulders, the warmth of his palms on my hips, the nearness of his freshly shaved neck, the scent of his deodorant.

The way nothing separated us but fabric.

"If we're going to pretend to date, Christabel, you should probably stop calling me 'rookie.'"

I tried to focus. "What else would I call you?"

"How about my name?"

Finally, I met his eyes. "What *is* your name?"

He pulled back to give me a frown. "You know my name," he said.

"Callaghan," I said.

"My first name."

I studied his face for a minute. Then I shook my head. "Nope. Nothing."

He flared his nostrils. "Try."

This was good. This was helping me focus. Now my brain had a task—and that task was teasing him. "Felix," I said, mentally trying it out on him.

"Seriously?"

"Frank!" I tried. "Melvin."

"Melvin?"

He actually looked a little perturbed. This was fun. "Reginald," I offered. "Maximilian. Jebediah."

He set his jaw with a kind of grudging respect for my obnoxiousness. "Jebediah Callaghan."

I was delighted by his irritation. "It has a ring to it."

He let out a good sigh. "It's Owen. My first name is Owen."

"You want me to call you Owen?" I asked, like it was the craziest idea ever.

"Yeah, actually," he said. "I kind of do."

I gave him a serious nod. "Okay, Oscar," I said. "I respect that."

He didn't let himself correct me.

Triumphantly, I rested my head on Owen's shoulder—and that's when I saw his whole family watching us.

"All that worry for nothing," I said then. "Your mom is fine."

"She's always fine on the surface," Owen said. "I'll get an earful later, though."

In truth, I was glad to have him to hold on to. I felt a little woozy.

"Hey," I said then. "Is there any chance those virgin daiquiris I just shotgunned weren't totally virgin?"

Owen stretched up to take a look at the bar. "That's my cousin Alex bartending at a party full of Irish, so, yeah, actually, there's a pretty good chance."

But the wooziness wasn't alcohol. I knew that.

It was Owen. I was drunk on Owen. His name, his tie, the ironed, slim-fit dress shirt clinging to his pecs. His kindness. His hands on my hips.

The song was ending.

"Are you okay?" he asked. "Do you want to get some air?"

I nodded, and he led me off the floor.

Word about us had spread like a gas fire. As we made our way back across the room, Owen got high fives and cheek slaps from his cousins, and comment after comment, like, "Nice work, buddy," and "Better lock that up," plus plenty of teasing, like, "Your fly's unzipped."

We had the exit in our sights when I caught the edge of my platform shoe and my leg went out from under me. I twisted and fell, but Owen caught me right before my knee hit. I started to say, "Thanks," and scramble back up, but his arms locked, and he held me right there in place, my eyes even with his belt buckle.

I got my feet under me, and I was just about to push up and say, "What the hell, man?" when I heard Owen say, "Hello, Captain Murphy."

Then I heard Murphy's voice, like a nod. "Rookie."

I froze.

Then, after a second—and presumably after taking in the sight of my head at Owen's crotch, the captain went on. "Looks like you're having a fine evening."

"Yes, sir."

"See you next shift."

"Yes, sir."

A beat, and then I felt myself hoisted up, clutched against Owen's chest, and hustled straight into a coat closet.

The door clonked closed behind us.

"What the hell?" I said, as Owen released me, blinking my eyes in the blackness.

He sounded amazed that I would ask. "That was the captain."

I knew that already. "I thought he RSVP'd no."

"He *did* RSVP no."

"But now we're stuck in a closet."

"*You're* stuck," Owen pointed out.

It was so dark, we were nothing but voices. Owen was tapping around the doorframe for a switch. "We could be in here for hours," I said.

His voice was a little teasing. "You say that like it's a bad thing."

I was mad, and the teasing made me madder. "I'm serious."

"We'll figure this out."

"How?" I demanded. "You said we wouldn't get caught!"

"We won't!"

"Hello!" I said. "The captain just saw us!"

"But there's no way he recognized you."

"Why?"

"Trust me," Owen said. "You look nothing—*at all*—like you do at the station."

Was that an insult or a compliment? I frowned. "I'm recognizable, though. I'm not in a clown suit."

"Whatever he saw out there, it wasn't Hanwell the firefighter."

"What did he see?"

"He saw me holding a sexy drunk girl who was all legs and hair."

"I'm not drunk!" I blinked. "Or sexy!" Did he just call me sexy?

"That's my point. That girl out there was the opposite of you."

Guess not. "Thanks."

Owen had already shifted into problem-solving mode. "There are a million ways to get you out of here. We just have to take a second to think it through."

I didn't want to have to solve this problem. "What was I thinking coming here?" I demanded into the darkness. "This was the dumbest thing I've ever done."

"You were helping me out," Owen said.

But I was just getting started. "I knew this place would be lousy with firefighters. Even if the captain wasn't coming, there was no way we weren't going to get caught somehow, by somebody. I knew that, but I came anyway. My captain in Austin specifically told me not to do this. Of all the ten thousand things I was *not* supposed to do, this—right here—was number one! But here I am, like a chump. Sabotaging everything I've ever worked for. I've never even been kissed, and now I'm going to get fired for sleeping with a rookie!"

The rookie held very still. "Wait. You've never been kissed?"

I gave an angry sigh. Tried to think of a way to backtrack. Then gave up. "Not properly."

"How is that possible?"

"I've been busy, okay? I've been working."

"Yeah, but—no one's that busy."

Silence.

"What?" I said.

"Nothing."

"What?" I demanded, stepping closer. My eyes had adjusted now. I could see him.

"It's just," he said, shaking his head like he was trying to shake the idea out, "hearing that makes me want to kiss you."

"Don't kiss me," I said, pushing him by the chest back up against the closet wall. Our faces were just inches apart. I stood my ground.

Was I trying to put out a fire? Or trying to make it worse?

I should step back, I thought. But I didn't.

"I will get you out of here," the rookie said then. "I promise."

And that's when I kissed him.

He was startled but not too startled. In a flash, his arms were around me and he was kissing me right back—and not just with his mouth, with his whole body: arms, legs, shoulders, hands. He leaned into that kiss so hard that we stumbled backwards and bumped against the back wall of the closet. Then he was pressing against me, running his hands all over that silk hankie dress, and up my shoulders, and behind my neck, and into my hair—and I was doing all the equivalent things right back.

It was like a wave crashing.

And I got swept right in.

Is it too dramatic to say time stopped?

Because time stopped.

Maybe kisses are special for everybody, I don't know.

But this was my first one.

My first good one, anyway.

When the rookie's mouth touched mine, somehow everything in me that had been aching—for years, it seemed, now that I noticed—got soothed.

I felt some new kind of joy that I'd never felt before.

Was this what love was?

I had no idea.

I did know that this kiss, this moment right here, was something special. I'd seen and done and felt a lot of amazing things in my twenty-six years. But nothing like this.

The rookie slowed down but pressed closer. I tightened my arms around his neck. I touched my fingers to the velvety hair at the back of his head. I slowed down, too. Savoring. Relaxing into the moment.

He was kissing me. And I was kissing him back.

Impossible. But true.

Somehow we slid against the closet door, and he pressed up against me and brought his leg between mine, wedging us together in a way that made every cell in my body hum. I started melting like a stick of butter in a hot pan. I just dissolved into him and gave in to all of it—all this amazing, heart-thumping, breathless goodness.

This was what I'd been missing. All this time. Huh.

The thing that would astonish me later, looking back, was that nothing was bad. Not one part of this unbelievable moment in the story of my life felt scary or creepy or painful. And for a minute there, as I gave in to every good thing about it, it felt like nothing could ever possibly be bad again.

Until there was a loud knock on the closet door.

The same door we were pressed up against.

The knock reverberated through my rib cage.

We startled out of the moment and looked around.

"Are you guys in the coat closet?" came an annoyed voice.

The rookie gave a sharp sigh. "Go away, Shannon," he called.

"Everybody thinks you're having sex in there."

"Nobody is having any sex. Scram."

"There's a betting pool, actually," she went on. "I put fifty bucks on you."

"I mean it, Shannon," Owen said again, louder this time.

"Fine," she said, "but don't let us all down." Then she leaned very close and fake-whispered, "Alex has a big box of condoms, if you need them."

The rookie and I were both out of breath. When she was gone, he said, "She's a world-class pain in the ass."

I felt like a person waking from a deep sleep. I blinked and looked around. Reality came back into focus. The moment was definitely lost. I was in a coat closet. With the rookie. Not good.

I pushed against Owen's chest ever so slightly, and he got the hint and stepped back.

He straightened his clothes, and I straightened mine.

"That was surprising," I said.

"I agree," the rookie said.

"Probably a very bad idea."

"Not on my end. Just saying."

"I'll likely get fired now."

"That's not going to happen."

"Yeah, well," I said. I knew how life worked. I knew how things were. This wouldn't end well for me.

Then the rookie did something that surprised me. He grabbed my hand and squeezed it, leaning in to meet my eyes in the shadows. "I will never tell anybody about this. Please know that you can trust me, okay?"

I nodded.

"Okay," he said then. "Let's get you out of here."

"How?" I said.

He shrugged, like it was easy. "I'll carry you out of here over my shoulder, and that mane of hair will hang down over your face, and even if the captain sees us, he'll never know it's you."

Eighteen

THAT NIGHT, WINDOWS open, I lay in bed watching the pom-pom curtains flutter in the breeze, with my heart gusting around inside my body like a kite.

The rookie. I'd kissed the rookie. Very well. In a coat closet.

I might have expected some mixed feelings on kissing, given how long and how hard I'd avoided it.

But I had none.

I felt thrilled. I felt *enchanted*.

Nobody could have been more surprised than me.

So this was what it was like. This was how I could feel.

I'd thought for so long that I'd lost all capacity to feel all these good things.

Do I have to describe what Heath Thompson did to me on the night I turned sixteen? Do I have to lay out all those details?

Let's just agree that it was bad—very bad. So bad that "bad" isn't even a bad enough word. So bad that it left a black vortex at the center of my heart that I'd spent every day since trying not to look at, or think about, or get too close to for fear I'd fall in and disappear. So bad that I closed off my heart entirely—I never went on another date, or kissed anyone, or even had a romantic thought for ten solid years.

Until now.

Until the rookie.

Who had given me something undeniably *good.*

I would have told you I was fine before. I *was* fine. I was functioning, I was strong. I paid taxes and changed the oil in my car and bought organic eggs at the farmers' market. I was a self-defense instructor, for Pete's sake. Some people get derailed by trauma. Some people are crushed by it and never recover. I get it. I understand. But I was lucky. It took so many years I could barely tell it was happening, but I was able to put my life back together. I was able to finish high school, go to college, and make a living helping people.

I'd wanted to die for so many years.

But I didn't die. I survived.

More than that, I thrived.

Before the awards ceremony, I would have told you I was completely recovered.

Until Heath Thompson showed up on that stage and *dared to touch me*—and then we both found out exactly how strong I'd become.

Maybe too strong for my own good.

It had felt like self-sabotage in the aftermath. I had been so worried, as I drove across the country alone, that I was at the beginning of the end. And maybe it was the end of something. But it was a beginning, too. One with the potential to make things better—or possibly so much worse.

But so far so good. I had kissed Owen—in a no-holds-barred, full-body kind of way, and it had been good.

All violence is bad, of course, but what Heath Thompson had done to me was an attack on love itself. It took one of the best parts of being human and ruined it.

I'd gladly given up all hope of love for a guarantee of never having to relive even a part of that memory again.

Here was the astonishing thing: Nothing about what had just happened with the rookie reminded me of that night. It didn't cause flashbacks, or spark terror, or—worst-case scenario—make me want to die. Quite the opposite, in fact.

It wasn't terror, it was joy. It wasn't agony, it was pleasure. There were mouths involved, yes, and hands and arms and bodies touching—but the context was so different, there with a person I'd come to like and admire and absolutely trust, there was just no comparison.

The kiss itself was a big surprise.

But the discovery that kissing wasn't agony? Even bigger.

It felt almost nostalgic, like remembering what it felt like to believe that the world was full of good things and good people and good luck. It tasted bittersweet, because it insisted there was so much to look forward to—even when I already knew there was far more to dread.

Somehow, what the rookie made me feel was the kind of hopefulness you could only get when you didn't know any better.

Even though I did know better.

And worse.

I wondered if that was it: Maybe I only liked him so much because I couldn't have him. I could not have chosen a more forbidden, off-limits, never-gonna-happen guy to obsess over than Owen. We couldn't be together.

In a way, he was a safe choice.

In another way, it was more dangerous than anything I'd ever done. Because now I knew what I'd been missing. Now I just wanted more.

And now I was crying in my bed. So much my hair was wet on the pillow below. I'm not exaggerating at all when I say that I was a person who never cried—but there they were: tears.

I'm not even sure I could've told you what they were *for.* There were so many different emotions making up their alchemy, I had no idea how to separate them out. There was sadness in the mix, for sure. And anger. As well as relief and joy and longing and anxiety. Tears of *everything,* I guess. They were tears of intensity. Tears of coming back to life.

Nineteen

THE NEXT MORNING, the captain called me into his office and yelled at me. But not for what you think.

When I entered his office, he was at his desk.

"What the hell were you thinking, Hanwell?" he demanded, without looking up.

I froze.

Oh God. This was it.

When I didn't answer, he looked up—then stood up. "Well?"

I shook my head, like I didn't understand.

"There's no way this was an accident!" he said then. "Because there is no way you don't know the rules."

I held still.

"And if you know the rules," he went on, "and you broke them anyway, that's insubordination." He took a step closer. "And you know how I feel about insubordination."

I blinked.

"Are we clear?"

We weren't. Not at all.

Ever so slightly, I shook my head.

"You don't know what I'm talking about?" he said.

I shook again.

He reached out and picked a package up off his desk. "I'm talking about this." He held it out, like incriminating evidence.

I frowned.

Then I realized what it was.

It was a cyanide-poisoning antidote kit.

That's what he was mad about? The relief hit so hard, I felt dizzy for a second. But it passed.

"Do you care to explain this?"

I took a breath. "Looks like we got a cyanide kit," I said. I checked his desk for another package. "There should be two."

"So you admit you're responsible."

My name was right there on the mailing label. "Yes?"

"Hanwell," the captain said then, tossing the package back on his desk and crossing his arms. "As you keep reminding me, you are not a newbie. You know how things work in a fire station. So what I can't figure out is how you could possibly have imagined you were allowed to order fire equipment without my permission."

"I didn't order it," I said. "I applied for a grant."

"And who told you to do that?"

"You did, sir."

He gave me a look that said he could not be bullshitted.

"Remember?" I said. "Way back, on my first day. I asked if we had cyanide kits at the station, and you said no, and I said we needed them, and you said, 'Find me two thousand dollars a pop and we'll get some'?"

He squinted at me. "Vaguely."

"Well," I said. "I found you two thousand dollars a pop."

"I don't understand."

"I applied for a grant from FEMA. For the station. For money to buy two kits. And we got it."

"You applied for a grant?"

"I applied for a bunch of them, actually," I said, feeling the tiniest bit of pride in my initiative. "From different places. Funding for new paint, new mattresses, better lighting. Also, for a new gear dryer and new lockers. A better vent for the engine bay. A bunch of stuff."

I'd assumed, honestly, that if any of the grants came through, that would unequivocally be a good thing. How could it not be?

But as I watched the captain's face, it was clear: not good.

The captain stood up. "Is writing grants part of your job description?"

"No, sir. I just—"

"We have a chain of command here, Hanwell. You do not apply for grants, or decide we need new mattresses, or even get us new toilet paper unless I tell you to."

"Yes, sir, but you yourself said—"

"This firehouse," he went on, "has been standing here, on this very spot, for one hundred and twenty years"—

Oh God. I'd offended him.

—"and we've survived all of them, every damn one, without your help."

"I just thought—"

"You thought you'd come in here with your compost heaps and your solar panels and show us all how it's done."

"No, I—"

"Don't you see how that's a little insulting?"

"I just—"

"Has it occurred to you that you might not know everything about everything?"

He waited for an answer on that one.

I lowered my eyes. "I was just trying to make myself useful, sir."

"Maybe the newest person on a crew shouldn't start changing everything right away. Maybe the newest person on a crew should spend a little time at the station before deciding to repaint it."

There are no words to describe how much I had not expected this reaction from him.

"I'm sorry, sir."

"You bet you are."

"Should I—" I began, amazed that I was even asking the question. "Should I send the kits back?"

"It's not about the kits, Hanwell," the captain said. "It's about respect for the chain of command."

"I respect the chain of command, sir," I said.

"Do you? Because what do you do when a ranking member of the crew tells you to do something?"

He blinked at me, waiting for an answer.

"You do it, sir," I said.

"And what if a ranking member of the crew *doesn't* tell you to do something?"

I sighed. "You don't do it, sir."

"We're clear on that?"

"We're clear."

He turned back to his computer. We were done here. "Good," he said then. "Now scram."

I walked to my locker feeling stunned—but also very lucky that I hadn't been in trouble for what I thought I'd been in trouble for. Maybe the rookie was right. Maybe our going on a date would not lead inevitably to the end of my career.

Maybe we were going to get away with it.

Or maybe not: because when I opened up my locker, I discovered that somebody had scrawled graffiti all across the inside. Very specific graffiti that made it clear somebody somewhere knew something.

In terrible handwriting, in five-inch-tall letters, in Sharpie—there was one word: *Slut*.

I SLAMMED THE door shut the second I saw it.

I felt a sting of panic through my body. Not cool. Not fair. Not even, you know—accurate. Not even close.

Six-Pack looked over. "Everything okay?"

"Yep," I said. But I was breathing fast.

The timing was uncanny.

Six-Pack was still eyeing me.

"The lock sticks sometimes," I said, leaning hard against the door, breathing.

Had the captain recognized me? Was that why he was so weirdly mad that I had just earned the station four thousand dollars' worth of safety equipment? Or had there been someone else there we didn't see? Or maybe word of mouth? Of course, by the end of the party, every single person there knew that Owen had screwed a very drunk girl in the coat closet.

All anybody had to do was recognize me.

I'd been warned, of course. Captain Harris had warned me—as had a lifetime of being female. If we broke the rules, I would be the one punished. I had known the risk I was taking when I went to that party with him, though I had not truly been able to imagine what the consequence would feel like. But I'd persisted. Like a fool.

Now, pressed up against my locker, frozen against it, really, my heart racing, my adrenaline on high alert, I was starting to get it.

This was not good.

Six-Pack frowned at me.

The thing was, though, this actually was not the first time in my life that I had opened a locker and seen the word "slut" inside. The last time, it had been high school, and it had been scratched into the orange paint on the inside of the metal door. This time, it was dark black Sharpie ink. It seemed like such an impossible coincidence. What were the chances of getting harassed like that—even once, much less twice?

Although, maybe the playbook for harassment just isn't all that varied. Maybe the type of people who do this kind of thing don't dig deep into creativity.

Seeing that word, scrawled there so angrily, left an afterimage in my eyes that I couldn't blink away. It shocked the hell out of me, honestly—both in the real moment of my current life, and in a way that felt like a reverberation from high school.

Somehow, it made me angry at Owen. If he hadn't been so irresistible, and so likable, and if he hadn't frigging *asked,* I would never have gone with him to that party in the first place. Today could have been just another plain old regular firefighting day.

It also made me angry at myself. What had I been thinking? How cocky was I—how flat-out stupid—to think that I could just do what I wanted? I knew what world I was living in. I had willfully, stupidly broken the rules, and now I'd have to suffer the consequences.

And last, though not at all least, it made me angry at whoever had done it. Someone had gone to some trouble to figure out my combination and find a time when the locker room was empty. Someone had done something to hurt me. Intentionally. With malice.

That was a horrifying feeling. Somebody out there had come after me.

And I didn't even know who it was.

I spent that entire day rigid with rage at every living human being on earth, including myself. I glared at patients. I evaluated every guy on our crew suspiciously. My thinking and my emotions were totally jumbled all day, but one thing was clear: I needed to stay as far away from the rookie as possible.

So . . .

If he came into a room, I went out.

If he asked me a question, I turned away.

It was a way for me to reclaim a sense of strength. I could survive this. I was tougher than this. One piece of graffiti wasn't going to shut me down.

Then, once the guys had gone to bed, and I could hear the reliable rhythm of their snores, I snuck back down to my locker.

I couldn't sleep anyway.

I opened it up and peered in. Part of me hoped that maybe if I just checked again, it might be gone.

Nope.

There it was. *Slut.*

The handwriting was rounded and pointy at the same time. The *T* almost looked like an *X*. It looked more like *Slux*, really. Terrible penmanship. *Come on.* If you're going to do it, do it right.

Though it was a clue. Maybe there'd be some way to get a peek at some of our paperwork from the captain's office—or maybe four graffiti letters wouldn't be enough to settle it.

I drew in a long, scratchy breath, then let it back out. I just let my head lean forward until it was resting in my hands. I closed my eyes. I felt so tired.

That's when I heard a sound in the doorway.

I snapped to attention and slammed the door closed in one motion.

It was Owen. Sleepy looking, hair a little mussed, in his undershirt and, I guessed, recently slid-into work pants.

"You okay?" he asked.

"Fine," I said, leaning back against my locker now, to block it even more.

"What's going on?"

"Nothing."

We hadn't spoken since he'd dropped me off after the party, a hundred years ago, when my whole body was still molten with delight over all the fun we'd had in that coat closet. The last time we'd spoken, every molecule in the air between us had shimmered with possibility.

But everything was different now.

And that made me angriest of all.

"Were you—" He searched for the word. "Praying? Or something?"

I want to state for the record that I knew intellectually that the rookie was not attacking me in any way.

Still, I felt a little bit attacked. Couldn't I just get a couple of minutes to process this by myself? The feeling was compounded, I'm sure, by the fact that the graffiti *was* actually an attack—though not, of course, coming from Owen. Although, who knew? Could have been anybody. Maybe this was his evil plan all along: Gain my trust by seeming all nice and sweet and mouthwatering, kiss me into oblivion, and then sabotage me behind my back.

Ridiculous.

Then again, this whole situation was ridiculous.

"I was *thinking*," I said, sounding more annoyed than I expected to. "You've heard of that?"

"Sure," he said, frowning at me. "Huge fan of thinking."

"What are you even doing awake?"

"Wakeful," he said, shrugging, like, *The usual.* "I might go bake some chocolate chip cookies."

I stared at him.

"Want some?" he asked. "If I do?"

Even the idea of him baking something as comforting and delightful as cookies felt annoying. "Nope," I said.

"Really?" he said, like I was acting odd.

Later, I'd try to figure out why I felt so mad at him in this moment. I didn't really think this whole situation was his fault. I knew he was just trying to be a friend. But that was it, right there. That was the problem. Did I want a cookie? Of course! Did I want to be able to tell him what was going on and hash it all out with a pal? Of course. But the rookie, despite being the one person I wanted to talk to, was the last person I could talk to.

Off-the-charts frustrating.

What can I say? It came out as anger.

"You've been acting weird all day," he said then.

"So?" I demanded.

"So . . . are you okay?"

"No. Okay? I'm not okay. And no, I don't want to talk about it, or rap it out, or have a feeling circle. Just leave me alone. Just go."

The rookie held his hands up, like, *Easy.* "Hey. Okay. No problem. I'm gone."

"And no cookies!" I called after him.

Then he actually was gone. He left the room, just like that—which I'd just asked him to do—but it still surprised me.

Alone again. I was exactly as glad that he'd left as I was disappointed.

I tried cleaning the Sharpie marks off with alcohol, but it didn't work. Finally, after trying Windex, then WD-40, and scrubbing with steel wool and Comet, I hung the beefcake calendar from my old Austin station over the word with duct tape and called it a day.

It was a pretty good solution, covering the graffiti with Hernandez's shirtless, bulging form. But it also made me homesick.

After that night, I struggled for weeks to hold on to my equilibrium—on runs and workouts and parkour jaunts. I struggled with it every minute of every shift. I struggled with it as I fully, solidly ignored the rookie with such vigor that it was like he didn't even exist. And I struggled with it as we went out on call after call, helping an elderly man with chest pains, a mother who had driven her car into a ravine, a teenager who gave birth without ever having realized she was pregnant.

I couldn't make sense of anything anymore.

It violated everything I knew about firefighters to think that one of them would stoop to such a thing.

Here's the most essential truth about firefighting: It's a helping profession. People get into it because they want to help others. Yes, okay, maybe they also want to wear the bunker gear, or bust things up with axes, or drive a big red truck with a siren.

But firefighters are basically good guys at heart. I'm not saying they don't get into trouble, or have difficulty processing their feelings, or harbor a little unexamined sexism—or other isms. They're human. They're messy and imperfect and mistaken. At their cores, though, they're basically good people.

This was the crux of it.

If *firefighters* weren't the good guys, then maybe there just weren't any left.

IN PRACTICE, THE weeks at work that followed were not all that different from the weeks before. I still got to work on time and did all my chores and duties with care. I still ran calls and took care of patients and brought my A-game. I still took a six-mile run every day. I still practiced parkour and studied the course whenever no one was looking. Maybe I ignored the rookie a little harder than I had before, but it wasn't like I'd ever actively sought out his company. For various reasons.

On the surface, things probably looked about the same.

But nothing was the same.

That night with the rookie had opened me up in the most profound way. It's like I was a flower bud on a time-lapse camera and I just exploded into petals and tenderness and color.

I keep thinking that if I'd walked into that locker room the next morning as my usual, armored self, seeing that graffiti would have smarted, yes. But it wouldn't have shredded me like it did.

What choice did I have but to retreat after that? What choice was there but to armor back up? It was self-preservation.

But now I knew what I was missing. Now I remembered what it felt like not to be alone.

And now that I knew, it was unbearable.

But I bore it anyway. That's what we do, isn't it? That's the thing I always love best about the human race: how we pick ourselves back up over and over and just keep on going.

Still, the loneliness after I turned away from the rookie was so excruciating, so physical, that I actually felt like I might wither and die.

And so, the next best thing: crochet club.

Maybe, I thought, if I soothed the loneliness elsewhere, I could find a way to be okay.

Josie and Diana were always delighted for me to join them, and they gave me a giant basket of yarn balls to wind. And even as I marveled at how low I'd sunk—winding yarn balls!—I had to admit that the softness and the rhythm of the motion were pretty soothing, after all. Especially the chenille.

To be truthful, it wasn't just crochet club. I looked for every opportunity to be around either of them. I started showing up at the kitchen table for coffee. I helped prepare dinner. I volunteered to help Josie in her shop. When Diana invited me to go to the movies, I said yes. When she asked me to help in the garden, I did that, too. And when she hugged me, as crazy as it sounds, I hugged her right back.

It was like I was starving for human connection—and had been, all along—but I'd only now just figured that out.

My plan was to feast on friendship at home so that I'd be satiated when I got to the station.

It kind of worked.

Except that I never seemed to get satiated. The more connection I got, the more I wanted. You know, like when you take a nap, but when you wake up you're somehow sleepier than you were before? That was me, all the time—with humanity.

To everyone's astonishment, after Diana and Josie had failed to even coax me out of my room for so long, now they couldn't get rid of me. To my relief, they were delighted. And they were also hell-bent on solving the Case of the Slutty Locker.

They treated it like a Nancy Drew moment, and they questioned me about each guy on the crew, trying to nail down our suspects.

"It could have been any one of them," Diana announced one night.

"I say it was the captain," Josie said. "He's the one who saw her at the party giving the rookie a blowjob."

"Can I just reiterate that I did not give the rookie a blowjob?"

"Not *yet*," Josie said.

"The captain *does* make a good suspect," Diana said, totally unflummoxed by the topic.

"Well," I said, "he doesn't think women should join the fire department."

"That's suspicious right there," Josie said.

"Is he mean to you?" Diana asked.

"No, he's mostly very nice. In his gruff way."

"Is he harder on you than on everybody else?"

"He actually tends to use me as an example of how everybody should be doing things."

"Does he like you?"

"I don't know that I'd go that far."

"But he admires your work?"

"Frequently."

"Does he realize that you're a woman?"

"He says I'm the exception that proves the rule."

"Whatever that means," Diana said.

"If he knows you're onto him," Josie suggested, "he could fire you."

"He's not going to fire me," I said.

Josie smiled at me. "You're adorable. Yes, he is."

Diana nodded in agreement. "Yeah, he's probably going to fire you. If it was him."

"Who else could it have been?" Josie asked.

I shrugged. "It could have been anyone, really. Six-Pack has lost a ton of money—hundreds—betting against me. I absolutely annihilated Tiny in a game of hoops one time. DeStasio and Case were never thrilled to have a woman around. But there's no obvious villain. They've all been surprisingly nice to me."

"They underestimate you," Diana pointed out.

"But not in a vicious way," Josie said. "In a chivalrous, slightly patronizing way. Not mean-spirited."

"Maybe it was the rookie," I said then, and they both lowered their crochet.

"Absolutely not," Josie said.

Diana shook her head, too. "Impossible."

"Why not? It's the perfect alibi. Pretend to be allies and then do a double cross. Oldest trick in the book."

"He's not pretending. I saw the way he looked at you."

True enough.

"Why do you want to work with these guys, anyway?" Josie asked. "They seem very high maintenance."

I shrugged. "I love the job."

"And she's good at it," Diana added.

"I love the job *because* I'm good at it."

"Maybe it's the fact that you're so good at it that's the problem. It's got to be someone who's jealous of you. Or who feels threatened by you," Diana said.

"That could be anyone," I said.

"Maybe you could lay some kind of a trap," Diana said. "Maybe rig a squirt gun full of paint to go off when somebody opens your locker."

"That's a little flawed," I pointed out. "*I* have to open my locker."

Diana and Josie thought I should report it, but I couldn't.

I couldn't go to the higher-ups, because that would be not just complaining but also squealing and breaking ranks. I couldn't confront the stalker, because I didn't know who it was. In different circumstances, I might have just worked harder, tried to get better, in hopes that whoever didn't like me might come to see my value.

I suspected that Graffiti Guy had never wanted me there and had expected me to burn out on the job and quit. Well, I hadn't burned out. And once he realized I wasn't going to fail on my own, he'd decided to make me so miserable I'd have to leave.

I wasn't going to do that, either.

But how bad did things have to get before he got it?

I worried about it constantly.

Until the captain gave us something else to worry about.

Twenty

ONE EVENING, AFTER we'd cleaned up from supper, the captain called us all to order at the dining table.

"I just had the strangest phone call of my career," he said.

We all waited.

"Apparently, the city's got a budget shortfall. Nobody's exactly sure what happened, but there was some graft, some corruption—some bad investments made. Somehow, the projected city budget is not what it should be, and not what it was last year. There's an investigation, blah, blah, blah—but the long and the short of it is, they're cutting city services."

We waited.

"Cutting staff on city services, is what I mean." He cleared his throat. "I've never seen anything like it. They hired some planning consultant to come in and advise them on how to make up the gap, and his recommendation is to cut two percent of teachers, police, and firefighters in the city. Among many other things."

The captain looked down at the floor and shifted his weight.

"They're retiring some old-timers early," he continued, and just as I glanced over at DeStasio, who was the oldest guy on the crew, the captain went on, "and they're suspending the contracts of some of the newest hires."

Everybody looked over at Owen and me.

"What I'm saying," the captain went on, "is that two of the city's newest contracts are on our shift, and it looks like we're not going to get to keep both of them."

"You're letting them go?" Case asked.

"Just one," the captain said, like that was an upside.

"Which one?" Tiny asked.

Before the captain could answer, the guys all started shouting out their suggestions.

"Keep the girl!" DeStasio shouted, just as most of the others shouted to keep the rookie, and I felt a spark of gratitude toward him before I wondered if he was being sarcastic. Also: *Really? The girl?* I'd been working here for five months. Didn't I get a name?

"He can't sack the rookie!" Case was shouting. "That's Big Robby's kid."

"Well, there's no way he's keeping the girl." That was Tiny.

The guys all started debating our various merits and drawbacks, all at once, everybody talking and nobody listening. My upsides were, apparently, competence and skill, while pro-rookie arguments seemed to stress that he was "a good guy." The captain let everybody vocalize for a few minutes before shutting us up again.

"It's a tough situation," he went on. "I don't know who I'm letting go, but I do know it's going to mean we'll have a reduced crew on this shift and several others. That's unsafe for us, and it's bad for the community—but there's nothing to do about it right now. We've just got to roll with it until they get this thing sorted out. Nobody here is a stranger to hardship. We'll handle it."

"But who are you firing?" Tiny wanted to know.

"Normally, I'd just fire the newest guy, but these two"—he gestured between us—"started on the same day. The chief's given me a few weeks to decide—and despite what you might be thinking, my mind is not yet made up. It'll be a hell of a decision."

For a second, I found myself wondering if the captain was the stalker, and he was just making this all up as a ruse to get rid of me, but then he showed us the letter from the chief laying the whole situation out. I had to admit it seemed pretty official.

The captain didn't seem as mad at me lately, anyway. Despite the scene he'd made about the cyanide kits, in the end, he'd put one on each apparatus—the engine and the box. Other things had arrived, too—the gear dryer, three infrared cameras, a voucher for seven new mattresses at a local store—and he'd kept them all.

As gruff as he was, I knew he liked his new mattress.

That might work in my favor.

The captain shifted his weight, looking not too happy about the situation.

"What happens to the one you let go?" Tiny asked.

"He or she," the captain said carefully, "will have to find another position. You can bet I'll write 'em one hell of a recommendation letter."

The captain looked up and met my eyes for the first time, then Owen's. "I hate to have to do it, but I've got no choice. I'm putting you two on notice. From now on, every choice you make, every patient you interact with—it's all being monitored and evaluated. So bring your A-game. When the time comes, I'll make the call. But I'll tell you something straight. I wish like hell I didn't have to."

AS I WALKED out to my truck to head home after shift, I had the worst feeling about what was going to happen.

The captain was going to pick Owen. I tried to imagine being Captain Murphy and making his choice between Owen—a young, fit, friendly hard worker, son of a captain from Boston FD, sired from a long line of heroes, a local boy with the exact same Massachusetts accent as the captain himself—and me.

What did the captain see when he looked at me? A Texan, a foreigner, a newbie.

But mostly, a girl.

And we all knew how awful girls were.

I just knew. I was going to lose my job.

I'd been so stupid. This moment was just a crystallization of what I'd known all along. The rookie would be my downfall, one way or another.

For so many months it had been my job to train him, to break him in, to bring him up to speed. I'd been helping him. I'd let myself think of us as being on the same team. In theory, it only helped the crew for him to be stronger, and it helped the patients, too. He was a good guy. I wanted him to succeed.

But not in place of me.

That was the downside to helping him. My place here had never been safe, and that fact was just hitting me as I reached my truck and saw that the tires had been slashed.

All four of them.

There was a note under a windshield wiper in Sharpie with some simple advice: *Just quit you bitch.*

It was hard not to get judgy with the grammar, and the comma that should have been there. Not to mention the handwriting. It looked like a preschooler had written it. Once again, the *T* looked like an *X*: *Just quix.*

Still, I got the message.

I crumpled the note up in my hand and stared at the tires. Totally flat, all four. That would be a hundred dollars apiece, at least—money I did not have. But the immediate problem was how was I getting home.

Like with the locker, I had no intention of telling the crew about this. No way was I going to self-identify as the weakest of the herd—especially not now. Luckily, most of them had gone home already, and because Owen and I were the two newest members of the crew, we had the two farthest parking spaces.

Maybe no one had noticed.

I was counting that particular blessing when I heard footsteps behind me.

The rookie.

"What the hell happened?" he demanded, staring at the tires.

I had no idea what to say. I just shrugged.

"Somebody did this?"

It was a funny question. Of course somebody did it. "Looks like it," I said.

"Who?"

"I don't know."

"Someone from the neighborhood, I bet," he said. "Some dumb kid."

"I don't think so," I said.

He turned to me. "What do you mean?"

I gave him the crumpled note and watched him uncrumple it.

As soon as he read it, he looked up at me. "What the hell?" he demanded.

I shrugged.

"Who wrote this?"

I shrugged again. "I found it under my windshield wiper."

He was so shocked, it made me wonder if he was faking. "Someone put this under your wiper?"

I nodded.

"You have to tell the captain."

"I am not telling the captain. Ever. And neither are you."

The rookie walked over to my truck, studying it for other clues and thinking. Then he came back to study my face. "This isn't the first time."

"For what?" I said, stalling, knowing full well.

"The first time someone's messed with you like this."

I shook my head.

"What else? What else has happened?"

I sighed. No sense hiding it now. "Somebody wrote the word 'slut' in my locker."

Owen frowned and took a few steps closer. "When?"

"The first shift after your parents' party."

I watched that sink in. I saw him click the pieces into place. "That's what happened. Somebody scared you."

"Nobody scares me," I said. "It was a good reminder, that's all."

"Of what?"

"That I'm here to work. Not to"—but then I couldn't think of a good word. "Do whatever that was we were doing."

"What we do or don't do," Owen said, holding up the note, "has nothing to do with this asshole."

"I think the asshole sees it differently."

"Why didn't you tell me?" He was angry. I could see it in his eyes and the tension in his shoulders.

I, in contrast, was doing that thing where I decide I'm not going to have any feelings. "I felt my best option at the time was distance." I sounded like a robot, even to myself.

"We need to figure out who this is."

"What do you think I've been trying to do?"

But his mind was racing. "We need to check security camera footage. We need to set some kind of trap. We need to question all the guys—"

"No. We're not questioning anybody."

"But how can we find him if we—"

"I don't know. But the last thing I'm doing is telling the whole crew."

"But we—"

"And stop saying 'we'! This is not your problem. This is my problem."

"But I—"

"Cut it out!" I snapped. "Stop trying to rescue me! I can rescue my own damn self."

Owen blinked. Then closed his mouth. Then nodded. "Okay," he said. Then he handed the note back to me. "I won't rescue you," he said.

"Great. Perfect. Thank you."

"Just let me point out one thing."

"What?"

"You're going to need a ride home."

* * *

ON THE DRIVE, Owen told me he had a cousin with a wrecker service. "He'll handle it for you," he said.

"What does that mean?" I asked.

"He'll pick up your car, and get you some new tires, and bring it to you. I already texted him."

"I'm not sure I can afford new tires."

"He's not going to charge you."

"For the tires?"

"For any of it."

"Why wouldn't he charge me?"

Owen smiled. "He owes me a few favors. More than a few."

I didn't respond to that, just leaned back against the seat, trying not to let my mind drift back to the last time I'd been in the rookie's truck with him.

"Let's talk about something else," I said, when the silence had gone on too long.

"Like what?"

"Anything. Anything distracting."

"There is actually something I need to share with you."

"*Share?*" I asked. That would be distracting. Firemen didn't share.

"It's relevant to our positions here."

"Our positions?" I didn't look back. "You mean me, the desperately overqualified and yet somehow underrated newcomer—and you, the rookie who wants my job?"

"Yes."

I looked out the window. "Bring it on, pal."

"First of all," he went on, "I want you to know that I know that you are a better firefighter than I am."

That caught my attention.

"I know it," he went on. "Everybody knows it. If it were up to me, I'd just back out of this whole situation and let you have your rightful place."

"Great," I said.

"But I can't."

"It's not up to you?" I asked.

"Not entirely."

"Who's it up to?"

"That's what I want to talk to you about."

"Okay," I said. "Talk."

But he hesitated. "I'm about to tell you something I've never told anybody."

"Maybe you shouldn't," I said.

"I think I want to. Have wanted to for a while, actually," he said.

"You've been wanting to tell me your biggest secret for a while?"

"Someone, at least. But when I started thinking about who I could trust—you were at the top of the list. Actually, you *were* the list. Just the whole list."

The whole list? I squinted at him. "Parents?"

"Not for this."

"Sisters?"

"Nope."

"Friends?"

"You're my friend, aren't you?"

"Friend-slash-enemy."

"Fair enough."

He was stalling. "Out with it, then."

"Okay," he said. He adjusted his hands on the wheel. "When I was a kid, I used to hang out with these two boys from my neighborhood. I was the youngest of a bunch of kids, and all our parents worked, and these kids and I just kind of ran around all summer pretty much unsupervised. We didn't misbehave, we just did kid stuff. Looked for bottle caps. Collected sticks. Set up toy soldiers. But our favorite thing to do was set little fires and put them out—and it was especially my favorite thing to do because my dad was a firefighter and so the other boys, even though they were older, totally deferred to my expertise."

"Okay," I said, wondering what any of this might have to do with me.

"Anyway, there was a warehouse district just past our neighborhood with lots of abandoned buildings. We weren't supposed to go there. Our moms had drawn a line at Battle Street that we were never, ever supposed to cross. So of course we crossed it all the time."

"Of course."

"And one day, one of us—and I'm not even sure, honestly, who it was—decided we should set a matchbox on fire and toss it through the window of one of the empty warehouses."

I felt a tightness in my chest. This was not going to end well.

"I was eight," Owen went on. "My details are really fuzzy, but we slid open the drawer of a matchbox, and then we tilted the matches up out of it and closed it again just enough to hold the matchsticks out, in a spray. And then we lit them. And then one of us tossed the whole thing through a broken window, and we took off running."

This was starting to ring some bells for me. This story sounded familiar.

"What were we thinking? What were we expecting? What were our goals? I think we hoped the building would shoot up like a Fourth of July firework.

"We'd played in that warehouse before, lots of times," he went on. "The ground floor was empty, for the most part. I've thought about it so often, and I can't imagine how the matches didn't just burn themselves out on the concrete floor."

"But they didn't."

He shook his head. "They didn't. Turns out, it was an old paper factory."

I turned to look at him.

Oh God. I knew that fire. Everybody knew that fire.

I turned to him and met his eyes. As soon as I did, he knew I knew.

I lowered my voice—for no reason. "We're talking about the Boston Paper Company fire?"

He nodded.

"You started the Boston Paper Company fire?" I asked.

He nodded again, then went on. "Walking home at sunset, we saw it. There was fire coming out of every window, black smoke everywhere, and a funnel-shaped tornado of fire rising from the roof. Every company in the city was called to that fire. The streets were closed off. They had to turn off the electricity to ten city blocks. It was unstoppable. The upper stories were all filled with reams of paper—dry, brittle paper. We watched it burn. We could feel the heat. It sounded like a freight train—so loud, I could feel the roar on my skin."

"I remember. It was too hot for water. It had to burn itself out."

He nodded. "And when the walls finally collapsed, they took the surrounding buildings down with them."

"A firefighter was killed by one of the falling walls."

The rookie nodded. "But not just any firefighter," he said. "My uncle."

A long sigh seeped out of me. Not just any firefighter. His uncle.

He ran a hand through his hair. "An eyewitness said she'd seen two boys running from the warehouse—not three, two. The other boys were brothers, and their mother watched them staring endlessly at the coverage and somehow, in that way moms have, she just knew. She got them to confess, but they never ratted me out. Nobody looked for a third kid. The official story was 'two boys.' The media circus was so insane, they wound up moving away—down to Florida, I think."

"And you never told anybody you'd been there."

He shook his head.

"That's why it took you so long to join up. Even with your dad pushing."

He tapped on the steering wheel. "It was like that day sealed me into an impossible fate. To spend the rest of my life avoiding everything about fires—and to be duty-bound to join the fire service."

"Why are you duty-bound to join?"

A little shrug. "My dad wants me to."

"It's your apology," I said.

"It's the shittiest apology ever, but it's all I've got."

I studied him a second. "You just want to bake cookies."

"Pretty much."

"But you can't. Or you think you can't."

"I brought my dad indescribable grief."

"Are you atoning for the fire?"

He gave the tiniest shrug. "He's still grieving, in a way, my dad. Even now. If there's anything I can do, I have to do it."

"I get that," I said, and I really did. I wasn't sure I agreed with it, but I got it.

"I've never told anyone the whole story like that," Owen said then. "I can't tell you how strange it feels." He let out a big breath.

"You were a kid, you know. Kids do stupid stuff all the time. It was an accident."

"That may be true. But my uncle Ryan is still dead. My dad's only brother. Because of me."

I wondered if maybe he was emphasizing the wrong parts of the story. "That's just such a burden for a kid to carry."

"I'm not a kid anymore."

"For *anyone* to carry."

He nodded. "Anyway, that's why I can't quit the fire department. That's why I have to win that spot—even though I know you deserve it more. If the captain gives it to me, I have to take it. This is my dad's dream. And I have to make sure he gets it."

"Maybe your dad's dream is just for you to be happy."

The rookie looked at me like I was so wrong it was almost cute. "Nope. Firefighter first, happy second."

"You are talking to a person who has watched you turn pale, faint, or throw up on every medical call. Sometimes all three."

He let out a long breath. "I don't know what else to do."

"Well, first of all, I'd find yourself a therapist."

"Did that already," he said, like he'd already checked it off the list. "Third grade. I didn't speak at all for almost a year after the fire, and they made me see a grief expert twice a week."

"Did you talk about what happened?"

"Parts of what happened."

"The important parts?"

He shook his head.

"I think," I said then, "you should start thinking about forgiveness."

He raised his eyebrows like I was crazy. "Are you saying you think I need to tell my dad?"

"Have you thought about it?"

The rookie shook his head, like, *Nuh-uh. Nope. No way.*

I shrugged. "I don't know that you need to tell him, necessarily."

He frowned. "But you think I need him to forgive me?"

I shook my head. "No. I think you need to forgive yourself."

He was quiet, as if that thought had never occurred to him. Then he said, "I wouldn't even know where to start."

"It just so happens I could help you with that. My mother has been educating me on the joys and challenges of forgiveness."

He couldn't tell if I was joking.

"It's easier than it sounds," I said. "It's more a shift in thinking than anything else. You have to think about the person you're angry at—in this case, your eight-year-old self—and try to be compassionate with him. Empathy soothes anger, you know," I said, suddenly feeling very wise. "Then you have to work to find some good things that came out of what happened, even despite all the bad. And then you have to decide to let it go."

"That's good advice," he said.

"I am full of good advice."

"Doesn't really change anything about our situation, though, does it?"

"Not at the moment," I said. "No."

"You still want this job, and I still need this job."

I kept doing that: forgetting who he was. I nodded, like, *That's right.* "We're still enemies."

He frowned at the word choice. "Friendly rivals," he corrected.

"To-the-death combatants," I said.

"Sparring partners."

"Look," I said, "no matter what we were before, now we're enemies. We're competing for the same position."

"You really love that job, huh?"

"What's not to love?"

"I don't know," he said, looking out the window. "The blood? The guts? The diarrhea?"

"The heroism? The camaraderie? The saving people's lives?"

"Sure," he said. "There's that."

I looked him over. "I've seen worse rookies," I said.

He gave a nod, like, *Maybe.* "I'm throwing up less often now," he said. "But you're the one they're going to keep."

I honked out a laugh. "*You're* the one they're going to keep."

He looked at me like I was crazy. "The captain's not going to choose me."

"I think he is."

He shook his head. "Why would he do that?"

"Because." I shrugged. "Because you come from a long line of brave heroes. Because the captain knows your dad. Because you are fun and friendly and easy to get along with. Because you look like a firefighter—like a Norman Rockwell painting of a firefighter, actually, crossed with a *GQ* cover. And because the captain doesn't think women should be in the fire service."

"He can't think that."

"He does. He told my old captain, back in Austin. They only took me because they were desperate."

"That was before he'd seen you in action. There's no way he still thinks that now."

"Wanna bet?"

"He knows you're good. He knows you're better than half the guys in there."

"*Half* of them?" I said. "All of them."

"You could dead-lift Case under the table."

"Anybody could dead-lift Case under the table."

"You deserve that job," Owen said.

"I do," I agreed. "But you're the one who's going to get it."

Twenty-one

A FEW DAYS later, just before dawn, the stalker threw a brick through my mother's kitchen window.

That really happened.

It was a shift morning. Still dark out. My alarm hadn't even gone off yet. The shattering sound woke me up, and I sprinted down two flights of stairs in my bare feet only to stop short at the kitchen threshold when I saw glass pieces glittering all over the counter and the floor.

Diana was right behind me.

The sound of it had been shockingly loud. So loud, in fact, that it woke Josie next door. She showed up in her robe not long after, after I'd found some flip-flops and started sweeping up the mess. Diana watched from the doorway, and Josie watched from the back door.

My mom's kitchen window, in her historic little home, had not been safety glass. I found razor-sharp shards in every nook and cranny, even one impaled in a loaf of banana bread on the far counter. I swept three times, dry-mopped twice, and then wet-mopped, and I'm sure it took me a while, but I don't remember time passing. Anger, I think, burned away all sense of time from that memory—and all details other than the way my hands started aching from their death-clamp on the broom handle.

Only when I'd gone over every surface did I let Diana and Josie step in.

"I don't think it's ever been this clean in here," Diana said.

"It was my stalker," I said, pointing at the brick on the counter.

Josie peered over. "At this hour?" She frowned.

Diana chimed in. "Who has that kind of energy?"

It was appalling. And incomprehensible.

Josie decided to make coffee—checking the inside of the pot for glass shards first. "How much anger does this guy have to get up before dawn to go terrorize somebody?"

"Nothing gets me up before eight," Diana said, lifting up the brick to get a look. Then she added, "Other than terrorism."

"Careful," I said.

"There's a note," Diana said, turning it over. Sure enough, there was a note rubber-banded around it.

I just stood there, staring. Did I want to read it? I wasn't sure. Of course, that's what he wanted us to do—and part of me didn't want to give him the satisfaction of scaring us more than he already had. What if we ignored him? What if we refused to be terrorized?

I wasn't sure of the best course of action.

Finally, Diana made the decision for me. She pulled off the rubber band, unfolded the note, and read it out loud. "It says, 'Just quit you wore.'" She looked up, frowning. "You wore what? What did you wear?"

Josie leaned over to take a look. "I think he means 'whore.'"

"Oh!" Diana said, checking the note again. "He forgot the *H*!"

"Not a great speller," I said.

"Not great at punctuation, either," Josie said, holding it up as evidence. "There should be a comma after 'quit.'"

"And probably an exclamation point at the end," Diana said. "For emphasis."

Josie took another look at it. "Not going to win any prizes for penmanship, either. That *T* looks just like an *X*."

And then Diana and Josie started laughing, that odd, minor-key laughing that you do sometimes when things are the opposite of funny. But laughing all the same.

"So," Diana said, still laughing. "Not an English teacher."

"Or a calligrapher," Josie added.

"Or a preschool graduate."

They were cracking themselves up. They had decided to think it was funny. Which I admired.

But I didn't think anything about this was funny. And it was time for me to go. Past time. I was going to be late for work. For real this time.

"YOU'RE LATE, HANWELL," Captain Murphy said, when I showed up in the kitchen. "Again."

The guys were all there. DeStasio was already starting breakfast.

I didn't respond to the captain. Instead, I held up the brick. Lifted it up high over my head until all the guys fell quiet and gave me their attention.

This was it. We were done here.

Ignoring it hadn't worked. Waiting for it to blow over hadn't worked. It was time for the nuclear option.

Though I wasn't totally clear what that might be.

I'd figure it out as I went along.

What could I do? Demand that a whole room of dudes be *nicer* to me? Sit them all down and walk them through how strange and unsettled and fragile I'd been feeling ever since I left Texas? Talk to them about guilt and regret? About missed opportunities? Get vulnerable with them?

Firefighters didn't do vulnerable.

Life in the fire service revolved around not being vulnerable. It was about being tough, and brave, and strong. Someone needed saving, so you saved them. Something was on fire, so you put it out. Were you scared? It didn't matter. Did you have feelings about it? Irrelevant. You did your job, and you did it well, and that was all there was to it. People who wanted to wrestle with complicated emotions became therapists, or poets. People who wanted to keep things simple became firefighters.

I wanted to keep things simple. But life wasn't letting me. Someone at the station, in particular, wasn't letting me.

I walked up to the head of the table.

"At five o'clock this morning, someone threw a brick through my mother's kitchen window. Someone from our shift. And I want to know who it was."

I studied their faces. Everybody looked shocked—except for the rookie, who looked angry, and DeStasio, who looked bored. I'd hoped I might be able to spot the guilty one right away, but I should have known better than to think things could be that easy.

Captain Murphy stepped forward. "You think it was someone from our shift?" His voice made it clear that he thought I was completely bananas.

"I do," I said.

The accusation offended them.

I let them be offended for a second, and then I said, "I wasn't going to say anything. I was going to let it blow over. I'm not a complainer. I can take it, of course. I'm not here for myself. But I draw the line at throwing a brick through an old lady's window. Mess with me all you want—but do not fuck with my mother."

The guys blinked at me. *Language!*

"No one was hurt, if you're wondering," I said. "But glass went everywhere—and not safety glass, either. And a lovely historic window is destroyed."

I checked all their faces, one by one. Sympathetic. Concerned. Shocked.

But somebody here was responsible.

"So who was it?" I demanded. "Who the hell thought terrorizing a sweet old lady was a good idea? Who in this crew wants to get rid of me so badly that they're willing to do that?"

“It’s terrible,” the captain said. “But it wasn’t us.”

“I think it was.”

“Why would you think that?” Case said, sounding hurt.

I was pacing around now. “A few weeks ago, somebody broke into my locker here at the station, and scrawled the word ‘slut’ in Sharpie across the back wall.”

That got their attention.

“I ignored it. I tried to clean it off. I hung an old calendar from my station in Austin over the spot. I didn’t complain. But then, this week, somebody slashed all my tires—four hundred bucks’ worth of tires!—and left a note on my windshield that said, ‘Just quit you bitch.’”

The guys looked around at each other, like, *What the hell?*

“Fine,” I said. “I ignored it. It’s not the first time I’ve been called a bitch. Whatever.”

I looked around.

“But then, this morning—my mother. *My mother,* you guys.” I looked around. “This one had a note, too.”

“What did it say?” the captain asked.

I held up the note.

The captain leaned closer and peered at it, reading and frowning. “‘Just quit you wore’? What does that mean? What did you wear?”

“I think he means ‘whore,’ Captain,” Tiny said.

“Can’t spell for shit,” the captain said.

For a second, my throat felt like it was closing up. I held very still to let it pass. I would not cry, or let my voice break or even tremble. All emotions but anger right now were unacceptable. This moment had to be a show of strength and defiance and absolutely nothing else. But I would tell them about my mom. Maybe it would shame them into behaving better, or maybe it wouldn’t—but by the time I finished talking, they would know the truth.

“She’s sick,” I said, surprising even myself with the crackle of emotion in my voice. “That’s why I came here. She lost the sight in one eye after an operation, and her sight’s not great in the other one. She gets headaches. She wears an eye patch. Her depth perception's all messed up, and she has trouble with the stairs, and she can't drive at all. That's why I'm here."

The guys were dead silent.

I was not going to cry.

I went on. "And somebody threw a brick through her window. Somebody here. Somebody who has dedicated his life to helping others. Somebody who's supposed to be a hero."

I started pacing.

"It doesn't matter that I'm not actually a whore—whatever that even means. It doesn't matter that I'm not even remotely intimidated by this bozo. It doesn't even matter that there's no point in going after me like this. It's—*what?*—weeks before the captain makes his decision between me and the rookie. We all know what he thinks about women. We all know what we *all* think about women. I'm out. I'll be gone before you know it anyway. So whoever this asshole is, he's going to a lot of trouble to accomplish something that's already pretty much a done deal.

"Here's what does matter: What this guy is doing is *wrong*. You can't do what we do and see the kind of suffering we see every damn day and still want to create more of it in the world, can you? You can't do what we do for a living and not know the simple difference between right and wrong. That's what has me so, so pissed. We're supposed to be the heroes. We're supposed to be the helpers. The caretakers. The good in the world. What the hell can I believe in, if I can't believe in you?"

Oh God. Now there were tears on my face. Humiliating.

It just made me angrier.

"I know we're all just human. I don't expect you to be perfect. But I expect you, at the very least, to be better than that."

And that's when I had an idea. Not a perfect idea. Maybe not even a good one. But it was the best I could come up with in the moment.

"So I'm making everybody a deal," I said, wiping my face again. "Pick your best guy, and let's go outside right now to run the course. I will beat him. I'll beat anybody here. I'll prove myself to all of you—again, for the thousandth time. And if I don't win, I'll quit. I'll quit right now, this morning, and you'll never see me again, and all your lady problems will be over."

The guys were all frowning at me.

"But I will win," I went on. "And when I do, the asshole stalker in this room needs to make a choice to be a better human being—and cut it the hell out."

The guys looked around at each other.

"And if he doesn't—if he manages to run me out of here in the end? At least every single one of us will know that I deserved to be here."

I was so angry, but the guys just looked sorry. They'd been standing at ease, but then, almost like a school of fish in unison, they all took a few steps closer. Then the captain, of all people, was holding his arms out to me. "You know what you need, Hanwell?"

"Group hug," the guys all assented, lifting their arms, too.

Were they mocking me? Were they being sarcastic? They looked so earnest, but that couldn't be right. I smeared the tears off my face with my impatient hands, then pointed at them all, like, *Keep back.* "Do not hug me. Nobody in this room hugs anybody."

Then I took a few steps backwards, as if my pointing finger were a gun and I was the villain making my escape.

One by one, I made eye contact with every guy in the room.

That was my goal, I guess. To make sure that no matter what, everyone would know exactly what they'd lost.

The guys were all silent at the notion.

Then the captain said, "Is this really necessary?"

Case jumped in with, "You're too short to beat anybody on that course, Hanwell."

"Don't do this," Six-Pack said.

"There's no way you can win," DeStasio said.

That's when the captain stepped forward. "Nobody wants you to quit, Hanwell. You don't have to do this."

"Apparently, I fucking do," I said. "Now, pick somebody. And then send him outside."

* * *

I STOOD OUT back in the parking lot, surveying the course, and waited.

A few minutes later, the captain showed up and said, "That was a hell of a speech."

I held still, eyes on the course.

"It could be somebody on a different shift, you know."

"It could be," I said. "But it isn't."

"I can't imagine any of our guys would do that to you."

"Maybe it was you," I said, not looking over. "I'm pretty sure you told my old captain that women in the fire service would be the downfall of human civilization."

The captain leaned forward until he caught my eye. "It wasn't me, Hanwell. Do you want to know why?"

I shrugged, not looking over.

"I did say that to your captain. But in the short time you've been here, you've made me change my mind."

I looked down.

I believed him. But I wasn't going to give him the satisfaction of admitting it. "So you say," I said.

"The guys don't want to take your challenge. They say you don't need to prove yourself. They want me to give you a pass."

"I won't take it."

"That's what I told them."

"Go back in and tell them to pick somebody, then," I said.

"Who gives the orders here, Hanwell?"

"You do, sir. So go back in and act like it."

The captain went in, and a few minutes later, they sent out Case.

"Nope," I said, the minute I saw him. "That's just insulting."

"I'm the choice," Case said with a shrug. "Deal with it."

"Case," I said, "you could not run this course if your life depended on it."

"That's why we all picked me," he said. "Nobody wants you to lose."

"I'm not going to lose," I said. "Now get back in there and pick somebody real."

A few minutes later, the rookie came out.

"Why didn't you call me?" he asked, referring, I supposed, to the brick.

"What would you have done?"

He shook his head, looking out at the course. "I don't know. Helped you sweep up, maybe."

"Maybe it was you who threw it," I said then.

"You couldn't possibly think that." He searched my eyes.

I shrugged. "Maybe you've been nice to me this whole time to throw me off your trail. Maybe you secretly want me gone."

"Trust me," he said. "I want you the opposite of gone."

I looked away. "I don't trust anybody anymore."

"You don't have to do this," Owen said. "Nobody wants you to."

"Why are you out here, anyway?" I asked. "Shouldn't you be inside, deciding?"

"They've already decided."

I turned to him. "Who is it?"

He shrugged. "It's me."

I let out a bitter laugh. "Of course it is," I said.

"What does that mean?" he asked.

I was marching toward the course. "Call the guys. Let's get this done."

The guys gathered near the pull-up bars.

"Who's got a stopwatch?" I said.

Tiny raised his phone, open to the stopwatch setting.

It wasn't a perfect plan, of course. But I just needed to do something. Anything.

The rookie and I took our places.

I'd been practicing as inconspicuously as possible. I worked on elements of the course when the guys weren't looking, mostly because I never wanted them to see me do anything I wasn't good at. Twice a year, the captain had said, we'd run it together, and I didn't want to be embarrassed. More than that, I wanted to kick ass.

So now, suddenly, it was that day.

Time to see if all that on-the-sly practice and self-taught parkour would do the trick.

Necessity, as always, was the mother of invention.

I'd watched the guys do the course before. When they jumped to grab the bar, they grasped with their hands and hoisted up against gravity. But I didn't have the option of jumping for the bar. The only way for somebody my size to grab it was to do a wall run up the pole, then a turn vault.

It was the only way for me—but also a better way.

The momentum would do most of the work for me. I wasn't crawling up over the bar so much as grabbing it as I went by. The guys started with their heads below it, but using the pole as a kind of springboard helped me grab the bar with my head already above—then it was just a little farther to pop up into a hip catch, and then I could spin over it and drop.

I used some version of a wall run to approach every tall structure on the course, using it to shift my momentum from forward to upward. I used the cat leap to get myself over that eight-foot wall. I used the thief vault and the lazy vault to sail over most of the log hurdles, adding a pop vault for the tall ones. Who says hours watching YouTube are wasted?

I also used the lache technique to swing across the eight parallel bars. Of them all, this one probably saved me the most time. The guys would hang from the bars, reaching forward to grab the next bar before letting go of the first one. I didn't have that option because my arms were not long enough to touch both bars at once. I had to propel myself forward, using legs and momentum, and "fly" from bar to bar. If you get the rhythm right, you never slow down, just zip along under the bars, arms pumping. The guys never had to trust themselves to fly.

Even my landings were better. The guys would drop, absorbing a little impact with their knees, and then keep lumbering forward. I would land like a cat and spring back up, catching that momentum to propel myself ahead.

So I felt pretty confident standing there, about to start. Owen was the youngest, and probably the fittest, of the guys.

But I could still beat him.

CASE CLANGED A metal pipe against another as our starting gun.

"Go!" he shouted, and we were off.

I didn't even look at Owen, I just launched—hoisting and spinning, vaulting and leaping into a massive lead over him before we were even halfway done.

I worked the course like a pro. It was more like ballet choreography than anything else. I skimmed under the monkey bars, vaulted over all the logs without ever breaking stride, and scaled the eight-foot wall without faltering.

At the top of the wall, with only the rope climb left to go, I had a good one-minute lead on the rookie.

But then I landed wrong.

Maybe I had too much momentum. Maybe I was distracted by all the guys watching, but when I hit the ground on the other side of the climbing wall, rather than shifting straight into a parkour roll, I caught the side of my foot and felt it bend under me.

I heard a crack.

I felt the pain sear up to my brain and then reverberate back down—and I'll admit, it threw me off. I made a quick self-assessment. Definitely sprained. Possibly fractured. I heard a clonk to my right and looked up to see Owen hook over the top of his wall and drop down. I took off running, limping badly, and he scrambled after me.

One final thing: the rope climb. Parkour couldn't help me too much with this one. It just called for the standard technique of wrapping the rope in a J-hook around one foot. I'd done it before, but this time my injured ankle wasn't quite working right.

I'd tell it to push, and it would just kind of disobey.

The rookie had a real advantage over me here. Not only did he have two working ankles, he also had big guy shoulders. I was strong for a woman, but his shoulders were twice the size of mine. There really was no way I could beat him up the rope. But I wasn't giving up.

The rookie and I were neck and neck when I gave up on my legs and just started climbing arms only, hand over hand, letting everything else dangle below me. It was harder, and slower, but it was my only option, and the truth is he beat me to the top. But then, in his haste to drop back to the ground and head for the finish line, he dropped too fast. He hit the ground hard and fell on his side. I dropped fast, too—rope-burning my palms as I went—but I never lost control. I landed on one foot, just as he was getting back up, and I took off running, ignoring the searing pain shooting from my ankle all the way to my hip, and crossing the finish line a good two seconds before him.

Here was the weirdest thing about winning that race. There was no cheering, no hugs, no high fives. There was just me, and my throbbing, angry ankle, as I collapsed on the ground, and a whole crew of firefighters surrounded me in disbelief, admiration, and maybe even a little respect.

"Does it hurt?" Six-Pack asked.

It hurt like hell. "Nope," I said.

"We're going to need a medic," Case called out, and all the guys raised their hands to volunteer.

"Let me guess," I said. "You're going to make the rookie do it."

They did.

Six-Pack and Case lifted my arms around their shoulders and helped me limp back to the station. Tiny went off to find me a set of crutches.

Had I solved all my stalker problems?

Maybe not.

But I'd impressed the guys. I'd maimed myself to do it, but I'd impressed them.

And even better: Nobody had been willing to bet against me.

It felt pretty good to hear that.

"You wouldn't really have resigned, would you?" Case called out.

"I would have," I said, dead serious.

"I wouldn't have accepted it," the captain said.

"Maybe not this week," I said, reminding him of the choice he still had to make.

Back inside, the guys were back to their rowdy selves, already retelling the tale, and imagining how it would have gone if Case had been my competition, hooting wildly at the idea of his round body trying to hoist its way over the hurdles.

Owen tended to my ankle.

As the guys got louder, my little corner with Owen seemed to get quieter.

I watched his hands wrapping cold packs around my ankle. They were pretty scraped up.

"You okay?" I asked.

"Fine," he said. "*You* okay?"

"Totally fine," I said.

The rookie smiled. "That was unbelievably amazing, by the way. How did you learn to do all that?"

I shrugged. "YouTube."

As I watched him work, my brain kept circling back to one moment during the course. The moment when he'd fallen at the bottom of the rope. Something about the way he'd fallen seemed strange to me.

"Why did you fall at the bottom of the rope?" I asked then, quietly.

He kept his head down, wrapping my ankle with a bandage. "Just hit too hard, I guess."

"Did you hurt yourself?" I asked.

He kept his head down but shook it. "Nah."

"Weird," I said.

"Lucky," he said, still not looking up.

I was studying him. "If you hadn't fallen right then, you would have won."

"You don't know that," he said, head still down.

"Rookie," I said then, lowering my voice. "Did you fall on purpose?"

He finished wrapping and taped it in place. Then he lifted his head and looked straight into my eyes—and I knew the answer.

"Rookie," I said, gearing up to scold him.

But he leaned in. "There was no way in hell you were quitting the department today. Not if I had anything to say about it. You deserved to win, and you won. Now shut up."

I could have kissed him.

I also could have argued. I could have insisted that he come clean to the guys. I could have demanded a do-over—at some future date when my ankle was healed.

I didn't get a chance to do any of those things.

Before I had time to respond at all, my phone rang. It was in my bag across the room, but Six-Pack jogged it over to me.

It was Josie. "Hey," I said.

"Hey. I'm sorry to call you at work."

"It's okay," I said. Something was wrong.

"It's about Diana," Josie said. "She collapsed. Actually—that's not right. She had a seizure."

Twenty-two

SHE HAD A *seizure.*

Normally, a word like "seizure" would prompt my usual sense of calm-in-the-storm to kick in.

That's not what happened this time.

I was always at my best in a crisis. But not today.

This time, kind of like when you see lightning flash, and then you hear a clap of thunder, panic flashed through my chest, and then I heard it in my voice. "What happened?"

"She was making breakfast, and the seizure hit. She fell to the floor, but she smacked her head on the counter as she went down."

My brain was like a lightbulb with a short in it. "You called 911?"

"Yes. We're already at the hospital. Rockport County."

That counter was granite. "Does she have a concussion?"

"They're assessing her now," Josie said. "She has a bruise on her forehead the size of an apple."

"Better to bruise on the outside than on the inside," I said, to comfort her. And myself.

Josie was pretty flustered. "She was making French toast," Josie said, her voice incredulous at the memory, "and then she froze for a second, and then she kind of snapped in half and dropped. It was so fast. And the sound of her head hitting that counter . . ." Josie made a sob-like noise. "I ran to her, but I didn't know what to do. I'd never seen anything like it."

"She's lucky you were there," I said. "How long did it last?"

"I don't know," Josie said. "Two minutes? Three? It felt like a thousand. Can you come?" she asked. "Right now?"

"Of course," I said. "I'm on my way."

Before I'd even pressed END, Owen was helping me to my feet. He knew something was up, but he didn't ask. He handed me the crutches Tiny had found.

I moved toward the guys, who were all still gathered around the table. My whole body felt wobbly, but I forced it to work right, mind-over-matter style.

"Could I speak to you, Captain?" I asked.

The guys all fell silent. They recognized the sound of panic in my voice. They all turned to watch me.

The captain heard it, too. "Shoot," he said.

"My mother's had a seizure," I said.

He nodded, all business. "Is she at Fairmont?"

"They've taken her to Rockport County."

The captain nodded. "We've got you covered, Hanwell. Get your things, and we'll call in somebody from B-shift."

"Thank you," I said.

As I hobbled away, getting my bearings with the crutches, the captain called out after me, "Hanwell!"

I turned back.

"Anything you need, anything at all . . . it's yours."

Then the captain told Case to give me an escort. And to use the lights and sirens.

AT THE HOSPITAL, Josie was waiting outside my mother's room, nursing a paper cup of tea with the tag still hanging over the side.

"What happened to you?" she said, when she saw the crutches.

"Tiny sprain," I said. "Don't even feel it."

I moved toward the closed door, but Josie whispered, "She's sleeping now."

"Any word on the assessment?" I asked.

Josie said, "No head injury that they can see."

"That's good," I said, nodding in approval.

"They want to keep her overnight," Josie said, "for observation."

Josie looked shaken. Her expression had that intensity people get in emergencies—when every detail matters. It hadn't been an easy few hours, and that kind of stress is never good for you, but when you're just into your third trimester, it's maybe a little worse.

The sight of her gave me an impulse that I gave in to: I volunteered for a hug for the first time in a decade. "You did great," I said, wrapping my arms around her and giving a squeeze. "You did just fine."

"I needed that," she said when I let go.

I smiled. "I'm out of practice."

"But talented."

"Go home now," I said then. "Get some rest. You've had a rough day so far."

Josie nodded. "Not a big fan of hospitals."

"I've got this," I said, trying to sound way more at ease than I felt. "I do this for a living."

Josie took my hand and held it, and then peered at me like she was making a decision. Then she said, "She turned around, you know."

I frowned, thinking we were talking about the seizure. "She turned around?"

"On your birthday. The day she left. She drove for hours, crying the whole time, until finally, somewhere in Arkansas, she decided to turn around and go back. She couldn't do it, she decided. She couldn't leave. She pulled off at a truck stop, planning to get back on the interstate going south instead of north.

"Before she even finished at the pump, she got a call from Wallace. He was just checking in. Just saying hello. But the sound of his voice stopped her. She stood there for several minutes after they hung up. Then she called it: She couldn't leave him to face it all alone."

"And she kept going."

Josie nodded. "He needed her."

"*I* needed her," I said, almost a whisper.

"But you had your dad. She told herself you'd be all right."

My throat tightened. Oh God. What if she had turned around? What if she had showed back up at our house that night? Could my life have unfolded in a completely different way?

But it wasn't a real question. Even if she'd come back, it would have been too late. Even as she stood by the side of the highway in Arkansas deciding what choice to make, I had already made choices of my own.

There was no changing it. There was no possibility of a different story.

There was only what had happened. And how to carry on.

I looked up to see Josie smiling at me. Then she reached out and tucked a wisp of hair behind my ear. "She believed you'd be okay," she said again. "And she was right."

JOSIE WAS BARELY out of sight when a doctor appeared beside me.

"You're the fireman?" he asked, looking me over.

"I'm the fireman," I said, looking him over right back.

"She told me about you."

He had a couple of black nose hairs poking down out of his right nostril. "What happened?" I asked, staring at them.

"Fairly common, in her situation," he said. "I'm surprised it hasn't happened before."

I looked up. "You mean the eye? The blindness?"

"It was an occipital seizure," he confirmed. "That explains the hallucinations and the blurred vision afterward. Also the headache. All very common with this region."

Hallucinations? Blurred vision? "I don't understand how blindness in an eye could cause seizures."

He frowned at me. "It's not the eye causing the seizures. It's the tumor."

I stopped breathing.

Didn't breathe, didn't blink.

The tumor?

The doc walked me over to a computer station in the hallway and pulled up her CT-scan images on the screen. He circled a white area inside my mother's skull about the size of a Ping-Pong ball with his pen—as if anyone with eyes could miss it. He motioned for me to lean in. If he had any qualms about doctor-patient confidentiality, or the fact that she clearly had not told her daughter the fireman about the situation inside her skull, he did not mention them.

"Holy shit," I said, and I realized I was having the same feeling I'd had back at the station when Josie had called. Not clarity, but the opposite.

He nodded. "It's a doozie."

I didn't know what to say. But I felt like I should have something to say. Professionally, anyway. I scanned through my knowledge of types of brain tumors. "Glioblastoma?" I finally asked.

He shook his head. "It's not primary. It's secondary. A melanoma recurrence many years later. But it's large enough now to impact the brain."

Wait—she'd had a melanoma? Hospitals mixed up charts all the time. Maybe this doc was thinking of another old lady with a homemade calico eye patch.

"Is it malignant?" I asked.

"Oh, yes," the doctor said. He looked almost excited about it. And I got that. When you see these things all the time, sometimes the people behind them start to seem like a whole different story.

I shifted back a little.

"I'd say she has a few months," the doctor said, still staring at the screen. "A year at the most."

I felt a sudden collapse in my chest. *A year at the most.*

The doctor glanced over at me, read my face, and seemed to remember he was talking to a human. "I'm sorry," he said. "I guess she hadn't told you."

"She had not told me," I confirmed, keeping my eyes on the films in front of me, like I was studying them. Which I wasn't.

It seemed impossibly rude that he hadn't bothered to trim his nose hairs before delivering information like that—as if it were just some ordinary moment in some ordinary day.

The doc stared at the films alongside me, but I got the feeling he wasn't studying them, either.

I felt sorry for him, in a way. He never expected, popping in, that he'd be delivering this kind of news to an unsuspecting family member. I knew what it felt like, how it jolted the system. I knew how you had to gird yourself for it—go in fully armored. It was always the moments you didn't expect that haunted you the most.

I'd given bad news to hundreds of people over the years. Sometimes they collapsed to the floor. Sometimes they screamed, or erupted into sobs. Sometimes they went eerily silent. One woman had slapped me across the face.

For a second, I thought more about what that doctor must have been feeling in that moment than what I was.

Until he said, "Well. The good news is, she seems to be otherwise healthy. As far as we can tell."

I felt sorry for him right then, trying to come up with some good news. But I felt sorrier for me. Because there really was no good news.

THE DOCTOR WENT into the room after that, but I stayed in the hallway. I don't remember saying good-bye to him, or thank you, or whatever I must have said. I just remember the most searing feeling of cognitive dissonance. A total stranger, with one unexpected sentence, had just irrevocably changed the story of my life.

On the way into the hospital, I'd thought I might ask for an X-ray, but now my ankle was forgotten. I'd worry about it later, if it didn't get better. It was all I could do to soak the news in. My brain couldn't understand it. It was like a white fog inside my head where the comprehension should be.

A year at the most.

She'd known this whole time. She'd known, and she hadn't told me.

I felt my knees start to tremble, and because I wasn't ready to face her, I found a sitting area in the hallway. My brain didn't understand, but my body did.

Why hadn't I tried harder? Why hadn't I demanded to look at that eye? All the clues clicked into place, and I felt like an idiot for not having put it all together sooner. I had seen all the pieces, but I had refused to assemble them.

Maybe I hadn't wanted to. Things were different sometimes when the heart was involved.

But now I knew. There was no way to unknow.

I needed the details. I needed charts and histories and information. I wanted to see all her films, get the records of the surgery. I wanted to gather it all up and spread it out on the dining table like a code that I could read just right—better, smarter, than anybody else—and crack for her. I needed to know what was going on. How could I help her if I didn't have the full story? But maybe not even she had the full story.

I noticed, the way you might with a patient, that my breathing was accelerated.

Some part of me understood that she was beyond help. That doctor had not said, *Get her into surgery, stat!* He hadn't talked about any treatments at all. If this were something that could be cured—they would be trying to cure it right now. The fact that we were crocheting baby blankets for preemies at the hospital instead of going there for radiation treatments seemed to confirm that there weren't any treatments left.

It all made sense now.

How thin she was. How vague she'd been on all the details. The goofy collection of eye patches. This was why she'd called me here. This was why she'd asked me to give up my entire life. This was what we'd been doing all this time.

We were saying good-bye.

Why hadn't she told me? It seemed so unfair—that I hadn't been informed.

I might not have done anything differently. But I might have thought about things differently. I might not have wasted so much time.

It filled me with panic. We were running out of time! What was she doing sitting around in the garden and making soup and crocheting blankets with a deadline like this? There had to be something more important for her to do with her time than watch '80s rom-coms. Weren't there people to see? Conversations to have? Travel?

Or maybe she just wanted to sit in the garden and breathe.

Complicated—always so complicated with Diana.

I don't know how long I sat out in that hallway with my head in my hands. An hour? Two? All I knew was, once I went into her room and saw her again, knowing what I knew now, it would be real. And I didn't want it to be real.

I stalled as long as I could. I stalled so long that when I finally forced myself through her door, she was asleep for the night. The lights were all dimmed, and the room was shadowy. I could make out the bruise on her forehead easily—it was almost black—but I didn't get too close. I didn't want to wake her.

Also, she wasn't wearing her eye patch. It was the first time since I'd arrived that I could see her face, unobstructed. Would I have been able to tell, if I'd seen? Maybe. I could see that the eye itself was a bit distended. But otherwise, there she was.

My mother. Exactly the same as always—and totally different.

I lowered myself into the visitor's chair beside her, held very still, and watched her sleeping face. I tried to imagine a world without Diana in it, but I couldn't. I just couldn't.

How had I wasted so much time? How had I let one disappointment shape the course of our relationship? More than that, why had I decided to blame her for everything that happened with Heath Thompson? Stupid. And wrong. Why hadn't I tried harder to see things clearly? Ten years I'd simmered in my own self-righteousness, holding my grudge against her as if the only way to win was to stay mad the longest.

As if there had ever been anything to win.

As if you don't always lose by definition when you push the people who love you away.

All she'd wanted was forgiveness. And I had flat-out refused to give it to her.

I will always remember that moment of my life—that night in the hospital, crouched in a chair in my mother's gray room, groping my way through the news of her death sentence, feeling it all, but completely numb at the same time.

I see it frozen in time, as if it's a painting.

In the memory, it's not my adult self, in my Lillian uniform with my crutches, that I see in that chair. It's me as a child, wearing my favorite nightgown from when I was about eight—the one with ruffles and little hearts. I'm barefoot, with those soft, chubby feet children have. My hair is long, and my mother has just brushed it before bed. And then I stand up in the painting and walk out of my place. I crawl into the hospital bed beside her, suddenly as small and lost as I'd ever been, trembling, gasping for air, seeing it all, every implication of everything I'd just learned, and at the same time, blinded by a fog of incomprehension.

I wedge myself between her and the railing.

I press against her soft warmth.

And I beg her with everything I've got not to leave me.

THE NEXT MORNING, when my mother opened her eyes, I was standing by her bed, assessing her bruise.

She met my eyes. Then she said, "Oh, sweetheart. They told you."

I nodded, trying to stand up taller—as if that might make me braver.

She held out her hand to me.

I took it. "Why didn't you tell me?" I asked.

"I just wanted to have some fun while we could." She gave me a smile. "This kind of news can be so depressing."

I gulped a little unexpected laugh.

"I just wanted to see you," she said, squeezing my hand. "I just wanted a little taste of how it used to be before . . . I knew Wallace was dying when I married him. But sometimes I wish I hadn't known. It's so hard to feel happy and sad at the same time."

Suddenly, I felt for her. For the first time ever, I looked at that moment when she drove away through her eyes—and with her heart. What must it have felt like to give up her husband and child for a man she knew she would also have to lose?

It must have been agony in every direction.

For the first time, I understood. In all the times I'd remembered that story, I'd experienced every single part of it from my own perspective, standing in my own sixteen-year-old shoes. Now, for the first time, I saw it unfold from a new angle. Hers.

And it changed the story.

I felt a wash of forgiveness through my body.

Now it was me, suddenly, who wanted forgiveness.

"I'm sorry I was so angry at you for so long," I said then.

She was ready for it. She patted me, like, *Nonsense.* "You were a kid. Sometimes it's easier to be angry."

"I was so stupid. I blamed you for things that weren't your fault."

"You were standing up for yourself. That's a good thing."

I hadn't thought of it that way.

She went on. "You thought I had rejected you, so you rejected me harder. It was very sensible, really. Self-protection. I admired it."

"But it was more complicated than that."

"You did what you needed to do to be okay. I always believed you'd come back to me. I just ran out of time to wait."

"I get it now, I think," I said. "I get what you said about love being powerful."

She nodded. "I bet you do."

I rubbed my eyes. "I wasted so much time."

She squeezed my hand again. "That's just the human condition, sweetheart. We're always doomed to waste our time."

My brain was circling around, trying to put all the new information together. "That's it, then? You're not doing any treatments?"

"Did the doctor show you the brain scans?"

I nodded.

She gave me a look like, *Well, there's your answer.*

"I don't know what to do now."

"Just be here," she said. "Just be nearby."

More tears from me.

"It's okay. It's better in a way," she said. "We aren't meant to last forever. I wouldn't have wanted to spend my last year getting cut up and drugged. I'd much rather be in the garden. Or painting pottery. Or walking by the ocean."

Of course, you can't argue with walking by the ocean, but when the end result of that is dying, it sounds a little less ideal.

"There's nothing else to try? Nothing even experimental?"

"There was some experiment I could have joined, but I declined. It sounded awful."

I sat up. "What? Really? What was it?"

"Some new drug. Some clinical trial. I said no."

"What? Why would you say no?"

"I don't want to take any more drugs. I've had enough medical intervention for a lifetime."

"But it's just medicine."

"With gruesome side effects. The least gory of which is 'fatal skin infection.'"

"I'm just saying, what if it worked?"

"What if it didn't? And then I'm killed by my own skin?"

"At least that way, there's a chance."

"Not one worth taking."

In that moment, it seemed like she wasn't trying. "You have to try it! Call them back! Tell them you've changed your mind! You can't be a quitter. You have to keep fighting!"

She shook her head, infuriatingly calm. "I am fighting. In my own way."

"How?" I said. "How are you fighting?"

She looked me straight on. "I've been meditating three times a day since my last checkup."

"Meditating? You're fighting recurrent melanoma with *meditation*?"

"I think it's working," she said.

"What's working?"

"I should have had many more seizures by now, in fact. That's a very promising sign."

"What are you talking about?"

My mom gave me a smile. "When I first got the prognosis, I read everything I possibly could about it—like you do."

I nodded.

"And one of the articles I read was about a French woman with basically my same situation who had managed to halt the growth of her tumor through creative visualization."

I shook my head. "What did she visualize?"

"She mediated three times a day, and she very specifically imagined a hard shell growing around her tumor—so hard that it was compressed inside and couldn't get any bigger."

I made a conscious effort not to roll my eyes.

"It *worked*," Diana said. "She'd been going downhill rapidly—but then her decline slowed, then stopped entirely. She didn't die for another seven years, and that was in a car crash. Totally unrelated! When they autopsied her tumor, guess what they found?"

"What?"

"A shell. A hard shell around it. And it hadn't grown at all."

I shook my head. "That's urban legend. That can't be real."

"It is real. It's documented."

"You can't just imagine a tumor away!"

"Maybe not," she said. "But there's certainly no harm in trying."

Twenty-three

AND SO WE went home. And made supper. And sat in the garden while the sun went down. There was nothing else to do.

It hit me in strange waves. There were moments when I felt gutted, and moments when I felt almost normal; moments when I felt at peace with Diana's acceptance, and moments when I felt panicked to do something; moments when I felt like somehow, when all was said and done, everything would be okay, and moments when it seemed like nothing would ever be okay again.

Remember when I was all about trying to keep my life from getting destabilized?

Yeah, that whole concept got shot to hell.

I had four days before my next shift. Four days to figure out how to face the rest of my life. So I just helped Diana weed her garden, and I helped her make supper. We looked through old photo albums and sang Christmas carols, even though it wasn't Christmas. She showed me her old diaries and old portfolios from art school. She walked me through her jewelry box and tried to educate me about which long-gone relatives had owned which rings and necklaces and charm bracelets. We drank a lot of coffee and made a lot of tea. We made sure not to miss the sunsets.

I tried, with at least partial success, to savor the time we had left. That was the goal, anyway—to enjoy her living presence near me and not fixate so much on the sorrow to come that I forgot to pay attention. To learn to make the best of things. As fast as I could.

Every night that week, after supper, the rookie showed up at the front door, wanting to check on us, or do something for us, or help.

But I wouldn't answer it.

He came anyway, though, and left tubs of scones and muffins and cookies for comfort.

We brought them in later and arranged them on the kitchen table. But I couldn't eat.

Finally, on the last night before our next shift, he knocked—and kept knocking.

"Me again," he said, when I finally opened the door.

He'd been texting me, too—to see how my mom was, and how my ankle was, and how I was doing about the brick. He'd left a few messages. But I hadn't answered anything.

I wasn't ignoring him, exactly. I just had no idea what to say.

How could I put any of this into words?

The sight of him there, in the doorframe, felt like salvation. I wanted to grab onto him like a life preserver in an empty ocean.

Instead, I made myself keep treading water. If I stopped, I'd never start again.

"You can't be here," I said to him, like the threshold was some great barrier neither of us would ever cross.

"I need to talk to you."

"I can't. You know? It's too much."

"I know. You just got this stalker thing dealt with—I hope—and the last thing you need is me showing up like a pain in the ass."

"It's not that."

"I just need to see you."

I shook my head.

"Five minutes. Please."

I'd been afraid to leave the house since finding out about my mom. Afraid she might . . . disappear, maybe. But she'd gone to bed for the night already—cranked up her white noise machine and closed her door. What was I going to do? Sit in the hallway and guard the stairs while she slept?

I could give Owen five minutes.

I hung the dish towel on the coat rack and stepped over the threshold.

Owen backed up less than he should have, and then there we were, standing way too close.

"What now?" I said.

"I just want to see you."

I held my arms out like, *Voilà.*

"Can we just . . . talk? I have questions for you."

"Fine," I said, and started down the front walk. I didn't even limp. I wondered if he'd forget about my ankle.

"How's your ankle?" he asked then.

"Fine," I said. "I've been off the crutches since yesterday."

"Actually fine?" he asked. "Or firefighter fine?"

"Firefighter fine," I conceded. "But it's much better than it was. I'm being careful."

"You're limping a little."

But I disagreed. "I'm not limping at all."

"You're walking gingerly, then."

Funny to start with the ankle. It was the least of my worries now. "Next question."

"Okay," he said, following. "Tell me how your mom is."

I took a deep breath. Then I just said it, fast, like ripping off a Band-Aid. "She has a brain tumor. That's what caused the seizure. It's a recurrence of melanoma. It's malignant and very aggressive. She has a year to live at the most."

The rookie had not been expecting that. He was quiet for a minute.

I intended to keep walking, but when I got to the garden gate, I slowed to a stop.

The rookie stopped beside me. "Did you know?" he asked, his voice softer.

"I didn't know anything. She didn't tell me. She actually told some fibs to throw me off. But I knew something wasn't right."

"How is she?"

"Weirdly, she's okay most of the time."

"How are you?"

My voice caught in my throat. I felt myself straighten and stiffen, like that might help. "I am struggling," I said.

"Now you really need that hug," Owen said.

Maybe I did. Somehow, though, it felt like that would make things worse. I shook my head at him. "Don't hug me," I said, and started walking again.

"Okay."

We walked awhile without talking. Honestly, how could you follow that? Hell of a conversation killer.

So we didn't talk, but Owen stayed right there with me. In this moment, given everything, it was better than talking.

After a good while, Owen asked, "Should I distract you? What can I do?"

"What were your other questions?"

"They all seem stupid now."

"Ask me anyway."

"Okay. Do you know how much you shocked the hell out of everybody on the course the other day?"

I smiled a little to myself. It seemed like a different life, but the memory of it felt strangely good. Like it broadened my perspective to remember other things that mattered.

"They can't stop talking about it," he said. "You're a legend."

"That works," I said. "I'm good with 'legend.'"

It felt like maybe that was it for his questions. We walked a little longer, until we made it out to the spot where the road ended and the rock jetty began, and then we sat on one of the benches there, at the turnaround at the end of the road, watching the evening sky over the water.

It did feel good to get out. The wind. The ocean. The stars. The universe. I was surprised how soothing it was to be in the presence of things greater than myself.

"I also wanted to tell you," Owen said, after a while, "that I talked to my father. About the fire."

I looked into his face for the first time since he'd arrived. "You did?"

He nodded. "We had a few beers first, but I told him everything."

"I wasn't pushing for that, you know."

"I know. But it felt like the right thing to do."

"How did he take it?"

"It was rough," he said. "At first, he kept shaking his head and saying, 'But there were only two boys.' But I kept repeating that the witness had been wrong until it sank in. It stirred a lot up for him about my uncle. His voice got gruff, and his eyes got pretty red."

"Was he angry?"

"I don't think so. Though it can be kind of hard to tell with my dad."

"What did he say?"

"Actually, I told him that I'd always worried I might have been the one who threw the matchbox. That I'd been trying to remember for twenty years if it was me or not. But he said no. He was there in the room when my friend Stevie gave his testimony, and Stevie described throwing the box. My dad remembered it specifically because what Stevie had said was so odd: He said that as soon as he lit it, he thought it looked like a flaming hedgehog. And then, the minute my dad said that, I remembered something: I saw a flash in my memory of Stevie throwing the box and shouting, 'Hedgehog!' It all came back."

I let out a long sigh of relief. The rookie hadn't thrown the box. He hadn't started the fire—not directly, anyway. What inexpressible comfort he must have felt to know that.

"So now you know it wasn't you," I said.

He thought for a second. "I was still a part of the group. But it's nice to know I didn't actually throw the hedgehog."

I pushed my hands down into my pockets and turned toward the water.

The rookie leaned toward me. "Anyway, thank you. I've done a lot of thinking about forgiveness since I talked to you that day. I've tried to come up with good things that came out of what happened, even as bad as it was."

"And?"

"I'm starting to think maybe the aftermath of it all wound up shaping my life. In good ways, as well as bad. I couldn't change the past, but with every choice going forward, I tried like hell to do the right thing." He gave a little shrug. "It definitely forced me to define who I wanted to be."

"And do you feel better?" I asked. "Since telling your dad?"

"I think so," he said, nodding. "Although I still have one thing left I need to tell him."

"What's that?"

He hesitated a second, and then he said, "I'm quitting the fire department."

Wait—*what?*

"I need to talk to my dad first, of course. He and my mom are down in Boston this week, but I'm planning to cook them dinner once they're back and break the news. You know, delight them with some amazing meal, and then say, 'That food in your belly? I want to do that all the time.' Then I'll make it official with the captain."

I was still catching up. "Wait. You're—what?"

He nodded. "You were right. I should be cooking."

I was right? I didn't want to be right! That was the last thing I wanted—no matter how much I'd benefit. He was my favorite person in the firehouse. He might be my favorite person, period. Suddenly, words my captain in Austin had said to me flashed into my head: *Find one person you can count on.*

I took a step back. "Can't you do both?" I asked. Most firefighters had two jobs. Some had three.

He shook his head.

I knew my reaction was totally irrational. We couldn't both stay. If he stayed, if he fought for his position and won, then I would lose. Him leaving meant I could stay. It might well have been part of why he was doing it—to do something kind for me.

I knew all this in my head.

But, in the moment, given all the sadness that already surrounded me, all I could focus on was *the leaving.* My heart rate sped up. Was it panic? Was it anger? All I can say is, I just wasn't sure I could take one more person leaving me.

Not today.

"I'm no good," he said, giving me a look. "You know that."

"You can practice!" I said. "You can work to get better!"

He shook his head. "I don't think I want to get better."

Really? He wasn't even going to try? Hadn't we become friends? Hadn't we—I don't know—come to matter to each other?

"Where will you go?" I asked. "Back to Boston?"

He gave a shrug, like he wasn't sure.

I felt a sting in my chest, right behind my sternum. Owen was leaving. With the possible exception of the night I watched my mom drive off down our street, it was the sharpest feeling of abandonment I could ever remember.

But I'd never been comfortable with sorrow. I'd much rather be angry. So I just stood up and walked away, as fast as I could while still being careful of my ankle.

"Hey!" he said, following after me. "Where are you going?"

I kept walking. "It's fine. Go to Boston."

"I'm trying to help you!"

"I don't need your help!"

"You of all people know I'm not right for this job," he said, like there was some kind of logical argument to be made.

"That's not a reason to quit. Is that who you want to be? A quitter? I've spent months trying to help you. I've got veins like Swiss cheese from all those sticks. I've taught you everything I know. But here's something else I know. You can't make people stay if they don't want to. People leave all the time. They look around one day and say, 'You know what? Never mind. I'm out.' I certainly can't stop you, and I'm sure as hell not going to try."

"Hey," Owen said, trying to grab my arm to turn me around.

I yanked my arm out of his grasp.

"Hey!" he said, trying again. "I'm not finished!"

I yanked away again. "I am."

And then I took off running, ankle and all. He wanted to leave? Fine. I would leave *harder.*

But he took off running, too—right behind me. His feet smacked the pavement right behind mine. I sped up—or tried to, though I could tell my ankle wasn't going to put up with it much longer. Was getting away worth reinjuring myself? Who cared? *Good. Fine. Whatever.*

That's when Owen caught me. Reached out and grabbed the back of my T-shirt and broke my momentum—and as soon as he did, it was like snapping a rubber band. I stopped running altogether and turned to face him, right there in the middle of the road, panting.

"What?" I said, more like a yell.

"Cut it out! You're going to sprain the other one."

"I don't care."

He was panting, too. "Can I just talk to you?"

Here's what I was doing: shutting down. When I watch that moment in my memory, knowing everything I know now, it seems so crazy to me how angry I was. He was trying to help me. He was making sure I could keep my job. He was giving me the thing I wanted most in the world.

Except the thing I really wanted most was him.

All I can say is, I wasn't good at feelings. I'd spent my life carefully avoiding them. And now, since moving to Rockport, it had been one tidal wave of them after another—the crush, the kiss, the stalker, my mother . . . It's easy to heckle the screen of my memory and say, *Just let the man talk!* But in the moment, I truly felt like I might drown in emotion—as all the feelings of loss and abandonment unleashed—and so I did the only thing I could think of to rescue myself, the thing I'd always done for all these years to stay safe . . .

I shut it down.

"No," I said. "I have to go."

"I just—"

"Nope," I said, turning and striding back toward Diana's front door. "I can't."

I expected him to follow me.

But he didn't.

He let me go.

When I got to the door and pressed against it, gripping the handle, I turned halfway back, ready to tell him to leave again, and I was surprised to find myself all alone.

A second of relief—and then disappointment.

I turned farther, and I saw him walking away.

My shoulders sank.

I watched him unlock his truck and get in. I heard the ignition come on. And then he started driving off.

Good. Great.

But it didn't feel better to be rid of him. It felt worse.

"Wait," I whispered, staring after him, watching his taillights.

And then it was almost like he heard me.

His brake lights came on. And just stayed on.

I stepped away from the door to get a better look.

Then he was hooking a U-turn and driving back up the street toward me.

He stopped a few houses away and flipped off his lights, and before he'd even opened his door, I was moving through the garden and down the road to meet him. Ankle be damned.

I stopped when I got close.

He shut the truck door behind him, turned to face me, and then leaned back against it.

We faced off like that for a minute.

Finally, he said, "Did somebody hurt you, Cassie?"

I felt a flash of alarm, as if I'd been found out. "What?"

"The way you push me away," he said, "it's like you think other people are dangerous."

"Other people *are* dangerous," I said.

He waited for more, and when it didn't come, he said, "So. Did somebody hurt you?"

My first idea was to say some tough-guy thing, like, "Please." But that wasn't going to work, because there were already tears on my face.

I'd already answered his question. There was no sense in pretending.

So, very slowly, I just nodded.

"Was it a guy?"

I nodded again.

"Was it bad?"

I nodded again.

And then he knew. All the pieces clicked into place for him, and he just knew.

"I don't want to talk about it," I said.

"You don't have to talk about it."

"Good," I said, wiping my cheeks with my palms.

In my whole life, there was nobody who knew, except maybe my old captain in Austin, and possibly—once they'd seen me beat the crap out of Heath Thompson—my old crew, and then, I guess, by extension, the entire ballroom of the city's bravest who'd been in attendance that night.

Still, it felt like a milestone.

The rookie didn't take his eyes off me. "Can I tell you something?"

"Okay."

"I'm not going to hurt you."

"Everybody hurts everybody," I said, "eventually."

"Fair enough," he said. "I might do stupid things. I might forget to pick up milk at the grocery store, or step on your toe when I'm not looking, or do something I don't even understand, like I just did tonight. But I'll never be cruel to you. Not knowingly."

No sense arguing. I knew that was true.

Then I did a crazy thing. I hugged him.

This wasn't the first hug I'd initiated lately—I'd given quite a record number to Diana and Josie in the past few days—but it was the first hug

I could remember in years that I wanted for myself. Something about the expanse of his chest, so close to where I was standing, looked so solid and reassuring—and like a place I just wanted to be. I leaned in to rest my head against it, and the rest of me just followed.

We leaned against the car like that for a good while. I listened to his heartbeat, and his breathing.

Then, through his chest, I heard his muffled voice. "And there's one more thing."

I lifted my head, stepped back a little to see his face.

He took a deep breath, like he wasn't even sure where he was headed. Then he said, "I am in love with you."

I don't know what I was expecting—but I promise this wasn't it.

He went on. "It's bad. And that kiss that night—it only made things worse. That's why I'm quitting—partly, anyway. It's that bad. It's made things kind of unbearable for me at the station. I suspect you've known all along. It must have made you so angry. You're there to do a job—and you've got this house full of guys who underestimate you like every minute of the day—and the last thing you need is some rookie mooning over you."

Now he was making me smile. *"Mooning?"*

"Pretty much."

"Since when?"

He met my eyes. "Since the first day."

"The first day?" I asked. "The first day at the station?"

He nodded.

"The day they sprayed you with the hose?"

He nodded again.

Holy shit.

He went on. "Nothing would ever happen. Of course. I wasn't ever even going to tell you about it. Can you imagine the guys? If they even suspected—even if you didn't condone it or even know—they'd give you endless shit about it. They'd make the firehouse a living hell. For both of us. Right?"

"Right," I said.

"So I had to stamp it out. Or hide it so well nobody would ever guess."

I kept my voice cool. "I did not guess."

"I was doing okay," he said. "I was really working on it."

"Working on what?"

"Um," he said. "On not letting myself talk to you except when absolutely necessary. Not touching you unless forced by the captain. Not following you around. Not asking for advice. Not, you know, staring at you longingly—or even stealing glances the way I might've if I were the only person at stake. And just basically trying not to even think about you." He gave a little shrug. "Failing most of the time on that one, but genuinely trying."

He looked down at his shoes. "But then—that kiss. It kind of broke everything. It made me wonder if maybe I wasn't totally alone in all that stuff."

Um, no. He was not totally alone. But I held still.

He went on. "So that's why I'm telling you. Because I'm never sure, when you push me away, if you really want me to go."

I took a step closer, and then another, until my body was right up against his, like it had just been—except this time, rather than curling down against his chest, I reached up, stretched against him, and brought my face close to his.

A very different vibe.

Then I looked straight into his eyes.

"I don't want you to go," I said.

And then I wrapped my arms behind his neck, pulled him closer, stood up on my tiptoes, and kissed him.

I never even made a choice—or maybe I'd made the choice long before.

I kissed him there in the street, up against his truck, as long as either of us could stand it. I leaned in. I owned it. I pressed against him and tried to absorb that solidness of his chest. I caressed him and tasted him and just let myself fully melt into the moment. Then I pulled back, a little breathless, and said, "If I took you upstairs, could we keep doing what we're doing?"

He gave me a wry smile. "I am very grateful to be doing what we're doing."

"But," I added, wanting to be clear, "not go any further."

"Just kiss, you mean?"

I nodded.

"You're asking if I'm willing to go up to your room and kiss you?"

I nodded again. "For a good long while."

He kissed me again. "I am definitely willing to do that."

"I'm going to have to take things very slow, is what I mean."

He nodded. "Of course."

"Could we go upstairs and sleep together—actually sleep?"

He smiled bigger, all teasing. "Firefighter Hanwell, are you proposing that we *snuggle*?"

I gave a barely-there smile of my own. "I guess that's one way to describe it."

"I'll take anything. I'd sleep on a bed of nails to be next to you."

I turned and started pulling him toward the house. "That's actually perfect, because my bed is made of nails."

"Sold," he said. "I'm in."

I led him through the garden, over the threshold, up the slanted stairs, and through my attic door. We kissed and stumbled the whole way.

It's amazing how brave you can be when you feel safe. I walked him backwards to the foot of my bed, and I tugged on him to sit down. When he sat, I climbed on top of him, perching on his thighs, my arms around his neck, my face right there with his.

We just kept kissing. And the more we kissed, the more I relaxed into the moment, and the more I gave in to all the goodness of being close to him. It was like a tiny, wordless negotiation: Each time I took a step closer and he met me with tenderness, I took another step closer. The closer I got, the closer I wanted to be.

I pulled his shirt off and threw it on the floor, and then there he was, half-naked, all smooth skin and contours. Then I pulled my own shirt off, and there I was in my sports bra—exactly as I'd been with him so many times at the station, as he put EKG pads on me or checked my spine.

Of course, this was nothing like those other times.

When he ran his palms up, then back down, the skin of my back, he wasn't checking my vertebrae. He wasn't working to maintain professional distance. He was doing the opposite. He was trying to get as close as possible.

And so was I.

I ran my hands over him, just absorbing the warmth and the softness, and the landscape of his muscles and the miracle of getting to touch him at all.

Then I pushed him back until he was lying down.

I scooted forward and traced his six-pack with my fingers.

His breath came out like a shudder.

It's amazing how much context matters. I knew Owen. I'd seen him in action. I'd worked with him all these months, and I'd seen him make the right, kindhearted, compassionate choice time and again. The man spent his free time baking cookies, for God's sake. He brought puppies home in baskets. I trusted him. I cared about him. And the more I kissed him, the more I wanted to kiss him.

"Thank you for coming upstairs," I said.

He met my eyes. "Thank you for inviting me upstairs."

"This is a big deal for me."

"For me, too."

"But you've been in a girl's bedroom before."

He shook his head. "Not in the bedroom of a superhero."

"I'm not a superhero."

"You're pretty damn close."

"I'm the opposite, in a lot of ways."

"It's possible that you don't fully know how awesome you are."

"That's distinctly possible."

He met my eyes. "But I do."

The intensity of his gaze made me feel shy.

"I think about you all the time," he confessed then. "In between shifts, all I'm doing is waiting to see you again. Then, during shifts, I can't concentrate. I'm supposed to be filling out time logs, but all I can see is that one wisp of hair you can't seem to keep in your ponytail holder."

I started to lean in for another kiss, but he stopped me.

"I think you are so beautiful," he went on slowly, deliberately, "that it's blinding. But it's not just that. When I look at you, I just see all the things I admire. It's all the badass stuff about you, sure, like the way you're so calm when all hell's breaking loose, and the way you can toss a three-point shot backwards without even looking and make it with nothing but net, and don't get me started on the one-arm pull-ups. It's how you never panic and nothing scares you. But it's also that your first career goal was to be the Tooth Fairy. And that you hum to yourself when you're washing the dishes. And that when you laugh really, really hard, you run out of breath and start squeaking like a mouse."

"I don't squeak like a mouse."

"There's all this toughness about you—but the most impressive thing about that toughness, I think, is that you built it to protect the tenderness."

I blinked at him. Who was this guy? "It's not true that nothing scares me," I said then. "You scare me."

He let out a laugh. "I am far too lovesick to scare anybody."

I had to clarify something. "Are you lovesick?" I asked.

He met my eyes. "Horribly."

"About me?" I asked, just making sure.

He gave me a look like I was adorable and ridiculous and lovable, all at once. Then he nodded and got serious again. "Every single minute of every single day."

"It's not you that scares me," I said. "It's the things I feel about you."

"The things I feel about you scare me, too," he said, looking very serious. "We'll just have to be very careful with each other."

"Okay," I said. Agreed. Next, I kissed him breathless.

"We can stop whenever you want," he kept saying.

"Okay," I'd say, and keep going.

The official plan was to snuggle. But I just kept kissing him instead.

I don't know how long this had been going on—an hour, maybe?—when I started tugging at his pants, like I wanted him to take them off. I'm not even sure what my plan was, exactly. I just wanted there to be fewer barriers between us. I just wanted to get rid of everything that was in the way.

He shook his head. He didn't break the kiss, but he pulled my hand away. "Nope. Not a good idea."

I went back to tug some more. "Why not?" I said, not breaking the kiss, either.

"Because we had an agreement. And I'm trying to stick to it."

"But the agreement was more about me than you."

He squinted at me, like, *Kind of.* "True. Ish."

"So if anyone should be allowed to amend the agreement, it should be me."

"We're not amending the agreement."

"Because we don't have protection?"

At that, Owen squeezed his eyes closed.

"What?"

"We do, actually, have protection."

"We do?"

He put his hand over his eyes. "My cousin Alex put a condom in my pocket at the party."

I thought about that for a second. Problem solved. I went back after the pants.

"Nope," the rookie said.

"Why not?"

"I don't want you to regret anything."

"I won't."

"You don't know that."

Maybe he was right, but I was willing to find out. "Don't you want to?" I asked.

He honked out a hoarse laugh. "There are not enough words in the universe to describe how much I want to. But we can't."

"I think we can."

"Cassie," he said, lifting up on his elbows, "I don't want to mess this up with you."

His saying no had the opposite of the effect he intended. It didn't discourage me. It freed me up to go forward.

His saying no just made me say yes harder.

I pushed him back down on the bed and started working on him to change his mind. I kissed him with new purpose. I ran my hands through his hair. I draped myself over him.

He kept talking. "We don't have to rush things."

But I could tell he'd closed his eyes. And the way he was breathing—so deep and fast—I could tell that I was melting his resistance.

"We can do this anytime," he went on, still protesting. "Life is long."

"Life is not long," I said, running my hand over his torso. "It's short."

"I think we should wait," he said, kissing me back just as hard.

I was winning. Or maybe we both were. But I could feel him giving in.

Then I pulled back and looked him in the eyes. I had a serious question. "Do you think, if we got started, but then it wasn't good for me, you could stop? After starting, I mean?"

He gave me a serious answer. "If we got started and it wasn't good for you, I wouldn't want to do anything *but* stop."

"I might need to stop," I said. "I don't know. But what I do know—right now—is that I'd really, really, really like to get started."

WE DIDN'T STOP.

I never even thought about stopping again after that.

All that closeness, and trust, and time we'd spent together—plus the fact that he was a Nobel Prize–level kisser—made it easy. There were fumblings and mistakes, and moments of self-conscious laughter. The point is, we laughed a lot, and we stumbled along, and we took things slow, and fast, all at the same time. At one point, he accidentally pulled my hair. A little while later, I accidentally elbowed him in the cheekbone. Somewhere in there, for a few scary minutes, he thought he'd lost Cousin Alex's condom—which, laughing with relief after he found it, we decided would be a great name for a garage band.

But as goofy and silly and fun as everything that happened between us in that room, that night, on my virginal white bed, was—it was serious, too. And had nothing to do with the past or the future. We were just alive, and together, and happy—right then and right there.

Would it always be just exactly like this? Of course not.

The rookie was leaving, my mother was dying, and the world was full of monsters. Good things didn't last, people hurt each other every day, and nobody got a happy ending. But that night with him made me see it all in a new way. All the hardships and insults and disappointments in life didn't make this one blissful moment less important. They made it *more.* They made it matter. The very fact that it couldn't last was the reason to hold on to it—however we could.

Yes, the world is full of unspeakable cruelty. But the answer wasn't to never feel hope, or bliss, or love—but to savor every fleeting, precious second of those feelings when they came.

The answer wasn't to never love anyone.

It was to love like crazy whenever you could.

So I kissed him back. And I made a choice to believe in that kiss. I stripped us down until there were no barriers left, and I made a choice to get started and see what happened.

What happened was good. What happened was just exactly what I needed.

There was something powerful between us, and I had this unshakable feeling that it could rebuild something essential that had crumbled inside me—the same way that laughter soothes sorrow, or company soothes loneliness, or a good meal soothes hunger.

It was a profound thing to realize. Love could heal me. Not the rookie, not some guy, but love itself—and my impossibly brave choice to practice it.

It really did turn out to be power, not weakness. The power to refuse to let the world's monsters ruin everything. The power to claim my right to be happy.

I made a choice to trust the rookie, but it was the choice that mattered the most.

I won't lie. Sleeping with the rookie that night was the hardest thing I'd ever done.

But it was also, without question, the easiest.

Twenty-four

THE NEXT MORNING, I woke up with a naked rookie in my bed.

I guess there's a first time for everything.

Woke up *late,* I should add, because, understandably, I'd totally forgotten to set my alarm.

Nothing about this situation alarmed Owen—but everything about it alarmed me.

"Get up, get up!" I said, pulling the blanket to wrap up in. "My mom's downstairs! It's morning! We're late! We're on shift today! Come on, come on!"

He opened his eyes and took in the sight of me with a look I could really only describe as blissed out.

"Come on, man! You're going to get me fired!" I stepped to the bathroom to run the shower, and when I came back in, he was just standing there, again, still, totally naked, fumbling for his pants. "Oh my God," I said, slapping my hand over my eyes. "You're so naked."

"That tends to happen when you take off your clothes."

I peeked through my fingers. "Do you want to know how many naked men I've had in this room?"

"Not really."

"Zero!"

"Until today."

"Until today."

"You're naked, too," he pointed out as he buckled his pants. "Under that blanket."

"We're going to be late," I said, back to business, "both of us, at the same time. They'll totally know what happened."

"They will not. I have a legendary poker face."

"I don't!" I was panting just a little. "Neither of us is ever late! Both of us late—together? We're screwed."

"Don't panic," he insisted, all chill. "I'll text the captain. I'll tell him your car broke down and I'm giving you a ride."

Actually, that was a good idea.

Plausible, at any rate.

"Go take your shower," he said then. "I'll make coffee." I started to turn, but then he said, "Wait! One quick thing!"

And then he was beside me, no shirt, no shoes, and he was wrapping his arms around me and the blanket. He pressed his face into my hair at the crook of my neck. "Thank you," he said then. "For everything."

THE GUYS DID not suspect us.

If they had, they would have teased us mercilessly. I waited for it all day, but it never happened.

So I just did what I do best: ignored the rookie and did my job.

It was a week before Owen would have a chance to talk to his dad, so we'd have at least two full shifts of doing this before anything changed. Whatever "this" was. It wasn't dating, that was for sure. I'd forbidden him to come near me again until this whole situation was resolved. I guess we were just keeping a shared secret. Or maybe nurturing a mutual crush. Or having flashbacks—luxurious, shocking, delicious flashbacks—of that glorious night in my attic room and the way the breeze had ruffled the pom-pom curtains.

Or maybe quietly, without even doing anything at all, we were just making each other happy.

It was weird to feel happy—especially when there was so much trouble and sorrow around us. But I just couldn't seem to help it.

So I let it be what it was. I let it alter my experience of being on shift in ways that didn't matter and ways that did. I was supposed to be a robot, but I'd become the opposite of that. Instead of metal and machinery inside my rib cage, it was music and motion and color. It was grief about my mother, and euphoria about Owen, and hope for the future and regret for the past—all swirling together in some relentless symphony.

Distracting.

I wasn't sure it made me bad at my job, though.

If anything, it seemed to make me better—more committed, more alert. More alive.

It wasn't easier. It was harder.

But it was better.

I made it through a whole week like that, trying to let everything that had happened soak in and start making sense in my head. It did and it didn't, and my mom insisted that was okay. That's just how the heart worked, she said—more in circles than straight lines.

Owen kindly respected my wishes and did not come to see me on our days off.

But he called every night at bedtime.

And I'd lie in my attic bedroom on the phone like the hopeful teenager I'd never really had a chance to be, my bare feet against the window, watching the moon through the curtains for hours, as we talked ourselves to sleep.

THEN, DURING THE last shift before Owen would explain everything to his dad and officially resign, we got a call for a structure fire.

This was not a little garage fire on the edge of town. This was a grocery store, right in the middle, and a fire that had started in the early hours of the morning and built momentum until sunrise, when the manager witnessed a black column of smoke rising from the roof as he pulled in to work.

When we arrived, a crowd already lined the road. We were the first crew on scene.

This was a big fire.

The sight of a blazing structure fire is really mesmerizing. There are always crowds, and the crowds are stupider than you might think. Sometimes they harass the firefighters, sometimes they try to help, sometimes they try to get close up to take selfies.

We took a few minutes to assess the situation.

We were going to need backup. Lots of it.

The captain called in a second alarm. The fire chief was already en route, but he was headed in from Central, farther away. We got word from dispatch that Station Three was also on the way. Gloucester, too.

The unventilated building had spent the morning smoldering, filling with dark smoke. It was a 1960s-style box store with one entrance of glass doors at the front, and probably a door and a loading bay at the back. Windows don't break until temperatures get to around five hundred degrees, and the row of windows across the front of the store was still intact.

It was a pretty simple layout, but what made the scene complicated was that road access to the front and the back of the store was interrupted by a solid concrete block wall. The front opened onto a highway, but you could only get to the back of the store by going around the block to a backstreet.

From the looks of the smoke, the fire was concentrated toward the back.

The captain grabbed three guys—Tiny, Case, and Six-Pack—to drive around back, closer to the source. He ordered me, DeStasio, and Owen to stay in front with the ambulance, manage the crowd, and direct the chief and all backup crews around back when they arrived. "This is a defensive fire," the captain said as they loaded up, pointing at us. "No interior operations."

Meaning, *Don't go inside.*

No argument from me. That building was a deathtrap.

We waited out front, the three of us, but kept busy. The rookie kept an eye on the crowd, I manned the radio, and DeStasio went to inspect the building.

I don't remember now how we divvied up those jobs. I don't remember any discussion. Though later, I would find myself wishing that DeStasio had taken any other job at all.

Because as DeStasio inspected the entryway and the windows, he saw something that would change all our lives.

He saw a little boy inside the building.

Bystanders falsely see "someone in the building" all the time.

The smoke, the heat, the way it bends the air—it can make you see things. You can think you see a face at the window, but it's only smoke. You can think you hear someone screaming *Help!* but it's only a whistle of steam. Panic can crimp your mind. I've seen it happen over and over and heard plenty of stories. When a civilian says there's someone in the building, you say thanks and keep on doing what you're doing.

But when a firefighter says it, that's a whole different thing.

DeStasio showed back up out of breath. Like he'd been running. And firefighters never run. "You saw him, right?" DeStasio said. "You saw him?"

"Saw who?"

"Inside the building. Just inside the window. A boy."

I studied the windows. I couldn't see anything. "I don't see anyone," I said.

He looked over to Owen. "You saw him, right, rookie?"

Owen shook his head.

But DeStasio was already pulling on his bunker coat. "Let's get moving."

I started to get a bad feeling. "You want to go in?"

"There's a child in there," DeStasio said, like, *Duh*.

"We don't have the right equipment," I said, shaking my head. "We have to wait for backup."

Something flashed over DeStasio's face then—some kind of rage that I had never seen before. If I had to guess, I would say maybe being told he "had" to do something by a nonranking member of his crew—and a female, at that—didn't sit too well with him. It's also possible that he sensed I was doubting him about the child. I'd checked those windows, and I hadn't seen anything—and why would a kid be inside a grocery store at this hour of the morning? It didn't add up.

"What we have to do," DeStasio said, in a voice tight with outrage, "is get in there. Right now!"

"We've got orders to stay out," I said. "Backup will be here in ten minutes."

"No," DeStasio said. "We don't have time to wait."

Here was part of the problem: DeStasio, as he was constantly reminding me, had a lot more years in the department than I did. He was senior to me in every way—except one. I was a fully trained paramedic, and he was only an EMT.

Technically, even though he was the senior crew member, that made me the ranking medic on the scene.

Which might also account for some of that rage.

DeStasio turned toward Owen. "Get your mask on. We're going in."

"We have orders to stay out!" I said.

DeStasio leaned in, his eyes wild and vicious. "Radio the captain."

So I tried.

I grabbed my handheld and fired it up. "Captain," I said, "we've got a possible child trapped in the building. Over."

I waited for a reply, but I could only hear static.

I tried again. "Captain, requesting permission to enter the structure and check for victims. Over."

This time, his radio crackled to life, but it was half static and only half words. I couldn't tell what he'd said—and, in truth, it sounded more like I was overhearing him than receiving a message from him.

I looked at DeStasio. "I am not reading you, Captain," I said into the radio. "Please repeat. Over."

Another long blast of static. Could he read me?

"That's it," DeStasio said. "We're going in."

"We have orders *not* to go in," I said.

"Ask me if I care."

"That's insubordination," I said.

"Tell that to the dying boy inside."

DeStasio was already moving toward the building. He grabbed Owen as he went and pulled him along. Owen, of course, would have no choice but to follow DeStasio's orders. That's the essence of the paramilitary structure. DeStasio may have ranked below me, but Owen ranked well below us both.

"We have orders to stay out!" I shouted, again, following.

"That's not what I just heard."

"You heard static!" I said.

"We always go in. If there's even a chance someone's inside, we go in."

"Do not go in there!" I shouted. I ran past them and put my body between DeStasio and the entrance, standing my ground.

But there was that rage again. DeStasio came at me, shouting, his face red, spit collecting at the edges of his mouth.

I'd never heard DeStasio shout.

"I've been with this department longer than you've been alive!" he said, his face like a mask of agony. "When I started working with this captain, you were in diapers! We've fought more fires together than anybody can count! Don't tell me what we need to do! I know what to do! I could follow our captain's orders in my sleep! There's a boy in that building! We don't have time to wait! 'To Protect and Serve!' You want me to leave that little boy to burn to death, but I won't do it!"

"You can't go in there!" I shouted.

"You can't stop me!" He smacked Owen on the shoulder. "Rookie, come on."

In slo-mo, I watched as the rookie started to follow him.

"Rookie!" I shouted. "What are you doing?"

He turned and shook his head. "It's a deathtrap in there."

"Yeah," I agreed, raising my hands like, *What the hell?* "It's a deathtrap in there."

Owen shook his head, dead serious. "Can't let him go in alone."

Shit.

I checked the road for any sight of backup on the way. Still nothing.

And that's when I realized the crux of it. The rookie wasn't going to let DeStasio go in without him, and I wasn't going to let the rookie go in without me.

This was happening.

We were all doomed.

I tied a guide rope to a pole near the entrance, then turned on our PASS safety devices and secured our masks and air tanks. Sometimes, in a well-vented structure, you don't have to turn on your air right away—but this place was the opposite of well vented. I opened the valve on DeStasio's tank, DeStasio opened up Owen's, and Owen opened mine.

Time for a quick reminder. "Rookie," I said, "what's the average time the air in a thirty-minute canister lasts in a working fire?"

"Fifteen-point-six minutes," Owen answered.

"Very good," I said, tugging on the guide rope to make sure it was secure. "At the eight-minute mark, we come back out for new canisters—no exceptions. Even if your low-air alarm isn't going off yet. Even if DeStasio won't come with you. I am not letting you die today, got it?"

The rookie nodded.

I glared at the back of DeStasio's helmet. "This is the stupidest thing I've ever done at a fire," I said to Owen. "Stay at the perimeter of the building on the front wall. Stay in physical and verbal contact with me at all times. And whatever you do, do not get off the guide rope."

We might be okay.

Maybe.

We pushed open the sliding doors. Smoke came billowing out like from a dragon's mouth.

When you're working inside a burning structure, you can't expect to be able to see. The smoke is thick and dark and fills up the rooms. If the windows blow out, sometimes the smoke will dissipate, and if you stay low, you'll have some visibility—but there are no guarantees, and you find your way by feel. That's a particular skill: the ability to visualize rooms and construct mental floor plans in totally unfamiliar spaces without using your eyes. There's definitely a spatial relationships component.

Also a not-freaking-the-hell-out component.

The heat pushes you down anyway, and you sweep the rooms on all fours, keeping contact with the walls. In residential structures, you have to check under beds and in closets, because when kids are scared they tend to hide under furniture and in toy boxes or laundry hampers. But where would a kid hide in a grocery store? Where would we even start looking?

DeStasio had seen him at the front window. That's where we'd start, at the front perimeter. We'd have to stick together. The rookie had never been in a hard-core situation like this, and though we'd driven him through countless blindfolded drills, it wouldn't be the same. The heat, the time pressure, the blackness.

It's a whole different thing when you do it for real.

Normally, you never enter a structure without a hose line, both as a source of water to hold back the flames and as a lifeline back to the place where you entered. You stay on the hose—always, always—or risk getting lost in an unfamiliar space. You feel the couplings to know which way is out.

But we didn't have a hose. The hose had gone around back with the pumper.

Here's some irony: We'd ordered new radios, but they hadn't come yet. Even good radios were hard to work in tough conditions, but the static on the captain's line had been unacceptable. I read once that most firefighter deaths came back to communication problems, and that didn't surprise me at all.

Did I think what we were doing right now could lead to firefighter deaths?

Yes.

But we'd just have to work like hell and hope for the best.

And find the boy, if we could.

Inside, we worked our way around magazine stands and lines of carts.

I kept one glove on the guide line at all times, and alternated the other between feeling around the space and keeping contact with DeStasio's boot up ahead. The rookie was behind me, doing the same.

I worried about our air supply.

We'd been in five minutes. The smoke was thick. Somewhere, a window blew out, but the smoke didn't thin.

We kept crawling. I could only see filtered light down low and blackness up top.

Soon, I could see flames rolling across the ceiling.

It was going to be time to get out soon. I'd been in bigger fires than this, and hotter fires than this, but I'd never been so ill equipped. I remembered an old-timer back in Austin telling me when I was a rookie, "It's an emergency until you get there. Then it's just work."

Somehow, this felt like an emergency.

Sixty more seconds, I thought, *and then we're out of here.*

That's when I heard Owen's voice over my radio. Laughing. Actually, more like *giggling.*

"What's funny, rookie?" I asked.

But no answer. Only more laughter. Why was he on the radio?

I turned back to reach for him, but he wasn't there.

"Rookie?" I said. "Rookie, are you on the guide line?"

"I think I see a bunny rabbit," Owen said, through the radio. Or—that's what it sounded like.

"What is he babbling about?" DeStasio shouted, still moving forward.

More laughing through the radio.

There was no reason—*at all*—for the rookie to be laughing. Firefighters do plenty of laughing, but never, ever when they're working a fire. "It could be cyanide poisoning," I said. I'd learned all about it when I applied for the antidote kit. "It makes you kind of drunk at first before the real symptoms kick in."

In theory, Owen had been breathing the air from his canister. But we'd moved fast getting in here. His breathing apparatus could have been ill fitting. Or leaking. Or knocked loose without his realizing it.

"Rookie, where are you?" I couldn't see him. I beamed my flashlight behind me. But he wasn't there.

I felt a sting of panic in my chest. "DeStasio, stop! The rookie's off the guide line!"

DeStasio stopped.

I panned my flashlight around. Nothing but smoke. "Rookie, where are you?" I said into my radio. "What can you see?"

"Fluffy stuff," he replied.

I tried to make my voice so authoritative that he would obey me. "Look for the beam from my flashlight and move toward it!"

Then I saw him. Crawling toward me around the end of an aisle, maybe ten feet away.

Relief. Visual contact. All I had to do was get to him and bring him back to the perimeter.

I started to move toward him.

But then two things happened, one after the other. The rookie—who must truly have been not right in the head to do this—stood up, like he was just going to walk over.

And then the ceiling collapsed.

Twenty-five

THE SOUND WAS unreal—like a thousand cannons going off at once. The ground shook like in an earthquake for much longer than it should have.

Then stillness—and the room went white.

I couldn't see anything. Not even my hand in front of my face. I crawled toward where DeStasio had been, but I found an overturned shelf. I shouted into the radio, "Are you conscious?"

"I'm okay," he shouted back. "But something got my shoulder."

"Stay there, okay? I'm getting the rookie. I'll come back for you."

As I crawled through the whiteness, my radio crackled with a long blast of static—the captain, asking everyone in the crew to report their status. I reported in as I kept crawling, though I suspected the captain couldn't hear me.

Next, another blast of static, most likely the captain calling a Mayday—and then, seconds later, the sound of all the engines outside blowing their air horns at once for forty-five seconds. The sound that means, *Get the hell out. Now.*

But I was focused on another sound.

Because in the seconds before the air horns started, I heard something more urgent. The rookie's PASS device started going off. PASS devices let out a shriek if you're still for too long.

I'd heard the sound before, but never like this.

It meant he'd been still for at least thirty seconds.

And that could mean anything.

I kept crawling, unable to see anything at all in the whiteness, navigating my way through the spacc using my memories of what I had seen before the collapse to form a mental map. Was I going the right way? I had no idea. Had I passed right by Owen without even knowing it? Anything was possible.

But I couldn't change the visibility. All I could do was focus like hell. I could have been off by aisles, but there was nothing to do but try. If I was right about the cyanide poisoning, every second counted.

People say that emotions muddy your decision-making, but that wasn't my experience that day. How I felt about Owen—and the sound of that PASS device—sharpened my purpose to a knifepoint. It's like an article I once read about a teenage girl who'd lifted a car off her father after an accident and saved his life. Those were some pretty herculean feelings.

I thought about my mom saying, *Love makes you stronger.* And then I couldn't help but understand—clearly and brightly and inescapably—right there in the middle of it all, that I loved Owen. I loved him. And it wasn't stupid, or girly, or a waste of time. It was the thing that was going to save his life.

I was going to get him out of here.

Or die trying.

The white powder was starting to clear. Through the fog of it, with my flashlight, I caught a glimpse of what looked like Owen's boot. I felt it to confirm, and then I felt all around.

It was him.

Ceiling debris had come down on him, and I had to shove it aside before I could start dragging him back toward the exit.

It's a little bit ironic that the "fireman's carry"—that iconic image of firefighters throwing victims over their shoulders—is not actually a technique we use in fires. Heat rises, after all. You have to stay low. You'd never stand up with a victim over your shoulder.

So how do you get people out of burning buildings?

You drag them.

That's what I did with Owen.

Bunker gear even comes with a built-in strap behind the coat collar for that very purpose. Pull it, and webbing in the coat tightens around their body. I'd never had to use the strap before, but I found it in seconds and pulled.

The rookie weighed a thousand pounds, but I didn't even feel it. I stayed low and leaned all my weight back in the direction I needed to go, dragging him after me in short yanks, using every fiber of strength in my thighs, butt, torso, and shoulders to push us backwards like a machine and pull his dead weight behind me.

We made it to the exit just as DeStasio did, too.

"I told you to stay put," I said.

"I don't take orders from women," DeStasio said.

Guess how much time I had for that nonsense?

The sliding doors were still pried open, and together we dragged Owen out into the open air.

Backup had arrived, big-time. The scene outside was an absolute carnival of medics, pumpers, and rescue personnel. As soon as they saw us, they leapt into action. Some took DeStasio, and some came for me, but I deflected them.

I was fine.

A couple of medics grabbed Owen and hoisted him onto a rolling gurney.

I barely had time to get a good look at him before medics started working him right there, but I will never forget what I saw. His helmet was melted, and so was his mask.

His bunker gear was smoking, too.

There must have been a flashover when the ceiling fell.

The crew moved like lightning—ripping off his mask and helmet, pulling off his air tank, ripping open his gear, feeling for a pulse. I could see soot around Owen's nose and mouth—and second-degree burns at the edges of where his mask had been.

It's true that firefighters never run, but I knew this crew didn't have a cyanide kit on their box, because we were the only crew in Lillian that had one. Somebody needed to get it—stat—and that somebody was me.

I took off sprinting, grabbed the kit, and then sprinted back, just as a medic jumped on the gurney, straddled Owen, and started pumping compressions for CPR. "No pulse," he called out. "No respiration."

I glanced at Owen as I ripped open the kit box with my teeth, used the transfer spike to add sodium chloride, and rocked—but did not shake—the vial to mix the solution. Unconscious. Unresponsive. He was most likely in cardiac arrest.

I heard somebody say Life Flight was inbound.

Real CPR in a real emergency is nothing like anything you've done in a class on a dummy. It's ugly—almost brutal—and this is especially true when firefighters are working on one of their own. They don't hold back.

Another medic checked the defib monitor to see if we could shock him with the paddles. Yes. The rhythm was right. Everybody stepped back. Three quick shocks, and then they were back to CPR.

I grabbed Owen's arm and found a vein. I got the IV started, a perfect stick. The antidote can't be given in one injection. It has to enter the system slowly, over a period of ten minutes.

But no way was I going to stand there and hold an IV bag, especially not when the medic next to me, trying to pump air into Owen's lungs with a hand-squeezed bag, was having trouble. He listened to Owen's lungs with a stethoscope.

"Nothing's going in," he reported. "No movement."

"Tube him," I ordered, and he turned to find an airway kit.

But I stopped him. I handed him the antidote IV bag. "Hold this."

"I have to tube him!" he protested.

"I've got it!"

He stepped back, and I pulled out a pediatric airway kit. If the rookie's airway was burned, it could be swollen, and it's hard enough to intubate a normal airway.

The medic on top of him was still working his chest.

Others had removed Owen's bunker pants and were wrapping his lower half in a cold gel blanket to try to bring down his body temperature.

In my memory, this whole scene always replays itself in slow motion. I can see every detail, hear every word, stretched out and slowed down. In reality, it lasted barely a few minutes, and everything happened at once.

I stepped in, tilted the rookie's neck just right, started working the tube.

I heard Life Flight arrive, but I stayed focused.

The medic doing compressions kept his eye on me. "Come on, come on," he whispered.

It's hard enough intubating people—without the added pressure of it being another firefighter, a guy with your same job. A guy you know.

And if you happen to have slept with the person you're trying to tube? Even harder.

Anybody could find it freaky.

Fortunately for the rookie, I'm not anybody.

I eased the tube in like a pro. Three seconds flat.

I told you. You just know when you're good.

Another medic was listening with a stethoscope. "We've got air," he called out, just as Life Flight settled to the ground in the parking lot beside us.

With the air came the heartbeat.

"We've got a rhythm," the medic with the stethoscope called next.

It was only a short distance to the Trauma Hawk, and we all pushed the gurney toward the Life Flight crew. They took it like a baton in a relay, and we followed, shouting stats and information about his situation—

explaining the cyanide poisoning and antidote protocol, handing off the IV bag, making sure they knew everything.

As they loaded him up in the chopper, I took one second to find Owen's hand and give it a squeeze.

And then I had no choice but to let him go.

Twenty-six

LIFE FLIGHT TOOK Owen to Boston, and all I wanted to do was follow.

But there was still a fire to put out.

Our shift wasn't over.

The medics from Station Three treated DeStasio, who turned out to have a broken collarbone, and transported him to Fairmont Methodist. I was fine, and once they cleared me, I got back to work.

We still had a job to do.

No one else on our shift was injured. On the other side of the building, separated by that concrete wall and a faulty radio, the rest of our guys had followed the captain's orders, which had never changed: No internal operations.

It took four hours to put out the fire, even with crews from Gloucester and Essex pitching in. When it was out, there was still overhaul to do—making sure no pockets were still burning, and securing the site.

We were still on shift, after all.

Once word got out we had injured crew members, off-duty crews started showing up at the scene and then, later, at the station. That's what firefighters do. They show up. They offer relief. They look after each other. They help.

We got back to the station around four in the afternoon and found a makeup relief shift waiting for us. We couldn't have left to go home, or check on Owen or DeStasio, if they hadn't shown up.

I've never been more grateful to see anyone in my life.

Gray with soot, caked with salt and sweat, I knew that as soon as the adrenaline wore off, I'd collapse. There's nothing on this earth more exhausting than a big fire. Every foot of hose weighs eight pounds when it's full of water. We'd hauled 250 feet of hose that day, working the flames, feeding the line. No CrossFit regime or "fireman's workout" can even compare to what you're really doing when you work a fire. You come back blistered, chafed, and dehydrated from the inside out—with your shoulders, back, hands, and basically every cell in your body stinging and aching.

At first you barely feel it. Adrenaline distracts you.

Then it hits.

Despite it all, after we got off shift, all the guys were heading to Boston to check on Owen. The chief and the captain were already there—had gone straight from the scene. I headed toward my truck a few steps ahead of the guys, but Tiny and Six-Pack followed me and climbed in the passenger side without even asking.

We drove in silence. The sky drizzled rain the whole way, and I remember thinking how strangely loud the wipers sounded. I'd never noticed how loud they were before.

The captain had sent group texts to our entire shift several times with updates, but they were vague: The rookie's heart rate and breathing had stabilized, but he had a collapsed lung. They were keeping him in a medically induced coma for the foreseeable future. They were going to treat him in the hyperbaric chamber and then take him to the ICU.

My brain jolted around from thought to thought. I'd see the rookie, sleeping safe and alive in my bed, and then the channel would skip to his melted mask and his smoking gear. I'd feel the memory of his mouth on mine, and then I'd flip to the moment when I tubed him. When panic threatened to freeze my chest, I'd focus on the good signs. "We've got air," the medic had said.

We had air. We had a pulse.

As far as I knew, that was still true. Now I just needed to get to Boston.

I held Owen in the front of my mind, as if that might help him somehow.

But somewhere in the back of my mind, other questions waited to be answered.

Why had we gone into that building at all? What could DeStasio have been thinking? What the hell just happened?

There was no "little boy" in the fire. I'd dreaded finding a body all day, but there was never any sign of a child. Had DeStasio hallucinated it? Had he panicked? He'd fought way too many fires to be fooled by a shadow, and it left me with a question I couldn't answer.

What, exactly, had DeStasio seen in that window?

BY THE TIME we stepped off the elevator at Mass General in Boston, the waiting room was packed standing room only with Owen's extended family, the entire guest list from his parents' party—from sisters to cousins to friends called "uncle"—plus about fifty retired firefighters right out of Central Casting in their FD shirts and dad jeans.

Friends of Big Robby's, I supposed.

I remember it now as a blur of navy-blue station shirts, overgrown mustaches, Dunkin' Donuts cups, and cigarettes.

Could you smoke in the hospital waiting room?

No.

Did those ornery old firefighters give a shit?

Hell, no.

The wives were all on one side of the room, sitting in chairs, leaning toward each other, talking and gabbing and worrying. The guys were all crammed in the hallway, standing close, faces somber.

I was the last one off the elevator, and after the guys had melded themselves into the group, I looked up to see the whole crowd fall quiet to stare at me.

Like, no talking, no coughing, no moving. Except the one person who half-whispered, "There she is."

She? Only one "she" had just stepped into the room.

At first, I wondered if maybe they recognized me as the drunk girl from the party, and now my identity as a firefighter was being revealed.

But then I remembered I was a smoke-stained mess.

I hadn't showered or changed. My skin was smeared gray with soot, and my shirt was stained and blotchy with salt. My hair was matted. I reeked of smoke and sweat and muck. My uniform was damp in some places and soaked in others from sweat and hose water.

I looked nothing—at all—like the girl who had showed up with Owen that night.

I felt nothing at all like her, either.

My next thought, looking at all those stricken faces, was that Owen must have died.

I held my breath.

But then the captain pushed through the crowd, came up to me, clamped his arm around my shoulders, and steered me off in the other direction down the hall.

"Let's talk," he said.

"Is he okay?"

The captain sensed my anxiety. "He's fine," he said, and I closed my eyes, and my whole body felt like it was full of water. "Well," the captain corrected, "not *fine.* They've had him down in the hyperbaric chamber since he got here, but they just brought him up for the night. We'll see how he does for a while. He's got edema of the upper trachea and second-degree burns on the face, a couple of broken ribs, and a collapsed lung."

"So," I said, "the opposite of fine." More like fighting for his life in the ICU.

"He's a strong kid," the captain said. "He's got everything to live for."

I had a sinking feeling. "What's the prognosis?"

The captain let out a long sigh. "Maybe fifty-fifty. He needs to make it through the night."

I took a minute to concentrate on breathing. How did it work again? In, then out—or the other way around?

The captain gave my shoulders a final, awkward squeeze and then released me. "Good thing DeStasio caught that cyanide situation, huh?"

I looked up. "DeStasio?"

"If he hadn't caught it," the captain went on, clearly trying to stay positive, "we'd be facing a whole different deal right now."

"DeStasio didn't catch it," I said. "I caught it."

The captain frowned at me, like I'd taken leave of my senses. "Hanwell," the captain said, like I needed to stop playing around, "DeStasio already filed his report."

Was that supposed to explain anything? "Okay," I said.

"He emailed it to me from his hospital room. I read it on my phone."

"Why did DeStasio even fill out the report?" I asked. "He wasn't the ranking medic on scene."

"He was the senior firefighter," the captain said, as if that mattered.

"What did his report say?"

The captain studied my face. "It says that he identified symptoms of cyanide poisoning while still inside the structure, and he instructed you to administer the antidote as soon as possible."

I actually shook my head to try to clear it. "That's not true. I'm the one who recognized the cyanide poisoning."

"That's not what the report says."

"Then it's incorrect."

"Are you saying DeStasio filed a false report?"

That would've been a hell of an accusation. "I'd have to see it," I said. "Maybe he was disoriented from his injury."

"He seemed pretty coherent to me," the captain said.

"Can I see the report?"

The captain shook his head. Then he gave a quick glance down the hall at all the people milling around the waiting room.

"That's what I want to give you a heads-up about, Hanwell," he said then. He took a step closer and lowered his voice. "It's pretty damning."

I frowned. "Damning?"

"You made a lot of mistakes today—rookie mistakes, really. I'm surprised at you. And though I'm sure you never meant to—"

I broke in. "What mistakes? I didn't make any mistakes!"

The captain gave me an uncomfortable look that had a lot of pity in it.

"What mistakes did DeStasio say I made?"

The captain took a breath. Then he put on his reading glasses and lifted up his phone, presumably to read from DeStasio's report. "Well, for starters, the way you insisted on entering the structure, even though—"

"*I* didn't insist on entering the structure! That was DeStasio! He said he saw a child inside."

"The report says you saw the child."

"It was *him*."

"Either way, you had standing orders not to go in."

"That's what I told DeStasio!"

"But you went in anyway."

"DeStasio wouldn't wait. He was going in with or without me—and taking the rookie."

"You should have waited for orders."

"We were running out of time. I radioed you at each decision point."

The captain shook his head. "I had no radio communications from you."

"I tried. There was only static on our end."

"The report states that when DeStasio tried to stop you from entering the building—"

This was insane. "*I* was trying to stop *him* from going in!"

"You had no water, no backup, and insufficient equipment—and you recklessly endangered the lives of all three crew members."

What the hell was going on? "That was *him*!"

"He had the presence of mind to tie a guide rope to a pole before following you—"

"I tied the guide line!"

"—but when the rookie became disoriented and showed clear signs of cyanide poisoning, you still refused to exit the structure."

"What?"

"Then DeStasio pulled the rookie to safety and ordered you to give the antidote—over your objections."

"He's lying!" I shouted, and when the crowd down the hall turned to look our way, I lowered my voice. "He's confused."

The captain looked offended for DeStasio's sake. "What are you saying, Hanwell?"

"I'm saying that's not how it went down, sir." I stood up a little taller. "I was the one who tried to protect the crew and not override your commands. DeStasio insisted he'd seen a boy's face inside at the window, but I didn't see anything. I tried to talk him into waiting for backup and a hose. I tried to radio you for orders. When it became clear that DeStasio was going in with or without me, and taking the rookie in with him, I made the call to go in as well, for crew integrity. I'm the one who tied the guide line. I'm the one who recognized the rookie's cyanide poisoning. I dragged the rookie to safety, by myself, after the roof collapse. DeStasio did nothing today but lie, disobey orders, and put us all in danger."

The captain looked concerned. "That's exactly what his report says about you."

"Fuck the report!"

The crowd gasped. *Language!*

Apparently, they were listening.

That's when I got it. They knew about the report. They'd known when I walked in. The captain must have told Big Robby, and then things must have spread, like they do.

That's what the silence was about. They thought Owen was in here because of me.

The captain already knew all that. He went on. "You expect me to believe you dragged the rookie out of a collapsed building by yourself? He must weigh two hundred pounds, and you're one-thirty dripping wet."

"You think DeStasio did it? A sad old man with a broken collarbone?"

"He claims his injury occurred after he got the rookie to safety."

"How, exactly?" I demanded. "By slipping on a banana peel in the parking lot?"

The captain gave me a look.

I went on, determined. "DeStasio and the rookie were injured at the same time—when the roof caved in. I found DeStasio under an overturned checkout aisle shelf, and I found the rookie—by feel—under ceiling debris. Sir."

But the more I talked, the worse I made things.

The captain was a reasonable guy, but I was calling his friend a liar, and the more I did it, the more he wanted to defend him.

"I've known DeStasio for almost forty years, Hanwell. We met at the academy, and I've seen him just about every day since. I was with him when he lost his son. I was the first person he called after his wife walked out. I have never known him to lie. About anything."

The captain stared me down, but I stared back just as hard.

"There'll be an investigation, of course," the captain went on. "No matter"—he glanced in the direction of the ICU—"how this turns out. But I've got to warn you, Hanwell. Until we know the true story of what happened, I have to suspend you from duty. If DeStasio's report checks out, we're talking gross insubordination. And if the rookie . . ." He hesitated. "If the rookie doesn't pull through, we might be talking manslaughter as well. You'll have more to worry about than your career. Either way, you're probably going to need a lawyer."

A *lawyer?* How could this be happening? How did DeStasio's lies become the truth? Wasn't the truth supposed to set us free? A lifetime of movies where the good guys won in the end had not prepared me for this. How, exactly, did the liar get to be the authority?

Lots of reasons, of course. DeStasio was from here, and had lived his whole life here, and raised his own boy here. He'd been here forever, and he was fully involved in this world with all his boyhood friends and cousins. I was an outsider and a newcomer and an uppity girl. Any one of those reasons would have been enough to give his version of the story the edge.

But maybe more important than any of that: He got there first.

"It won't check out," I said. "Every detail in that report is false."

"For your sake," the captain said, looking tired to the bones, "I hope so."

I took a few breaths. I felt woozy. "I will fill out my own report tonight—a correct one—and file it with you in the morning."

"That'll be fine, Hanwell."

And now, at last, for the question that had brought me here. "Can I see the rookie?"

The captain shook his head. "Family only."

I shook my head. "I need to see him." And before I knew it, I was walking away from the captain, walking straight down the hall, back toward the crowd.

"They haven't even let me in, Hanwell," the captain said, following me.

"But I'm the one who saved him," I said.

"So you say," the captain said, catching up, "but you're also the reason he's in here."

It was all I could do not to punch the wall. "I am *not* the reason he's in here."

"Either way," the captain said, "they've only let in his parents and sisters." Then he remembered: "And his girlfriend."

I froze in my tracks. I turned. "Girlfriend? What girlfriend?"

The captain looked over my shoulder to spot her.

"The rookie doesn't have a girlfriend," I said. Other than me.

The captain spotted a girl standing by the swinging doors of the ICU. He nodded at her. "His girlfriend might disagree."

"That is not his girlfriend."

"Close enough. Word is, they're almost engaged."

It had to be Amy. Perfectly nice, nothing-wrong-with-her Amy. The very image of clean, ironed femininity. She was wearing a pink tank top and khaki shorts.

I hated her on sight.

"Amy?" I said, stepping closer.

She looked up, but she didn't know me. Of course. What did she even see in that moment? Some grimy, sooty, filthy, sweaty female in a firefighter's uniform. The sight of me seemed to shock her a little.

I could tell she had no interest in talking to me. I seemed like nobody to her.

To everybody in the room, actually.

"I thought you moved to California," I said, bewildered by this turn of events.

She looked around, like, *Who is this?* "I'm home on vacation."

"Why are you here?"

In the second that followed, the whole room, including me, wondered if I had the right to ask her that question. But then she answered it anyway. "Colleen called me."

It felt so weirdly disloyal of Colleen. She knew Owen was with Christabel now—even if Christabel didn't exist. And even if nobody in this room seemed to recognize her without her poofy hair and hanky dress.

It pinched my heart to remember that night.

I turned back to the captain. "I need to see him."

"You can't."

But I did need to see him. Who cared about hospital rules?

I moved toward the ICU doors, but then I felt the captain's hand clamp my arm.

I'll tell you something. I'm strong, but the captain is stronger. No way was I getting out of that grip.

Now I was right next to ex-girlfriend Amy, close enough to confirm that she was exactly as garden-variety as the rookie had claimed, and the whole crowd was craning to see what would happen next.

I didn't know what would happen next.

I couldn't make sense of things. The whole situation felt like a dream—or more like a nightmare. Nothing felt real. Keys jangled. Voices murmured. The ex-girlfriend stared at me like I'd escaped from the loony bin.

Only a few things were clear:

DeStasio had blamed me for everything he did—and everyone who mattered believed him.

I was suspended from my job. And I was going to need a lawyer.

My mother was dying. My dad was three thousand miles away.

And Owen, my Owen, the one guy who was always on my side, was on a ventilator. In a medically induced coma. With a fifty-fifty shot at survival.

"I just need to see him," I said in a voice that I didn't even recognize. "Please."

"Hanwell, you're exhausted," the captain said. "We're all exhausted. Go home and get some rest."

"I need your help," I said to the captain.

But he was already shaking his head. "I can't help you. There'll be an investigation, and whatever happens will happen."

"Not with that," I said. "I need to see the rookie."

"No can do," he said in a voice like, *We've been over this.*

I wasn't getting anywhere.

Time to do something really brave.

I took a deep breath. "I love him," I told the captain.

He frowned at me. "Who?"

"The rookie!"

"Everybody loves the rookie," he said.

"No," I stared at him, like, *I. Love. Him.*

But the captain wasn't having it. "Come on, Hanwell. Keep it together. Now's not the time to develop a crush on the rookie."

I stood up straighter. "It's not a crush," I said. And then, knowing exactly how ridiculous these words would sound to the captain and every single other person in the room, including the guys on our crew, and even myself, I said, as steadily as I could, "When I say I love him, I mean I am in love with him."

The crowd burst out with gasps and whispers and cries of, "What?"

A mixed reaction, but I'd say the general consensus was that I'd just made myself the butt of every joke forever.

I could read the captain's response in his face. *We never should have hired a girl.*

No way out but through. "That," I said, gesturing at Amy, "is not his girlfriend. I am his girlfriend. It's not a crush. And I'm not the one who started it, either."

The captain frowned. "Are you telling me that you and the rookie fell in love with each other on C-shift? In my firehouse?"

Knowing that I was pretty much ending my run in the Lillian FD by confessing this—no matter what happened with DeStasio's report—I nodded.

He shook his head. "What the hell were you thinking?"

But I had to call him on that. "Are you really going to stand there—you, married *thirty-six years*, a guy who'd do anything for his wife and his four kids—and tell me that love doesn't matter?"

That got his attention.

"When I say I'm in love with him," I went on, my voice shaking, "I mean that he's the person I want to marry and spend my life with. He's the person who makes everything else matter. But I never told him that. I was afraid of losing my job. Or of losing the guys' respect. I know what you all think, that love is weakness—because I thought it, too, and I never questioned it. But I'll tell you something, as of today I know for sure that it's the opposite. I would have lifted that entire building off the ground to get the rookie out of there today, and I will do the same to get into that ICU right now."

The captain closed his eyes and shook his head.

"I need to see him," I said, my voice starting to crumble.

"Oh, no," the captain said. "Do not cry."

"I'm not crying," I said, as I wiped my face.

Worse and worse. My captain from Austin's words ticker-taped through my head: *Don't have feelings. Don't talk about them, don't explore them, and whatever you do, don't cry.*

I never cry, I'd said. So cocky. Just begging for life to teach me different.

"Women," the captain said, taking in the sight of me, shaking his head. "This is what I'm saying."

I stepped closer. "No. Don't do that. Don't roll your eyes. Help me get in, or tell me to go home, but don't stand there blocking the door while the rookie is fighting for his life and act like caring about other human beings doesn't matter."

The captain blinked. Then he cleared his throat. Then he said, "Fair enough."

For a second, I thought he was going to help me get in.

But then he just sighed and said, "Hanwell, go home."

Twenty-seven

I WENT, BUT not willingly.

I went, but only because the captain steered me by the elbow down to the parking lot and made a highly compelling argument that whatever had happened at the fire, and whatever my feelings about the rookie might or might not be, and regardless of whether human connection actually had any meaning, the rookie's parents needed all their strength and all their focus—and no distractions—if they were going to get him through this alive.

"So I'm a distraction?"

"You are a massive distraction."

"I can help," I said. "I was there."

"None of that matters at this point," the captain said. "Like it or not, the rookie needs his parents right now. There are big decisions to be made, and Big Robby's not in great health, and Colleen is about two inches away from losing it. If you hang around here, she's going to go over the edge, I promise you—and I've known this woman a long time. Go home. Let them cope. I'll be here, and I'll call you as soon as there's news."

* * *

I WENT HOME. What can I say? The adrenaline had worn off, and I was too tired to fight.

But I snuck back later.

I got home, showered, put on my softest sweats, and lay in bed.

But it was the bed I'd slept in with Owen. Owen, who was now fighting for his life in the ICU. Owen, who I could not bear to lose.

I didn't sleep. I wound up writing my far-too-detailed report for the captain instead, and emailing it off at midnight.

They were keeping him in a medically induced coma, letting the tissues heal and also offering him the mercy of sleeping through some of the pain. I thought back through what I knew about what happened. In addition to the cyanide poisoning, his airway had been burned by the hot air in the flashover. The swelling had caused respiratory arrest, which led to cardiac arrest—though I had no idea how long he'd gone without breathing. Five minutes? Ten? It's hard to tell time in a fire.

They say you can only last six minutes without breathing before incurring brain damage, but it really can vary a huge amount from person to person. A fit guy like Owen, I kept telling myself, could amaze us all. I thought about a story I once heard about a two-year-old boy who was drowned in a frozen river for over half an hour but walked away just fine.

The rookie could be okay. It wasn't the most impossible thing I'd ever tried to hope for.

Or maybe it was.

Finally, at two in the morning, I couldn't take it anymore.

I snuck down the stairs, past Diana's white noise machine, got back in my truck, and drove down to Boston.

The waiting area was mostly empty now. The rookie's parents were asleep on the one available sofa—his mother sideways with her head on his dad's thigh, his dad with his head tilted back against the wall. Somebody had put blankets over them.

I tiptoed past, and I pushed through the double doors into the restricted section.

There are no rooms in the ICU, just beds separated by curtains. I checked one chart after another until I saw CALLAGHAN. But before I could slide the curtain back, a nurse stopped me.

"No visitors at this hour," she said, slipping between me and the curtain.

"Hi. Yes, I just—"

"You'll have to come back tomorrow." She looked me over. "And then only if you're family."

How to describe myself. "I'm his girlfriend," I said.

"Then you can come during visiting hours."

"It's complicated," I said. "I'm not sure I can."

She stepped back and looked me over. "You're his mistress?"

"No!"

"But his family doesn't like you?"

I sighed. "They think I'm the reason he's in here."

Her eyebrows went up, like, *Are you?*

"But I'm not! I'm the one who saved him!"

I was ready to launch into the whole story—but one look at her face told me she didn't want the story. She had work to do, and she needed the person breaking the rules to get out of the way.

Instead, I summed up: "I can't be here during visiting hours. But I need to see him. Five minutes—please. There's something I need to tell him."

Her face pinched up. She didn't really have time for this nonsense. But as I waited for her verdict, tears started filling my eyes and spilling over. For a person who never cried, I sure was turning out to be good at it.

Finally, she'd had enough. "Five minutes," she said, pointing at me. "And don't try to sneak in here again."

BEHIND THE CURTAIN, the rookie was hooked up to every tube and machine possible. He was on a ventilator, and the paper tape holding the tube in obscured much of his face. His eyes were taped shut. His face was red with second-degree burns where the edge of his mask had been.

Thank God for the movement and the noise of the ventilator, because everything else was as still as death.

But his hand was there. Someone had tucked his blankets carefully up under his arms and laid his hands at his sides. I reached over the rail. It was warm and soft. Alive.

And then I didn't know what to say. Faced with the chance to talk to him, my mind went blank. I'd planned a whole speech on the drive down—one inspiring and powerful and motivating, one he would hear through the fog of his coma and grasp on to for the will to live.

But now I was here, and the clock was ticking.

"It's me," I said. "They won't let me in to see you. DeStasio filed a false report, and now everybody thinks I'm the reason you're in here. Looks like I'm going to lose my job. But I don't care about any of it. The only thing I care about is you pulling through." I stepped a little closer, still holding his hand but reaching out to stroke his forehead, too. "You're really something special, rookie. The world needs you. I know you're fighting. Keep fighting. Don't give up."

I leaned down and kissed his forehead.

"They only gave me five minutes—and I'm not allowed to come back. But just know that my whole heart is with you. Apparently, I need a medically induced coma to spark enough courage to say it, but—" I took a shaky breath. "I love you. I told the captain, and the whole crew, and the entire waiting room. So now, everybody knows but you. That's why you've got to get better—so I can tell you for real."

AFTER THAT, I stayed away.

I kept my phone on me at all times, waiting for texts from the captain. He was group-texting the whole crew with any information that he got, but after my enormous and dramatic confession in the waiting room, I kept thinking I'd receive something a little more personal.

I didn't.

Not the first day. Or the second. Or the third.

I only got the basic updates sent to the group: His parents were keeping vigil in the ICU. His mother hadn't changed clothes in days. His health was touch and go, and there were moments of encouragement and moments of worry. The collapsed lung and facial burns were improving, but the real concern was the damage to his trachea.

I wondered if ex-girlfriend Amy was still lurking around, abusing her mistaken status as "family." But the captain didn't mention her.

I didn't hear much from the guys. Let's just say heartache wasn't exactly their area.

Those first days back home, banished from the hospital, melted into a blur of sleeplessness. And worry. And anger.

And utter, agonized dismay at the rubble around me.

I wanted to shut myself up in my room and lock the door and stop eating and curl up on the bed in a fetal position.

I wanted to—but to my credit, I didn't. When Diana came in to sit by me, I didn't send her away. When Josie showed up with a homemade smoothie, I took a few sips. I'd tried coping in isolation before, and I knew firsthand that it didn't work.

I felt desperate, restless, lost. I needed to help, but there was nothing to do. I needed to move, but there was nowhere to go. I was more exhausted than I've ever been, but I couldn't rest.

When Diana and Josie had crochet club, I made myself go sit near them.

They wanted to get to the bottom of what had happened at the fire. They wanted to figure out why a seasoned guy like DeStasio would have put us all in danger like that—and why he would lie about it afterward. They pieced clues together and analyzed details and floated theories. I participated, but in a strange, detached way—talking, and answering questions, and providing clues, but only halfheartedly, as if I were in shock. It all mattered, I supposed, but nothing really mattered until I knew Owen was okay.

Still, we now had a pretty good theory on who my stalker had been. I just didn't exactly have the energy to care.

It was all I could do to stay away from the hospital.

A WEEK WENT by.

I stayed home. I updated my charts on Owen's health. I waited for texts. I slept late and stayed up late, worrying too hard to fall asleep.

Then, on Friday, my mom had a doctor's appointment. A checkup.

And she insisted she needed me to go with her.

"I can't," I said, shaking my head.

"You can," she said. "And you will."

I hadn't showered in a week. "I'm useless."

"Look," she said, "if you don't drive me, I'm not going."

Well played.

I drove her. It was time for Diana to get a scan to see how she was doing, and Diana resented it like hell. "There's no point," she said in the waiting room.

"We have to know your status," I said. "We need to know what's going on."

"Why?" she asked. "Why do we need to know that?"

Why did anybody need to know anything? "Because we do."

"This is a waste of a whole morning," she said.

"It's going to give us critical information about what's going on with you."

"Critical, how? Is there even a possibility that we'll do anything differently?"

There was a possibility, I figured. It was possible that hearing how much the tumor had grown would inspire her to consent to experimental treatments. A little fear could be very motivational. And then it would also be possible that one of those treatments might buy her some time.

I couldn't help but root for that, now, after spending all these months with her. Was it wrong to want a little more time, even if there were downsides? Maybe it was selfish. She had chosen quality of life over quantity with no hesitation. In theory, it made sense. In practice, I just wanted her to hang on as long as she could.

"They bought all those big fancy machines," she said, "and now they have to find a way to pay for them."

"Are you really arguing against CT scans? They're a miracle of modern technology. They save lives all the time."

"Not mine," she said.

All in all, adding up drive time to the little outpatient center, waiting room time, and time for the scan, it took about two hours before the radiologist called us in to give us some information.

My mother had all her clothes back on by then, and she was so eager to get home that she almost left without waiting for the report.

When it came, the report was not at all what we'd expected.

The doc, who was about my mother's age, shook her head in wonder as she showed us the films. "You're not going to believe this," the doctor said. "I don't believe it myself." She brought up two side-by-side scan images on a screen and gestured between them. "There has been no growth at all since your last scan," she said.

Diana and I blinked at the screen.

"When was your last scan?" I finally asked my mom.

"Just before I called you in Austin," Diana said.

"There's been no growth in all that time?" I asked.

"Not that we can measure."

I looked at the doctor. "I don't understand. A 'very malignant' tumor just stopped growing?"

"Sometimes this happens, but it's highly uncommon," the doc said.

"Sometimes what happens?" I asked.

"An aggressive tumor like this will just sort of take a break."

"For how long?" I asked.

She shook her head, like there was no way of knowing. "It's so rare, we don't have much data. Only anecdotal accounts."

I looked over at Diana and her blue floral eye patch. If you didn't know her, you'd think she was just impassively listening, taking in the information. But I could tell from something about the crinkles at the edge of her one good eye that she was pleased.

"You can't take credit for this," I said on the drive back. "I know what you're thinking."

"I can take credit for it, and I will."

"Doesn't that seem a little cocky?" I asked. "To think that you can just personally tell a malignant tumor what to do?"

She touched her fingers to the car window. "I think it's the opposite of cocky. I am humbled by the wisdom of the body to take care of itself."

"We don't even know what caused the pause," I said.

"That's right, we don't," she said. "So that leaves me free to choose an explanation."

"Maybe you're just very, very lucky."

"I am definitely very, very lucky."

The doctor had given Diana a new prescription for some super-strong painkillers, not believing that she hadn't even dipped into the first bottle. While we drove, she folded the paper into an origami bird.

When I noticed what she was doing, I said, "You might need that, you know."

"Nah," she said. "This stuff'll kill ya."

"So will a brain tumor."

She gave me a look. "I read up on these pills. Nasty stuff. You get hooked, even if you follow all the rules. Then you get angry. You start lying. Your whole personality changes."

"I know," I said, nodding. We'd had to study it all for paramedic certification. She wasn't wrong. "Even people who know better get addicted."

She nodded, like wasn't it a shame, but I suddenly found myself sitting very still—looking straight ahead at the answer to a question I didn't even know I was asking. *Even people who knew better got addicted.*

Maybe DeStasio was addicted to painkillers.

It wasn't all that uncommon with firefighters, given all their on-the-job injuries. DeStasio's back pain was legendary—and so was his ability to endure it. Add to that the loss of his son, his problem drinking, his wife leaving—and the pieces seemed to fit together. Possibly.

I felt a strange twinge of worry. Not that DeStasio deserved it.

"It just hit me, right now, that DeStasio might be addicted to painkillers," I said then, out loud.

My mom looked over. "Why?"

I walked her through my thinking.

"That's a pretty good list," she said.

"Maybe I should go check on him this afternoon," I said.

"You want to go check on the guy who stalked you, lied about you, and ended your career?" she said.

"I'd been planning to go over there anyway," I said, nodding at the turn of events. "But the plan was to yell at him."

"Maybe you could bring him some soup instead."

Safe to say, I had a lot of mixed emotions toward DeStasio at that moment. But I knew him too well to just decide he was evil and leave it at that. It was unequivocally not okay that he was taking it all out on me, but I could know that and also know that he was in pain. Both could be true at the same time.

I wasn't sure if he deserved my compassion, but I did know I wanted to be the kind of person who would offer it. It's not the easy moments that define who we are. It's the hard ones.

DeStasio was clearly at the end of his rope. The addiction, the losses. There was nothing left of his life but smoldering rubble. I tried to imagine being him—being in that situation—and then having somebody like me show up at the department to break apart the last bricks in the foundation.

In his shoes, I might have made some bad choices, too.

Though probably not *that* bad.

"I think," I said carefully, "that I've got a workable plan. First I'll go over and punch him in the jaw. Then I'll force him to stand face-to-face with his cruel, stupid behavior and hold him accountable. Then I'll give him some homemade soup. Just to cover all the bases."

"You're forgetting something," Diana said.

I glanced over and shook my head.

"What are you going to do after you yell at him—before you give him the soup?"

"I don't know," I said.

"I think you do know," Diana said, setting her little bird on the dashboard. Then she reached over, put a hand on mine, and said, "You're going to forgive him."

I shook my head. "I'm still bad at forgiveness," I said.

"Well, then," she said. "This is a great chance to practice."

Twenty-eight

DESTASIO DID NOT answer his door.

I stood on his porch with a massive thermos of beef-and-vegetable soup on my hip, and I knocked and knocked.

Something didn't feel right. His sedan was parked carefully in the driveway.

I set the soup down on the steps and went to the window to peer in.

The inside was dark. The place was a mess—papers everywhere, trash, several meals' worth of old plates of food on the dining table. Suspicions about DeStasio's quality of life confirmed: He was not doing well.

That's when I spotted him at the far end of the living room, laying back in a recliner.

He wasn't just ignoring me. He was unconscious. The skin around his lips was blue.

When you've seen it enough times, you just know.

He'd OD'd.

I ran to grab the trauma kit in my car, and then, before I broke out the window, I went ahead and tried the front door. It was unlocked.

Something a firefighter would do—make it easy for the medics when they discovered the body.

I got to him in seconds, and he was bluer up close than he had seemed from the window. There was a note on the table next to him with two words on it: *I'm sorry.*

I started an IV push of Narcan, which is an antidote to opiates. It's amazing stuff, really. Seconds after you give it, the patient wakes up—a little groggy, but completely fine. If you give it in time.

That's what happened with DeStasio.

He opened his eyes. Blinked a second. Took a few deep breaths.

It was that easy.

Then he looked at me. "What are you doing here?"

"Saving your life," I said. "Apparently."

I picked up his note and showed it to him. If I'd had my mother's origami skills, I might have made it into a bird.

"That's private," DeStasio said.

Underneath the note was a sealed envelope addressed to Captain Jerry Murphy. I stared at it for a second as I took note of his handwriting: The *T* in "Captain" looked like an *X*.

It was one thing to have guessed it, but quite another to know for sure. I felt a spark of anger burn through me. It had been him. All along.

I held it up. "Is this private, too?"

He studied my face. He could tell I knew. "Get out of my house," DeStasio said.

"I just saved you. Do you have any idea how lucky you are that I showed up when I did? Another hour and there'd have been no bringing you back."

"I didn't want to be saved."

"Too fucking bad."

DeStasio looked over at the wall and kept his eyes there.

"You don't want to be saved? You think you can just take a pass on all your consequences? You almost killed us all. The rookie's still in the ICU—in a coma."

"I've seen the texts."

"And then you lied about it. You lied about me, and everybody believed you. The guys believed you. The rookie's parents believed you, and now I can't even get into the hospital to see how he's doing. The captain believed you, and now I'm suspended, and my career's probably over, and they've told me to get a lawyer. But we both know the truth, don't we?"

"Get out of my house, or I'm calling the cops. You want an arrest on your record, too?"

"Call the cops! I've got nothing to lose! What'll you tell them? 'A mean lady just saved my useless life'?"

DeStasio closed his eyes.

I waved the envelope for the captain at him. "Is this your confession?"

"You wish."

"But that's not all. It wasn't just one bad day. You've been stalking me for weeks. Messing with my locker. Slashing my tires." I pointed at the *T* on the envelope. "This is terrible stalking. Your handwriting's totally obvious. *I* could have done a better job of stalking me than you did. This is Stalking 101! Cut the letters out of newspaper headlines!" I said it like, *Duh*.

DeStasio wouldn't look at me.

I leaned closer. "You stood outside my dying mother's house and threw a brick through her window."

"I didn't know she was dying."

"What is wrong with you, man?" I shook my head. "Firefighters are supposed to be the good guys."

DeStasio was quiet for so long, I was starting to think he was about to share something honest about what he'd been going through the past years. Instead, he went with anger and blame. "The department is the only thing I have," he said. "And you took it from me."

"I wasn't trying to take it from you," I said.

"But you did."

So he wanted to make it all my fault. "Why couldn't we share it?"

"Just by coming here, you changed things. The station I loved disappeared."

I gave him a look. "That's a bit extreme, don't you think?"

"You walked in, all ladylike—"

Now I was offended. "I am hardly *ladylike*."

"And you changed everything."

"Um," I said, counting off on my fingers, "the building was still there, the people were still there. Even the porn was still there."

He pointed at me. "But it was hidden. We never had to hide the porn before."

"That's what drove you to the dark side, man? Because you had to hide your porn?"

"Not just that!" he said. "I've been here thirty-eight years. I've been at this station—day in and day out—longer than you've been alive."

"So you've said," I said. "Many times."

"I was proud to go there. I was proud to be part of that brotherhood."

I sighed. "Why can't the brotherhood have a sister?"

"Because it can't."

"Think you might need to check some of that sexism, buddy."

"It's not the same with a woman around," he insisted.

I sighed again.

As weird as it sounds, I actually did know what he meant.

A station that had women working at it could not possibly be a guy-fest in that old-school way. It did have to be something different. It could still be great—I'd seen that in Austin. Better, even. Stronger, as everybody contributed their own personal and gender-based gifts. But he wasn't wrong. It would be different. "I hear you," I said. "I probably slightly altered the vibe of the station."

My empathy just pissed him off. "Damn right, you altered it! And I want it back the way it was!"

Now he sounded like a child. My empathy disappeared. "There are lots of things I want that I can't have," I said, making my voice infuriatingly calm. "But I don't go around terrorizing people and lying."

"Not yet," he said. "Give yourself time."

"Maybe. Maybe when I'm your age I'll be a bitter old liar. But I hope not. I'm going to fight like hell not to let that happen."

"Good luck."

"Maybe you need to find something new to add to your life, instead of just clutching so hard to the past that you strangle it."

"I didn't strangle the past," he said, not looking my way. "I strangled you."

"You strangled *yourself*," I said. "You let your grief make you bitter. You let your suffering make you cruel. Want to know what that makes you? A villain. That's every comic book villain ever! They suffer, and then they inflict suffering on others. Good guys do the opposite. Good guys suffer, too—but they respond by *helping*. I know you started out a good guy. You wouldn't have joined up otherwise. But you gave it all up the minute you broke into my locker with that Sharpie."

DeStasio wouldn't look at me. He kept his eyes pointed at the window.

The sight of him like that, so defiant, so unwilling to acknowledge his own role, made me want to push him into a state of empathy. It felt vital not to waste the moment. Before I even realized what I was doing, I said, "That wasn't the first time somebody wrote that word in a locker of mine, you know. Some girls at my high school beat you to it by like ten years. You're like a sad knockoff of a mean girl."

DeStasio didn't respond.

"Are you wondering why kids at school would be that vicious toward another kid?" I went on. "Or maybe that doesn't surprise you. Maybe when you look back on your life, all you see is cruelty. But I'll tell you something. It still shocks the hell out of me. I see that sixteen-year-old I used to be, and she's so young. So tragically unprotected."

I let my gaze drift away from DeStasio. I really could see her.

"That's what I see when I look back. It's her sixteenth birthday, a Saturday, and her mother is leaving town that day—that *same* day—to move across the country. Her mother is leaving her dad for someone else, and that's the day she picks to leave, because of 'scheduling,' she says. Hell of a birthday present.

"Can you imagine how angry this girl is? How gutted? When her mother tried to bake her a cake and give her presents the night before, apologizing again and again that 'the timing isn't great, honey,' she wouldn't touch either. She will never open those gifts, or taste that cake. They will sit on the kitchen table for at least a week, maybe longer, before the girl shoves every item on that tabletop into the kitchen trash.

"Can you imagine what it feels like for your mother to leave you at all, much less on your birthday? Can you even conceive of the abandonment that girl must have felt as she watched her mother drive away?"

Of all the people to share the memory of that moment with . . . DeStasio. But I needed to make him understand.

I went on. "But then imagine this. Later that day, she gets a text from a boy she's had a crush on for months—stealing glances at him and doodling his name in notebooks. He's older. A handsome alpha male, a senior. Totally out of her league. But he tells her he's noticed her watching him in the hallways, and then he invites her to a party at his house that night. And she wonders if maybe the universe is apologizing somehow. And she puts ice packs on her puffy eyes and she takes a shower and flosses and blow-dries her hair. He says to meet him there, so she walks to his house. It's at least twenty blocks away—but she doesn't have a ride. His parents are out of town, and the whole high school has converged on his house, like something from the movies, but far louder and more terrifying. And then when he sees her, he drapes his heavy arm around her shoulders and stays like that for the rest of the night, talking to his guy friends and handing her cups of spiked punch, as if she's something that belongs to him.

"And the whole thing is so weird and foreign and not quite what she wanted, but she's so lost and heartbroken and it feels so nice to belong to someone—she stays.

"You know it's not going to end well, right? No love story starts out like this. You've been on enough calls to know exactly where this night is headed. But she doesn't know. She's never even been kissed, not really. She thinks she's on a date. She thinks she's had a stroke of good luck. I want to march right in there and grab her stupid, naïve hand and drag her outside to safety. Dumb girl. I'd slap her right now, if I could. I'd shout some sense into her.

"But then, when she's good and dizzy, he says he's going to take her home. She's thinking he's going to drive her. She's hoping to get a good-night kiss—her first, by the way, besides a few party games. But instead, he steers her out behind his garage. She giggles at first, like he's made a funny mistake. But then he pushes her down into the mud next to a dead rosebush, and when she tries to get away, he grabs her hair in his fist and tilts her head back so far, she thinks he might break her neck.

"That's what she's thinking, on her sixteenth birthday, in the mud: *This is how I'm going to die.*

"Do I have to tell you what he does next? He pushes her face down so it's half buried in the mud. Mud fills her nose and her mouth and her eyes as he stops laughing and gets to work. She could have suffocated in that mud, for all he noticed or cared. But she didn't.

"She won't remember how she got home. That part goes black. But when she finds herself outside her living room window, her dad is in there watching TV, waiting for her to get home. She waits, crouched down by the back steps, until he gives up, turns off the lights, and goes to bed.

"She thinks she might have to go to the hospital, or the school nurse, if she doesn't stop bleeding—but it stops eventually. She won't get sick, or pregnant. But she will never go on another date—or even want to—again. And she will never, ever tell anybody what happened to her. Not until right now. This moment. Right here. To a bitter, vicious old man.

"But you can bet the boy told people what happened. Lots of people. Except he makes up a story that 'she begged for it.' Guess what word he uses? *Slut.* Guess how many people he tells? Everybody. Anybody. And guess what the mean girls decide to scratch into the metal door of the girl's locker with a set of keys?"

I waited then, as if DeStasio might actually take a guess.

Which he didn't.

But I gave him a minute.

I gave us both a minute.

Then I said, "Yeah. *Slut.* Very cliché for high school terrorism. Been done to death."

I kept my eyes on the distant shape of a tree out the window. Of all the people in the world to finally, finally share that buried secret with, why the hell had I chosen DeStasio?

I waited to regret it. I expected it to hit me like a head-on collision.

DeStasio was quiet a long time—so quiet, I started to wonder if he'd dozed off or something.

Finally, in a scratchy whisper, he said, "I am sorry."

"What?" I said.

"I didn't realize."

I nodded.

Then DeStasio said, so softly I could barely hear him, "It was Tony I saw in that fire—my boy. It was Tony when he was about ten or eleven—the year he got a buzz cut. He was wearing his Little League cap. And the shark's tooth necklace we got at the shore that summer. I saw him. He was right there, just on the other side of the glass. I *saw* him. My little boy. He was calling to me for help."

I turned from the window to look at DeStasio. He looked frail.

He went on. "When your child calls you for help, you go. Even if you know you can't help, you go. Even if you know he's not really there, you go. You go, no matter what the cost." There were tears on DeStasio's cheeks now. "My life got away from me somehow. I lost hold of it. I lost everybody. Everything that mattered." He closed his eyes. "Then, there he was. I couldn't leave him there. I couldn't let him die."

He wasn't looking at me, but he didn't have to. Something about that idea—of DeStasio so desperate to save a child who was already lost—made me feel his sorrow as clearly as my own.

It's a big deal to share your grief with other people—to give them a glimpse of the pain you carry. It connects you in a profound way. That's why you usually only do it with friends. DeStasio and I were not friends. Mostly, we were the opposite.

But part of what made us enemies to start with was this pain he was describing now. It wasn't just this conversation that would connect us; it was everything that had come before it. Our lives were already tangled up. But what I'd just told him, and what he was telling me in this moment—these were bedrock truths about our lives. The kind of truths that could force us to understand each other better. The kind with the raw power to change how we saw each other, and even transform all that anger into something different—something more like understanding.

Could that happen? Could DeStasio and I become friends? Could I even consider not hating someone who'd treated me so viciously?

I wasn't sure. But I felt too much empathy for him right now to say never.

"You couldn't leave him there," I said, my voice as soothing as I could make it—validating his choice to put us all in danger in a way I wasn't even really sure I agreed with. Maybe he just needed someone to understand him. "I get it," I said.

Maybe we could both overcome all our bitterness.

Then, after a good pause, DeStasio said, "Piss off. I don't need your approval."

Maybe not.

Now I could see what a friendship between us would look like. Equal parts hostility and grudging acceptance. Equal parts deep understanding and pure misunderstanding. Equal knowledge that I'd saved his life, and that he'd borne witness to the worst moment of mine, and no matter what else happened, that connected us.

Of course. One conversation might have bonded us, but it sure as hell wasn't going to shift his entire personality from crabby-old-troll to sensitive-New-Age-guy-friend.

"It's fine. Be your bitter self," I said. "I didn't even come here for that, anyway."

"What did you come here for?" he asked.

"To bring you soup," I said with a shrug. "To find out how your collarbone was healing. To be a frigging human being." I met his eyes. "Also, because it suddenly occurred to me that you have a painkiller addiction."

DeStasio let that land. Then he said, "Fuck off."

"You fuck off."

He closed his eyes.

"It's so obvious now that I see it," I went on. "The lying, the aggression, the secretiveness, the hallucinations . . . How did it take me so long to catch on?"

DeStasio just glared at me.

"I don't need you to admit it," I said. "It's plain to see."

"I'm not going to come clean to the captain, if that's what you're thinking," DeStasio said. "I'm two years from retirement. You think I'd give up my pension?"

"I never expected you to come clean."

He'd as much as admitted it. If this were some other version of my life, I'd be wearing a wire, and I'd now have his confession on tape. I'd take it to the captain, exonerate myself, get my old job back, triumph, and roll credits.

But life's not the movies. And that wasn't why I'd come here.

What I was trying to do was bigger than that.

DeStasio tried to pretend I was only there for self-interest. "A thermos of soup's not going to get me on your side."

But I wasn't having it. "You're already on my side," I said. "You just don't know it yet."

I thought I saw the tiniest flicker of a smile. Though maybe it was a wince. Always a fine line with him.

"On that note," I said, "I have some good news. I forgive you."

He gave a tiny snort, like an eye-roll. "For what?"

"For all of it. For disliking me. For being so small hearted and mean. For stalking me, and scaring me, and making me the target of all your misdirected rage. For blaming me for your grief. For taking the one thing in my life that made me feel strong and safe and happy and trying to rip it apart. I forgive you for all of it. I forgive you."

He studied me for a long time. At last, he said, "Why the hell would you do that?"

"Because that's who I want to be," I said.

And it was.

"Guess what else?" I said, on a roll now. "I don't just forgive you. I forgive myself."

For a second, he looked almost grateful before he turned away. "You can't forgive me," he said. "I won't let you."

"It's not up to you."

"I forbid it," he said.

"I'm not doing it for you," I said then. "I'm doing it for me."

"Get out of here," he said. "And take your damned soup."

"I'm not taking the soup," I said.

"Well, I'm not frigging eating it."

"Fine," I said. "Pour it out! It's homemade by my dying mother, you bitter old pain in the ass, but pour it out."

"Get out of my house!"

"I'm going," I said, packing up my bag.

"And take your forgiveness with you!"

"No way in hell. The forgiveness stays!"

"Leave. Right now."

"I am," I said. But instead of moving away, I stepped closer. "I'm leaving. But I'm taking you with me."

DeStasio checked my expression to see if I meant it.

I did.

I expected him to fight me, but as I reached out my hand, all the fight just seemed to drain out of him. Like he'd been fighting way too hard for way too long, and right at that moment, he decided to surrender.

Was it okay, what he'd done to me? Or to Owen? Or to himself? Did an addiction excuse everything? Did losing his son, and then his wife, give him the right to violate all standards of human decency? Of course not.

But did I suddenly want to do everything in my power to make sure that I never let my own grief and rage and disappointment do the very same thing to me?

You bet.

"Come on," I said, helping him up.

He didn't resist. "Where are we going?"

"I think you know where we're going," I said.

He took a second to get steady on his feet. "You're taking me to the captain, is that it? Or to the police?"

"Neither, old man," I said, shaking my head. "I am taking you to rehab."

Twenty-nine

I FINISHED THAT day feeling strong.

True, DeStasio wasn't going to confess anything. True, I wasn't getting my job back. Technically, other than the fact that DeStasio wasn't dead, I hadn't accomplished all that much by confronting him.

It didn't matter. I was proud of myself. I was proud of how I'd handled it all. I'd brought him soup, and gone to check on him, and chosen, over and over, to be compassionate, and to be human, and to do the right thing—no matter if he deserved it or not.

I'd risen above my anger. It wasn't all gone yet, but it didn't have to be.

I'd forgiven him. Or tried, at least.

When I'd spoken the words, honestly, I'd been faking. I'd said them on principle, not expecting to feel them. I'd expected the feeling would only follow later. Possibly years later. If at all.

But saying the words had somehow sparked the feeling, too.

Words were powerful, I realized in a new way.

No denying it now.

I had told my story. I had put it into words, at last. For *DeStasio,* of all people—but you can't have everything. He wasn't the only person to witness that moment, anyway.

I was there.

Telling the story changed the story for me. Not what had happened—that, I could never change—but how I responded to it.

It was like I'd been averting my eyes from that memory for ten solid years, but I'd finally forced myself to look again. And what I saw, at twenty-six, was so different from what I remembered from when I was sixteen.

Even though nothing about the story had changed, I had changed.

I'd begun telling that story to DeStasio because of how I wanted him to feel. I wanted to force him to recognize how hurtful his actions had been. Maybe he did, and maybe he didn't. What I know for sure is that I felt something, hearing the story—something I never would have expected to feel for that stupid, naïve girl I had been: compassion.

Looking back, I saw her—that teenage me—with different eyes. I saw her in the story as young, and trusting, and inexperienced—but not stupid. Not contemptible. Now, all these years later, she was someone I could root for, and understand, and hurt for. And in this crazy way, the fact that I could look, and listen, and care about her, and ache for her, and defend her—even if I couldn't change anything at all—the fact that someone *heard her*, could stay in that moment with her and bear witness, meant that she wasn't alone.

She wasn't alone anymore.

She'd been so alone all these years, endlessly facing the worst moment of her life and completely abandoned by everyone. Even me.

All that changed when I told her story.

Now, she had me on her side—too little and too late, but right there at last, all the same.

Putting that long-unspoken night into words changed the memory. It was no longer some kind of poison gas that snaked around my consciousness, formless and uncontainable and lethal. Now it had words. Now it had a shape.

A beginning, a middle—and, most important, an end.

* * *

IT TAKES A lot out of you, confessing your darkest secret. I went home and slept like the dead.

And when morning came, something about me was reborn.

I lay in bed under a pattern of sunshine from my window and marveled at my capacity to do the impossible. *I'd told the story of Heath Thompson.* I'd told the whole soul-destroying story, and I'd lived to see the dawn. Of all the brave things I'd done in my life, that one was the bravest.

If I could do that, I could truly do anything.

And now I was going to the hospital to see the rookie, no matter what anybody said.

Just try to stop me.

But when I headed downstairs, I found that my mother's house was full of firefighters.

Not just any firefighters, either. Station Two, C-shift. My crew.

They were doing chores.

Six-Pack and Case were in the kitchen, repairing my mother's broken window. Tiny was on a ladder in the living room, replacing the lightbulbs in a ceiling fixture. And the captain was sipping coffee at the kitchen table with my mom, in her bathrobe.

"Oh, honey," my mom said when she saw me. "You're up."

The captain turned, saw me, too, and stood up. "Morning, Hanwell."

As soon as the guys heard him, they all called out, "Morning, Hanwell!"

I wasn't sure what to make of them all. "What are you doing here?"

"It's a long story," the captain said.

"They showed up here at seven forty-five and started fixing my broken window," my mom said. "Then they asked me to make a list of every single honey-do I could think of for them, and they've been hard at work ever since."

I looked at the captain like, *What the hell?*

"These guys," my mom went on, chirpily, gesturing at Six-Pack and

Case, "are going to repaint my garden fence. And this one"—she gestured at Tiny—"adjusted that broken gate latch out front, tightened the loose cabinet door, and fixed the leak behind the toilet."

She looked pleased.

I frowned at the captain. "Why?"

He looked right at me. "By way of apology."

"What are you apologizing for?" There were so many possibilities.

"DeStasio throwing a brick through that window, for starters," the captain said, nodding at it.

I blinked. "You knew it was him?"

"I do now."

"How?"

"The rookie and I kind of pieced it together."

I walked closer. "He's awake? He's okay? You saw him?"

He nodded. "Last night. They just moved him from the ICU."

A funny little sob of relief passed through me, and then my eyes filled with tears—but I squeezed a tight blink to push them back. "How is he?"

"He's on the mend," the captain said. He shook his head at Diana. "Youth."

I smiled and wrapped my arms around my waist. "You talked to him?"

"Yep. He asked after you."

"He did?"

"He wanted to know if you'd been to see him."

I felt my expression harden. "Did you tell him why I had not been to see him?"

"I did."

"And what did he say?"

"He said DeStasio's account of what happened at the fire was—his words here: 'an utterly false pack of bitter-old-man lies.' Then the rookie ranted and raved on your behalf and accused DeStasio of lying and being a sleazebag reptile. He got so agitated he gave himself a coughing fit."

I smiled a little. "He called DeStasio a sleazebag reptile?"

The captain smiled a little, too. "He's on a lot of medication."

"Sounds like he's feeling better."

The captain went on. "When he'd settled down, I told him the department was handling it, that there would be a full investigation, and that we'd get to the bottom of everything, for sure. I meant to reassure him, but he kept pushing for information, and when it came out you'd been suspended, he quit."

"He quit?"

The captain nodded, impressed with the gesture. "In protest."

Good thing the captain didn't know he'd been about to quit anyway.

"Anyway, I thought you were nuts when you confessed"—he cleared his throat—"your, uh, special feelings for the rookie. But now I'd say, just based on our conversation and, uh, his body language, it seems pretty mutual."

That was it. Time to go. I needed to get dressed.

I turned toward the stairs.

"Wait!" the captain said.

I kept walking. "I'm going to Boston," I said. "I've waited *more than* long enough."

"But that's why we're here," the captain said.

I stopped and turned around. "Why?"

"To take you to Boston."

I angled back toward him. "Wait—why are you here?"

"To apologize to you," the captain said, "and to your mother. And to try to make things right."

"What are you apologizing to me for?"

"Suspending you, for one. You're unsuspended, by the way."

"What does that mean, 'unsuspended'?"

He gave a little shrug. "You've got your job back, if you want it."

That didn't feel like a question I could answer just yet. I looked around at the guys. They'd all stopped working, and they were watching us.

The captain continued. "I also apologize for doubting you when you were telling the truth."

I stared at him. How did he know I was telling the truth?

"The rookie confirmed every detail of your story," the captain said.

"Every detail he was conscious for, anyway. But then, on top of it, I got a phone call from DeStasio last night. From rehab."

DeStasio had called the captain from rehab? Were phone calls even allowed?

"He confessed everything. The false report. The locker, the tires, the brick. His OD, and the painkillers. He's been stealing painkillers from our supplies for months."

"Wow," I said. "He did confess everything."

"He also told me that you saved his life."

That was unexpected. "Twice," I confirmed. If you counted not letting him roast alone inside a burning grocery store.

The captain went on. "He's withdrawn his initial report about what happened at the fire and will submit a new one."

I lifted my eyebrows.

He nodded. "It will corroborate yours and make it clear that you put your own safety at risk for others that day, acting with extreme courage and pretty much saving his life and the rookie's."

"So he's admitted everything he did wrong?"

"I think so," the captain said, "unless he's leaving something out."

"He swore he was never going to confess," I said.

"I guess he changed his mind."

"But—will he be suspended?"

"He will."

"Will he lose his pension?"

The captain nodded. "Probably."

"Why would he give all that up? He was getting away with it."

"He said he owed you big-time," the captain said. Then he added, "He said he didn't want to be a villain."

I didn't quite know how to feel.

"I was a stupid idiot," the captain said then. "We were all idiots. We underestimated you and didn't trust you. And now we're going to put things right."

I wasn't sure things could ever be put right. It made me feel worse, almost, to hear him admit it. But only almost. "How exactly are you going to do that?" I asked.

"I'm not entirely sure," the captain said. "But I know we're going to start by driving you down to Boston. With lights and sirens."

ON THE ROAD, we hashed it all out. We all piled into the captain's Suburban—the captain and Tiny up front, and me squeezed between Six-Pack and Case in the back. I talked them through exactly how I'd figured out what was going on with DeStasio, describing all the clues and how they all just fell into place.

"He would have died if you hadn't showed up," the captain said.

"Probably."

"He would have died if he'd gone into that building alone," Six-Pack said.

"Definitely."

On the drive down, the guys acted like things were totally normal—like I'd never been under suspicion, never been shunned or doubted. In fact, things were better than normal. Something about the whole ordeal seemed to have broken some final, unseen barrier that I hadn't even realized was there. The guys joked around, and teased me, and thanked me, and apologized, and called themselves idiots over and over.

They mostly teased me about the rookie.

Yeah, no way was I getting out of that one unteased.

"We need to combine your names," Six-Pack said.

"'Cassie' plus 'rookie,'" Case said. "'Cookie.'"

"I called it from the beginning," Six-Pack said.

"You never saw it coming," Case said, reaching around me to punch him.

"Shut your yaps," Tiny said. "It was an epic secret love. Nobody called it."

"Mentally," Case said. "To myself. I said, 'Those two will be in the sack before you know it.'"

"Nobody's in the sack," I said, my ears getting a little hot.

"Not at the moment, anyway," Six-Pack said.

"Not for a couple of weeks," the captain advised from the front seat. "Give the poor guy a little time to recover."

"Poor Loverboy," the guys all chimed in.

"Oh God. Please tell me you're not going to start calling him Loverboy."

"Too late," the guys said, and roughed each other up some more.

OWEN'S SMALL HOSPITAL room was so full—his parents, his sisters, their husbands, at least a few cousins, and a handful of retired firefighters—it was like stepping into a crowded elevator.

Captain Murphy and the guys hustled me in. "We brought you a present," the captain said, as the guys from my crew cheered, and the crowd parted, and I found myself standing beside Owen's bed.

He was alive. He was awake. He was okay.

He was the most beautiful sight in the world.

I caught my breath, and then I held it.

He looked up and met my eyes.

"Hey, rookie," I said.

"Hey, Cassie."

His voice was hoarse from the tube. His face was still burned, a little red in places, but not bad. His hair was adorably mussed.

He reached out his hand over the bedrail, and I took it.

But then I heard Colleen. "What's she doing here? I told you I don't want that girl in here."

I looked up and saw her face, and I knew the captain had been right. She had not been coping well. Her eyes were bloodshot, and her hair was limp. She clearly hadn't slept in a week.

"It's okay," the captain said. "We brought her."

Colleen glared at him. "Why would you do that?"

"We were wrong, Colleen," the captain said. "DeStasio filed a false report. She's not the reason your son got hurt. She's actually the reason he survived."

Colleen looked me over, suspicious.

"You remember when DeStasio hurt his back in that roof collapse?" the captain asked.

Nods and murmurs all around.

"Looks like he got hooked on some of the painkillers they gave him. Then, after Tony died, it got worse. And then Annette left him, and it got even worse. Bad enough that his judgment was off. Bad enough that he started lying. Bad enough that he hallucinated the boy in the fire. He dragged the rookie into that structure, and she"—the captain gestured at me—"dragged him back out. She recognized the cyanide poisoning. She put her own life at risk to find the rookie—unconscious, with his PASS device sounding—under the rubble. She administered the antidote, and she tubed him on scene when he was unconscious and unresponsive with no air and no pulse."

He made me sound pretty great.

"I'm telling you, Colleen," the captain went on, "if this girl hadn't been watching out for him, we wouldn't be at a hospital right now, we'd be at a funeral."

Colleen stared at me for a second.

Then she made her way around the end of the rookie's bed, pushing through the crowd. When she got to me, her face was covered with tears. She pulled me into a full-body hug and didn't let go. I could feel her trembling. She held on and whispered, "Thank you," in my ear.

I hugged her back with one arm, but I kept hold of the rookie's hand with the other.

"Wait a second," one of the rookie's sisters said, watching the scene. "Isn't that Christabel?"

Colleen let me go to get a look.

The captain shook his head. "She's Cassie."

"She's both," the rookie said, his voice raspy, and everybody turned to stare at him. "She is both the best firefighter on our shift"—he met the captain's eyes, and then looked over at his folks—"and my date to the anniversary party."

"It wasn't a date," I said to him, giving him an eyes-only smile.

"It didn't start out as a date," he said, a little flirty, "but it sure wound up that way in the end."

The guys on the crew started whooping and cheering.

I looked down.

"We thought the coast was clear," the rookie said to the room, "but then the captain showed up."

The captain stared at me. "Hanwell was the drunk girl?"

Owen nodded. "Yep. Except not drunk. Just pretending so you wouldn't recognize her."

"It worked," the captain said, impressed.

"We gave her a false name so word wouldn't get back to the station."

Everybody in the room got that. Every single person there knew what a scandal that would have been. Firefighters didn't *date.*

"But why would you even have brought her, son? Why take the risk?"

The rookie looked around at everybody, like, *Duh.* And if it embarrassed him to say this, to admit it out loud for everybody to hear, he sure didn't show it: "Because I'm crazy in love with her," he said with a shrug. "I have been since the first day."

The room went quiet.

Then everybody at once seemed to look down at us holding hands.

Then the guys all burst out cheering, slapping each other on the back like we'd all just won the lottery.

"It was all those blood draws," Six-Pack called out.

"It was when we duct-taped them to the pole!"

"Or when we trapped 'em on the roof."

Here's what surprised me: how cheerful the guys were about it. They seemed so pleased at the idea of Owen and me—and so eager to take the credit. All this time, I'd expected to be reprimanded, at the minimum, and probably more like shunned, if we were found out. But the guys were all for it. They seemed not just okay with it but delighted—a whole crew of firefighter yentas.

Maybe they were just glad the rookie wasn't dead.

Or maybe I'd misjudged them, too, in my way.

We really do see what we expect to see.

The rookie tugged me a little closer. "Come here."

The room quieted as I stepped closer.

"I've got something for you," the rookie said. Then he reached toward the tray where his breakfast still sat and he picked up a little silver ring.

Made of tinfoil.

I stared at it.

"I made it from the applesauce top," he said, meeting my eyes. "It might be a little sticky."

I held very still. "What's this for?"

He held it up. "I promised myself that if I lived, the very first thing I'd do was ask you to marry me."

"Guess he likes you back, Hanwell," someone shouted.

"Will you marry me?" the rookie asked, holding up the tinfoil ring, his gaze pinned on mine.

I nodded before I could find the words. "I will."

And then he was tugging me closer, and then sliding that homemade ring on my finger, and then he kissed my hand in a way that inspired the captain to start hustling everybody out of the room.

"All right, all right," the captain said. "Let's give these two kids a moment of privacy." The rubberneckers weren't easy to herd. "You!" The captain pointed at the closest guy to the door. "Let's move!" Then, to another guy, "You! Out! Let's go!"

Once the crowd cleared out, the captain put his arms around the final two stragglers, Big Robby and Colleen. "Let's give Loverboy a minute and take you two for some coffee."

The door closed behind them, and we were alone.

The rookie tugged at me to sit beside him. "Get down here."

I let his bedrail down and sat. "They wouldn't let me in to see you," I said. "But I snuck in anyway."

"I thought I dreamed that," he said.

"No. It was real."

I didn't even realize my face was covered in tears until the rookie reached up to brush them off.

"I'm so glad you're okay," I said, and my voice was so shaky, the words trembled, too.

"Thank you for not letting me die," Owen said.

"Thank you for not dying."

"Thank you for agreeing to marry me."

"Thank you for asking."

"If I could lean forward and kiss you some more right now, I would."

I smiled. "I'd kiss you back."

He nodded. "But I can't. You know—because of the ribs."

"I get it," I said.

"So if you want to get kissed," he went on, eyeing me, "you have to do all the work yourself."

I leaned in. "I don't want to hurt you," I said.

"But you do want to kiss me."

"I really, truly do."

"Be careful, then," he said.

So I kissed him. Carefully. Supporting my weight on one arm, and resting the palm of my other hand against the contour of his unshaven neck. I could feel his pulse, simple and steady, and I let myself feel so grateful—so unabashedly grateful—that it was there.

When I pulled back to take in the sight of him, he said, "Don't stop."

"The captain says I have to go easy on you."

"Don't go easy on me."

"I should probably let you rest."

"Don't let me rest."

"I should probably go."

"Definitely don't go," he said.

He looked tired, as if even just a little bit of flirting and kissing was enough to knock him out. But I didn't want to go. Instead, I shifted to lie beside him in that skinny little bed, slow and careful not to hurt him anywhere, nestled between him and the railing.

When I finally got settled, my head against his shoulder, as if it were the most natural possible next step in the conversation, Owen said, "We should do it today."

I lifted up my elbow. "Do what?"

He smiled and met my eyes. "Get married."

"Here? In the hospital?"

"I'm sure they've got a chaplain or something."

"No," I said.

He met my eyes. "No, you won't marry me?"

"No, I won't marry you today. In a hospital."

"Why not?"

"Because it's too many good things at once. I want to keep something to look forward to."

He smiled, lay back against the pillow, and closed his eyes. I laid my head beside him. I thought he was almost asleep when he said, "Trust me. You have so much to look forward to."

"I agree," I said.

But anything could happen. I knew that, too.

I knew too much about life to pretend that it wasn't half tragedy. We lose the people we love. We disappoint each other. We misunderstand. We get lost and lonely and angry.

But right now, in this moment, we were okay.

Better than okay.

My mom was in her garden with plans to see Josie for lunch and a newly repaired kitchen window. The guys from the firehouse were out in the waiting room telling bawdy jokes. DeStasio was getting a second chance to pull himself together. Big Robby and Colleen were sipping a couple of hard-earned coffees. I had my job back—if I chose to take it.

And the rookie was alive. And I was next to him, holding his hand, feeling his chest rise and fall like the most amazing miracle in all of time. I'd take it. I wouldn't complain.

I'd forgiven us all, and I'd do it again.

Maybe everybody was just foolish and doomed. Maybe nobody got a happy ending in the end. Maybe all happiness could ever hope to be was a tiny interruption from sorrow.

But there was no denying what this was. A genuine, blissful moment of joy.

It couldn't last, but that's what made it matter.

And that just had to be enough.

Epilogue

I NEVER MADE it back to Texas.

But I did see my crew from Austin again, a year later, when the rookie and I got married in Rockport on a warm summer evening at sunset. The whole gang drove up from Texas in a caravan of pickup trucks after agreeing to be my bridesmaids. Hernandez vied for position as maid of honor, but Josie beat him out.

Josie made my wedding dress, too. As thin as a slip, but with lots of ruffles. Her mystery husband wound up holding their squirmy baby during the ceremony while she held my bouquet. Hernandez talked his cousin into driving his shiny Airstream taco truck across the country to cater the reception for us—so he wound up in a position of honor, too. Cousin of Taco Truck Guy. He wanted us to note it in the program.

But we didn't.

He brought us Austin's new firefighter calendar as a wedding present.

Our crew from Lillian served as the rookie's groomsmen, and all his sisters stood up with him, too. We had a parade of little flower children. And we couldn't decide between Captain Murphy from Lillian and

Captain Harris from Austin to officiate, so we asked them both, and they both got certified, and they took turns.

What can I say? When it came time for us to stand up and make our vows to each other, we had a lot of great people standing with us.

My dad and Carol flew in for the wedding, and my mom and dad gave me away together. My mom wore a white silk eye patch that Josie made her with remnants from my dress.

Later, my mom told me that she'd found a moment to take my father aside and apologize to him. For leaving him, of course, but also for the way that she'd left him—with so many questions so unanswered for so long. "You know that I never cheated on you, right?" she'd asked him, leaning in to study his eyes.

But he hadn't known. All that time, he'd thought she must have cheated. For years and years, he'd just assumed that she'd betrayed him as well as abandoned him

"No," she said, taking his hand and squeezing it. "You were abandoned. But not betrayed." Then she shook her head and looked out at the ocean. "Not that it makes a difference now, really."

"It does make a difference," my dad told her, and he squeezed her hand back. It didn't change the past, of course, but it mattered.

Colleen and Big Robby were there, of course, and the rookie's cousin Alex bartended for free and handed out condoms on the sly. I invited the ICU nurse who'd sneaked me in, and I'm pretty sure the two of them hooked up.

Did we invite DeStasio?

We did.

His attitude toward me improved quite a bit after I saved his life.

And mine improved toward him after he got out of rehab, showed up at my place to sincerely apologize, with actual tears of regret, and made a pledge to spend his retirement years volunteering at the local women's shelter as a way of atoning for his mistakes.

In acknowledgment of his personal growth, I got him a T-shirt that says THIS IS WHAT A FEMINIST LOOKS LIKE.

It didn't change what he'd done, of course, but it mattered.

Plus, he'd started dating someone—the director of the women's shelter, in fact, which improved his personality quite a bit. I could almost see why people liked him now. Almost.

I WANT TO tell you that Diana managed to permanently kick her cancer through sassiness and sheer force of will, but she didn't. Even before the wedding, the tumor had started growing again, and she already had another grim diagnosis.

But, in that way of hers, she didn't tell me.

She let me have that one beautiful, breezy night to stand in my white silk gown and drink champagne and look fully forward to all the blessings that lay ahead.

She never officially told me, actually. She never spoke the words. She knew that once the tumor was back in action, I'd figure it out. In the end, we got a year more than we'd hoped for. And she knew that neither one of us took even a single day of that extra time for granted.

She'd hoped to see a grandbaby before she was gone, but we couldn't get that done in time. I did manage to get pregnant, though—just barely—before we lost her. Somehow, she knew before I did.

"Guess what?" she said, on the day before she died.

"What?"

"You're pregnant."

The rookie and I had been trying for a baby—with enthusiasm—but nothing had taken yet. Several months of clockwork-like periods had left me a little discouraged.

I wrinkled my nose. "I don't feel pregnant."

"But you are," she said, closing her eyes. "And it's a girl. And you will love her more than you love yourself. And you'll disappoint her, too—and never live up to the standards you set for yourself. But don't worry. She'll be okay."

"Yes," I said, shoving tears off my cheeks. "She will."

Diana did wind up leaving Wallace's house to me, and the rookie and I wound up moving in, and we now have two toddlers ransacking the place on a daily basis. But we figure if that place could handle Samuel and Chastity McKee, and those eight children, and all the countless fish they pickled, it can put up with a few Hanwell-Callaghans.

We kept the pottery shop open for a while, to sell off what was left of Diana's stock to fans and friends. Some of the loveliest, most special pieces, we kept to display in an antique hutch with glass doors that lock with a skeleton key. Those, we'll hold on to. But the rest of them, we use. She wanted us to use them. They are the bowls and plates our kids are growing up eating on.

Eventually, the rookie converted the old shop into a lively little restaurant with seven tables. We stay open year-round, and there's always a line out the door. DeStasio helps in summer, during the busy season. It's hard work, but the rookie doesn't mind.

And yes, we all still call him the rookie.

I went back to my job in Lillian. Eventually. After they groveled for a while.

It's actually a pretty good schedule for a mom. I only work two days a week—twenty-four-hour days, but still . . . Josie managed to have two more babies, and her mystery husband wound up shifting jobs after that to be home a lot more. Her littlest one and my oldest were born just days apart, and we've worked out a kid-sharing co-op to cover the evenings when I'm working and the days when Josie is. Between us all—as well as the world-famous C-shift babysitting crew of Lillian's bravest—we get it done.

It really does take a village. And a half.

SO I FORGAVE my mother. And my dad did, too. And the rookie forgave himself for once having been a very dumb kid. And I forgave DeStasio for recently having been a very dumb adult. And all in all, as a group, we pretty much mastered forgiveness.

I even read a whole book on the psychology of post-traumatic growth, and how, in the wake of the terrible, traumatic, unfair, cruel, gaping wounds that life inflicts on us, we can become wiser and stronger than we were before.

Am I wiser and stronger now?

Without question. Even in the wake of it all.

I've spent so much time wishing that what happened never happened.

But it did. And the question I try to focus on is, *What now?*

Now that I'm older, and better, and have done so much healing, I do try to think about the bigger picture. I pay attention to politics, and I vote for candidates who care about safeguarding women. I taught self-defense classes in Texas, and I'll teach them again here once my kids get a little older and I have more time. I always make sure in my job to treat victims of assault with special compassion and tenderness.

And I've started volunteering with a nonprofit group that asks survivors of rape and assault to go into schools, prisons, and colleges, and tell their stories. To girls—but, equally as important, to boys.

It's terrifying.

I go once a month without fail, and I have to stop on the drive home every single time to throw up by the side of the road.

But I do it anyway.

I do it because I believe that human connection is the only thing that will save us. I do it because I believe we learn empathy when we listen to other people's stories and feel their pain with them. I do it because I know for certain that our world has an empathy problem with women, and this is one brave thing I can do to help fix it.

Honestly, I tell myself, if I could share my story with DeStasio, I can share it with anyone.

I hope those kids hear me. I hope they come away resolved to be better people. To be more careful with one another. To try like hell to use their pain to *help* others rather than harm them.

Maybe they get it, and maybe they don't. All I can do is try.

But when I get home, Owen is always there, waiting for me. He makes sure he has dinner ready—something warm and soothing and buttery. On those nights, I play with our kids and kiss their chubby little bellies until bedtime, and then he takes them up to their little attic bedroom with pom-pom curtains and tucks them in. When he comes back down, he brings me a blanket and a mug of tea, and we sit on the sofa and talk about the day. He tries his best to make me laugh. Sometimes he gives me a foot rub with lemon-scented lotion. Sometimes we watch bad TV.

He can't fix it, but he tries to make it better.

And then, when it's our bedtime at last, he falls asleep in my arms, and I fall asleep in his.

Unless I can't get to sleep right away.

Then, just like I've done for so long, I close my eyes and imagine making chocolate chip cookies. I measure out the chips. I crack the eggs. I watch it all churn in the mixer. It's the same as it always was. Except now it's different.

Now, it's not just me baking cookies alone. Now, I always imagine my sixteen-year-old self there, too—right beside me.

When the cookies are ready, we pull them out, sit side by side on the sofa, and eat them—still warm and gooey—and drink glasses of ice cold milk. Sometimes I put my arm around her. Sometimes I say compassionate, understanding, encouraging things. Sometimes I lean in and promise her with all the conviction I possess that what happened to her won't destroy her life. That in the end, she will heal, and find a new way to be okay.

She never believes me, but I say it anyway.

I know these moments don't really happen. I know I can't truly step back in time and mother my long-lost self. I know the teenage me and the current me can't actually hang out like that, eating cookies and rolling our eyes at the world like besties.

It's pure fiction. Of course. I'm just telling myself stories.

But that's the life-changing thing about stories.

We believe them anyway.

* * *

BUT, HOLD ON—*did I ever forgive Heath Thompson?*

Not exactly.

I forgave *myself,* at last. Even though I'd done nothing to require forgiveness.

I didn't really forgive Heath Thompson.

With him, in the end, I guess you could say I chose revenge.

I don't know if you read about it in the papers, but he wound up going to jail for a long time.

And not for what you'd expect, either.

Tax fraud.

Though, in that same month, in a front-page story, he was outed as a patron for an expensive prostitution ring. And then, in the wake of that, he was sued by thirteen different women for assault. And then his wife left him—but not before posting some deeply, eternally humiliating photos of him in some very embarrassing outfits on the internet.

We'll leave it at that. Use your imagination. Then make whatever you're picturing a hundred times more humiliating and try again.

But what did he go to jail for? *Tax fraud.*

On top of it all, he turned out to be embezzling city money to pay settlements to the women who were suing him.

Which the good people of Austin, Texas, did not take too kindly to.

Yeah, he went down in flames.

One of the women he'd assaulted ran for his city council seat—and won.

All this was in the papers and on cable news for months. But somehow I missed it.

I must have been too busy being happy.

Honestly, I didn't even hear about it until years later—when Heath Thompson tried for parole and was soundly rejected, and the whole series of scandals churned back through the news cycle.

I spent some time after that wondering if I should have spoken up—and wondering why I hadn't. Partly, I just didn't know about the lawsuits, way back home in Texas. I'd like to think I would have joined them if I'd known.

But I can't know for sure.

For so long, it was everything I could do to keep my head above water.

Sometimes I wonder, if I'd been able to tell someone sooner about what he did, if I might have been able to protect the women he harmed after me. Maybe. Maybe one brave voice could have stopped him. Or maybe, just as likely, I'd have been blamed and humiliated and ignored—and he'd have gotten a pass.

I know why women don't speak out. It's hard enough just to survive.

And, by the way, the blame for what Heath Thompson did to all of us sits nowhere but on his shoulders.

The morning I discovered all the news about his scandals, I took a few minutes to enjoy his spectacular downfall, and then I got right back to making us all heart-shaped pancakes for breakfast.

I had more important people to think about.

I guess it really proves the old saying: "The best revenge is marrying a kindhearted guy with a washboard stomach who brings you coffee in bed every morning."

Wait—is that the saying?

Maybe it's "The best revenge is spending your life in a cottage by the ocean with a world-champion kisser who takes the phrase 'with my body, I thee worship' literally."

That might not be it either.

How about "The best revenge is flying kites on the beach with your chubby toddlers." Or "The best revenge is dancing to oldies in the kitchen with your goofy friends."

Or maybe "The best revenge is to love like crazy."

Gosh, what is that darned saying? "The best revenge is . . ."

"The best revenge is . . ."

Oh, well . . .

I forget.

Acknowledgments

I started dating a cute, funny, mischievous paramedic right after I graduated from college, and I've been with him ever since. All these years later, he's now a history teacher, but he still volunteers as a firefighter/EMT. All to say, when I started writing a book about a firefighter, I knew exactly how much I didn't know.

So glad I found Gary Ludwig's book on life in the fire service: *Blood, Sweat, Tears, and Prayers*. I was also lucky that so many firefighters were willing to let me visit their stations. I am so grateful to the many folks at the Houston Fire Department who answered so many questions: Captain Jerry Meek and the great guys on the D-shift at HFD Station 11 for their warmth and candor and hilarious stories. Kevin Brolan, retired Chief Investigator, Arson Bureau, HFD, was very helpful as well. Maria Jordan at HFD Station 17 graciously talked with me about what it's like for women in the fire service. Thanks also to Kristi Baksht's friend Kim, who introduced me to her husband, Andrew Eckert, a firefighter/EMT at HFD Station 16—who gave me a tour of his station, answered a thousand questions, and even demonstrated a pole slide.

I also want to thank the authors who kindly recommended my last book, *How to Walk Away*, to readers. It takes a village to get the word out, for real, and I'm grateful beyond words to Emily Giffin, Nina George, Elinor Lipman, Jill Santopolo, Graeme Simpsion, Karen White, Brené Brown, Jenny Lawson, Catherine Newman, and Taylor Jenkins Reid. Sincere thanks also to novelist Caroline Leech for coaching me in Scottish. A hundred grateful hugs!

Thanks also to Vicky Wight and Bridget Stokes of Six Foot Pictures, who have seriously given me the thrill of a lifetime this year by turning my novel *The Lost Husband* into a movie.

To all my pals at St. Martin's Press: I am so devoted to you! I've been writing novels a long time, and I know exactly how lucky I am to have your support. Sally Richardson, Rachel Diebel, Jessica Preeg, Erica Martirano, Karen Masnica, Jordan Hanley, Lisa Senz, Janna Dokos, Elizabeth Catalano, Devan Norman, Brant Janeway, Meghan Harrison, Olga Grlic, Danielle Fiorella, India Cooper, and Andrew (and Katherine) Weber—I seriously love you. And a special, sincere, adoring set of thank-yous to my agent, Helen Breitwieser, who believed in me all along, and my editor, Jen Enderlin, who took me on and changed everything.

Hugs to my fun family: Shelley and Matt Stein (and Yazzie), Lizzie and Scott Fletcher, Bill Pannill and Molly Hammond, and Al and Ingrid Center. Sincere thanks to our bookkeeper, Faye Robeson, who is not quite family, but pretty darned close.

Thanks to my genuinely delightful kids, Anna and Thomas, who are so patient with me when I think in circles instead of straight lines, and who crack me up every day. I am so grateful to get to be their mama.

Thanks to my amazing mom, Deborah Detering, who has doggedly refused to ever give up on me. Everything I know about believing in myself, I learned because she showed me how.

And, at last, a thousand heartfelt thanks to my husband, Gordon. He's one of the world's true good guys, and I'm more grateful than I can say. For everything.

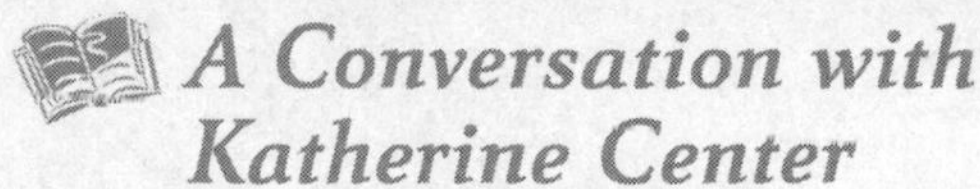

A Conversation with Katherine Center

Why do you think you became a writer? What turned you into a writer?

Lots and lots of reasons! I'm a talker from a family of talkers. I've always loved words, and I frequently just stop to notice them and admire them and say a word out loud and kind of feel the experience of making the sound ("astonished" is a perennial favorite). I love syllables. I love the music of language and the rhythm. I love conversation—chatting, gabbing, bantering. I love joking around with people. I have a whole mental collection of memories of funny things people have said, and sometimes I'll crack myself up while brushing my teeth in the morning as I go back and remember them. It's really been a whole lifetime of just loving words and sentences and paragraphs and stories—and being endlessly fascinated by different ways of putting them together. My parents loved books and stories (my mom has a master's in library science, and my dad was a journalist and then a lawyer), and I had great teachers who encouraged me. But I think the thing that really turned me into a writer—maybe more than anything else—was keeping a journal. I started keeping journals at the age of twelve and wrote in them constantly for ten solid years. Malcolm Gladwell says you have to practice for ten thousand hours to master something, and that's definitely where I put in my time!

You often describe your books as "bittersweet comedies." Where did that term come from—and what does it mean to you?

THINGS YOU SAVE IN A FIRE

by Katherine Center

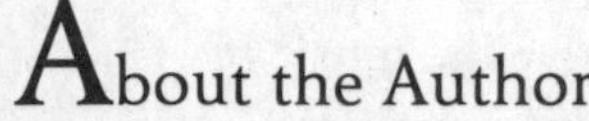

About the Author

• A Conversation with Katherine Center

Keep On Reading

• Recommended Reading

• Reading Group Questions

A Reading Group Gold Selection

Also available as an audiobook
from Macmillan Audio

For more reading group suggestions
visit www.readinggroupgold.com.

ST. MARTIN'S GRIFFIN

When I first started writing novels, I couldn't find the right category for classifying them. They didn't seem to fit anywhere just right . . . and so I just made up a category. The stories I write are half comedies and half tragedies. They feature characters who really have to struggle and cope with genuinely hard things—but they do that by cracking a lot of jokes. We have a tendency to separate stories into "tragedies," down at one end of the spectrum, and "comedies," down at the other, as if they are totally unrelated things. But in my experience, comedy and tragedy live shoulder to shoulder. Jokes are an essential coping mechanism for stress and sorrow and worry and grief. I truly think that comedy exists because of tragedy. We invented it to help us cope with all the suffering life throws at us. That's my favorite kind of humor—the kind that's fueled by heartbreak. So it doesn't seem strange to me at all to write "laugh and cry" books. Because to me, life is always both, just right at the same time.

You've said that your battle cry is "Read for joy." How did you come to that idea? What does it mean to you?

I used to read for joy—for fun, for delight—when I was young, but as I got older, I stopped. I got into high school, and reading became about serious work and hard-core achievement. For years, I thought of reading as work. Then, on my fortieth birthday, the present I gave myself was that, for the whole year, I wasn't going to read any book that I thought I "should" read. I was only going to read books that I wanted to read. I barely even knew what it meant to read for fun anymore, but I decided that if a book felt like homework, I couldn't read it. I gave myself a fifty-page rule—if a book hadn't grabbed me in fifty pages, I had to start another one. There's value in reading difficult, uncomfortable books, of course. But that's not the only way to read. There is also value in reading something that just takes you away, and immerses you, and delights you. There's value in following your own compass about what stories resonate for you and matter to you at different times in your life. I went through an intense period of de-snobification that year, and it was one of the best things that ever happened to me. I read twice as much now as I did before—and I have a lot more fun, too. The more I talk to people, the more I think my experience was not all that uncommon. A reader wrote to me one time and said, "My husband even loved your book, and he hates feel-good reads." And I wrote back and said, "Nothing wrong with feeling good once in a while." I wish I could give us all that permission—to just read for joy. It's life-changing, I swear.

What was the inspiration for* Things You Save in a Fire*?

My brilliant editor, Jen Enderlin, noticed Cassie—who has a very minor part in my novel *How to Walk Away*—and wanted to know more about her. Honestly, when Jen suggested that I might make Cassie the main character of my next book, I was hesitant. My husband has been a volunteer firefighter/EMT for many years, and as much as I admire him, I've always had a hard time relating to how he could want to put on a hundred pounds of bunker gear on a hot Texas day and walk into a

burning building. And if there's one thing I really have to do with my main characters, it's relate. I don't have to be exactly like them, but I need to understand them. I need to get it—why they want what they want and what they're willing to do to get those things. I just couldn't imagine wanting to work that hard and be that hot. But then I talked with my husband, and he said, "What if she's just really, really good at it?" And suddenly, I got her. I know what it's like to want—so badly—to reach your potential. I know what it's like to try and try and not give up because you love what you do so much. That's me with writing. Once I had a way in, the story just kind of wrote itself.

What kind of research did you do before writing this novel?

So much research! I knew just enough before I started to be intimidated. I knew exactly how much I didn't know. The world of firefighting is a very specific, rather closed culture, and I knew I wasn't a part of that world. I read memoirs and watched documentaries. I put on my husband's bunker gear and tried to move in it (not easy). I visited firehouses and interviewed firefighters. At one house, they announced my presence over the speaker system—"lady in the house"—so the guys would know to be on their best behavior. I felt a little shy going to do those interviews, but the firefighters were universally welcoming and very forthcoming—and utterly hilarious. It was particularly fun to talk with my husband about all of it—which I did constantly during the writing process—because though I'd been hearing his firefighter stories all these years we'd been together, I'd never tried to get inside them before. I'd never tried to listen so closely that I could picture myself there. He read draft after draft for accuracy, and he kept saying, "I love it. More firefighting." He had so many great stories, and the more we talked, the more tempted I was to work them in. But finally, when it was time to turn the book in, my editor read it and she said, "I love it. Less firefighting." So not all those stories made it in.

What's next for you? Are you currently working on another book?

I have a new book on the way! It's called *What You Wish For*, and it's the story of Samantha Casey, a librarian at a historic school in the sleepy island town of Galveston, Texas. When Duncan Carpenter, an old teacher friend of hers (and a former crush she hasn't seen in years) gets hired as the school's new principal, she thinks his arrival will be great for the school . . . until she discovers that he's changed beyond recognition: from fun, wacky, and warmhearted to cold, tough, and warden-like. When, in the name of safety, Duncan wants to basically turn the place into a prison, Sam needs to find a way to stop him—and stand up for the kids, the teachers, herself, and everything that really matters.

I'm extra excited about this story, because Duncan was a minor character—the annoying younger brother of the main character—in my novel *Happiness for Beginners*, and I've always wanted to give him his own story. *What You Wish For* is set ten years after *Happiness*, and Duncan has grown up a lot—maybe too much. It was such a treat to

hang out with Duncan again and get to know him better—and to get a little visit with Helen and Jake (the main characters from *Happiness*), too. I've always wanted to set a story on Galveston Island as well—it's the beach I grew up going to, and the place where I still do the majority of my writing.

I'm also just getting started on my next novel! It woke me up this morning—writing itself in my head!

Recommended Reading

Why We Love: The Nature and Chemistry of Romantic Love
Helen Fisher

This fascinating nonfiction read looks at the role of romantic love in human life. Researcher Helen Fisher put people in love in brain scanners and watched what happened when they looked at photos of their partners. The scans showed activity in the oldest parts of the brain—and Fisher takes a long, thoughtful look at what this means about who we are and the importance of love in our lives.

The Storytelling Animal: How Stories Make Us Human
Jonathan Gottschall

This fascinating book tries to get at the role of storytelling in human life and describes stories as "the last bastion of magic." For anyone who's interested in how stories work and why they're so powerful, it's a great read.

David and Goliath: Underdogs, Misfits, and the Art of Battling Giants
Malcolm Gladwell

Of all of Malcolm Gladwell's books, this one, for me, is the most moving. It looks at the phenomenon of strength—and how it can so often be misunderstood. Advantages can hobble us in unexpected ways, and disadvantages can work in our favor.

Know My Name
Chanel Miller

Chanel Miller is the woman whose victim

statement about her sexual assault by Brock Turner was posted online and went viral—read by millions of people in a matter of days. I was one of those people, and I read it with tears running down my face. At the time, she was known as Emily Doe. Here, in her memoir, she takes back her name and tells her story in her own voice.

The Nightingale
Kristin Hannah

For a page-turning read that really showcases both physical and emotional courage, you can't beat *The Nightingale.* A historical novel about two sisters in France during World War II who survive the occupation in ways that require courage of every kind. Very inspiring—and an absolutely gripping, up-all-night reading experience.

Why Marriages Succeed or Fail: And How You Can Make Yours Last
John Gottman, Ph.D.

One of the reasons the rookie is so dreamy, to me at least, is that he really appreciates Cassie. John Gottman is a researcher who looks at what marriages need to thrive, and one of the many things he talks about is creating a "culture of appreciation" in a relationship—where partners focus on and savor the things about each other that they love. I thought about this book when I was writing the rookie. I wanted him to be an absolute genius at the act of appreciation—for Cassie's sake, if nothing else.

1. At the start of the story, Cassie pummels a city councilman onstage after he touches her inappropriately. How did you react to that? Did it make you like her more—or put you off? What did you think of that moment once you knew the full story?
2. Cassie spends the early part of the story avoiding a phone call from her mother—which turns out to be a plea for Cassie to move across the country and help her with her health issues. What did you think of Cassie's reluctance to go at the time? What was Cassie afraid of?
3. After the debacle at the awards dinner, Cassie is called into Captain Harris's office, and the captain gives her some pretty intense advice about how to survive in an all-male fire station that doesn't want her there. Could you relate to some of her "rules" for Cassie? Have you ever been in a work situation where you had to monitor your own behavior in similar ways?
4. Cassie's goal when she arrives in Rockport is to do her duty and nothing more. She doesn't want to bond or be friends with her mother, no matter how much her mom might want to. Why do you think Cassie works so hard to keep her mom at arm's length? What's at stake for her?
5. Cassie's captain has warned her that there's one thing she absolutely *cannot* do in her new firehouse: Date firefighters. Cut to Cassie laying eyes on the dripping-wet rookie on her first day in the firehouse and feeling a powerful attraction to him. As the story

progresses, he becomes one of her favorite things about her workday—and, at the same time, the biggest threat to her job. When she goes with him to his parents' anniversary party, she knows she's putting herself in danger. Why does she do that? Is it a total mistake—or is there some wisdom there, too?

6. Cassie is better at firefighting than the rookie is. Nothing fazes her, but he passes out taking blood, goes pale riding out to calls, and throws up after his first fire. What did you think of this dynamic? How is the rookie good for Cassie? How is she good for him?
7. The guys at the fire station have a lot of mixed feelings about Cassie being there, and yet it's not the outright hostility she'd feared. In what ways do their attitudes make things harder? Are there any ways that they help her? It takes them a while to get past their assumptions about her, but it also takes her a while to do the same thing with them. In what ways did the firefighters surprise you?
8. Cassie is a master of physical courage—but her movie to Rockport forces her to explore emotional courage. Diana insists, "Choosing to love—despite all the ways that people let you down, and disappear, and break your heart. Knowing everything we know about how hard life is and choosing to love, anyway . . . That's not weakness, that's courage." How does falling in love with the rookie help Cassie learn about emotional courage? How does falling in love with the rookie impact her relationship with Diana?

9. As cruel as DeStasio is toward Cassie, he's got a tragic story of his own. Why doesn't he want Cassie's forgiveness? Why does Cassie forgive him anyway? Would you have forgiven him? How do you manage forgiveness in your own life?
10. Cassie's dad says, "The best revenge is forgetting," and Cassie says, "The best revenge is marrying a kindhearted guy with a washboard stomach who brings you coffee in bed every morning." What *is* the best revenge? Does Cassie get her revenge in the end?

Turn the page for a sneak peek at Katherine Center's next novel

Available July 2020

ONE

I WAS THE one dancing with Max when it happened.

No one ever remembers who it was now, but it was me.

Actually, pretty much everything that night was me. Max and Babette had gone on a last-minute, two-week, second honeymoon cruise around the boot of Italy that they'd found for a steal—and the return date just happened to be two days before Max's sixtieth birthday party—smack in the middle of summer.

Babette had worried that she couldn't book a trip with an end date so close to the party, but I stopped her. "I've got this. I'll get everything ready."

"I'm not sure you realize what a big undertaking a party like this is," Babette said. "We've got the whole school coming. Three hundred people—maybe more. It's a huge job."

"I think I can handle it."

"But it's your summer," Babette said. "I want you to be carefree."

"And I want you," I said, pointing at her, "to take a dirt-cheap second honeymoon to Italy."

I didn't have to twist their arms. They went.

And I was happy to take charge of the party. Max and Babette were not technically my parents—but they were the nearest thing I had. My mom died when I was ten, and let's just say my dad was not my closest relative.

Actually . . . technically he *was* my closest relative.

But we weren't close.

Plus, I didn't have any siblings—just a few scattered cousins, but no family anywhere nearby. God, now that I'm laying it out like this, I have to add: no boyfriend, either. Not for a long time. Not even any pets.

I did have friends, though. Lest I make myself sound too sad. Especially my friend Alice, six feet tall, friendly, and relentlessly positive Alice, who was a math specialist and wore a T-shirt with a math joke on it every day to work.

The first day I met her, her shirt said, NERD SQUAD.

"Great shirt," I said.

She said, "Usually, I wear math jokes."

"Is there such a thing as math jokes?" I asked.

"Wait and see."

To sum up: Yes. There are more math jokes in the world than you can possibly imagine. And Alice had a T-shirt for all of them. Most of which I didn't understand.

We had almost none of the same interests, Alice and me, but it didn't matter. She was a tall, sporty, mathy person, and I was the opposite of all those things. I was an early riser, and she was a night owl. She wore the exact same version of Levi's and T-shirts to work every day, and every day I put together some wildly different concoction of clothes. She read spy novels—exclusively—and I read anything I could get my hands on. She played on an intramural beach volleyball team, for Pete's sake.

But we were great friends.

I was lucky to be a librarian at a very special, very legendary elementary school on Galveston Island called the Kempner School—and not only did I adore my job, and the kids, and the other teachers, I also lived in Babette and Max Kempner's garage apartment. Though, "garage apartment" doesn't quite capture it. The real term was "carriage house" because it had once been the apartment above the stables.

Back when horses-and-buggies were a thing.

Living with Max and Babette was kind of like living with the king and queen. They had founded Kempner, and they'd run it together all these years, and they were just . . . beloved. Their historic mansion—that's right: real estate is super-cheap in Galveston—was just blocks from school, too, so teachers were constantly stopping by, hanging out on the porch, helping Max in his woodshop. Max and Babette were just the kind of people other people just wanted to be near.

The point is, I was glad to do something wonderful for them.

They did wonderful things for me all the time.

In fact, the more I thought about it, the more it seemed like a rare opportunity to really astonish them with the greatest party ever. I started a Pinterest board, and I went through magazines for décor ideas. I got so excited, I even called up their daughter Tina to see if she might like to do the project together.

Ironically, their daughter Tina was one of the rare people in town who *didn't* hang out at Max and Babette's all the time. So I didn't know her all that well.

Also: she didn't like me.

I suspected she thought I was trying to take her place.

Fair enough. She wasn't totally wrong.

"Why are *you* decorating for my dad's party?" she said, when I called—her voice tight.

"You know," I said, "just—timing." It's such a disorienting thing when people openly dislike you. It made me a little tongue-tied around her. "They're on that trip . . ."

I waited for a noise of recognition.

"To Italy . . ."

Nothing.

"So I just offered to get the party done for them."

"They should have called me," she said.

They hadn't called her because they knew she wouldn't have time. She had one of those husbands who kept her very busy. "They wanted to," I lied. "I just jumped in and offered so fast . . . they never got the chance."

"How unusual," she said.

"But that's why I'm calling. I thought maybe we could do it together."

I could feel her weighing her options. Planning her own father's sixtieth birthday party was kind of her rightful job . . . but now, if she said yes, she'd have no way to avoid me.

"I'll pass," she said.

And so the job was mine.

Alice wound up helping me, because Alice was the kind of person who was always happiest when she was helping. Babette had been thinking streamers and cake, but I couldn't leave it at that. I wanted to go big. This was *Max*! Principal, founder, living legend—and genuinely goodhearted human. His whole philosophy was, *Never miss a chance to celebrate*. He celebrated everybody else all the time.

Dammit, it was time to celebrate the man himself.

I wanted to do something epic. Magical. Unforgettable.

But Babette had left an envelope on her kitchen table labeled "For Party Supplies," and when I opened it up, it held a budget of sixty-seven dollars. Many of them in ones.

Babette was pretty thrifty.

That's when Alice suggested we call the maintenance guys to see if we could borrow the school's twinkle lights from the storage facility. When I told them what we were up to, they said "Hell, yes," and offered to hang everything for me. "Do you want the Christmas wreaths, too?" they asked.

"Just the lights, thank you."

See that? Everybody loved Max.

The more people found out what we were doing, the more everybody wanted in. It seemed like half the adults in this town had been Max's students, or had him for a baseball coach, or volunteered with him for beach cleanups.

I started getting messages on Facebook and texts I didn't recognize:

The florist on Winnie Street wanted to donate bouquets for the tables, and the lady who owned the fabric shop on Sealy Avenue wanted to offer some bolts of tulle to drape around the room, and a local seventies cover band wanted to play for free. I got offers for free food, free cookies, free booze, and free balloons. I got texts from a busker who wanted to do a fire-eating show, an ice-sculptor who wanted to carve a bust of Max for the buffet table, and a fancy wedding photographer who offered to capture the whole night—*no charge*.

I said yes to them all.

And then I got the best message of all. A phone call from a guy offering me the Garten Verein.

I'm not saying Max and Babette wouldn't have been happy with the school cafeteria—Max and Babette were pretty good at being happy anywhere—but the Garten Verein was one of the loveliest buildings in town. An octagonal, Victorian dancing pavilion built in 1880, now painted a pale green with white gingerbread. Nowadays it was mostly a venue for weddings and fancy events—a *not-cheap* venue. But several of Max's former students owned the building, and they offered it for free.

"Kempner class of '94 for the win!" the guy on the phone said. Then he added. "Never miss a chance to celebrate."

"Spoken like a true fan of Max," I said.

"Give him my love, will ya?" the Garten Verein guy said.

Max and Babette were too jet-lagged by the time they came home to even stop by school, so the change of venue took them completely by surprise. That evening, I met them on their front porch—Babette in her little round specs and salt-and-pepper pixie cut, forgoing her signature paint-splattered overalls for a sweet little Mexican-embroidered cotton dress. And Max looking impossibly dapper in a seersucker suit and a pink bow tie.

They held hands as we walked, and I found myself thinking, *Relationship goals.*

Instead of walking two blocks west, toward school, I led them north.

"You know we're going the wrong way, right?" Max stage-whispered to me.

"Don't you just know everything?" I teased, stalling.

"I know where my damn school is," Max said, but his eyes were smiling.

"I think," I said then, "if you stick with me, you'll be glad you did."

And that's when the Garten Verein came into view.

An arc of balloons swayed over the iron entrance gate. Alice—amateur French horn player and faculty sponsor of the fifth-grade jazz band—was already there, just inside the garden, and as soon as she saw us, she gave them the go-sign to start honking out a rendition of "Happy Birthday." Kids filled the park, and parents stood holding glass champagne flutes, and as soon as Max arrived, they all cheered.

As Max and Babette took in the sight, she turned to me. "What did you do?"

"We did not go over budget," I said. "Much."

We stepped into the garden, and their daughter Tina arrived just behind us—looking svelte and put-together, as always, with her third grader, Clay, holding her hand. Babette and Max pulled them both into a hug, and then Max said, "Where's Kent Buckley?"

Tina's husband was the kind of guy everybody always called by his first and last name. He wasn't ever just "Kent." He was always "Kent Buckley." Like it was all one word.

Tina turned craned her neck to look for her husband, and I took a second to admire how elegant her dark hair looked in that low bun. Elegant, but mean. That was Tina.

"There," she said, pointing. "Conference call."

There he was, a hundred feet back, conducting some kind of meeting on the Bluetooth speaker attached to his ear—pacing the sidewalk, gesticulating with his arms, and clearly not too pleased.

We all watched him for a second, and it occurred to me that he probably thought he looked like a big shot. He looked like he was kind of proud of how he was behaving, like we'd be impressed that he had the authority to yell at people. Even though, in truth, especially with that little speaker on his ear, he mostly just looked like he was yelling at himself.

A quick note about Kent and Tina Buckley. You know how there are always those couples where nobody can figure out what the wife is doing with the husband?

They were that couple.

Nobody could figure out what on earth Tina was doing with Kent Buckley. Most of the town liked her—or at least extended their affection for her parents to her—and it was a fairly common thing for people to wonder out loud what a great girl like that was doing with a douchey guy like him. I'm not even sure it was anything specific that folks could put their finger to. He just had a kind of uptight, oily, snooty way about him that people on the island just didn't appreciate.

Of course, Tina had never been "a great girl" to me.

Even now, beholding the party I'd so lovingly put together, she never even acknowledged me—just swept her eyes right past, like I wasn't even there. "Let's go in," she said to her mom. "I need a drink."

"How long can you stay?" Babette asked her in a whisper, as they started toward the building.

Tina stiffened, as though her mother had just criticized her. "About two hours. He's got a video conference at eight."

"We could drive you home, if you wanted to stay later," Max said then.

Tina looked like she wanted to stay. But then she glanced Kent Buckley's way and shook her head. "We'll need to get back."

Everybody was setting out their words carefully and monitoring their voices to keep everything hyper-pleasant, but there were some emotional land mines in this conversation, for sure.

Of course, the biggest emotional land mine was the party itself. When we stepped inside and Max and Babette beheld the twinkle lights, and the seventies band in their bell-bottoms, and the decorations, and the mountains of food, Babette turned to me with a gasp of delight and said, "Sam! It's magnificent!"

In the background, I saw Tina's face go dark.

"It wasn't just me," I said. And then it just kind of popped out: "Tina helped. We did it together."

I'd have to apologize to Alice later. I panicked.

Babette and Max turned toward Tina for confirmation, and she gave them a smile as stiff as a Barbie doll's.

"And, really, the whole town's responsible," I went on, trying to push past the moment. "When word got out we were planning your sixtieth birthday party, everybody wanted to help. We got deluged, didn't we, Tina?"

Tina's smile got stiffer as her parents turned back to her. "We got deluged," she confirmed.

That's when Max reached out his long arms and pulled us both into a bear hug. "You two are the best daughters a guy could have."

He was joking, of course, but Tina stiffened, then broke out of the hug. "She is not your daughter."

Max's smile was relaxed. "Well, no. That's true. But we're thinking about adopting her." He gave me a wink.

"She doesn't need to be adopted," Tina said, all irritation. "She's a grown woman."

"He's kidding," I said.

"Don't tell me what he's doing."

But nothing was going to kill Max's good mood. He was already pivoting toward Babette, snaking his arm around her waist and pulling her toward the dance floor. "Your mama and I need to show these whippersnappers how it's done," he called back as he walked. Then he rotated to point at Tina. "You're next, lady! Gotta grab you before you turn into a pumpkin."

Tina and I stood at a hostile distance as we watched her parents launch into a very competent set of dance moves. I spotted Alice across the way and wished she would come stand next to me for some emotional backup, but she made her way to the food table, instead.

Was Alice's party attire jeans and a math T-shirt?

It was.

The shirt said, WHY IS 6 AFRAID OF 7? And then, on the back: BECAUSE 789.

I was just about to walk over and join her, when Tina said, "You didn't have to lie to them."

I shrugged. "I was trying to be nice."

"I don't need you to be nice."

I shrugged again. "Can't help it."

Confession: did I want Tina to like me?

I absolutely did.

Would I have given anything to be a part of their family—a real part of it? I would. Even if the most Tina could ever be was my bitchy big sister, I'd take it. My own family was kind of . . . nonexistent.

I wanted so badly to belong somewhere.

I wasn't trying to steal her family. But I would have given anything to join it.

But Tina wasn't too keen on that idea, which seemed a little selfish, because she was never around, anyway. She and Kent Buckley were always off hosting charity galas and living a fancy, ritzy social life. You'd think she could share a little.

But no.

She didn't want them, particularly, but she didn't want anyone else to have them, either.

She resented my presence. She resented my existence. And she was determined to keep it that way. All I could think of was to just keep on being nice to her until the day she finally just gave up, held out her arms for a defeated hug, and said, "Fine. I give up. Get in here."

It was going to happen someday. I knew it was. Maybe.

But probably not tonight.

After a very long pause, I said something I thought she'd like. "They adore you, you know. And Clay. They talk about you both all the time."

But she just turned toward me with an expression that fell somewhere between offense and outrage.

"Did you just try to tell me how my own parents feel about me?"

"Um . . ."

"Do you honestly believe that you're qualified to comment on my relationship with my own parents—the people who not only brought me into this world but also spent thirty years raising me?"

"I . . ."

"How long have you known them?"

"Four years."

"So you're a librarian who moved into their garage four years ago—"

"It's a carriage house," I muttered.

"—and I am their biological child who's known them since before I was born. Are you trying to compete with me? Do you really think you could ever even come close to winning?"

"I'm not trying to—"

"Because I'll tell you something else: My family is not your place, and it's not your business, and it's not where you belong—and it never, ever will be."

Sheesh.

She knew how to land a punch.

It wasn't just the words—it was the tone of voice. It had a physical force—so sharp, I felt cut. I turned away as my throat got thick and my eyes stung.

I blinked and tried to focus on the dance floor.

An old man in a bolo tie had cut in on Babette and Max. Now Max turned his attention back toward Tina and swung an imaginary lasso above his head before tossing it over at her to rope her in. As he pulled on the rope, she walked toward him and smiled. A real smile. A genuine smile.

And I—resident of the family garage—was forgotten.

Appropriately.

It was fine. I never danced in public, anyway.

That night, Max mostly danced with Babette. It was clear the two of them had done a lot of dancing in their almost four decades together. They knew each other's moves without even thinking. I felt mesmerized, watching them, and I bet a lot of other people did, too.

They were the kind of couple that made you believe in couples.

Max lassoed a lot of people that night, and one of them, eventually, was me. I was surprised when it happened—almost like I'd forgotten I was there. I'd been watching from the sidelines for so long, I'd started to think I was safe—that I could just enjoy the view and the music without having to join in.

Wrong.

As Max pulled me onto the dance floor, I said, "I don't dance in public."

Max frowned. "Why not?"

I shook my head. "Too much humiliation as a child."

And that was true. I loved to dance. And I was actually pretty good, probably. I had good rhythm, at least. I danced around my own house constantly—while cleaning, and doing laundry, and cooking, and doing dishes. I'd crank up pop music, and boogie around, and cut the drudgery in half. Dancing was joyful, and mood-elevating, and absolutely one of my very favorite things to do.

But only when I was alone.

I couldn't dance if anyone was looking. When anyone at all was looking, the agony of my self-consciousness made me freeze. I couldn't bear to be looked at—especially in a crowd—and so at any party where dancing happened, I just froze. You'd have thought I'd never done it before in my life.

And Max knew enough about me to understand why. "Fair enough," he said, not pushing—but not releasing me, either. "You just stand there, and I'll do the rest."

And so I stood there, laughing, while the band played a Bee Gees cover and Max danced around me in a circle, wild and goofy and silly—and it was perfect, because anybody who was looking was looking at him, and that meant we could all relax and have fun.

At one point, Max did a "King Tut" move that was so cringingly funny, I put my hand over my eyes. But when I took my hand away, I found Max suddenly, unexpectedly, standing very still—pressing his fingers to his forehead.

"Hey," I said, stepping closer. "Are you okay?"

Max took his hand away, like he was about to lift his head to respond. But then, instead, his knees buckled, and he fell to the floor.

* * *

THE MUSIC STOPPED. The crowd gasped. I knelt down next to Max, then looked up and called around frantically for Babette.

By the time I looked down again, Max's eyes were open.

He blinked a couple of times, then smiled. "Don't worry, Sam. I'm fine."

Babette arrived on his other side and knelt beside him.

"Max!" Babette said.

"Hey, Babs," he said. "Did I tell you how beautiful you are?"

"What happened?" she said.

"Just got a little dizzy there for second."

"Can somebody get Max some water?" I shouted, and then I leaned in with Babette to help him work his way up into a sitting position.

Babette's face was tight with worry.

Max noticed. "I'm fine, sweetheart."

But Max was not the kind of guy to go around collapsing. He was one of those sturdy-as-an-ox guys. I tried to remember if I'd ever seen him take a sick day.

Now Max was rubbing Babette's shoulder. "It was just the long flight. I got dehydrated."

Just as he said it, a cup of ice water arrived.

Max took a long drink. "Ah," he said. "See that? All better."

His color was coming back.

A crowd had formed around us. Someone handed Max another cup of water, and I looked up to realize at least ten people were standing at the ready with liquid.

He drank the next cup. "Much better," he said, smiling up at us, looking, in fact, much better. Then he lifted his arms to wave some of the men over. "Who's helping me back to my feet?"

"Maybe you should wait for the paramedics, Max," one of the guys said.

"You hit the floor pretty hard there, boss," another guy offered, as an answer.

"Aw, hell. I don't need paramedics."

The fire department was maybe four blocks away—and just as he said it, two paramedics strode in, bags of gear over their shoulders.

"Are you partying too hard, Max?" one of them said with a big grin when he saw Max sitting on the floor.

"Kenny," Max said, smiling back. "Will you tell this batch of worriers I'm fine?"

Just then, a man pushed through the crowd. "Can I help? I'm a doctor."

Very gently, Max said, "You're a psychiatrist, Phil."

Kenny laughed. "If he needs to talk about his feelings, we'll call you."

Next, Babette and I stepped back, and the paramedics knelt all around Max to do an assessment—Max protesting the whole time. "I just got dehydrated, that's all. I feel completely fine now."

Another medic, checking his pulse, looked at Kenny and said, "He's tachycardiac. Blood pressure's high."

But Max just smacked him on the head. "Of course it is, Josh. I've been dancing all night."

It turned out, Max had taught both of the paramedics who showed up that night, and even though they were overly thorough, everything else seemed to check out on Max. They wanted to take him to the ER right then, but Max managed to talk them out of it. "Nobody's ever thrown me a sixtieth birthday party before," he told them, "and I really don't want to miss it."

Somehow, after they helped him up, he talked them into having some snacks, and they agreed to give him a few minutes to drink some water and then reevaluate.

They took a few cookies, but even as they were eating, they were watching him. Babette and I were watching him, too.

But he seemed totally back to his old self. Laughing. Joking around. When the band finally started up again, it was one of Max's favorites: ABBA's "Dancing Queen."

As soon as he heard it, Max was looking around for Babette. When he caught her eye about ten feet away, he pointed at her, then at himself, then at the dance floor.

"No," Babette called. "You need to rest and hydrate!"

"Wife," Max growled. "They are literally playing our song."

Babette walked over to scold him—and maybe flirt with him a little, too. "Behave yourself," she said.

"I'm fine," he said.

"You just—"

But before she could finish, he pulled her into his arms and pressed his hand against the small of her back.

I saw her give in. I felt it.

I gave in, too. This wasn't a mosh pit, after all. They were just swaying, for Pete's sake. He'd had at least six glasses of water by now. He looked fine. Let the man have his birthday dance. It wasn't like they were doing the worm.

Max spun Babette out, but gently.

He dipped her next, but carefully.

He was fine. He was fine. He was absolutely fine.

But then he started coughing.

Coughing a lot.

Coughing so hard, he let Babette go, and he stepped back and bent over.

Next, he looked up to meet Babette's eyes, and that's when we saw he was coughing up blood—bright red, and lots of it—all over his hand and down his chin, drenching his bow tie and his shirt.

He coughed again, and then he hit the floor.

The paramedics were back over to him in less than a second, ripping his shirt open, cutting off the bow tie, intubating him and squeezing air in with a bag, performing CPR compressions. I don't really know what else was going on in the room then. Later, I heard that Alice rounded up all the kids and herded them right outside to the garden. I heard the school nurse dropped to her knees and started praying. Mrs. Kline, Max's secretary for thirty years, tried helplessly to wipe up a splatter of blood with cocktail napkins.

For my part, all I could do was stare.

Babette was standing next to me, and at some point, our hands found each other's, and we wound up squeezing so tight that I'd have a bruise for a week.

The paramedics worked on Max for what seemed like a million years—but was maybe only five minutes: intensely, bent over him, performing the same insistent, forceful movements over his chest. When they couldn't get him back, I heard one of them say, "We need to transport him. This isn't working."

Transport him to the hospital, I guessed.

They stopped to check for a rhythm, but as they pulled back a little, my breath caught in my throat, and Babette made a noise that was half-gasp, half-scream.

Max, lying there on the floor, was blue.

"Oh, shit," Kenny said. "It's a PE."

I glanced at Babette. *What was a PE?*

"Oh, God," Josh said, "look at that demarcation line."

Sure enough, there was a straight line across Max's rib cage, where the color of his skin changed from healthy and pink to blue. "Get the gurney," Kenny barked, but as he did his voice cracked.

That's when I saw there were tears on Kenny's face.

Then I looked over at Josh: his, too.

And then I just knew exactly what they knew. They would wipe their faces on their sleeves, and keep doing compressions on Max, and keep working him, and transport him to the hospital, but it wouldn't do any good. Even though he was Max—our principal, our hero, our living legend.

All the love in the world wouldn't be enough to keep him with us.

And as wrong as it was, eventually it would become the only true thing left: We would never get him back.

A PE TURNED out to be a pulmonary embolism. He'd developed a blood clot somewhere during the flight home from Italy, apparently—and it had made its way to his lungs and blocked an artery. Deep vein thrombosis.

"He didn't walk around during the flight?" I asked Babette. "Doesn't everybody know to do that?"

"I thought he did," Babette said, dazed. "But I guess he didn't."

It didn't matter what he had or hadn't done, of course. There would be no do-over. No chance to try again and get it right.

It just was what it was.

But what was it? An accident? A fluke? A bad set of circumstances? I found myself Googling "deep vein thrombosis" in the middle of the night, scrolling and reading in bed in the blue light of my laptop, trying to understand what had happened. The sites I found listed risk factors for getting it, and there were plenty, including recent surgery, birth control pills, smoking, cancer, heart failure—none of which applied to Max. And then, last on the list, on every site I went to, was the weirdest possible one: "sitting for long periods of time, such as when driving or flying." And that was it. That was Max's risk factor. He'd sat still for too long. He'd forgotten to get up and walk around during the flight—and that one totally innocuous thing had killed him.

I couldn't wrap my head around it.

An entire lifetime of growing up, learning to crawl and then to toddle, and then to walk, and then run. Years of learning table manners, and multiplication tables, and how to shave, and how to tie a bow tie. Striving and going to college and grad school and marrying Babette and raising a daughter—and a son, too, who had joined the Marines and then died in Afghanistan—and this was how it all ended.

Sitting too long on a plane.

It wasn't right. It wasn't fair. It wasn't acceptable.

But it didn't matter if I accepted it or not.

People talk about shock all the time, but you don't know how physical it is until you're in it. For days after it happened, my chest felt tight, like my lungs had shrunk and I couldn't get enough oxygen into them. I'd find myself panting, even when I was just making a pot of coffee. I'd surface from deep sleep gasping for breath like I was suffocating. It left me feeling panicked, like I was in danger, even though the person who had been in danger wasn't me.

It was physical for Babette, too.

When the two of us got home from the hospital, she lay down on the sofa in the living room and slept for twelve hours. When she was awake, she had migraines and nausea. But she was almost never awake. We closed the curtains in the living room. I brought in blankets, and a bottle of water, and a box of tissues for the coffee table. I fetched her pillow off the bed upstairs, and some soft pajamas and her chenille robe.

She would sleep downstairs on that sofa for months.

She would send me to get anything she needed from their bedroom.

She would shower in her kids' old bathroom down the hall.

I mean, she was Max's high school sweetheart. Can you imagine? They'd started dating in ninth grade, when their math teacher asked her to tutor him after school, and Max had been right there by her side ever since. She hadn't been without him since she was *fourteen*. Now she was almost sixty. They had grown up together, almost like two trees growing side by side with their trunks and branches entangled.

Suddenly, he was gone, and she was entangled around nothing but air.

We needed time. All of us did. But there wasn't any.

Summer was ending soon, school was starting soon, and life would have to go on.

Three days later, we held Max's memorial service at the shore, on the sand, in the early morning—before the summer Texas heat really kicked in. The guys from maintenance built a little temporary stage in front of the waves, and in a strange mirroring that just about shredded my heart, Max got a whole new set of offerings from all those people who loved him: The florist on Winnie Street offered funeral wreaths and greenery. The photographer from the party gave Babette a great photo of Max to feature in the program. A harpist, who had gotten a D in his civics class but had loved him anyway, offered to play at the service.

There were no balloons this time, no fire-eater, no fifth-grade jazz band.

But it was packed. People brought beach towels to sit on, I remember that—and there was not an open inch of sand anywhere.

It's amazing how funerals even happen.

The party had taken so much work and planning and forward momentum, but the funeral just . . . happened.

I showed up. I read a poem that Babette gave me—one of Max's favorites—but I couldn't even tell you which one. It's crumpled in my dresser drawer now along with the program because I couldn't bear to throw either of them away.

I remember that the water in the Gulf—which is usually kind of brown on our stretch of beach, from all the mud at the mouth of the Mississippi—was particularly blue that day. I remember seeing a pod of dolphins go by in the water, just past the line where the waves started. I remember sitting down next to Alice on her beach towel after I tried, and failed, to give Tina a hug.

"She really doesn't like you," Alice said, almost impressed.

"You'd think grief would make us all friends," I said, dragging my soggy Kleenex across my cheeks again.

After the service, we watched Tina walk away, pulling little Clay behind her in his suit and clip-on tie, Kent Buckley nowhere to be found.

Once we were back at the reception in the courtyard at Kempner, Alice kept busy helping the caterers. I'm not sure the caterers needed help, but Alice liked to be busy even on good days, so I just let her do her thing.

I was the opposite of Alice that day. I couldn't focus my mind enough to do anything except stare at Babette in astonishment at how graciously she received every single hug from every single well-wisher who lined up to see her. She nodded, and smiled, and agreed with every kind thing anybody said.

He *had* been a wonderful man.

We *would* all miss him.

His memory would definitely, without question, be a blessing.

But how on earth was Babette doing it? Staying upright? Smiling? Facing the rest of her life without him?

Tina had her own receiving line, just as long, and Kent Buckley was supposed to be in charge of Clay . . . but Kent Buckley—I swear, this is true—was *wearing his Bluetooth headset.* And every time a call came in, he took it.

Little Clay, for his part, would watch his dad step off into a cloistered hallway, and then stand there, blinking around at the crowd, looking lost.

I got it.

I didn't have a receiving line, of course. I was nobody in particular. Looking around, everybody was busy comforting everybody else. Which freed me up, actually. Right then, surveying the crowd, I had a what-would-Max-do moment.

What *would* Max do?

He would try to help Clay feel better.

I walked over. "Hi, Clay."

Clay looked up. "Hi, Mrs. Casey." They all called me "Mrs."

He knew me well from the library. He was one of my big readers. "Tough day, huh?" I said.

Clay nodded.

I looked over at Kent Buckley, off by a cloister, was doing his best to whisper-yell at his employees. "Wanna take a walk?" I asked Clay then.

Clay nodded, and when we started walking, he put his soft little hand in mine.

I took him to the library. Where else? My beautiful, magical, beloved library . . . home of a million other lives. Home of comfort, and distraction, and getting lost—in the very best way.

"Why don't you show me your very favorite book in this whole library," I said.

He thought about it for a second, and then he led me to a set of low shelves under a window that looked out over downtown, over then the seawall, and out to the Gulf. I could see the stretch of beach where we'd just held the service.

This was the nonfiction nature section. Book after book about animals, and sea life, and plants. Clay knelt down in front of the section on ocean life and pulled out a book, laid it out on the floor, and said, "This is it," he said. "My favorite book."

I sat next to him and leaned back against the bookshelf. "Cool," I said. "Why this one?"

Clay nodded. "My dad's going to take me scuba diving when I'm bigger."

My instant reaction was to doubt that would ever happen. Maybe I'd just known too many guys like Kent Buckley. But I pretended otherwise. "How fun!"

"Have you ever gone scuba diving?"

I shook my head. "I've only read about it."

Clay nodded. "Well," he said, "that's almost the same thing."

Talk about the way to a librarian's heart. "I agree."

We flipped through the pages for a long time, with Clay narrating a tour through the book. It was clear he'd absorbed most of the information in it, and so all he needed was a picture to prompt conversation. He told me that the earth's largest mountain range is underwater, that coral can produce its own sunscreen, that the Atlantic Ocean is wider than the moon, and that his favorite creature in the Gulf of Mexico was the vampire squid.

I shivered. "Is that a real thing?"

"It's real. Its lower body looks like bat wings—and it can turn itself inside out and hide in them." Then he added, "But it's not really a squid. It's a cephalopod. 'Squid' is a misnomer.'"

"I'm sorry," I said, "did you just say 'misnomer'?"

He blinked and looked at me. "It means 'wrong name.' From the Latin."

I blinked back at him.

"Clay," I asked. "Are you a pretty big reader?"

"Yep," Clay said, turning his attention back toward the book.

"I don't think I've ever met a third grader who knew the word 'misnomer,' much less anything about its Latin origins."

Clay shrugged. "I just really like words."

"I'll say."

"Plus my dad does flash cards with me."

"He does?"

"Yeah. My dad loves flash cards."

Honestly, I'd never worked very hard to get to know Clay. He was in the library a ton—almost whenever he could be—but he knew his way around, and he didn't need my help, and, well . . . he was reading. I didn't want to bother him.

Plus, yes, also: I was afraid of his mother.

It's true in a school that even the kids who need help don't always get it—so a kid who *doesn't* need help? He's gonna be on his own.

At least, until now. Clay was going to need some love this year, and it would be right here waiting for him in the library, if he needed it.

I don't know how long we'd been gone—an hour, maybe—when Alice came running into the library, breathless, her face worried. She had on a black skirt and a black blouse—one of the only times I'd not seen her in jeans—and she almost didn't look like herself.

"Oh, my God," she said, when she found us, bending over to breathe for a second before grabbing Clay by the shoulders and steering him out. "They're looking for him everywhere! Tina Buckley is freaking out."

Oh. Oops. Guess we'd lost track of time.

"Found him!" Alice shouted as we strode back into the courtyard, shaking Clay's shoulders for proof. "Got him! He's right here!"

Tina plowed through the crowd to seize him in her arms.

"I'm sorry," I said, catching Babette's eye as I arrived behind them. "We went to the library."

Babette waved me off, but that's when Tina stood up and glared at me. "*Really?*" she said, all bitter.

I lifted my shoulders. "We were just looking through Clay's favorite book."

"You couldn't—I don't know—mention that to anyone?"

"Everybody seemed pretty busy."

"Clay's father was watching him."

Um. Sorry, lady. His father was not *watching him. His father was taking business calls on his cell phone. At a funeral.* "I'm sorry," I said again.

"You bet you are."

"I just wanted . . . to help."

"Well, you can't help. But here's one thing you can do. You can leave my family alone."

Leave them alone?

What did that even mean? I lived with Babette. Clay was about to be in my third-grade library class. "How would that even work, Tina? I live on your mother's property."

"Maybe you should find somewhere else to live."

But whatever this weirdness was with Tina, it had gone on too long. "No," I said.

She frowned. "No?"

"No. That's ridiculous. I'm not doing that. I love my carriage house—"

"Garage apartment," she corrected.

"And I'm not leaving. Why would you even want me to? Would you really rather your mom be all alone in that big house than have me nearby?"

We both looked over at Babette, who was back in her greeting line, now with her arm around Clay, who was watching us with his big eyes.

"She wouldn't be all alone," Tina said.

"Who would be with her?" I demanded. "You?"

Across the courtyard, Kent Buckley was back on another call.

I saw Tina's eyes flick from Babette to Kent. I saw her take in what he was doing. I saw her nostrils flare—just the tiniest bit, enough to ripple across her composure for a second. I knew she was suppressing some rage. Her husband was *talking on his cell phone during her father's funeral reception*. It wasn't just inappropriate, it bordered on pathological.

In a different context, I could have felt very sorry for Tina Buckley.

But not today.

She'd married that dude, after all—and no matter if it was a mistake, she chose to stay with him. Yes, I should have been more compassionate. But what can I say? I was grieving, too—and she'd done nothing all day but make it worse.

When her eyes came back to mine, I kicked my chin in Kent Buckley's direction, and then I said. "You think he's going to let you look after your mom? He didn't even let you out of the house when Max was alive."

Too much.

Too soon.

Tina went rigid. I saw her angry eyes turn to ice. And if I'd thought her voice had ever sounded vicious before, I now realized I hadn't known the meaning of the word. All that rage about her husband she was suppressing? She found a place to release it.

"Get out," she said, like a snake. "Get out of here."

I wasn't sure how to respond.

She stepped closer and her voice was all hiss. "Get out—or I will absolutely fucking lose it right now."

Now the ice in Tina's eyes had turned to fire. Crazy fire. Did I doubt that she would lose it? Did I think she was bluffing?

I did not.

I looked over at Babette—lovely, wise Babette, who was using every micron of strength she had left to hold it together. In the past decade, I knew, she'd lost her parents, a son, and now her husband. Did I want Tina Buckley to make things worse? Did I want to reduce the funeral of Max Kempner—the final punctuation mark on his long and extraordinary life—to a single image of his daughter screaming like a banshee in the courtyard?

No. On all counts.

And so I left.

And that's the story of how I got kicked out of Max's funeral.

Skylar Reeves Photography

Katherine Center is the *New York Times* bestselling author of *How to Walk Away* and *Things You Save in a Fire* and five other bittersweet comic novels. Her fourth novel, *The Lost Husband,* is soon to be a movie. Katherine has been compared to both Nora Ephron and Jane Austen, and *The Dallas Morning News* calls her stories, "satisfying in the most soul-nourishing way." Katherine recently gave a TEDx talk on stories and empathy, and her work has appeared in *USA Today, InStyle, Redbook, People, The Atlantic, Real Simple,* and others. Katherine lives in Houston with her husband and two sweet kids. Visit her online at katherinecenter.com